THE RAIN

BOOKS BY
JOSEPH A. TURKOT

THE DARKIN SAGA

A Journey East

The Prophecy of the Key

STANDALONE NOVELS

Black Hull

Neighborhood Watch

Wipe

The Rain

SHORT STORIES

House for Sale

THE RAIN

JOSEPH A. TURKOT

Published in 2023 by Blackstone Publishing
Cover and book design by Sarah Riedlinger

Printed in the United States of America

First edition: 2023
ISBN 979-8-200-83502-7
Fiction / Dystopian

Version 1

Blackstone Publishing
31 Mistletoe Rd.
Ashland, OR 97520

www.BlackstonePublishing.com

For the ones who are alone, still fighting to survive.

1
TANNER

There are a lot of stories about how the rain started.

It's not *how* that matters anymore, though—it's how much. After all these years, Russell still does the math, keeping track with that old formula—15 inches a day, 5,400 a year, and 19 years since it began. That's over 8,500 total feet of rain. We have no idea if it's accurate, but the numbers remind us to keep moving.

It came slow at first, not even every day. Russell likes telling that part, but I have a hard time believing it. I've never seen the rain stop. He's told me so many times—how no one even wore plastic yet, or worried about exposure, hypothermia, or the rubber flesh that forms and slides off like a glove. But soon, it became clear that the rain wasn't going to stop. It was just going to keep on coming. And everyone thought that there'd be some explanation, some solution. But there never was.

WE'RE CAMPED AGAIN today in the Bighorn Mountains, somewhere in Wyoming. A few peaks rise above the waterline. Most of them are just long islands of mud and rock that blend into the mist. We have no idea how deep the floodwater is, but it goes on forever in every direction. We call it the rain sea.

We're right at the edge of one of the islands, in case we have to push off quick. I squat by our tent, a leaky spread of canvas on some aluminum poles, to look in at Russell. He's breaking his own rule, sleeping during the day. And I'm anxious because we're wasting time.

We should be moving toward Leadville, my last shot at a life that's more than just survival. The highest-elevation city in America, the last place where it's not raining, and where the veneer is still thick.

"Russell!" I lift the flap.

He moans back at me. Words jumble into a cough.

"I'm freezing. It's time to go." I tap the canvas.

"Did you see them?" He opens his eyes.

"No."

"Maybe they drowned."

I shake my head. "I didn't see any bodies float by."

"Maybe they ate each other."

He's sick, and I know he's trying to buy more time to rest. I wish I could let him, but it's more than wasting daylight, and freezing to death, that I'm worried about—the last few times we rowed across the water, from one Bighorn to another, three face eaters rowed after us in a boat not much bigger than ours. Three of them, which means they can bail out the rain faster. If we hit a patch of water too wide, they'll catch us.

Ever since we came through Rapid City, the face eaters have stopped waiting for people to die before eating them. Now they kill for their meat.

Russell and I never eat people, no matter how they died or how desperate it gets. Besides caring for each other, it's the biggest part of the veneer we still carry with us. Russell doesn't do it because he promised god, and I don't because I'm afraid I'll lose part of myself. I want people to know I'm still human when we get to Leadville.

I sit next to him in the tent. Rain hammers the canvas.

He pulls out our map, soggy and hard to read. His finger rests on Philadelphia, where we started together seventeen years ago.

I point to a river there, hoping to get him talking so that he'll wake up more and we can get the hell out of here. "Is this where you found me?"

"You were crying so damn loud in that house." He nods. "A beautiful baby girl with bright blond hair, stuck up there in a cabinet like a sack of flour, the only shelf left above the water."

"You think they drowned?" I know he never saw my family, but I still ask sometimes, hoping he'll remember something new.

"I'm sure of it. It only takes two inches of floodwater to sweep a man off his feet," he says. "What matters is your family gave you a chance, right before the Delaware took them. I'm lucky the current slowed, otherwise we would've went with them."

"I wish I remembered what they looked like." I've tried to picture their faces. Nothing ever comes.

"I went back the next day to find someone. The whole block was gone, the river swollen into a great lake."

I know I was born in the rain, but that's never stopped me from wishing I hadn't been, that there was one moment I could say I was alive before all this. That I'd seen the world in Russell's stories, and my family. I shiver.

He points at the map to distract me, and his finger traces our route—Philadelphia, Pittsburgh, Indianapolis, the Great Lakes, Sioux Falls, Rapid City, northern Wyoming. He hangs on the Bighorns for a moment and then slides down to the Rockies. The last leg.

"Only a few hundred miles south. We can make it," he says. "Where's the sun?"

I look through the flap at the bright blur behind the clouds, enough for a general sense of direction. "Still pretty high in the west."

"Good. We'll keep it on our right all the way to Leadville."

"You think there'll be blue sky?" It feels like a crazy question. I've only seen blue sky once.

"Blue sky, and stars at night." He grins like life has come back into him. It gives me so much hope that I smile, too.

I imagine the kind of life he's told me about, life before the rain. It's just a dream to me. People living safely enough that they can risk the veneer—love and family and a future. But right now it's more than a dream. It's just a few hundred miles away.

When I poke my head outside the tent flap and lower my eyes to the horizon, I see the face eaters.

They stand on a muddy ridge a few hundred feet away, spot us, then start walking fast. The veneer's all gone in them.

Russell has his eyes closed again. "They're back!" I shake him.

He opens them slowly, as if he's still in a dream. When I check through the flap again, they're running.

"Russell!" I half pull him out of the tent so he'll see for himself.

"Where's their boat?"

He's right. They aren't hauling their boat with them, but I don't have time to wonder what's happened to it. We're at the water's edge, and our rowboat is right here. There's still time to get away.

He goes down the bank and unties the nylon rope. The rope's about as precious as our hardtack and beans. If we lose it, we lose the boat. He takes his time. He has to.

I break down the tent and fling it into the boat, then stand behind a boulder, keeping an eye on them.

Two run out in front. I think I see them squinting, and then one grimaces. He looks mad, like if he doesn't get us, he'll turn on his friends and start eating them right away. The one who lags behind just looks sick. Like Russell's started to look.

They trip a few times but keep getting up. When they're fifty feet away, Russell calls my name. I turn around and he waves me down. He's got the boat in the water. Eyes glued to the trash bags tied around my sneakers, I go down the bank. It's easy to slip on the rocks with plastic shoes, and it's even easier because the mud's flowing. I hear the face eaters shouting and I go faster, then too fast, and start to slide.

Somehow, Russell jumps out of the boat, steadies me, and guides me the rest of the way down. I don't know how he risked it, because the boat could have pushed off without us, but he did. I fall in and the boat rolls heavily to one side. Water splashes in. Immediately, I start bailing. With the rain on high, we're always bailing. The rain hasn't been on medium for days, so there'll be no break. It fills the boat hard and fast.

I dump water over the side with the bright orange bucket we picked up in Sioux Falls. It's the only color here. The rain on the floor of the rowboat starts to go down. I look up. Russell's coughing like he's about to choke, but he thrusts the oars through the water, pushing us away from land.

Bony faces stare at us from the bank.

I feel delirious from our escape, like I want to say something to Russell to make him laugh. But before I can speak, one of the face eaters wades in up to his knees, then dives forward, dropping into the frigid water.

His head pops back up about ten feet from the bank and he starts swimming in a direct line toward us. I glance around to see how far the next island is, but there's too much fog. The others, desperate but not as insane yet, watch with hope, as if they expect him to reach us.

Russell doesn't even look—he just keeps pumping the oars. His breathing sounds horrible. I think he's worse than he's been telling me, that maybe his infection is back. When our boat flipped in Sioux City, he sliced his leg open on a scrap of metal hidden under the water, and the damn thing just never healed right.

Rain pelts the back of the man's head as he emerges. He's swimming fast enough that he might have a chance. I want to yell at Russell to row hard like he used to, but I don't. Panic will just slow him down.

I try to speak calmly. "He's getting close."

The face eater plows forward with uncanny speed, making tiny swells. And then it happens. He starts to flounder in the water, suddenly out of strength, but he's too far out to swim back.

When the first gasp comes, Russell finally turns to look. He gives the face eater one second, just enough to see it's over, and then returns to the oars. He rows us through the water, no faster or slower than before.

The others stand limply on the rocky bank, making no move to help their companion. The hope in their faces starts to fade. I can't be sure, but I think one of them closes his eyes. The other pulls at his hair.

The gasps for air get louder and I can't take my eyes away from the drowning. The face eater's head is barely above water. He must realize how far he went, and how cold it is.

He stares at me with wild eyes. I hear a whimper and wonder if he's crying, but the sound isn't coming out clearly because of all the water he's spitting up. Maybe he's thinking about the mistake he made, how it will be the last thing he knows in the world.

His head goes under for the first time, and he makes a turn, like he's going to stroke back to land. But he can't—he doesn't even move that way. He jerks and rotates, his body writhing, clawing at the sky for anything to keep him afloat.

Something Russell once told me pops into my head. When the brain stops receiving oxygen, it's only a minute until lights out.

I shudder when I hear the scream, crystal clear. "Help!"

An intense sadness washes over me, like it has every time I hear one of them who's able to talk. It reminds me that they're still human, and it's the rain that's done this to them.

His head goes under for the third and then the fourth and final time. The last flailing is painful to watch. But then, right at the end, as he gently slides underneath the brown, it kind of looks peaceful.

The forms on the shore start walking back the way they came, a sad walk, maybe not because they lost their friend but because he was two days' worth of food. The face eaters have seemed less and less human since we reached the Midwest, and I wonder if the rumors—that they're on some kind of horrible drug now—are true.

Russell finally speaks. "They'll get their boat."

I already know that. I want to remind him he was wrong about them being drowned, mainly because I'm mad at how much he's coughing. Even though he's three times as old as me, he's never struggled this much to row before.

"Told you they were alive."

He doesn't look up. "Bail." His voice is gruff.

I dump water and watch the permanent clouds overhead. Always the same. They're deep gray today, except for the bright spot where they block the sun. It doesn't cheer me up like it usually does. I can't shake the fear of getting stuck on the water, but even more, I worry about tonight, and how we're going to fend off a second attack if the other two follow us.

A low island appears from the fog. It looks close enough that we could reach it in an hour. Beyond that, I don't see any more land. Just the flat rain sea and the gray haze that goes on forever, all the way to the Rocky Mountains. I'm told they exist somewhere that way.

There's no going back. I keep bailing.

2

ROOK

28 DAYS AFTER THE RAIN BEGAN

Rook tightened his fingers around the steering wheel as his 4Runner rolled to the bottom of Chester Avenue, wipers barely pacing the rain. The water ahead on Deacon Street looked higher than last week. Slowly, he pressed the brake.

A loud screech cut through the pattering rain.

Turning the wheel back to the center of the road, his feet tapped in concert—downshift, second gear, engine brake. The tires skidded to a stop.

He'd visited his parents every week since the rain started, driving the fifteen minutes from his Pueblo City apartment to their middle-class suburb, but the water was finally too deep to traverse Deacon Street. He'd have to go the rest of the way on foot.

Glancing at the house to his left, he saw four dark windows, no car in the driveway. Another evacuated family. Most of the street was empty now. The evacuee camps were swelling.

He walked through the mushy grass in tacky red rubber boots, pulling his black poncho tight. A downed power line snaked back and forth through the flood. The thought of electrocution drove him higher up the lawn.

It was eerie seeing the houses so dark. Of course, the blackouts hadn't deterred Rook's father one bit. He'd told Rook his generator would run for a year on the diesel he'd preserved. And if his mom wanted to go to a camp, he hadn't heard her say it. She was as stubborn as his dad. They'd probably stay until the water hit their front door.

Childhood landmarks came into view. On the left, a street sign for Kent Circle, his parents' cul-de-sac. Kent Circle rose uphill out of the flood, perpendicular to Deacon. If the water kept rising, even his dad's lifted, all-wheel-drive Ram would have trouble getting through.

On the right side of the street, the houses ended at Clover Park, where his older brother used to drag him—kicking and screaming from his computer—to get fresh air, to roughhouse and play sports. Now he barely recognized it. Construction signs floated in stagnant water near the entrance. The little yellow playground was missing its swings, chains dangling loosely in the wind. Behind the playground, the soccer field had become a swamp.

It was terrifying how quickly the rain had changed things. The way color had been drained, like everything was masked by some camera filter, glazed gray with vapor and fog.

The flooded park reminded Rook of how wrong his initial forecast had been. It was his job to evaluate Doppler radar images and write weather reports for Pueblo's Channel 4 News. That first prediction, *three days of rain*, seemed comical now.

After a week of the deluge, he'd convinced his producers to run a piece about the widespread earthquakes and their connection to the rain, pointing out research that linked the phenomena. Despite how wrong his first forecast was, the quake theory now seemed ominously correct. Four straight weeks of rain, and neither the quakes nor the rain were slowing. Volcanoes that had been dormant for hundreds or thousands of years were suddenly erupting. Something terrible was happening to the planet.

Rook shook his head in disgust. The heartfelt letters he'd written to Congress and the Office of Global Change, the donations to Greenpeace, investments in carbon trapping—all as useless as the storm drain by the curb, which now regurgitated water in a spumy fountain.

Turning up the cul-de-sac, he left the floodwaters behind. Ahead, someone under a black umbrella called his name.

"Mrs. Kilroy." Rook waved, recognizing his parents' elderly neighbor.

"Have you seen your parents?" she spoke between sharp breaths. "They didn't answer the door."

"Not since last week—that's where I'm going now." Rook glanced anxiously at their house.

Mrs. Kilroy's face sagged, her small glassy eyes falling to her feet. "Dick's gone. He went to Abbotsville yesterday and hasn't come back."

"Abbotsville?" Rook's heart sank. Hadn't his station reported a flash flood on Interstate 295 just yesterday? Poor Mr. Kilroy would have taken 295 to Abbotsville. A bridge had crumbled, and the highway was underwater now. He didn't want to panic her more. "Why did he go there?"

"The pharmacies in town ran out of his heart medicine. Abbotsville Walgreens said they had it."

Rook tugged anxiously at his stubble, wishing he could help. He had come to see his parents today to tell them he was leaving town, going to work for Yasper, to help people like Mr. Kilroy. The drug company was redirecting all its efforts to reach flood victims with food and medicines. They'd hired him just five days ago. If the company's venture proved successful, they'd prevent this exact kind of tragedy. Rook wanted to go; no, he *needed* to. The job would finally give him the power to make a real difference.

"You tried his cell phone?"

Fear scrunched Mrs. Kilroy's face. "It goes to voice mail."

"Did you call the police?"

"They don't have units!" Her arms flew up in frustration. "They're resigning—at a time like this, can you believe that? I thought your father would know something, being a retired sheriff."

Rook didn't want to believe it, but the despair in her eyes mirrored what he knew in his heart. Things were unraveling much too fast. "I'll make sure he talks to you."

She thanked him and hurried back inside her house.

Unlike his parents, Rook had always struggled to believe in a higher power, but the words echoed inside his head anyway, the residue of childhood Sundays spent in church: *God, help Mrs. Kilroy find her husband. Please let him be okay.*

Even though the coastal corridors of the country had been hit hardest, with endless quakes and torrents, the dangers inland were becoming unavoidable, too. A day before the bridge collapse, a colleague had died in a freak accident when a tree toppled onto the roof of her sedan. It took hours for paramedics to arrive. Even if they'd gotten to her in time, the hospitals were overcrowded, forced to turn people away.

That was the lead story yesterday: medical supplies low, doctors impossibly overworked, FEMA running low on money, waiting for Congress to raise the debt ceiling.

Rook knocked three times on the front door. No answer.

Where are you?

He anxiously fished his phone from his pocket and dialed his mom. No reception. It was the second time today he couldn't get a signal. *Christ, what if the satellites go next?*

Pushing the thought from his head, he walked around the bushes to peek in a window, his feet sinking into the soggy grass. Stepping on a tree stump, he peered inside.

Between two dark curtains, a face was staring at him.

3

TANNER

I watch the mountains recede behind us. They're the same dirt color as the clothes underneath my plastic rain suit. It's been three weeks since a change of clothes. Russell thinks that we'll get sick a lot faster if we don't find new ones soon, since there's bacteria festering under our plastic skin. I really don't give a shit about clothes right now though because he's barely rowing.

He slumps down, pushing the oars into the water, but it's like he can't find any strength to pull them.

"Do you want me to row?" I hold my hands out. "Here, give them to me."

He doesn't protest, sliding off the rowing bench and trading places with me.

I kick the food sack toward his legs. "I need you to bail."

"I will." He leans back. "Just a minute."

The island we're headed for is one of the lowest bumps of mud I've seen in the Bighorns. The water's calm and I'm sure we'll reach it, but Russell hacks and wheezes like he's about to die on me. I've never had to deal with the rain alone. The thought is terrifying.

I pull the oars and the familiar ache starts in my legs and back. The boat starts to move again. Beyond the mud island, there's nothing else in sight. A void of water and fog big enough that I know we won't make it without one of us bailing.

It's hard to fix my eyes on the island because I keep checking the water rising at my feet. With each stroke, the boat feels heavier, harder to push through the water.

"Russell!" I bang an oar against the rail. There's only the rain in response. Everywhere a million tiny splashes on the freezing cold water.

Finally his eyes open and he mumbles something about god, grabs the bucket, and starts to bail. He says it again. He's cursing god. After he clears some water he lies back, wrapping his arm around the rail. His head reclines and I can see the lines under his jaw. His too skinny neck. He breathes and I row.

He told me I should pray once, and after that, I pretended to do it for him sometimes. I could never help but feel like I was talking to nothing, though. Nothing except the rain.

"Russell, can you ask god to help get us there?" I try to keep him awake and bailing as I dig the oars deep and mumble my own prayer. Turning my head every few minutes to make sure the hump of land is still there, I repeat the prayer. This time, I ask Poseidon to help us.

"It was all that son of a bitch . . ."

"Who?" I need to keep him talking.

"His whole administration."

He means the people who did this, long before I was born. "Tell me the story again."

"Another record high—another record high—I hope you're alive to see what it cost us, you son of—"

Yes! He's alive again, railing at the dark sky, his face coiled with rage. When he tries to shout, the words scramble into a cough.

THE ISLAND GROWS BIGGER as we draw near. I pull the oars in to bail for a few minutes, listening to Russell cough. I've been ignoring his cold for too long, thinking it would go away like last time. But I've seen what a cough means for so many other people—the long fever, the sweating even when it's cold, the in-between place where life and death separate and leave a pale, rolling-eye nightmare that trembles through the whole body. But it can't happen to Russell. We need each other.

The island flattens down to the water at one spot, a good place to land the boat. It's mostly mud, like everything firm has been turned to mush. I steer hard into the gentlest slope and the boat lodges in.

"Russell, we made it." I look across the water. It's almost dark. Still no sign of another boat. "Get up."

He finds a jagged rock and ties the boat to it. I finish the second knot and help him walk up to where it's flat enough for the tent. Scattered stumps dot the island, the dead remains of a forest, but there's nothing high enough to hide us. If anyone comes this way, they'll see us from the water.

Russell drops the canvas and poles into the mud and sits down. I look at him and want to demand that he tell me what's wrong, but I don't want to hear about the infection, his refusal to take medicine. I set up the tent myself.

I've done it so many times that I could do it in the pitch black. Russell doesn't even get the food sack out of the boat. I go back down for it after the tent's finished.

Carefully stepping down to the water, I imagine how the slope I'm on descends for thousands of feet under the rain sea, to a graveyard of old cities and a million decomposing skeletons. Everything must be dissolved into salt by now. I'm almost to the boat when I slip. My foot digs in then slides, nothing firm to hold on to.

My shoulder smacks the ground and I tumble into the sea. Freezing needles stab me and water rushes into my nose. I can't move. My lungs won't work.

Get to the surface.

My feet kick down and find solid ground. I stand up, dripping and numb and with no sense of the cold anymore. Grabbing the nylon rope to steady myself, I reach the boat, lift it up enough to pull out our food bag, then let it drop down into the mud.

Russell's still lying outside the tent. I kneel down and study his face, a sinking feeling pinching my stomach.

"You can't sleep out here."

I put my hand on his forehead, like he's done so many times for me, but I'm no good at it. I can't tell if he's too hot. His eyes are sunken and his skin is puffy and gray. He's not even angling his face away from the rain.

"Russell." I feel my calm slipping away. If the face eaters appear out there, we're not running anywhere this time.

"Get inside." I nudge him. He still doesn't respond and I can't help it, I start yelling at him. "Get the fuck in the tent!"

Usually he gets annoyed when I swear, because avoiding it is something small we can do to keep ourselves close to the veneer. But I need to know he's alive, still feeling, and I curse again to get a reaction from him. Lately, he barely protests at all.

I grab his wrists and start to pull.

"I'm sorry." He digs his hands into the mud, pushing himself.

At first he sort of slides across the ground, but then he gets stuck a few feet away from the tent.

"You heavy bastard." My voice shakes. I whine and grunt and pull and curse.

Even though he's a skeleton compared to what he used to be, I can't move him. If he doesn't start moving on his own, he'll be stuck out in the rain. His cold will get so much worse. I start shaking him as hard as I can.

He cranes his neck up like he suddenly recognizes what I need him to do and finally crawls into the tent. I go in after him, closing the flap. He lies down on the mushy floor and I lie next to him.

My heart starts to slow down as I watch the dark splotches of rain blink on the roof, a hundred times a second, each one in a different place. Water drips through two holes, one right onto Russell. I roll him onto his side, forcing him as close to the wall as I can. He grins at me, face streaked with mud. "How do I look?"

"You're a piece of shit, you know that?" My desperation slides away at his smile.

"I just need some sleep." Then the smile's gone. He's out.

I push into his body as close as I can. Usually he's so warm, but now he's taking all the heat away from me. And I'm happy to give it, as long as he gets better.

He snores and I lie awake, watching patterns of raindrops dance on the ceiling. One constellation looks like a heart. It reminds me that love is part of the veneer.

Russell said he used to be in love. They planned to get married, but they could never get the money together. He always regretted that they hadn't just settled for a cheap wedding. I didn't really know what a wedding was, and he told me it was a giant waste of money. But it was part of the veneer, so he had tried to save up for it.

She died before they could get married though.

A picture fell out of his jacket once in Indianapolis, and he wouldn't even tell me who it was. When our boat flipped crossing the Great Lakes, he lost that picture for good. He was so sad at first. I asked why it bothered him so much and he told me it was his daughter. All that time with him and I never knew he had a daughter.

She didn't drown like his fiancée had. It was that there were no hospitals around to take her when she got sick. They'd all been abandoned. He finally got her antibiotics, but it was too late. That's why the stubborn son of a bitch won't touch our medicine. He thinks we need to save it in case I get sick. I've argued with him every day for the past week to take the fucking antibiotic pills, but he refuses. I'm going to have to shove them down his throat if he keeps being so difficult.

I push into him, hoping that the warmth returns. But his skin is cold everywhere. I watch the dripping roof until it gets too dark to see the raindrops.

We usually take turns on guard duty, but I don't have the energy to watch the water right now. We'll be easy prey, won't even hear their footsteps. But I can't leave Russell.

I take out my knife and run my finger gently down the six-inch blade. Still sharp. I accidentally bump Russell with the handle as I put it in my fist. He doesn't move, just breathes real soft.

"Sometimes I think you'd have gotten to Leadville already without me." I don't expect him to answer, but he surprises me.

"No," he mutters. "I would have died without you."

"Is it easy for you to see their faces? Your family, I mean."

"I see them all the time. Sometimes I wish I wouldn't."

I know it's veneer, and pointless, but I have to ask. "Will you always be with me?"

"Yes."

"Forever?"

"Forever." There's no hesitation, like he's certain of it.

I push my arms around his stomach, wrapping tightly to him. Then I reach up and put my fingers against his lips, waiting for breath. It rolls out, a small rush of warmth, and I know he's okay. That's when I hear something.

Splashing.

I shake him. "Did you hear that?"

He's really asleep this time. I don't think I can fend off two face eaters with my knife. I squeeze the handle and a dark thought comes in. Let them come kill us, end the rain forever.

I don't hear any more sound. And then comes a big splash. They're trying to land on the bank. They need to eat. We have hardtack and our bodies—that's what they're after.

"Russell," I whisper, my heart jumping, but he's useless now. I peel the flap back and poke my head out.

It's not the face eaters. Instead, a dark blue ridge skims over the water, ten times as long as our boat. I watch it glide higher. Suddenly, there's a loud rush of air as a fountain of water shoots into the sky and falls in a wide splashing arc. The ridge disappears under the water.

"Animal!"

I think about the big sea animals I've seen in pictures. Russell told me they probably died off from pollution. Magical creatures from the books he showed me when I was little—sharks, dolphins, squid. This one looked even bigger. I search for the right word.

Whale.

"It's a whale." I scramble out of the tent in stunned disbelief. "Come back!"

I stand for a long time in the rain, waiting, but it never returns. I wonder if the whale minds the rain and cold, if anything that's happened to the human veneer matters to it. No, I don't think it notices any of that.

I look in at Russell. He slept through it all. He needs rest too much, so I let him be and let the feeling wash over me, something like hope.

If one whale is surviving, despite everything, there must be more. Maybe the flood pollution is healing, and the whale has friends. Maybe *we* can come back from this, too. Find the veneer, and I'll be older and stronger and able to protect the things that are innocent, because Russell taught me how. That's what I want, once we reach the veneer. I'm going to protect the things that are innocent.

I look out over the dark horizon, one last scan for the whale, but instead, I see something else. I move down to the water, and all at once the fear from before jumps back into me, but twice as strong, because I realize it really is the face eaters' boat.

4

ROOK

28 DAYS

Rook's mother opened the front door wearing her faded-blue nightgown.

"Mom, you scared me!" As they hugged, he felt a sharp pang. This would be the last time he saw her for weeks, maybe months.

"I didn't recognize you in that new poncho. I'm sorry." She waved him inside, a frown forming on her face. "I told you not to come. It's too dangerous to drive from the city." She'd always looked younger than her age, but now she appeared worn and exhausted. "Have you heard anything from your brother?"

"Not yet. He'll get in touch as soon as he can. I'm sure he's fine." Rook kissed her on the cheek. "It has to be the blackouts and downed cell towers."

Of the whole Wallace family, his big brother was the toughest, hard as nails. Still, Rook was worried about his only sibling, so far away on the other side of the country, where the fault lines were exploding. They hadn't been on speaking terms before the rain started, and since then, no one had heard from him. No texts, no calls. His phone didn't even ring anymore, just an operator's voice saying the number was temporarily disconnected.

For Rook, the worry was laced with guilt. After all those years they had tried to get his brother help for his drug addiction, what other choice had there been but to cut him off, show him tough love? There was no way in hell his brother would still be holding a grudge now, though, not after what was happening to the country.

"And you're still going into work?" his mother scowled, pushing Rook's wet hair back from his face.

"Of course. I go in every day." He followed her to the stairs.

The living room was littered with supplies: rows of toilet paper; stacks of tuna fish cans; box after box of rice, couscous, quinoa, dry beans; batteries and flashlights. Despite his dad's hobby since retiring from law enforcement—extreme prepping—his parents had always been meticulously neat and organized. Now the prepping had won out, turning the house into a hoarder's showcase.

"Can't you take vacation time until this is over? The roads are a disaster."

"People count on me."

"To report the weather? Honey, it's *rain*—rain every day. Wait until there's something to report. Stay here with us." She stared at him like he was crazy.

He knew she didn't mean to mock him. She'd supported him through meteorology school at UCLA and always encouraged his obsession with science.

"I can't, Mom." His stomach dropped as he imagined how she'd react when he told her he'd be working for Yasper, even farther way.

From the top of the stairs, Rook heard rushing water. He went up to the bathroom to find his father bent over the tub. Milk gallon jugs crowded the tiny room, all filled with water.

"Rook!" His father's eyes lit up as he leaned in for a hug.

"Hey, Dad." Rook squeezed him back. "I saw Mrs. Kilroy outside. She told me you two didn't answer the door for her?" He realized the condemnation in his voice too late.

"With all the break-ins recently, we have to be careful who we open for," his mother said defensively from behind him.

Rook felt a tremor of apprehension. "Here?"

"For Chrissake, what kind of news company do you work for?

There've been three this week." His father maneuvered his large frame past them, down the stairs with four water jugs. "Grab a few, would you?"

"I didn't hear anything." Rook tried to remember his conversations with Kim, who covered crime. There'd been increases in store theft, and every day more violence, but only in the poorer neighborhoods. No home burglaries in the wealthier suburbs.

"That's because the police are quitting, and it's not getting reported." His father led them through the living room.

"She said Mr. Kilroy went to get medicine and hasn't come back yet. The police told her they didn't have enough units to help."

"Dick's missing?" His mother's voice jumped higher.

They walked through the kitchen, counters piled high with cereal boxes, granola, flour, and a pyramid of canned goods.

"I'll check on her first thing after I'm done here. Hell, even Gerry quit."

"Not Gerry?" Rook's apprehension solidified into dread. Gerry was his dad's best friend, a local officer who'd worked as sheriff's deputy for a long time and taken over the reins when his dad retired.

"Two others walked out with him. They're going to have a hell of a time finding replacements." His father opened the basement door and led them down.

"Why would they all quit?"

"Because it's gridlocked out there," he growled in frustration. "It's not like it was even two weeks ago. You can't get backup. Gerry had a robbery at Acme, this guy wearing a ski mask, hiding a snub nose under his shirt. He calls for backup and it takes *twenty minutes* for someone to respond! Finally, he goes in alone, confronts the guy. Turns out, the perp's out of money, trying to feed his family. Just drops his gun and starts crying. He'd been filling up a shopping cart, planning to walk out with it. Gerry let him go out of pity. But he knew how lucky he was. Next time he'll get shot. And if he does? The ambulances don't come. Hospitals are too crowded. It's mayhem."

"Jesus. I didn't think it was getting like that here."

"He told me he'll go back to work when the rain stops. But it's been a month."

Rook had seen the same Doppler images every day: constant rain systems moving in from the Pacific, stationary fronts banding across the country. Theories varied about what runaway chain reaction was acting upon the planet, but the scientific consensus was unanimous: it could have been prevented. Human-caused climate change had long been a partisan issue, polarizing enough to muzzle the scientists. Now, a month into the rain, their voices were loud and clear, and being heard too late.

"Looking good, isn't it?" His father swept his arms across the cluttered basement. A massive diesel generator took up half the room, yellow light illuminating neatly shelved supplies. Along the back wall hung five rifles.

Rook glanced at his father scribbling something on a pad. Tallies of food, water, ammunition, and miscellaneous supplies. It used to feel like a blemish on his father's otherwise exceptional character, this obsession with prepping. Now it was hard not to see it as a blessing.

"We could live without going outside for two years." His father's chest puffed proudly. "A few more trips, it'll be three."

Suddenly, Rook understood his parents' reluctance to answer the door. So much food in one place. It was probably happening in every household with the wherewithal to hole up and stockpile. The rain had been going long enough to make it a race.

"I tell him it's too much for us." His mom kicked one of the boxes softly. "It's not Christian."

"Didn't I ask Dick and Lilly to stay with us?" His father banged the table. "Believe me, we're going to share with refugees."

"The Kilroys are too proud." She set down a water jug.

"When Gerry and I go on search and rescue, we'll find plenty of people to take us up on it."

"You're going to search the floods with Gerry?" It was exactly the thing Rook would expect his father to do, but he hated to think of him risking his life.

"Just because I'm retired means I'm not going to help?"

"It worries me, too, but it's the right thing to do." His mother sighed.

"You're not going, are you, Mom?" Rook looked at her, her immense strength bottled in too small a frame.

"If she wants to come, that's up to her." His father put his arm around her and kissed her temple. "She's tougher than two of me."

She rolled her eyes, but she was smiling. "Do you want coffee?"

They went upstairs to the kitchen table. Through the window, pools swamped the backyard.

"Mom, Dad . . . I came over to tell you something." Rook's heart pounded with nervous energy. "Remember Yasper, the drug company I said was hiring?"

"Drug company?" His father's eyes narrowed. "Part of the reason we're in this mess. Look at what the Sacklers did to your brother! Only one thing motivates those people—greed."

It was one of the few things about Rook's father that upset him. He placed all his hatred on big business, but never on the elected officials in bed with them.

"They offered me a position. I've decided to take it." Rook watched the shock spread over their faces. "But I'm worried about leaving you."

"What did I tell you?" His father slapped a pistol on the table. Rook hadn't even noticed him carrying it. "Nothing's getting us, even if the rain never stops. You don't have to worry about your mother and me. I *am* interested to know what the hell you want with this drug company, though."

"They're starting a disaster branch to ship drugs and food to refugees, people stuck in flood zones and shelters."

His father leaned back skeptically. "Why would they be so charitable all the sudden?"

"The government's overloaded, so they're paying Yasper to do it for them. A *huge* grant."

"It sounds dangerous." His mother shook her head. "I don't want you going into those badly flooded areas."

Everyone had seen the videos on the news: lower-lying cities and towns across the country submerged under eight feet of water, refugees scrambling into makeshift settlements on higher ground.

"I won't be going out, the shipping team does that. I'll be at the headquarters as a meteorologist. It's located right next to the power plant, probably the safest place in the western United—"

"The new power plant? That's north of Denver!" His mother breathed out a frustrated sigh.

"It's his decision, babe." His father's face turned stoic. "When would you leave?"

The wind howled above the rain. Tree branches slapped into the house as Rook collected his courage. "I didn't want to tell you over the phone." He looked at his mother, hoping for her approval. "They're coming to get me on Thursday."

"In two days?" She turned away, sniffling like she might start to cry.

"All that matters is, do you really want to do this?" His father always cut straight to the heart of things.

"I've never done anything brave." Rook reached for his mother's hand. "This is my chance."

"Then it's settled. You go. End of conversation." He turned to his wife, her eyes already welling up.

"I'm sorry." She brushed away a tear and squeezed Rook's hand. "I'm proud of you for wanting to help. But you are brave, and you can live to be brave after this is over. Why *now*, when it's so bad?"

"All those years I studied, I always thought I'd do something really important, make a big difference. But I could never see how, or what I could do . . . Now here's this chance. I don't think I could live with myself if I didn't try."

Rook's father had protected lives as a sheriff, his mother had saved lives as a nurse practitioner, and his brother had toured the West Coast with his country rock band. Rook had always felt that he came up short in comparison. Watching life, safely behind a computer screen, never taking part in it.

"I just want you to be okay," his mother's voice cracked.

"Yasper is one of the best places I could be. The company's prepared for the worst. Almost as much as Dad has." Rook chuckled at his father.

His mother smiled, the tension finally easing.

"Like I said, don't you worry about us." His dad put his arm around her. "We want you to go."

She nodded, wiping her cheeks. "You better stay in touch. Can you come visit?"

"Eventually I can. I don't know how often, but yes. And of course I'll stay in touch." A tremendous sense of relief swept over him. He'd gotten through it, and more importantly, his parents both looked proud. His brother would be, too, he knew.

They finished their coffee, rehashing the president's most recent futile promises of aid. Rook reminded his father to talk to Mrs. Kilroy right away. Then he stood to say goodbye.

His mother hugged him at the door, sobbing gently. "I love you." She stood back and brushed his curly brown bangs out of his eyes. "You're my youngest baby boy. Please be careful, okay?"

"I will, I promise." Rook stepped into the rain. "I'll call soon."

His father followed him outside. "Don't stop trying to get ahold of your brother, you hear me?" It was his loud, stern sheriff's voice.

Rook nodded, watching sadness twist his father's face for just an instant, then walked down the cul-de-sac, looking back only once. His mother waved from the open door, his father already marching toward the Kilroy house.

By the time he got back to his SUV, Rook's fear of abandoning his parents had drained away, replaced by a new anxiety. The twilit sky looked like it was boiling upside down: dark tendrils of clouds, a mammatus formation, flashing red from within. A cumulonimbus was forming, the terrifying and beautiful base of a supercell thunderhead. Rook shuddered. Yesterday had been another record, nearly fourteen inches of rain. By the look of this storm, it would be broken by nightfall.

5
TANNER

I tell myself it's a different boat, but my eyes adjust to the haze and I know. It's the same shape, the one I've seen trailing us on the open water for days, and it's headed right toward us.

I almost sprint back to the tent, but I know that if I slip again, I might not come back up. I move slowly, climbing the sludge and walking around the streams so they don't send me flying into the brown rain sea.

Russell's still sleeping when I look in. I nudge him awake.

"Tanner?" He sits up right away this time, like he isn't sick one bit.

I try to choke out the words, but I feel like crying. It's a combination of the hope the whale gave me and the fact we're going to die anyway.

"They're back." I swing my head toward the water.

He pushes himself onto his knees, but then he grunts and flops back down.

"Give me a second," he moans. It takes him forever, but he finally gets his knife into his hand and rises again. I hold him upright until he can find his strength. I feel the boat getting closer.

He lifts his eyes. "How far?"

"A few hundred feet."

He walks on his knees to the flap, and as always, I get behind him, waiting for directions. I've never had to take charge against face eaters, and I don't want to start now. He'll tell me what to do—either we run or stand our ground. But I don't know how we can stand our ground, and I don't know where we can row in the dark. We've never been stuck on the water overnight.

Russell peeks first, then steps outside. I follow, locking my eyes on the sea. The boat's closer than I thought. The dirt yellow of the face eaters' rain suits stands out against the brown. One of the men is limp, lying against the rail, the other rowing.

"They're too low," Russell says.

He's right. The rail of their boat is close to the waterline, and the limp one isn't bailing. They're taking on too much rain. We stand still, watching them get closer.

"Should we go?" I squirm impatiently.

He's thinking slower than normal. Usually, there's a plan by now. But he just looks out there, judging something silently to himself.

"They're too low. They won't make it."

He brushes me off and walks down to the water's edge. I follow right after. Their waists look level with the water.

"What if they do make it?"

"You have your knife?"

I show him, trying to remember the way he taught me to fight. Swipe across, not down. Keep the blade pointed at your feet, not the sky. Slash, don't stab.

Closer up, the limp man looks like he's dead. He isn't moving at all, eyes closed. I wonder if he'll even try to get off the boat. The other seems to be in the same shape as the one who drowned earlier today—eyes spread wide, unblinking despite the heavy rain. It's like he's had one last shot of adrenaline, the final push before death.

Water starts spilling over the side of their boat. The whole thing wobbles and tips over. They fall out together with a quiet splash. The limp man doesn't even try to swim, he just sort of bobs for a bit, and then floats out into the brown, like the current's sucking him away. The other one knows how to swim, though, and isn't too tired to do it.

"He might make it." Russell stands straight, holds his knife ready, and looks at me. Life's back in him, a last fight.

I stand behind him, scared to death.

"Get beside me." He gestures.

I obey and we stand together at the water's edge.

The man makes good time swimming in. When he reaches a small jetty, he hoists himself up for air and sucks loudly for breath, breaking the steady taps of rain. Then he slips back under, swimming right up to our feet. His hand pops out onto the bank and finds a small root to cling to.

Russell steps forward and stomps down. The man screams. I cringe, unsure whether to jump in. Then, like the pain zapped him back to full strength, the face eater bursts from the water, ducks his shoulders down, and charges at Russell like a bull. Russell stumbles and the man falls on top of him.

I finally snap to life and run at them, but I can't tell who's screaming. As soon as I'm close enough to stab down, an elbow flies back into my head. A white flash of pain stuns my whole body. I can't see, can't tell if Russell is pinned. Mud sticks in my throat. There's grunting, a fight to the death. I scramble to my feet to save him as my vision returns.

Only Russell doesn't need my help. He stands up all on his own, rolling the man off his chest.

The man shrieks and flops over, both hands gripping the handle of Russell's knife, deep in his belly. There are no more sounds of pain, even though the sight of it hurts my own stomach. It's like he's numb to it. And he starts to rise again.

I know I should move closer to Russell, but I can't. I can't take my eyes off the face eater. He looks like a bloated corpse, skin puffed out around his beard, a gray mop dripping rain onto his gut where the red is streaming out. Both of his hands grab the knife handle like he wants to try to loosen it, but he just leaves it in, looking from Russell to me. He takes a step closer.

Russell hops toward me and slips. He smacks down hard into a mud stream and rolls all the way over the bank, splashing into the water.

"Russell!" I spin around. He's not moving.

I panic, certain the current will take him. Before I can move to help, heavy breathing sounds behind me. When I twist around, the man is coming at me, hands stretched out like claws.

There's a splash, movement at the bank. From the corner of my eye, I see Russell crawling on his hands and knees. The face eater turns just as Russell barrels into his legs.

I charge in too, grabbing the knife handle sticking out of his stomach and pushing as hard as I can, wedging it deeper. His skin has no measure of resistance anymore and it slides in, like he's one big sponge soaked in red water. The whole handle disappears inside him.

He falls on Russell and then rolls off to the side. I run to him and stomp on his face, over and over, until I slip and land hard on my side. Dirt smacks my mouth and I bite my lip. The metal taste of blood coats my tongue. I jump up immediately, all adrenaline, ready to fight, but the man is finally dead.

My body screams for me to act, to push him down into the water, but something stops me. A strange instinct I've never felt before.

For a split second, I think that he's food.

We have hardly any left, not nearly enough for the whole trip to Leadville. It's a wasteland out here, and there's a real chance we won't find more on the way. But I can't look at Russell, can't bear to ask. I know he'll refuse. And I don't think I could go through with it, even if it did mean getting to Leadville.

I follow my gut and kick the dead man, then drop down into the mud on my knees, rain smacking my back, and shove. I grunt and I cry and I roll him down into the water.

He floats away some, then drifts back to the bank, like the gravity of our living bodies is pulling him toward us because we need him for nourishment. Then he's finally sucked away, captured by the same current that took his friend. When he disappears, I realize I haven't heard Russell.

I race back up the mud, careless, forgetting to watch my feet so I don't tumble down into the water. It's getting dark but I can still see that Russell's eyes are closed. He's lying on his back and his chest looks still. *No*, I try to scream, but my throat catches. I reach him and crouch by his face as the rain pelts us.

6
ROOK

30 DAYS

The day of the appointment with Yasper had arrived. Rook cruised down the center of Main Street to avoid the water rushing along the curbside. Shimmering parking lots of flooded strip malls passed on his right, quiet residential homes on the left. A Walmart came into view, the parking lot packed so tightly with cars that there didn't seem to be a way in or out. One long line of umbrellas gathered by the foyer, a hundred different colors, probably waiting for a food truck to arrive. Not a police car in sight.

By the time the ugly orange stucco of the high school appeared on the right, Rook's mind had started turning against him. *Why hadn't his brother made contact yet?* If only his parents knew both of their children were safe, he would feel so much better about leaving them.

It wasn't fair. There should have been more time, time for the family to heal, to reunite before a catastrophe like this. What had happened?

"How many good summers do I have left?" Rook chuckled. It was one of the movie quotes his brother would bust out at the diner when they were little, those rare times the whole family was around the same table. He'd have everyone in stitches, and even back then, the way his brother thrived as the center of attention in a public place seemed so alien and inscrutable.

When they were kids, Rook had tried to do everything his older brother did: football, wrestling, camping, even dating girls. At least he pretended to try. Really, he hated those things, or was deathly afraid of them, and preferred to be studying or sitting behind his computer. But he wanted his big brother's approval, and for a few years, his brother had been happy to have him tag along, despite their eight years difference in age. They'd been so close then, and they were supposed to have a lifetime to nurture that bond. Now Rook didn't even know where his brother lived, whether he was still on drugs, whether he had even survived the earthquakes.

Passing the swampy grass that had been the school football field, he turned into an empty lot and parked. No sign of life, only the sheath of gray fog and the steady tap of rain. Would Yasper even show to pick him up today? The desolation made him feel vulnerable, and he fished for a radio station to distract himself. Nothing but static.

Ahead, Stone Hill stood tall. Behind it, Rook imagined the swollen Arkansas River, so wide now they would need to take a boat partway to the Yasper compound. He just had to stay calm and hope they came.

Voices startled him as the radio caught the sound of two voices.

"It's like the satellites just vanished," a man said. "Not communicating with the Earth anymore. One by one, they're going to blink out."

"God, I hope you're wrong." The other man sounded nervous. "There has to be a way to repair the damage to the upper atmosphere, if that's what's causing this."

"It's too late!" Rook spun the dial angrily until another station came in.

"How long can stationary fronts band the whole country?" a sad, whispery female voice asked.

"If the magnetosphere is too weak—I mean, if the sun really is burning up the oceans at the equator—it could go on for months," another woman said.

"And the European Union?"

"They can't even provide aid internally. The rain there isn't as heavy, but remember that their seismic activity is much worse. Italy has been cut in—"

The radio broke into fuzz. Before Rook could find another signal, a blue Ford truck caught his eye, rolling directly toward him.

He searched anxiously for a sign on the truck, any lettering or logo, but there was nothing. What if these weren't the Yasper men? *What if they're thieves?* He put his sweaty hand on the ignition.

An older man in a tan poncho emerged from the truck.

Rook saw the big Y logo on the plastic and heaved a sigh of relief. Rolling down his window, he waved. "Hey!"

"Rook Wallace?" The man squinted under his hood.

"Yes."

"You ready?"

Rook grabbed his suitcase and followed the man to the truck, where a younger guy sat in the passenger seat. The engine rumbled, and his old 4Runner faded into the gloom as they drove off. His dad had the spare set of keys. Would he remember to pick it up?

The driver eyed him through the rearview. "New meteorologist, right?"

Rook nodded.

"Thank god, we need all the smart people we can get." He reached back to shake hands.

"You're both with the shipping team?"

"Yes, sir." The driver jerked his head toward something out the window. "The ones you're going to protect from that shit."

Rook followed the driver's gaze to an ominously low formation of bubbling mammatus clouds.

"I'm going to try." His lifelong self-doubt, fomenting at the enormous responsibility that lay ahead, seemed only to grow. Doing something brave, he realized, at least the first step toward something brave, wouldn't make that doubt go away. He could only hope that if he kept doing the next right thing, his mind would eventually follow his body.

The men boasted about Yasper's successes delivering supplies until the banks of the Arkansas River finally came into view. A boat was anchored a few hundred feet away. Rook didn't know much about boats, but it looked new, with a long sturdy cabin so they'd be out of the rain.

Once inside, Rook peppered them with questions about company operations as the boat motored up the river. As he took in each detail, his stomach settled, and he began to feel a trickle of confidence again. He would learn quickly. He always had.

Soon the rain lightened, the river widened, and what had been mere images on the television and internet now appeared right before Rook's eyes: endless rows of homes submerged under the water, only their roofs visible. His heart sank. So many people were suffering without anyone to help. It made him even more eager to reach the compound and start learning.

After they had traveled north for a while, the river transformed into a giant lake with no end in sight. When he grew tired of watching the gray horizon, he tried to sleep on a bench.

Unlike his brother, the natural-born hobo, Rook had hardly traveled at all outside the familiar comforts of his hometown and the city of Pueblo. Just a stint at UCLA, where he'd practically lived in the library and on his computer. *Did you feel this scared each time you traveled somewhere new?* he found himself asking his brother. No, there was no way. It was one of the things he admired most about his brother, and always wished he'd been born with, too: undaunted courage and wanderlust.

Sometime during the evening, Rook awoke to a clatter and went on deck. The boat had stopped. Twenty feet away, on solid ground, was a waiting Jeep. They drove up winding mountain roads, shrouded by fog and high grass on both sides. Within an hour, the glow of the Yasper compound emerged from the dusk. After all the darkness and gray, he'd hoped it would cheer him up. But the only thing that kept running through his mind was how isolated the place was, just a speck of light surrounded by wilderness. At that moment, it was hard for him to imagine what good he could do at all, so far from everyone, and so completely alone.

7

TANNER

My hand touches Russell's chest, waiting for a breath. I feel almost faint with relief—it's there, the soft up and down.

He looks at me, struggling to make words. "You're . . . bleeding."

"I'm fine." I wipe my lip. "Are you okay?"

"Knocked the . . . wind out of me. You sure . . . he's dead?"

I can just barely make out the body, facedown in the water.

"He's dead. Come on, out of the rain before your cold gets worse."

He raises his hand in protest. "Catch my breath first."

Shivering, I look around, as if someone will spring out of the gloom and help me carry him to the tent. But there's nothing. Then it hits me as I stand up. I'm an idiot. I was almost ready to curl up on the mud beside him and let myself fall asleep, let the cold pull me gently into a permanent nothingness. It's so obvious I could slap myself.

Move the tent, not him.

The thought collapses my panic into purpose and I tread up the slippery bank. I pull out the tent poles, drag the canvas over, and set it up again. The angle makes it tough, but in five minutes he's under the roof.

The water's close enough that a mudslide could take the whole thing into the sea while we sleep, but it's the only thing left to do—hope that a night of rest will get Russell moving again.

I wrap myself around him, listening to him breathe, no more of the groans that were coming before. I share my warmth, timing his breaths to make sure they're coming evenly.

Behind closed eyes I see the face eaters' bodies floating away. What direction will the current take them? Will they pass through Colorado? And what about the whale?

Each time I've seen an animal alive in the rain, it makes me feel weak. They're supposed to be dead, but they're hanging on somehow, just like we are. They deserve someone's help, like Russell's always done for me. But even that's over, it feels like. He can't help me anymore.

I stop myself before I imagine him dying. I'm old enough and strong enough now. I'm not a little kid anymore. I can keep him alive.

Which means that after all these years following his direction, it will be up to me to decide what to do tomorrow—either we press on to Leadville, hoping for land and food along the way, or abandon our dream and follow the islands back to Rapid City, where they're murdering to feed themselves.

But at least there's the certainty of land that way. Backtracking might be Russell's only chance to recover. We could lay low on the edge of the city while he heals, and I could scavenge food, fuel for a fire. Steal if I have to. If we keep going toward Leadville, there's no guarantee of anything but freezing or starving.

Yet if we turn back now, it will be as if our struggle never happened. Every fire, clean pair of socks, cellar of food, battle for higher ground, and word of encouragement we ever said to each other—gone, like they never existed at all. He just wasn't supposed to get this sick.

I begin to understand the feeling the whale has given me—it's an ache for the life that Russell already got to live. It's selfish to want anything more than self-preservation in this world, but I hate that I never knew life before the rain. And we're so close now.

Take the chance, a voice starts in my head. *Go.* The words are so clear. *It's just a few hundred miles away. A city above the floods, with electricity, a community of people helping each other. Blue skies, green grass, and stars at night.*

The voice isn't mine, and suddenly I'm back there, five years ago, sitting by Timothy's fire.

TIMOTHY LIVED ALONE at the edge of a tarp town in Sioux Falls. No one hung around him because he smelled so bad, but we didn't mind. He was too old to hurt us, he was safe. Russell loved his stories, and they'd talk about the life only they knew. Russell and I both caught something worse than the flu from Timothy. We caught Leadville, Colorado.

"No one could have known how thin it was, how fast the rain would strip it all away," Timothy said one night.

"Strip what away?" I asked.

"The veneer, the way civilization was before the rain. A thin coating made up of all the human principles." His voice was deep and sounded like rust.

I tried to imagine what it must have been like, a life filled with a million hopes and dreams, not one about staying warm or dry. Then Timothy asked Russell to tell our story.

"Philadelphia when the earthquakes hit, on to Pittsburgh when the rain rose high enough to touch the Walt Whitman Bridge. After the high-rises collapsed into a lake of shrapnel, Indianapolis. We've been one step ahead of the water the whole way."

"What about your life before the rain?" Timothy looked into your eyes when he asked a question, and he didn't look away until you were done answering him.

Russell gave the longest sigh. "I was a handful growing up—drinking, drugging, fighting, stealing, the whole nine. Played in a few traveling bands. Wasn't too much older than Tanner here when I finally gave up my vices. It took a few years of trial and error, but I finally got myself into recovery, became a pretty good runner. I lived a great life for a long time."

He sounded like he was talking about someone who'd died.

"Tell us more." I felt brave because of Timothy's wine.

Russell leaned back and shifted his eyes to the sky. "I never thought I'd settle down, but I did, in Philly of all places. Do I look like a gym teacher?" He chuckled, the lighthearted laugh that used to come so easily and often. "Sold my guitars, gave up the traveling and the races. Met the love of my life and got a steady job. We had our baby girl and . . ."

The silence went on long enough that I grabbed his hand.

He took a deep breath. "That life's long gone. I've got Tanner now, and where we're going, there's a future for both of us."

Timothy waited for Russell to continue.

"When the TVs and phones were still working, the news said the flooding wasn't bad in the West. They reported that in one place it wasn't even raining. I heard people talk about a city, somewhere in Colorado—"

"Leadville?" Timothy leaned forward in surprise.

"I don't know. But we plan to get to Colorado eventually, and look for it."

Timothy drew a sharp breath and raised his arm into the firelight, rolling back the dirty plastic and the cotton underneath. There were numbers tattooed on his wrinkled shoulder.

"What does it mean?" Russell edged closer.

"Something came over the radio, a few years ago. A voice giving coordinates for a town in Colorado named Leadville, said it was a safe haven. That it wasn't raining there. A whole city, highest in the country, power working and all. A community of people still helping each other." Timothy let out a breath that sounded so painful. "Blue skies, green grass, and stars at night."

He leaned out of the firelight.

"Tanner." Russell grabbed my arm. "Maybe Leadville is our city!"

"The radio went silent, but I took the numbers down, right into my arm so I wouldn't forget. I thought I'd find a way to go, but it never happened. Was too old then, and I'm too old now."

Timothy fixed his eyes on me. I felt a chill down my spine as he spoke. "But *you*, there's still a chance for you to live a real life. Take the chance. Go."

That was the first time it really sank in for me. I knew all along what we were hoping to find, but it felt distant and cloudy. After Timothy said that to me, I never again thought it was out of reach. The chance was mine to lose.

Russell memorized the numbers on the spot. He says them out loud sometimes, like if he forgets, we'll forget where we're going.

N 39.2, W 106.2.

The way Russell looked at me when we got back to our tent that night made me shiver. "It's a sign, Tanner. There are no coincidences. Everything happens for a reason. We're meant to go to Leadville."

It sounded stupid to me at first—I had never thought there had to be a reason why things happen. But Russell bought into it, said it was our brightest hope. From then on, thanks to Timothy, we had a real destination. We were going where the veneer was still thick, a place where I could find a real life.

Not long after that night, we left Sioux Falls. It was horrible leaving Timothy. He was dying, cheated by the flu like so many others, yet we lived on. He wished us luck and said goodbye. That has to be the reason we're still alive, closer than ever to Leadville. To take the chance.

After a long night, going in and out of sleep, the canvas of the roof brightens. In the light of day, my decision becomes clear—we have to keep going. It's up to me to give us the final push.

I wrap my plastic suit tight and step outside to check the weather. The rain feels lighter and there's no wind. Hope floods my spirit for a moment.

"Russell," I call inside.

He jerks at his name and sits up slowly, rubbing his head. I put my hand on him. His forehead's hot, even I can tell.

I firm my voice. "You're taking the antibiotics."

He ignores me, crawls to the tent flap and looks outside. "Boat's still here." Then he sits down and coughs, squeezing his temples like there's a tremendous pain. "Christ, I feel like shit."

I grab our sack and root out the antibiotics, then hold up the bucket to collect water for him to swallow.

"Tanner, we're saving those for you." He sounds annoyed.

"Look, I'm sorry your daughter died!" My anger surprises me but I can't stop myself. "But I don't need them and you fucking do. I'm done arguing with you about it. And we're going to Leadville. There's enough food for a week. We'll find something by then. We always do. But not if you're too dead to bail."

"I don't know," he says after a long silence.

"You don't know what?"

"I'm afraid if . . ." His eyes hang with a tired expression, mouth open, waiting for words to come. "I've never felt this bad in my life. I don't want to let you down if we get stuck out there. Maybe we should go back to Rapid City until—"

"Go back to what?" I'm totally losing it. "Fighting to stay warm and dry and feed ourselves? Everyone who wants to take our shit? Our bodies? I won't go back to that anymore."

I expect him to lash out, but he doesn't. And for the first time, he doesn't argue about the medicine. He just takes one of the pills, drinks it down with water from the bucket, and starts to weep into his hands.

"I'm sorry." I kneel, wrapping an arm around him. "I didn't mean all that."

He sniffs, looking at me with a bright red face. "No, you're right. This was my idea. I wanted you to believe in Leadville as much as I did, and you do. We have to keep going."

"Look, all you have to do is bail for me when the water gets high, okay? Same as you did yesterday."

The oars slice easily once we're in the water and I row off with everything I have. I ask him to get me some hardtack out of the sack. After I eat two crackers, I hear water splashing behind me. I twist around, expecting to see him spilling into the sea. Thank Poseidon, he's bailing. We're going to make it.

I keep the sun on our left, leaving the Bighorns behind. The sun, just a bright splotch behind the thick clouds, wears across the sky, and soon the land behind us shrinks to nothing but the rain and the gray and the flat brown sea. I beg Poseidon that we don't get any waves.

Give us a strong current, help us reach land before dark.

My muscles feel strong, and I'm calm, in control. It's almost peaceful. Every time I start to get nervous about Russell, I call his name and he snaps to and bails out the water again.

There's no sign of land all day, and we drift through the night. I bail when the water gets high, too paranoid to fall asleep. By the time the morning comes, I'm tipping over with exhaustion. Russell promises me I can nap a little and he'll keep bailing. We trade throughout the day, stopping only to eat. Late in the afternoon, I'm back on rowing and bailing because he can't keep from shaking. My eyes hang on the ripples for a long time, trying to blank the thought of being stuck out here another night, of Russell's shaking getting worse, of being helpless as he dies in front of me. When I check the horizon, the sun is already sinking again.

And then I spot it. Just a small bump rising from the murk where the clouds meet the sea.

"Russell!"

He jumps for the bucket.

"No, look." I point.

"Is it land?" He squints, forming a halfhearted smile. "Don't miss it, Tan." Then his smile fades and he's out.

Renewed energy burns through me. I row and bail, even though my hands and feet are half-numb. I'm convinced I feel the rubber forming like a crust over my leg, and when I peel off the plastic suit, the pants, and finally look at my naked body, I'll see the markings, the rubbery pink welts, the sign that the skin is ready to come loose at the slightest prodding.

The sun sets lower, but as long as the water stays calm, and the current isn't pulling too hard, I'm sure I can get us to the island.

As we get closer, a long shock of color appears on top of the island. Blue, blinking with firelight. My heart jumps. They must be plastic roofs, a tarp city bigger than I've seen in years. Face eaters don't live in tarp cities—people do. Real, living people. I feel my muscles tensing with hope. The proof is right in front of us—I made the right decision. A small piece of the veneer is on that muddy rock, and I intend with the last of my power to get us there alive. I bail, and then I row.

"We're on our way, Russell." I think of how dry it will be under a tarp, how much food there must be for such a big camp.

Digging with the last of my strength, I stand up to stroke in, then hold the oar sideways to slow the boat. Rain punishes the muddy rise where I wedge us in. The hull sticks into the muck on the first try, and I collapse onto the bench.

"We made it?" Russell slowly starts to rise.

"Hold on." I check for my knife. Still in my pocket. "There are a lot of tarps up there."

"Tarps?" He surveys the barren slope.

"It looked like there was a big camp at the top."

I can't help but imagine the tarpers will have wood under their roofs, dry wood. The thought of fire gets me to my feet and I walk the nylon rope through shallow water to a large root slicing under the mud, raised enough to tie up the boat. A root's never as good as a rock, but I don't care. I tug the line and it feels stable enough.

"Wait here," I tell him. "I'm going up there to check."

"No," he grunts, grabbing my arm. "Too dangerous in the dark. We stay the night in the tent. I'll go with you in the morning."

I'm too exhausted to argue, and he's right. I'd be useless in a fight right now if anything went wrong.

Instead, I carry the tent to the first flat patch of earth, twenty feet from the shoreline. After double-checking the poles to be sure they're secure, I go back and hold my hand out for Russell. He moves rigidly, like his bones need oil. With his left palm on my shoulder for balance, we tread up the mud.

I pull the tent flap open for him and he wobbles down to his knees, dragging a streak of dirt across the floor of the tent. I pull the boat as far off the water as I can and flip it, then get inside with him. He's already curled in a ball against the canvas.

Before I let him sleep, I force him to take another antibiotic and eat some crackers. In a few minutes, the sun is almost gone and it grows dark inside. I rub the pruned grooves of my fingers, worrying they'll never be smooth again. But then the lack of motion, the pure stillness of the ground beneath my body, puts me into a trance. I can stop struggling now, and I can finally have a long, undisturbed sleep. No nightmares of face eaters hunting us or water slowly filling the boat. Just a dream of fire.

Even if it's just going to be us stealing fire, I'm excited for what's up on the hill. Anything's better than another night on the water. I push into Russell and loop my arms around his chest.

"We made it," I whisper.

He utters a long and deep *mmmm*, like he's as content as me to be on solid ground.

I wrap myself tighter, sharing my warmth, pushing us out from under the dripping leaks.

My body heat finally starts to come back, but my toes stay numb. For a moment, I think the hypothermia is setting in really hard, and the rubber skin, and it's no time to go to sleep. I should go get help right now from up the hill and gamble everything on a chance to be saved. But my closed eyes are an elixir I can't escape, my worn-out body finally at peace after days of rowing. The blackness pulls me quickly to the edge of the sweetest sleep I've ever known. We breathe in sync, and the sound of the rain on the tent fades away.

8
ROOK

2 MONTHS

Dear Mom,

I guess we're stuck writing good old-fashioned letters now that the phones and internet are down. Captain Lawrence, the head of shipping here, told me he'll deliver you my first letter, and you can reply by sending yours to any shelter we ship to.

To answer your last question, life here's exhausting, but in a good way. I think I've made a strong impression on my bosses. Mr. Marrow, the company owner, put me to work under Dr. Franklin, the head of meteorology. They both care a lot about the refugees. Marrow even had lunch with me so we could get to know each other. He started Yasper as a supplement business in his twenties (he's Dad's age now), and he filed twenty patents before one caught and the company took off. Anyway, he bought the power plant here two years ago as an investment in the energy sector, then built the compound around it. The plant was converted to run on its own microgrid, so we can keep going if we lose main power. A fleet of trucks comes in and out every day for shipments, and we're building a harbor and buying boats to maintain the distribution network in case the rain doesn't stop soon.

Dr. Franklin, my day-to-day boss, has degrees in spades:

meteorology, climatology, geology, and atmospheric science. He reminds me of Pop-pop with his long white beard and glasses, and he's just as intimidating.

Every morning I check the radars for low-pressure systems, then I overlay the images on our scheduled routes for the day. For each route, I predict total rainfall, soil saturation, and provide a percentage chance of flooding. The day shipments go out using my recommendations: either follow yesterday's route, make adjustments, or cancel the trip. We're reaching most of the Mountain Time Zone, so I check some routes in the middle of the night for morning returns.

Oh, and Dr. Franklin invited me to help with his side project. He's investigating the causes of the rain, long-term consequences, and possible solutions. I'll be able to do a lot of research because, though there's no more internet, the compound is equipped with a very fast intranet, which means everything already on our servers can be remotely accessed on our computers. Thankfully Franklin downloaded just about everything we'd need. Sorry for geeking out, but it's a very efficient setup, and even your nerdy son is impressed.

Maybe that's more than you wanted to know! Truth is I haven't had much time to myself, so work is all I think about. I did make a few friends, though, and we're going to start a weekly card game. Anyway, tell me how things are going at home with you and Dad. I can't wait to hear from you.

Love,
Rook

3 MONTHS

My Dearest Son,

It's wonderful to hear about your work, and I want to know everything! We're fine. The water got too high at home, so we're at Gerry's house now. I cannot count how many refugees your father has saved, with Gerry's help. It's a double-edged sword (as un-Christian as that sounds) because every time they go out, I worry myself sick.

Your father won't let me come with him anymore because every time I see a stray dog or cat hiding from the rain, I take it back with us, and it's getting too crowded here.

Do you remember the Arena Sportsplex? It's a shelter now, and from what we've heard, one of the best. It's big and at a higher elevation. The best part is that your company ships there directly. A big group already lives there, pooling resources and helping each other. It looks like that might be our next move.

It's a small miracle in an awful situation: at a time when you can't get police or ambulances, people are working together like family. I can see you rolling your eyes at this, but God is working through people!

I won't worry you with anything else. Remember, people are good at heart, and you are no exception. I hear all the time about the lives your company is saving. I'm so proud of you. I love and miss you terribly. Write soon, and tell me more about your work, about your new friends, and most importantly, have you heard anything from your brother? I've been feeling terrible lately about how things went between us and him.

Love,
Mom

4 MONTHS

Dear Mom,

Unfortunately, I haven't heard anything from big bro yet. Phone and internet probably went out more quickly on the East Coast. I know it's hard, and we all wish we hadn't been on such bad terms when this started, but we need to stay positive and have faith he'll contact us. It's funny, it used to annoy the hell out of me, but God, what I wouldn't give to have him busting my chops right now. He'd have us all in stitches in a minute. Sometimes I question whether it was right to cut him off, too, but I remind myself how many times we tried to get him help. Don't feel so bad about it. We had no choice, and we did the right thing. There's no way he'd still be holding on to resentment. I just hope he's safe and finds a way to reach one of us soon.

The thought of dogs running around you makes me so happy. Do you ever think of Bartleby? I still miss his fluffy butt. I'm glad you want to know more about work, because honestly, there's not much else I could write about.

Our compound is a close huddle of buildings next to the power plant, despite all the acres Marrow owns up here. I'm losing weight from walking a lot and eating only vegetables from our grow station. Marrow shipped in hundreds of fully grown plants, and he's talked about planting more. Maybe I'll end up becoming vegan? You know how eating meat always skeeved me a little bit. The power plant provides electricity, which from what Captain Lawrence says is getting rare out there. Does Gerry have a generator going?

Most of our shipments start on the river now, to be eventually picked up by people from the shelters at the closest passable land routes. There's a big map of the Mountain Time Zone states hanging in the lab, and we use thumbtacks to keep track of the refugee shelters and camps. It's a motivating reminder of how many people are struggling to survive. Each thumbtack has a radius penciled around it to show the distance that the refugees can travel to meet us for supplies. That way, we don't have to go all the way to the shelters themselves. The Arena Sportsplex has a wide circle around it, so I'm glad to hear that if you have to move, you'll go there.

I'm still helping Dr. Franklin investigate the rain. Our working hypothesis is that the earthquakes weakened the magnetosphere, which is what protects us from deadly solar winds.

Without protection, equatorial oceans are heating and the atmosphere is wicking up all the moisture and dumping it across North America. There's more water locked up beneath the Earth's crust than all the oceans combined. Between the warming, earthquakes, and volcanic eruptions, this water may be rising up, adding to the planet's water cycle, and magnifying the flooding exponentially.

What keeps me up at night is what triggered the earthquakes in the first place. It's controversial to link climate change to earthquakes, but it makes sense to me. We heated up the atmosphere with emissions, melted the glaciers, and the Earth's crust went bust. It drives me crazy to think it could have been prevented, every government competing for money to the point that we sacrificed our planet. I won't go on about it, but it still makes me so mad.

As for making friends, you'd be proud of your nerdy son! I've made quite a few, which surprised me a little, but I'm happy about it. There's Cleo, another meteorologist, who busts on me constantly, helping keep us both sane. Ed Bowling, head of chemistry, who's taught me how to play Texas Hold'em and subsequently taken all my money at our weekly games (money that's pretty useless right now anyway!). Gene, a chemist who's more concerned with his alcohol and tobacco stash than his work. He's a good guy, though, he shares everything but his Scotch. Dina is the power plant director. She's pretty nervous about her job all the time, until she starts rolling everyone with her stone-cold poker face.

Unfortunately, we just learned the government can no longer help us out. They hardly even respond to our radio communications. Rumors here are swirling that federal and state governments are dissolving fast. We're going to miss the resources we were hoping to receive: gasoline, food, medicine, vehicles, and equipment. I'm not sure what it means for Yasper long-term, but Marrow's confident we can find a way to continue our humanitarian efforts.

One more thing: Ed's creating a new medicine, designed to help people deal with the psychological effects of the constant rain and gloominess. Marrow's got so much raw material stored up from old medicines, decades' worth, that he's going to give it away free. Ed says it will be better than an antidepressant, a mood-lifting drug that also treats pain. I won't take it (you know how bad my hypochondria can get), but I think it could make a difference.

Stay warm and dry, and write back soon.

Love,
Rook

5 MONTHS

Beloved Son,

We're now at the Arena Sportsplex. It's a madhouse here, but people are friendly enough. The football field is covered in tents. Everyone's taken a shine to your father, naturally. They're calling him Sheriff. I think he likes it.

I've been struggling to get him to rest. They constantly go out in jeeps and boats, looking for people. Some refugees are living in settlements with nothing but tarps to keep the rain off. Even this place will be too crowded eventually, but what can we do? I can't tell him to stop rescuing people. God help me if I did.

A cold is spreading today. I feel sick and I would write more if I felt better. Thank God for your company (and you), because we have antibiotics. Truthfully, with all the death out there, this place is a bastion. And thank you for your heartfelt words about your brother. Keep him, and us, in your thoughts and prayers. You are always in ours.

Love,
Mom

7 MONTHS

Dear Mom,

Sorry I didn't write last month. There was a bad storm, and the ships couldn't leave. I'm glad you're safe at the Arena Sportsplex. The crowding worries me, though, and your cold. Please write back and let me know you're okay. I'd like to hear from Dad, too. I know he hates writing, but maybe you could get him to dictate a paragraph? Haha.

I keep having a recurring dream that all of this has stopped, and things are back to how they used to be. The whole family is together again in Pueblo. Even Bartleby is there. It's so perfect, and then so awful when I wake up. I promise though, I'm not as depressed as this might sound. Write back soon!

Love,
Rook

8 MONTHS

My Baby Boy,

Your father had to calm my panic when more than a month passed without a letter! I miss you terribly. I wish I could see you one more time, and just hold you. I miss my boys, but I don't want you to worry, or try to come here! Promise me you'll take no unnecessary risks.

There's something I'm hesitant to write, but I have to. We're planning to leave the Arena Sportsplex. There are too many people here, and everyone's goodwill is wearing thin. Fights have been breaking out, and as desperately as your father tries, he can't do anything to stop the growing lawlessness. I'm starting to get scared for our safety. The generator is running poorly, so we've been using fires. Unspoiled gasoline and dry wood are tough to come by, but your father somehow finds time to get fuel between search and rescue trips.

The storms have been rattling the rafters of this place. It gives me nightmares. I don't know where we'll go, or when, but I'll be sure to tell you soon. Write back and tell me how things are with your new friends!

Love,
Mom

9 MONTHS

Dear Mom,

I don't want you going to one of those tarp towns. I'm going to ask my boss if you and Dad can come live here. I have a small apartment, but if I sleep on the floor, there's plenty of room for all of us. I could easily split my meals.

The company has hardly any radio contact with anyone outside the Mountain Time Zone now. The reception goes in and out, and some repeater towers that amplify our radio signals have been washed away. Marrow's scrambling to import all the crude oil he can find and get a small refinery up and running here. It scares me to think of a world in complete darkness, unable to communicate. I love you both.

I'll write soon and let you know what Mr. Marrow says.

Love,
Rook

10 MONTHS

Mom,

Did you receive my last letter? The shipping crew said they delivered it, but they didn't get a reply. I'm worried sick. The crew said refugees were evacuating the Arena Sportsplex to higher ground and forming camps in the foothills. I hope you didn't go to a tarp town.

I'm sorry to tell you my request was denied. Mr. Marrow said if he allowed it for me, it would have to be for everyone. It pisses me off because we have enough resources to sustain so many more people than just employees!

There's one positive thing: the company is having success with the new medicine. It's called Red, after the pill's color, and the shelters receiving it have requested more. They told the crew it's making their lives "livable" again.

Please write!

Love,
Rook

11 MONTHS

Mom,

This is my last attempt to reach you by letter. It's been three months since I've heard from you. If I don't get a reply this time, I'm going to ask Captain Lawrence to look for you. If I can go myself, I will. I don't care what the risks are, I need to know you're okay.

Love,
Rook

9

TANNER

It's morning already, daylight beaming in through holes in the tent, when the sound of heavy breathing wakes me. I sit up, panicking that Russell is gasping for air, but when I look, he's fine, still sound asleep. The heavy breathing starts again, and I realize it's not coming from inside the tent. My whole body seizes up with fear as a large shadow streaks along the wall.

"Russell, someone's trying to get inside!"

The shadow passes by our heads. It huffs, pushing a long snout into the canvas.

"Russell." I shake him, excited and scared all at once. "There's a dog outside the tent."

I can't believe a dog is living here. My memories are cloudy because I was so little then, but I met a few dogs in Pennsylvania. I remember thinking they were friendlier than people, but as much as I want to meet this one, I'm frightened it might eat us, or bark and alert the tarpers. I fumble for my knife and prod Russell again.

He sits up and sees the shadow.

"I'll be damned." His voice sounds better until he coughs, and the dog jumps back and barks. Russell dives for the tent flap.

"What are you doing?"

He sticks his head out and shushes the dog. "I don't want it to attract attention."

The dog pokes its head right through the flap. A dirty blond mutt. Its fur is soaked through, but it doesn't look cold. It wags its tail as it comes in and starts licking Russell.

"Good boy." Russell's grin is bigger than I've seen in months, making me forget the danger we're in. The medicine must be working.

The dog pushes past Russell as soon as it spots me. A giant tongue lolls out and slides across my mouth. I back up and spit, but he's persistent and pushes in again, happy to meet me for some reason.

"Alright, let's go, boy. Out." Russell directs the dog's chest, but he doesn't want to go and Russell doesn't have the strength to make him.

Everything around us is awful, bitter cold and gray and desperate, but this dog is in ecstasy at meeting two strangers who, as likely as not, would eat him before petting him. But he stays anyway, wagging his whole body, expecting love.

And then I hear shouting.

It sounds distant, but loud enough, even with the smacking rain. The dog cocks his head toward the noise.

"Voley!" the voice hollers.

The dog looks confused, unsure whether to leave so soon, but a loud whistle sounds, and he darts outside.

Through the canvas I watch his silhouette bound up the hill and out of sight, and I hear talking. It's his master, asking what he's found.

Russell starts looking frantically for his knife.

"It's gone," I remind him, stuck in the face eater's chest, floating somewhere out on the rain sea. I watch the shadow of a person start down the hill. "Someone's coming."

Russell tries to go outside, but he's so slow and awkward that he slips.

"How big did this place look?" He sounds short of breath.

"Pretty big. The tarps at the top went as far as I could see. That's a good thing, right? Means they can't be face eaters?"

"Right." He doesn't sound convincing. "Give me your knife."

"You're too weak." I pull it away, scared but willing to slice anyone who comes at us.

"Who's in there?" It's the dog's master.

"Tanner, give me the knife." Russell tugs my arm.

I hang on to it and step outside the tent. I stand a better chance of protecting us now, and he knows it.

The dog is wagging its tail next to a man aiming a rifle at me. "Don't move! Tell me what you're doing here." He sounds young, but I can't tell how young because he's in a yellow full-body rain suit, his face half-concealed under a drooping hood.

"We're heading to Colorado. We got lost coming out of the Bighorns." I raise both hands.

"Drop the knife or I shoot."

I drop it.

He eyes our rowboat. "You came all the way from the Bighorns in that?"

"Yes." I try to sound calm as adrenaline buzzes through my body.

Russell hacks violently in the tent, and the man, unmoving, keeping the rifle trained on me, asks, "Who's we?" The dog sits obediently at his side.

"I'm Tanner, and Russell's inside. Just two of us. He's really sick. We need fire. We have a small bit of food we can trade."

The man walks down the slope but doesn't lower the gun, like he's expecting me to jump at any second. "Get him out so I can see." He gestures to the tent.

"I don't know if he can. He's really weak."

"Do it."

"Russell, can you come out?"

He must have heard everything because he's already crawling around the tent on his hands and knees. He stands up, leaning on me for support.

"We didn't mean to trespass." Russell gathers his breath. "We're just passing through to Leadville, Colorado."

The man studies us. He lowers the gun and takes off his hood. He's just a boy, no older than me, with dark brown hair across his face in a wet mess. And his skin is alive. Even from ten feet away, I can tell. Life is glowing in his dimpled cheeks, his wide-set hazel eyes.

"I'll ask my dad if we can let you rest here. Looks like you could use it. Can you make it up on your own?" He gestures to the hill.

"Yeah." I put Russell's arm around me.

"Stay in front of me and walk up."

He keeps his distance, never putting the gun away but no longer aiming at us, and we walk past him. Voley leaves his side and runs circles around our legs as if the rain's a playful thing to him and we're his best friends even though he just met us.

Every few minutes I look back and see the boy watching. Near the top of the hill, he passes us, probably frustrated with how long we're taking to climb the sludge.

I watch him move up the slope with ease. His body is fit, not emaciated like Russell's. I feel a strange energy rolling off him. It's the warmth. I can tell, even from way back here.

We reach a flat expanse and the blue tarps start to appear.

The boy stops us and raises his hand near my head. I flinch, then realize what he's doing. He pushes my hood up so he can see my face, then smiles like there's nothing wrong in the world.

"I'm Dusty, by the way." He looks at Russell. "Hopefully Dad can fix you a spot in the infirmary."

I wonder if this is all a setup to eat us. But his gun's lowered, enough that I could jump on him and wrestle it free if I didn't think the dog would rip my neck out.

"We don't expect anything for free," Russell rasps.

"That's good to hear." The boy nods.

We walk right into the camp. On either side of a main dirt road are rectangular tents, ten feet tall and quilted together into an endless row of blue tarp housing. The walls hang flat from angled tarp roofs, each tent with its own doorway slit, some tied open and others closed.

My hope spikes when I see one tent with smoke rising from a metal tube on its roof. As we pass its open doorway, I catch a glimpse inside.

There's fire burning in an oil drum. Two women who look about Russell's age and a much older man sit around the flames, all wearing thick gray sweatshirts, drinking from mugs. They look healthy like the boy. My instinct tells me none of them are face eaters.

The boy leads us to a tent on the left side of the road and pulls open a flap, tying it up to make a doorway, then leads us inside what must be his home. The floor is covered with the same blue plastic as the walls but darkened by a million muddy footprints. White plastic chairs and a small folding table take up the center of the room, and two more doorways look like they lead into connected tarp houses. Cans line a shelf along the wall, and I can't believe all the supplies sitting out in the open—rope, tape, cans, flashlights, knives, pans and pots, propane tanks, dry towels, clothes, cardboard boxes—all organized neatly, unruined by the wet.

"Wait here." The boy looks at me, like he wants to be sure we make eye contact. "The infirmary was full yesterday, but I'm going to get my dad and see if he can get an extra bed for you."

"Thank you." I'm too tired and stunned at his kindness to make the words sound grateful enough. I pull out a chair for Russell. He sits and lays his head in his arms.

"You did it," he mutters.

"We did." I squeeze his hand.

Voley sits by my chair and I pet his wet fur. He licks my hand and gazes up with a goofy open-mouthed grin, like he's never thought about the horrors of the rain. A beautiful melody floats in through the open doorway from the road. Someone on the street is whistling.

I watch the road through the door, waiting to see what they look like. A short woman walks by, curly white hair poofing out underneath her yellow hood, shoulders hunched over two large pails. I catch a glimpse of her brown face, haggard and wrinkled, a stark contrast to her vibrant melody. It's so happy.

"Russell, do you hear the whistling?"

He shifts his head. "Mm-hmm."

"Birds used to sing like that all the time?"

Then the woman is gone and a child walks past, following her.

She turns her head and looks right at me. It's a little girl, her rain suit way too baggy but clean yellow, like the woman's. Big green eyes stare at me.

"Hi." She waves.

I'm stunned. "Hi." I wave back.

"You're dirty." The girl stops walking and smirks. Voley darts out into the rain and rubs his nose against her leg. "Voley!" She bends and scratches his ears.

I notice the whistling has stopped. The girl runs her finger down Voley's snout but keeps eyeing us as the old woman returns, both pails in her left fist. She grabs the little girl's hand.

"Come on, Bryn, time to go to the greenhouse," she orders, then turns her soft face toward me. "Sorry to bother you."

"It's okay."

"You just arrived?"

"Yes."

"I'm Rose. Nice to meet you." The little girl tugs Rose's arm. "And this is Bryn."

"I'm Tanner. This is Russell." I glance at Russell, but he's asleep. The smell of smoke drifts past from some nearby fire. Voley runs back inside.

"If Voley likes you, that's good enough for me." She eyes Voley as he scoots up to my legs. "Daniel's a good man. He'll take care of you."

"Daniel?"

"Well, get yourself cleaned up and visit us at the greenhouse sometime. Come on." She tugs Bryn's arm and they're gone.

"We have bunnies!" the girl calls out.

I wonder if I heard her right. Did she say *bunnies*?

The smoke on the wind thickens, bringing the scent of something that makes my stomach rumble. Food cooking. The whistling starts again, and I listen, mesmerized until it fades into the patter of the rain.

I scratch my neck underneath my rain suit. My hand is brown from the dirt that must be caked over my entire body. It's been so long since I've seen myself, it scares me to think what I would see in a mirror.

I scan the ceiling for a leak but can't find a single hole, just patches of silver duct tape here and there. Even the floor is dry except for muddy footprints.

The luxuries this place might hold for us creep into the secret place where I hide my desires—a fire, a hot meal, a shower, a warm bed. And friendship. All the reasons I've been so desperate to get to Leadville are suddenly right here.

10
ROOK

2 YEARS

Ed Bowling slapped Rook's arm and hooted. It stung, but not as painfully as the embarrassment of all their faces staring at him. Still, it felt great to have his work recognized by his friends. It hadn't seemed likely he would make friends as close as these when he'd first come to Yasper, but after losing contact with his family, it was the best thing that had happened to him.

"Your buy-in's on me tonight, Rook." Ed smirked devilishly as he pulled a bottle of whisky from a bag. "And so is this fine Islay Scotch."

A dim electric lamp cast the poker table in bronze light, the whisky glowing gold.

"Where the hell did you get that?" Gene's eyes popped open, his hand reaching for the bottle. "You stole that from me!"

"I know better than to touch your liquor." Ed pulled the whisky out of reach. "This is courtesy of Captain Lawrence's personal stock, in honor of the ships, and lives, saved today by our very brightest—Rook Wallace!" Ed's salt-and-pepper goatee expanded with a pudgy-cheeked grin as he ruffled Rook's hair.

A round of clapping reverberated through the dusky cafeteria as Rook looked from face to face, overwhelmed with gratitude. Cleo, Ed, Gene, and Dina—they were all here. Rook's eyes hung a little longer on Cleo. She wasn't much older than he was, and he'd always found her attractive. Her beautiful amber skin, big brown eyes, and quick muscular frame had been the subject of many daydreams, but he'd never worked up the nerve to tell her. Besides, Yasper forbade romantic relationships, which made it easier to accept. Friendships had to be enough, and now, more than ever, they were.

"Gene, you're a real ass. You think Ed would steal from you? It'd be nice if you shared your stash for a change, like everyone *else* does." Cleo's smooth brown face crinkled into her joker smile, aimed at Gene, who rolled his eyes. Everyone but Ed, always the protective one, chuckled a little, but no one as loud as Cleo herself, who always had something smart to say, and always laughed at her own jokes.

Ed shook his head and fixated on his cards. "Don't start, Cleo."

"No, let her talk." Gene's green eyes seemed to glow against his reddening freckles. "What else you got to say, Miss Witty?" His tone had turned to indictment, and though Cleo never meant anything by her jokes, Gene was the most sensitive of the group, and she knew it.

"Come on guys, I'm right, aren't I?" Cleo cast her big brown eyes around the table for support, but everyone ignored her, focusing on their hands. Only Gene's eyes stayed up, glaring. "All I'm saying is if you were as careful with your bets as your liquor and tobacco stash, maybe you wouldn't lose your pay each week." She threw in another few chips. "I raise you."

Gene gave her a nasty look, ready to say something, but instead he folded his hand and pushed it to the center, then pulled a rolled cigarette from his shirt pocket and lit it.

No one spoke for a few seconds. Rook squirmed in his seat, preferring the embarrassment he was feeling earlier to this awkward silence.

"Look, everyone needs a distraction here," Dina spoke seriously, gray eyes narrowing as she raised Cleo's bet. "Gene has his liquor, so what? You have your childish sense of humor. And I take both of your paychecks every week." Her eyes rose to Cleo's with the same deadly poker stare she wore even when she wasn't playing cards.

Ed threw his cards down, folding. "What's on everyone's nerves today? Can we cut it out? We're supposed to be celebrating Rook."

Ed played peacemaker when things got testy. Too many hours around the same people, doing the same things, and adding alcohol, wasn't always the best mix. Maybe because Ed was the oldest, almost twice Rook's twenty-six years, he could sense when to bring everyone back before things went too far.

"You're right, I'm sorry, Gene." Cleo eased forward in her chair and offered a handshake. "I'll try not to bug you about your *distraction*." Her eyes widened with shock as he offered her his lit cigarette instead. "Whoa, this is a good start. Thanks."

Gene sighed and ran a hand over his high forehead, down through his stringy blond hair. "Dina's right. We all need distractions here, but I'll try to get better about sharing."

"What's Rook's distraction?" Cleo took a long drag and looked at him.

"His is pretty boring, I'm afraid." Ed's bushy black eyebrows rose as he put his arm around Rook. "Seems like his is just doing his job, huh?"

But Rook's distraction was all of them, their friendship. He almost said it, but he just nodded instead, throwing his hand down. "I fold, too."

Cleo put her elbows up and leaned into the table. "That's seven for Rook. Seven route cancellations where this punk made the override."

"Overriding Dr. Franklin this time, too. *Whoa, boy*." Ed side-eyed Rook, elbowing him. "It takes guts to do that."

"I know Captain Lawrence is keeping track of your work. Has to be twenty more lives saved just today." Dina fiddled with a radio on the table. An old blues song soaked the room with bass and electric guitar. "You still don't get to pick the music, though."

"Hey, you should get Captain Lawrence to run some favors for you, smuggle back more of this Scotch or something." Gene put the bottle to his lips.

The praise really belonged to Rook's insomnia, double-checking numbers at night when he couldn't sleep. It stopped him from thinking about his family. Most of the time he was catching his own mistakes that Franklin had missed anyway. There would be no whisky request, though, as Lawrence was already doing Rook a huge favor: going off-route and checking the small settlements surrounding the Arena Sportsplex, giving out a description of his mother and father in hopes someone had seen them. Although he'd given up on hearing anything from his older brother, Rook was still hopeful for word about his parents.

It was against company protocol to go off-route on a search expedition. Most employees had lost contact with loved ones, and if word got out, everyone would want Lawrence's help, and who knows how angry Marrow might get. Still, Lawrence had offered, wanting to repay Rook for saving so many of his crew's lives.

"Let's go, deal 'em!" Rook waved for some cards to get their eyes off him.

"Big blind." Cleo bounced two chips onto the table.

Gene threw in his chip. "Don't hurt as bad when it's funny money."

Ed dealt.

Rook took a sip of whisky. "Smoky peat, faint citrus, and the *memory* of salt," he imitated a Scottish brogue.

Cleo started to sing along to the music, then Gene and Dina joined in. "It's flooding this morning, come evening it'll be flooding again," they belted in an off-key harmony.

Rook stared down at two queens. *It's going to be a good night.*

BY THE TIME the dealer chip had gone around the table six times, Rook was up five dollars, humming along to the songs Dina played on the radio. He had begun to drift off, daydreaming about the time his brother taught him to play a blues scale on the guitar, when the sound of swearing brought his attention back to the table.

"They requested another fucking shipment already?" Cleo chuckled. "You really did good with this one, Ed."

Rook looked up. "What's that?"

"Red." Gene shook his head. "I'm the one who presses the pills, and *he* gets all the credit."

"No work talk, God help me," Ed protested. "This is the one night a week we can—"

Cleo cut him off. "When's Marrow gonna let us have some, too?"

She threw her ante into the pot. "I mean, I keep hearing it's a wonder medicine. Employee discount for when the Scotch is running low?"

"The medicine's really helping, huh?" Rook raised the bet, eyeing Ed. Of course he trusted Ed, but whenever drugs came up, Rook thought about his brother. During those first years of his addiction, money went missing from his dad's wallet, his mom's purse. Then pills from the medicine cabinets. It happened so fast. The carefree, loving, playful big brother he looked up to was never around, and when he was, he acted aloof, nervous, and withdrawn, his normally tan skin gone the color of a ghost. By the third family intervention and fourth arrest, Rook had read a dozen books about codependency and addiction. He'd finally understood the sad truth by that point: there was no way to help someone like that, even his own brother. Addicts could only help themselves. He'd never know if his brother had ever gotten clean.

"It sure is helping," Ed said compassionately, maintaining eye contact with Rook. "And the usage guidelines are clear, so it won't be misused." Ed was the only one Rook had trusted enough to open up to about his older brother's past, and Ed seemed to sense Rook's concern.

"You'd have to be one stupid fuck to start abusing drugs now, huh? When the whole country's drowning?" laughed Cleo. "Better off getting rid of those ones, anyway. That 'addiction is a disease' stuff is horseshit. It's about willpower, and only the strong are going to live through this."

Gene laughed, too, but it wasn't clear to Rook whether he was laughing with Cleo, or at her boisterous and slurred speech.

Ed sighed. "Really, Cleo? How much have you had to drink tonight?"

Rook felt the anger swelling up, harsh words crawling toward his throat, but just as he was ready to speak, Dina turned the knob on the radio. The music blared louder.

Rook looked at his new cards, a pair of aces, then flipped them over. "I'm done." He needed a walk to clear his head. Such a great day, ruined by one stupid comment.

Looking back, he stared at Cleo. "It *is* a disease." He stomped out into the rain.

HE'D JUST STARTED to cool off when a voice cut through the dark night.

"Rook!"

Someone on the main road was waving their arms, their face difficult to see through the downpour. The figure started to jog, slowing as Rook walked closer. Under the outdoor lights, he saw Lawrence's thick white mustache bent into a frown around his leathery cheeks, which were lined and chalky from constant exposure out on the boats.

"Captain Lawrence," Rook greeted him eagerly.

Lawrence shook his head slowly, his stony blue eyes sympathetic.

"You checked them, all the surrounding settlements?" Rook fought the truth written into Lawrence's expression.

"Every one within thirty miles of the Arena Sportsplex. They're not there." Lawrence's usually gruff voice was soft, compassionate. He placed his calloused fingers on Rook's shoulder.

Rook looked up and pulled his hood back, letting the rain sting his eyes. His parents were the last thread of the old world, and he'd clung so tightly to the hope that he would see them again. The hope snapped that quickly, and the weight of the truth came crushing down upon him. Between the alcohol, his anger at Cleo, and now this news, Rook couldn't stop the quick stabbing sob that cinched his throat.

"It doesn't necessarily mean they're dead," Lawrence said, sighing. "There are lots of smaller camps beyond my reach."

"I study the maps every day. The terrain surrounding the major shelter zones is covered in floodwaters, debris, crumbling buildings . . ."

"I know." Lawrence's wizened face remained calm. "Let me be dead straight with you, Rook. I didn't want to say this, but I think you need to hear—"

"Tell me!"

"I'm out there on those floodwaters every day. I know how hard it is to survive in one of those small camps. You need to decide if it's useful to keep holding on to this hope, Rook. I know it's difficult, but the odds are, they're gone. I had to go through it. I'm sure most of your friends have. You can let it torture you for years to come, but what I've learned is, it's better to let them go. Accept that they're dead, so you can find some peace."

Rook covered his face with his hand, muffling his sobbing. It wasn't right to take things out on Lawrence. He'd been kind enough to disobey protocol and do the search.

"I have to get back. Hang in there." Lawrence patted Rook's shoulder and walked back toward the apartments.

Rook stood alone in the rain, oblivious to the cold. His childhood, the happiest moments he'd shared with his family, flashed through his mind like a picture reel. Then, one frame froze.

It wasn't a happy memory. He was ten, lying in Children's Hospital with bacterial meningitis. It was the only time he'd ever heard his father cry, and the only time he'd felt certain he would die. He could see it on his parents' faces. Even on his brother's. They'd all tried to comfort him, but the way they'd looked at him, it was clear they didn't know if he'd pull through.

When he finally got home, his mom stayed at his bedside for a week, taking his temperature and bringing him soup and juice and Advil. His dad took a week off from work, and his brother told all his cool new friends he couldn't hang out because he needed to take care of his little bro. That look on their faces, there in the hospital, had scared Rook to death. But it had also been the first time he felt, really deeply *felt*, how much they loved him. And how much he loved them back. In his prayers, he'd promised himself to make sure they knew it when he got better.

But now, he wasn't sure if he'd ever shown any of them how much he loved them.

He was crying softly when someone touched his arm. It was Ed, his wiry goatee dripping with rain, eyes spread wide with concern.

"What are you doing out here? Is it what Cleo said?" Ed's face turned toward the road. "Was that Captain Lawrence?"

"They're gone." Rook wiped his cheek and pulled his hood down over his face. "I'm going to my apartment."

"What do you mean? Who's gone?" Ed's eyes searched Rook's face.

"He checked all the settlements for me. They're gone." Rook started walking toward the road.

"Oh no, no, no." Ed grabbed him by the shoulders. "I'm not letting you leave. You're hanging out."

"With Cleo? Did you hear what she said? And Gene laughed." Rook's disgust rushed back, directed unfairly at Ed.

"It was the alcohol. They'll apologize." Ed fidgeted. "She doesn't know about your brother. None of them do. Her and Gene probably never had a loved one who was an addict. They're just ignorant."

Rook forced a few deep breaths. Deep down he knew that, without his family, all he had left were his friendships at Yasper. If they broke too, everything was lost.

"I'll straighten them out." Ed hugged him. "I'm sorry about your parents."

Rook let Ed hold him. *I trust these people*, he reminded himself. *They're all that's left now.* The Yasper family, Marrow called it.

As they returned to the cafeteria, he thought about the pain he'd carried for his brother first, and now his parents. The mystery of their fates had haunted him for over a year. Maybe Lawrence was right. Maybe he had to accept that they were dead, learn to let go. But not tonight. Tonight, he was getting drunk.

"I need another drink."

"Drink all you want." Ed pushed the doors open. "You're a hero."

The whole group crowded the entrance. Cleo stepped forward and held out her hand. "I'm so sorry, Rook. That was a really dumb thing I said."

Gene put his hand on his heart. "I'm sorry I laughed."

The others chorused apologies, and their upturned eyebrows and somber stares cracked the last of Rook's resistance.

He shook Cleo's hand. "It's okay. Deal me those aces again, and get me a shot."

They clapped him on the back as he returned to his chair. The music blasted and the liquor worked quickly, dulling Rook's sadness. Cards were dealt, and soon everyone was laughing again.

But the drunker he got, the more something kept nagging at him. It was the feeling, deep in his gut, that Lawrence was right. For more than a year, he'd carried the certainty that one day life would return to what it *should* be: visiting his parents on the weekend, rehashing old times with his brother. With that certainty gone, he wasn't sure his friends here, the company's mission, would be enough. At bottom, the good he was doing at Yasper, he hadn't been doing it just for himself. He'd done it to make his family proud.

Fuck it. He took another swig. *I'll find out in the morning how this feels. Tonight, I want to feel numb.*

11
TANNER

Dusty returns with a wiry older man who must be his father, the same hazel eyes and strong nose as his son. There are only a few wrinkles around his thick gray-and-brown beard. It's hard to believe, but just like the others, he isn't wearing a rain suit, just a big sweater and a beat-up pair of blue jeans, both dry. Another sign of how well-maintained the roofs are here.

"This is my dad." Dusty smiles proudly as his father extends his hand.

"Daniel." He gives me a firm handshake. Russell tries to speak, but his voice cracks into a hoarse whisper.

"I'm Tanner." I nod to Russell. "This is Russell."

"You look like death." Daniel's eyebrows rise as he looks Russell over. "We're clearing a bed for you, should be ready in ten minutes. Dusty tells me you washed up in a rowboat. How long were you out there?"

I sum everything up for him in a minute, all the way back to Philadelphia.

"In a rowboat from Rapid City?" Daniel repeats like it's impossible. "Unbelievable." His fingers tug at his beard as if he can't make sense of us.

"Where are we?" I almost expect him to say Leadville, like we were wrong and it isn't the rainless city we imagined, but still closer to the veneer than anything we've seen in such a long time.

"You beached yourselves in Utah." Daniel spreads his arms.

Utah? I look at Russell's red face, his eyes still closed.

"Our camp's called Blue City. We're on the Wasatch Range, not far from Salt Lake City. I take it you didn't mean to come this way?"

"We're going to the Colorado Rockies," I say.

"You're damn lucky the current brought you here. I hear it's gotten cold as hell that—"

"We don't accept help unless we can pay for it." Russell jerks his head up.

Daniel chuckles. "Don't worry about helping until you come back to life some. We'll do what we can for you."

"How much trouble did you have on the way?" Dusty asks.

I tell them about how we lost Russell's knife.

"I wish I could say we didn't have that problem in these parts, but unless there's a place where the rain doesn't fall . . ." Daniel bends over Russell. "Russell, I'm gonna help you to the infirmary. Do you think you can stand up with me here?"

He lifts Russell out of the chair with ease.

"See that she gets cleaned up," Daniel tells Dusty. And then, with no protest from Russell, they leave together into the network of tarp tunnels.

A spike of panic gets me to my feet as soon as they disappear around a corner.

Dusty raises a hand. "No one's going to hurt him. Look, we help real people. You two were a pretty easy tell. Even the face eaters who still talk, they don't look like normal people."

He's right, they've always seemed like some critical part of the veneer is gone in them, like somehow you can tell just by their eyes.

"I need to get our stuff from the tent."

"I'll get it for you soon." He takes my hand and guides me back to my seat. The warmth of his touch stops my thoughts dead in their tracks.

I struggle for words. Just go with it, I tell myself. Try to remember how to have a conversation with a stranger, like you used to do back East, before things got so bad. "Did you grow up here?"

"My whole life. Dad grew up in Salt Lake City. When the rain first started, folks moved everything they could to the foothills. Eventually, they went higher into the Wasatch until they got here. There are a lot of camps in the mountains around here. Sometimes supplies come in from ships."

"Ships?"

"A merchant comes and trades with us."

"It feels so safe here."

"It is." Dusty sighs. "There've been attacks on smaller settlements nearby, but none here, thank God. We did have a few bodies wash up with teeth marks. Word is that the ones who aren't too far gone are hunting together now, attacking settlements and divvying up the bodies, I guess. That's why we approach castaways with a gun. I didn't mean to scare you."

"We don't eat people."

"Neither do we. I know there are desperate places, people are starving out there." He shrugs. "But it's evil to kill innocent people. My dad always says we're lucky the floods rose slowly in Salt Lake. A lot of religious folks from these parts were stockpiling food even before the rain. It gave them time to move supplies and keep everything together. We have a greenhouse here, with grow lights. Crops of beans, peas, broccoli, collards, radishes."

The bustling of people walking and talking outside the door distracts me. Someone laughs. A genuine, lighthearted chuckle. Leadville is supposed to be the only place left in the world where people can grow food, can trust each other, can laugh like that. This must be a dream, like the hundreds I've had before—I'll wake up with my face smushed in the mud, and my gut will be ripped out again by the sight of our flimsy tent walls.

Dusty's eyes widen. "What's wrong?"

"I'm just so . . . I thought we were dead."

"You're not going to die," he speaks seriously. "Tell me about your friend."

"Russell? I'm hoping it's just a cold. He might have a fever, I don't know, I'm no good at checking."

"No, I mean, who is he to you?" His hazel eyes study me, his smooth, bright face unworn by the rain. I struggle to answer him, to describe the person who means everything to me. I don't know how to explain the man who saved me, taught me to read and shoot, and watched over me for as long as I can remember.

"He rescued me from a flood when I was little," I finally say. "We've helped each other stay alive since then, since Philadelphia. We're going to Leadville together."

Dusty looks skeptical at my second mention of Leadville. "What's there?"

"The veneer," I blurt out the thing so obvious to me, so sacred to everything I've been chasing my whole life, that I'm almost afraid to describe it out loud, to share it with someone I've just met.

He softly shakes his head in confusion. "I don't know what that is."

"It's what makes people human, all the principles that held society together before the rain. Supermarkets and houses and doctors and schools and jobs and families and having a future where you can be anything you want." As I repeat what Russell's told me, the words feel like my own now. I believe them. For some reason, I want this boy to believe them, too.

He blinks a few times. "You think all that's in Leadville?"

"It's the highest city in the country. Not a tarp town, but a real town with brick buildings and electricity. And it's not raining there."

Dusty laughs and I feel like shrinking into the mud. I turn to the door and watch the smoke drift by, cursing myself for opening up. Then there's the warm touch again, his hand on my arm.

"I'm sorry," he says when my eyes return to his. "Look, I've never lived anywhere but Utah. I can't imagine traveling like you have, being out in the floodwaters." He frowns and looks at the ceiling. "We had a few castaways from Colorado, and they sure didn't want to go back that way. They said it was freezing cold, terrible storms. I just think it's crazy to go anywhere but west."

"Well I'm not trying to convince you of anything," I speak a little too sharply, feeling myself locking up. "And we don't take without doing something in return. I can work right away, anything you need." I feel desperate to prove my worth and buy time for Russell.

He laughs and waves his hand. "You need a hot shower. Come on."

I follow him through a corridor to a hanging flap. "Go inside and turn the knob on the left. You'll have hot water."

I don't know what to say, except that I can hardly believe him about the knob, that hot water will come out of this rusty pipe hanging over my head.

"There's a hook there, you can hang your clothes up. I might have some stuff that'll fit you. Just holler when you're done," he says.

As I hear his footsteps recede, I realize I need to thank him and actually sound grateful this time. "Thank you, Dusty!"

"No problem," he shouts back.

I know it's a risk, caring about people. Names that aren't Russell or Tanner are just missing pieces of the veneer, inconsequential and risky until we reach Leadville. There's no point in knowing any of them. They haven't mattered since Timothy. But maybe it's because we came so close to dying this time that some of my protection has broken down.

I take off my clothes slowly, peeling the plastic away first, then the wet cotton, dirtied and shredded in most places. I'm naked. I feel exposed for the first time in forever. Open and alone. I must really stink, but I can't tell.

I turn the knob and water comes out freezing cold. I jump back, knowing it was too good to be true. But then, it starts to steam, and gets too hot, and I turn the knob the other way. When I get under it, my whole body melts. There's nothing to clean myself with so I use my hands and turn the water as hot as I can stand.

How are they getting hot water?

But I can't stop to think it over—it feels too good. I run my hands over every part of my body and rub it all away, let the scalding water dissolve the dirt and grime and the rain. No welts on my legs, my arms. No rubber skin. I breathe easier. I open my mouth to the running water and let it pour inside. It bounces off my tongue and my shoulders and runs down my hair. Dirt-streaked water pools on the grated plastic board at my feet, but then it turns clear. I stop thinking about what's going to happen next. I become one with the water, and all I know or feel is the heat.

My mind stays completely blank, every muscle relaxed, until finally the water becomes warm, then cool, and finally cold. When I turn it off, I'm freezing.

"Dusty, I'm done!"

Already shivering, I feel a deep chill run down my spine. It's something he said, popping into my head uninvited. "*It was freezing cold, terrible storms. They sure didn't want to go back that way.*"

Maybe Colorado, but not our Leadville. They just didn't know where to go. I push the ugly thought away as I hear Dusty's footsteps approach.

12
ROOK

8 YEARS, 4 MONTHS

The aroma of smoke and spice permeated the noisy cafeteria as Rook tried to find Ed. It was their once-a-year Family Meeting, as Marrow called it. At least a hundred people waited patiently in folding chairs, staring ahead at the blank projector screen hanging from the rafters. In the throng crowding the food tables, Rook spotted Ed's distinct U-shaped bald spot.

"Didn't you have a full head of hair when I started here eight years ago?" Rook slapped his back.

"Yeah, and you weren't a prick back then either." Ed lifted a plate of lentils and chickpeas. Rook filled his own plate and followed Ed to the rest of the crew, seated near the front row.

"Hey, buddy." Cleo raised an eyebrow. She, Gene, and Dina filled out the row to the middle aisle, where Mr. Marrow was walking toward a pallet serving as a podium. "Would you look at that son of a bitch?"

"He loves showing off for the Family Meeting, doesn't he?" Gene pretended to fix a bow tie on his sweater.

Rook stopped eating to take in Marrow's dark ash suit and shiny black shoes, a stark contrast to his vibrant red hair and pale skin.

"Man knows his fashion." Cleo sounded pleased. "Let him dress up once a year if he wants. Hell, I wish I still had something to dress up for."

Rook was imagining what she would look like wearing a tight gown on her long, muscular frame when Marrow began to speak.

"Ladies and gentlemen." Marrow flashed white teeth. The crowd continued to chatter until he raised a hand. "Thank you."

The lights went out, and the projector whirred to life. An image glowed on the screen: pictures cropped together in the way that had once been common on social media. Two were of the East and South Harbors, both touching the bloated Arkansas River. The third was a bird's-eye view of the Yasper compound: the two L-shaped apartments, the long X-shaped laboratory, the fat square of the cafeteria with its teardrop greenhouse extension. The main road sliced between the buildings, ending at the power plant, with a small group of what looked like dots behind the plant, the spent nuclear fuel casks. Behind that, the electrical grid and crude refinery.

YASPER—HOW OUR MISSION IS CHANGING flashed in dark blue letters underneath. A soft uplifting piano track began to play.

"He's going all out this year," Cleo whispered. "Think he'll reveal the new iPhone?"

"As long as he brought liquor, I don't care what he reveals." Gene tipped an imaginary bottle. It was customary for Marrow to throw a party after his address.

Someone touched Rook's shoulder from behind. He turned to see Dr. Franklin.

"Can you help me with my presentation up there?" The soft, raspy question sounded like an order.

"Of course." Rook regretted his answer instantly. *In front of all these people?* The thought terrified him.

Ed cast a suspicious glance, gesturing at the stage. Rook shrugged in confusion.

"It's been many years since grant resources ran out and we were disconnected from the political forces that provided them," Marrow began. "They are no longer able to guide, or govern. At a time when it's never been clearer that we are truly on our own, when no other large organization exists in the West, we are continuing our mission. We are still—" Marrow's eyes swept proudly across his audience "—saving lives!"

Rook joined the others in clapping.

"We have long since transformed from a de facto arm of the Red Cross to a trade facilitator," Marrow went on. "Our infrastructure allows exchanges between most shelters within two hundred miles, giving them access to each other that would otherwise be impossible. In turn, we take only a fair share, enough to secure the future of the Yasper family." He stepped aside and pointed at the projector screen.

A map appeared, a computerized version of the one that hung in the lab. Rook's heart sank as he looked to where the Arkansas River bent east. His home, Pueblo, had become a permanent flood zone, both city and suburbs now dangerous graveyards that would lure only the most desperate souls to seek abandoned supplies.

It was hard to remember how the map used to look. The rivers, once pencil thin, now ran in thick heavy strokes, hundreds of miles wide, merging with thousands of fat lakes. There were only five big shelters left after the others were lost to flooding, forcing scattered refugees to form many smaller, disparate camps.

Large swaths of the map were shaded in gray, areas that no Yasper employee had directly observed. The gray surrounded the Mountain Time Zone states and stretched to the edges of the map. Dotted over everything were numbers too small to read: estimated water depths, many of them Rook's own work.

Suddenly, the map animated. The rivers grew wider and the lakes got fatter. Giant blue blobs engorged, connecting bodies of water, eating up most of the land between the highest elevations.

"I know this is frightening, but—" Marrow turned to Dr. Franklin, who stood just offstage "—this is what our meteorology team predicts the West will look like twelve years from now, after twenty total years of rain. As you can see, the only logistical impact for our compound will be losing a direct route to East Harbor. Fortunately, the flooding will bring South Harbor closer, and preparations are already underway to make it our primary departure hub."

Franklin walked onstage. "We believe the atmosphere is healing, simply because humanity is no longer polluting it with emissions. But there is no way to determine how long the healing will take." His eyes darted to Rook.

Oh God, no . . .

Franklin wiggled his finger, signaling for Rook. The room fell silent as he pushed his way past his friends into the aisle, feeling suddenly short of breath, each heartbeat loud enough for everyone to hear.

Franklin winked at Rook, "Tell them what we know."

Rook turned to take in the faces, too many of them, all concentrated on him. He gulped, refocusing on the doors in the back of the room.

"Dr. Franklin and I have been investigating what happened in the beginning, what's happening now, and where things are going." Rook rubbed his palms over his jeans. "We believe that years of eliminating environmental protections pushed climate change past the breaking point. Glacial melting and rising CO_2 have contributed to tectonic unrest in the distant past, so there's a precedent suggesting that global warming caused the initial earthquakes. Twelve thousand years ago, we know from geological records, the melting of half-mile-thick Ice Age glaciers led to fifty times the background rate of volcanic and seismic activity. Volcanic degassing is at the heart of the geochemical cycles that determine the planet's climate and atmosphere, and the most abundantly degassed vapor is water. Along with this, the upheaval of the Earth's crust depletes the magnetosphere, which is sustained by the stability of our planet's molten iron core. Without a strong magnetosphere, we are vulnerable to solar wind and overexposure along equatorial latitudes. The jet stream carried—continues to carry—moisture and dump it across North America. There is also the real possibility that vast stores of water, many times more than the world's oceans combined, are being released through earthquake fissures and volcanic activity. This means the surface water is rising not only from rainfall above, but also from sources below, enormous reservoirs of H_2O locked in the transition zone between the Earth's crust and mantle. There's no way of knowing when this will stop. It could be a year, it could be millennia. The truth is that we lack the equipment and scientific infrastructure that we once had to do the proper research. The most important thing we can do to keep ourselves safe, and continue our operations, is use the atmospheric data from the last eight years to predict future rainfall and to create these maps of what the country will look like if current trends continue. That's what you're seeing now." Rook turned to the map.

The crowd rustled with whispers and muted questions.

A hand shot up. "If the sun is hitting us harder, why is it getting colder?"

"The sun's hitting hardest along the equator. The climate is less uniform without the stability of the magnetosphere, and the cold here is what's bringing the warm air masses down in rainfall. We also have to consider the possibility that the geographical poles are shifting."

Dr. Franklin winked at Rook, dismissing him. More hands went up, but Rook was already rushing offstage, a tremendous wave of relief carrying him past his friends.

"Damn Rook, you need a flashier suit." Cleo nudged him. "But good job scaring the hell out of everyone."

Rook's mind turned to the alcohol. He didn't want to dwell on the fact that he'd probably soured everyone's mood with his ominous speech. Still, he'd been instructed to do it by Dr. Franklin. It hadn't been his decision to release the hypotheses they'd been exploring.

Marrow quieted the crowd as the projector flashed a bar graph.

"These columns represent the demand for our most valuable commodity, Red," Marrow continued. "As you see, we're having a lot of success. Although we no longer give it away, as the company would become unsustainable if we did, our evidence shows that the medicine is continuing to have a huge positive impact on refugee life. It's working so well, and we have so much of it, that I've decided to provide it—free of charge—to all employees. You may see Dr. Ed Bowling or anyone on his staff for dosages and guidelines."

As Ed pumped a fist into the air and the audience cheered, Rook couldn't help but join in, clapping for his best friend. Ed was a genius, and the medicine he'd created was a miracle, giving refugees the mental fortitude to endure the worst crisis in human history. Having battled his own depression since losing his family, Rook wondered if it wouldn't be worth trying Red himself. And for a second, he wondered sadly whether a medicine like Red could have helped his brother avoid years of destructive self-medicating.

"I will now go over some of the ways we'll strengthen our business," Marrow said, "as well as our collected store of supplies, which all of you, as employees, have a stake in."

Rook drifted off as Marrow droned on about route changes and fracturing shelters. He already knew all of it; he'd helped prepare the information. Instead he thought about Cleo, how great she looked, and that if Marrow ever allowed employee relationships, he would work up the nerve to ask her on a date. *The worst thing that happens, if she says no, is your life goes on just the same as it was before.* He could hear his brother's advice, the first time he chickened out of talking to a girl. *Nothing to lose by trying, but you might lose the love of your life if you don't.*

The crowd applauded as Marrow finished his presentation and walked to a table where alcohol was lined up. He popped a bottle of champagne, causing another cheer and a stampede toward the liquor.

"How bad was it?" Rook turned to his friends.

"You looked nervous as hell." Cleo raised her eyebrows in mock horror.

"Shut up. He did great." Ed brushed her away as Rook blushed. "Let's get a drink."

They fell in line, chatting about getting poker going after the party died down. Oldies music, the kind of rock and soul Rook used to hear his parents play, blared from a speaker somewhere. Cup in hand and about to pour a drink, he felt someone tug his arm.

He turned to see Marrow, his icy-blue eyes motioning Rook to step out of the line. His stomach dropped. He'd surely said something he shouldn't have, or provided too dark an outlook, but as they walked away for some privacy, Marrow beamed.

"That was great! I think you gave everyone some hope. Just reminding them that there's safety here with this company." Marrow's hand remained on Rook's shoulder. Before Rook could thank him, Marrow grew serious. "I know how hard it was for you after losing your parents. Dr. Franklin and Dr. Bowling told me how much depression you've worked through over the last seven years. You pushed through the pain and found renewed purpose in our mission here. Not everyone does that. We've had a few leave. God knows where they are now."

Rook couldn't help feeling a bit betrayed by his friends, but he kept his smile wide. "Actually, Captain Lawrence gave me some advice, a long time ago, that really helped. He told me I had to accept that they were gone in order to get over it. It took a few years for that to stick, but I've found peace. I believe so strongly in what we're doing. After we lost the grant, I worried our mission might get harder, but you've adapted so well. We're still the good guys."

"The reason I'm bringing it up," Marrow said, "is that I wanted to tell you . . . I went through the same thing. I lost everyone I loved in a single earthquake. I stayed in bed for a week, a complete breakdown. I wanted to kill myself, but I didn't. I realized that I had what so few others do, the power and influence to do something. Over the last eight years, my employees have become my new family. I hope you feel the same way." Marrow raised his glass.

Rook clinked it, and they drank. Before Rook could reply, someone else had already stolen Marrow's attention.

Rook slipped through the bodies and the noise. Boisterous voices called out to each other as friends gathered in circles, laughing and chatting. He didn't recognize many of the faces—the normally itinerant shipping crews, power plant workers he'd never met—but he did recognize the look on everyone's faces. It was pure joy. Rook felt like he was walking on air, replaying Marrow's praise in his mind, certain his family would be proud of him.

He spotted Ed standing on the edge of his own circle of friends.

His old buddy pulled him in. "Come on, hot shot, join us for a toast."

"To Rook, for doing such a *fine* job up there." Cleo held up her glass.

"Hear, hear!" Gene cheered. All faces were on Rook again, but after braving the podium, this was nothing. And maybe he did deserve it.

"No," he said confidently. "To *Yasper*, and to saving lives."

"To Yasper!" Ed clinked his glass into the others, spilling some liquor.

Marrow's words rang true: they *had* become family.

Once most of the crowd was gone, Ed set up the cards. It didn't take long for Dina to win the pot. Everyone else was too broke or drunk to keep playing.

Ed raised an eyebrow in concern as Rook stumbled toward his rain suit. "You want to wait a few minutes and I'll carry you home?" The others laughed.

"Yeah, I'm not trying to lose sleep because I have to dig your body out of a ditch in the morning." Cleo leaned back, somehow still drinking.

They'd already polished off an entire handle of whisky between them, and Rook hadn't been so drunk in years. But he felt okay to walk back home, if a bit wobbly. He shooed them off with a grunt and left, feeling the happiest he had in the longest time.

When he reached his hallway, something caught his eye. A white piece of paper stuck out under the door to his apartment. Bending down to pick it up, he found a sealed envelope, the front and back both blank.

He glanced up and down the hallway. No one was there. Everything was quiet. His heart racing, Rook stepped inside and ripped open the envelope.

DEAR SON,

I AM WRITING ONCE AGAIN, AS I HAVE EVERY YEAR, BECAUSE YOUR MOTHER REFUSES TO LOSE FAITH THAT YOU ARE ALIVE, AND THAT ONE DAY YOU WILL ANSWER US. THIS TIME IS DIFFERENT THOUGH. SHE IS VERY SICK NOW, AND WE ARE WITHOUT ANY ANTIBIOTICS. I FEAR THAT SHE WILL NOT LIVE TO HEAR FROM YOU AGAIN.

IF THIS LETTER SOMEHOW REACHES YOU, PLEASE FIND A WAY TO WRITE BACK AND LET US KNOW YOU ARE ALIVE AND OKAY. WE ARE HOLDING ON AS LONG AS WE CAN AT THE SETTLEMENT KNOWN AS CANVAS CITY.

LOVE ALWAYS,

DAD

13

TANNER

I bring the fresh clothes to my nose, taking in the scent of them. Dusty's extra pair of gray sweatpants, a sweater, boxer shorts, and dry socks. I put everything on, feeling good until I think of Russell, and that fast, the tranquility of the shower is gone.

Dusty gives me directions to the infirmary, and after winding through a few corridors, I enter a long room with three rows of metal-framed beds, each one with a patient under impossibly clean white sheets. A few people walk around the beds, wearing clothes as spotless as the sheets. Scanning for Russell, I spot Daniel, the only face I recognize.

"How is he?" Then I see Russell behind him on one of the beds.

"Gloria thinks he'll pull through fine now that he's on medicine."

Anxiety rushes out in a long exhale. "I don't know how to repay you."

"Well, Dusty always needs help in the greenhouse." Daniel seems preoccupied with a clipboard in his hands.

"Of course, I just need to talk to Russell first."

"You can try. He's been in and out." Daniel steps away to talk with one of the infirmary workers.

I lean over the bed. "Russell."

He comes to life, turning his head and opening his eyes. "It's warm in here." He smiles weakly.

"They're fixing you up." I grab his hand, freezing cold.

"They are?" He raises his eyebrows like he has no idea what's going on. "Tell them we're saving the antibiotics for you."

"I will." I press my lips against his forehead, so overwhelmed with everything, that we've arrived somewhere safe, warm, and dry. "I love you."

"Tan." His face grows serious as he glances around. "It's not Leadville. We'll get back in the boat tomorrow. I'm sorry I slowed us down."

I can't begin to answer him. It must be delirium. There's no chance he'll be ready to leave by tomorrow. And I can't stomach the thought of taking us out in that boat again so soon.

"It's okay." I squeeze his hand, knowing better than to argue. A short red-haired woman with thick-rimmed glasses walks over. She looks about twice my age.

"Hi, I'm Gloria," she speaks gently. "One of the nurses. Are you Russell's daughter?"

"Yes." It just comes out of me. When I glance to see Russell's reaction, he's asleep again.

"He has pneumonia. His fever was pretty high." Her tone grows serious. "And there's an infection in his leg."

I cringe. It's back.

She must sense my fear because she places her hand on my shoulder very gently. "We've given him the strongest stuff we have. He should pull through fine. I would let him rest."

Her confidence puts me at ease, reminding me that the veneer is here, even if just a little.

"Daniel said you washed up all the way from Philadelphia?" Gloria's face stretches in astonishment. "Well, you're very lucky, both of you. Blue City is good people."

"We'll pay you back, I promise," I stammer.

"I'm sure you will." She smiles warmly, then looks ready to ask another question when I hear my name.

"Tanner!"

I see Voley first, wagging his tail in the doorway. Dusty stands beside him in a yellow rain suit. I shove out my hand, rusty with my social etiquette, and Gloria shakes it as if I've behaved normally.

Dusty hands me a too-big yellow rain suit and a pair of rubber boots, better gear than I've had in forever. "Dad said you wanted to help."

Leaving Russell to get his sleep, I follow Dusty through the tarp hallways, pulling the suit on. Voley charges ahead, leading us outside onto the road. I catch busy movements inside some of the open doorways, loud talking, fires. Smoke puffs from thin pipes at the top of some of the tarps, bright white.

Dusty stops. "You must be hungry." Voley circles us and sits right in the mud, half his coat covered in it.

My instinct is to say no—we've accepted too much already. I haven't even done any work yet. But my hesitation must be enough for him to realize how ravenous I am. He tugs my hand toward one of the doors.

"Come on."

Inside, the smell of woodsmoke mixes with the scents of onion and garlic. Three long fold-up tables run the length of the room, a large silver kettle at the end of one. A few people sit, eating out of metal dishes.

Something else distracts me. There's music.

A young boy is sitting on a crate behind the kettle, picking a guitar. It's dented, with silver duct tape holding it together, but the sound is beautiful. My first thought is to tell Russell because he loves to play guitar, even though he hasn't had one since Pennsylvania when he used to sing me to sleep.

"Are you okay?" Dusty stares at me.

There's too much life, almost unbearable to my senses, and it makes me want to scream or run away.

"I hope you like spicy." He lifts two empty bowls, then gestures at the boy. "Tanner, this is Terry."

"Glad to meet you, Tanner." Terry's thin lips spread in a quick smile. He puts his guitar down, grabs a large steel ladle, then scoops thick glop into our bowls. I notice half the fingers on his left hand are missing. He looks younger than me, but his bronze skin is crisscrossed with scar tissue.

"Your playing is beautiful," I say.

"Thanks. You're new here?"

I nod.

"Well, enjoy the stew. You look like you could do with some hot food." And before I can say more, he picks up his guitar and goes back to the crate, like he's afraid he'll forget what he was playing. The plucking starts slowly until he has the same melody going.

I sit across from Dusty, wondering when the last time I complimented someone was. The luxury to give and receive compliments, with someone you don't even know—to care about beauty at all—has to be part of the veneer.

"Well?" Dusty stares, spoon halfway to his mouth.

I put the reddish-brown glop into my mouth. The texture is a little strange, but the spices are delicious.

"It's good," I say through a mouthful.

"You eat as fast as I do," he chuckles as I shovel everything down. "You can get more if you want."

The ultimate piece of the veneer—second helpings. But I shake my head. My stomach has shrunk. If I eat more, I won't be able to move.

Voley nudges my leg.

"He can lick your bowl." Dusty points down.

I lay the bowl at my feet. Voley shoves his snout in.

"How old is he?" I pet his ears.

"Seven now." Dusty's hand accidentally brushes mine as he pets Voley.

"I always wanted a dog." I pull away, startled by how warm his skin is. "How did you get him?"

Dusty's eyes light up, and he separates his hands by a foot. "He was this big when we found him."

I make a soft *aw*. It's surreal—being able to stop long enough to appreciate how cute something is, the image of a puppy Voley.

"The mother was already lost when Dad discovered the litter in a high-rise in Salt Lake City."

"What happened to his brothers and sisters?"

"They didn't make it." Dusty's smile fades. "But Voley did. It's so rare to see dogs. I think that makes it more important to spend time with them. To learn from them."

"Learn from them?"

"I think they teach us unconditional love. It's hard to remember that sometimes, with the rain."

I've never been close with a dog, and after how impressed Dusty was with my travels, I'm afraid to admit it. What a strange feeling—I know Russell loves me, but suddenly, I want Dusty to *like* me.

The music grows louder. Terry sings smoothly over the rhythm in a beautiful, gravelly voice.

"I met Rose and her daughter, Bryn, earlier." I sway gently to the guitar.

"Bryn is Rose's granddaughter. They're good people."

"She said something about bunnies?"

"Shit, the greenhouse." Dusty springs up. "We better go."

At the end of the road, I get my first glimpse of the open wasteland beyond Blue City. A long plain of mud stretches toward two hills that cut off the view, the same dead emptiness I've seen so often. I turn around and take in the shocking contrast—the bright and noisy settlement, fires flickering against the walls of blue tarp, creating an illusion of sky. A long building with a clear plastic roof juts from the end of the road, lit up too brightly to be another fire.

"I hope she's not mad." Dusty signals me to follow him inside.

The smell hits me first, sweet and strangely familiar. Flowerpots and Styrofoam squares litter the floor. Voley plops down by the door as Dusty leads me past large white bags filled with something. I poke one of them. My finger pushes in easily.

"Is this dry mud?" I can't believe how much there is.

"It's soil." Dusty spins, distracted by Rose waving at him from the brightly lit back section. "Sorry I'm late, we stopped to get something to eat." Dusty stands in front of Rose's small frame. Bryn is crouched farther back, and I can only make out the top of her curly black hair as she bends over something.

As they chat, I look directly at the artificial lights along the ceiling, bright as I've ever seen, and keep staring, certain that this is what the sun used to look like, until my vision starts to turn white.

"Are you okay, dear?" Rose sounds concerned.

I can't stop blinking at her. "I think I hurt my eyes."

"Don't stare at those lights then!" she laughs.

After a minute of rubbing, I can see again. There's a loud thrumming sound, and I spot the source—a wide, ribbed contraption with tubes running out the side and crawling up the walls toward the lights. "Generators—that's how you have lights!"

"One generator, to be exact." Rose crosses her arms.

"I haven't seen electric light since . . . I don't remember." I try to stay calm, but my voice cracks. It's more than the light, though. There's a row of plants stretching behind her. Some have colored leaves, some are low to the ground, and others are a few feet tall like small trees.

I feel myself slipping into a memory. It's when Russell and I first left Pennsylvania. Was I seven then? Ten years ago. The rich perfume of flowers. I'd forgotten . . .

"Will you help me?" Dusty kneels by a tray of pebbles.

He teaches me how to lay them at the bottom of empty pots to make filters. I have a million questions to ask, but he seems so focused, and Rose is already back to work, hovering over hanging baskets spilling with colorful petals.

"You okay?" Dusty looks at me as he finishes another pot.

"What does the pebble filter do?"

He lifts a pot with furry purple flowers and moves close to me.

"It's so the roots don't die." He lifts the plant out, revealing a tangle of roots. "If they sit on the bottom where water collects, they drown." He puts the pot back, next to a whole row of other purple-flowered plants.

"Where do you get the seeds to grow them?"

"Cuttings." His face lights up as he grabs another plant and rips off one of the stems. "It's pretty neat. You take a stem and cut it like this." He flicks a knife out of his pocket and grazes the stem until it waters up. "Roots grow from the wound, and it becomes a new plant."

"You can grow plants without seeds?" I'm dumbfounded.

He laughs. Rose turns like she's noticing us for the first time. "He's a smart boy. Thing is, you can't grow them without propane for the generator, to run the lights. And our supply won't last much longer."

"It's amazing you have any at all." I remember the stockpile of fuel preservative Russell kept with us, used to mix with fuel so it won't go bad, and how eventually, he traded it for next to nothing because we never had any fuel to mix it with.

"Rose taught me everything I know." Dusty smiles. He answers my next question before I ask. "These are sweet violets. They're good."

"*Viola odorata*!" Rose snaps.

Dusty shrugs. "I never remember the Latin names." He hands me a petal. "Go ahead, you can eat it."

The flesh of the petal is so soft between my fingers. I feel sad destroying something so pretty, but even Bryn has turned around to watch. I place the petal on my tongue.

"It's sweet," I say, but when I swallow, it turns bitter.

"She's lying!" Bryn shrieks.

Rose turns sharply to her granddaughter. "Don't be rude." Then to me, she says, "Tastes better after we turn it into syrup." She chuckles, returning to the baskets. Dusty's already adding pebbles for another pot. I force myself to put off the rest of my questions until we're finished working.

After twenty minutes, I'm in a rhythm, keeping up with Dusty, fifteen pots made between us. A groan from Rose breaks the pattering rain. I look up, rubbing sweat away and pulling out of a trance.

"It's quitting time for me," Rose says, stretching her arms.

"Alright." Dusty doesn't look up from his task.

Rose nods in approval at my pots as she passes. "Bryn!"

"I want to stay, Mammy." Bryn is even dirtier than Dusty, and it makes me jealous for some reason. I want to lie in the dry soil, press my nose into it.

"Alright, walk home with Dusty then." She kisses her granddaughter on the top of the head and leaves.

A full-body chill runs through me. My own mother kissing me on the head, a memory that I know I must have, is buried somewhere. Before I find it, a thought interrupts—Russell saying we will get back in the boat tomorrow. I try to silence it because I don't want to leave these flowers, these kind people, but it keeps repeating. Then I hear Dusty's voice, saying no one ever wants to go back toward Colorado, that it's freezing cold there, with terrible storms.

Stop it, I scold myself. Leadville is what matters most, the dream we've worked so hard for. I grab a fistful of pebbles, filling pots until I'm distracted enough to stop thinking about the future.

When we're finally finished, I'm drenched in sweat. Dusty lets out a long sigh, and Voley trots over to us.

"Good work." Dusty slaps me a high five. "We'll add soil tomorrow. Let's go home."

Bryn springs up. "You can't leave without seeing the bunnies!" Behind her is a patch of vibrant green, several feet long and wide, that I hadn't noticed.

"Grass!" I rush over.

"Okay, the bunnies, then we have to go." Dusty leans on a table, wiping his forehead.

I bend down in the soil next to the grass, unable to believe I'll see two animals in one day. My hands knead the dirt. I feel it sift through my fingers, so soft. Then I lie flat by the edge of the grass and press my nose in. Dusty laughs but I don't care. The smell of grass. *The smell of grass.*

"Look here, Tanner!" Bryn jams her finger toward a small patch of silver fluff.

"Oh my god." I crawl close. A fat gray rabbit is hidden behind the highest stalks of grass. With one hand, Bryn caresses the rabbit, and with the other, she delicately lifts a tuft of its fur covering a hole in the soil.

"They're underground," she whispers.

And then I see them. Eyeless little creatures, long ears stuck to the sides of their tiny heads. There are three of them, four, too many to tell, balled together under the soil. They come to life, wiggling little feet, stretching, and rolling onto their pink tummies.

"Okay, that's enough," Dusty says sternly. "Put the gate up, Bryn."

"Aren't they cute?" she replaces the tuft of fur that was covering them. The mother rabbit remains motionless, small black eyes watching us.

"Yes, they are." I step back, unable to look away. I wonder if they're going to be eaten, but I stop myself before asking in front of Bryn. I can't imagine what else they would be for, and it makes me sad because they're so beautiful and innocent.

Bryn rolls out a long mesh wire fence, wraps it around poles at the corners of the grass, and then we leave.

She hums softly on the road home and Dusty tells me about the work I can help with tomorrow. The flickering blue tarps look magical against the dark sky. When we stop at the flap to Bryn's home, a shadow emerges.

"Thank you, Dusty." It's Rose.

Bryn pauses in the doorway. "I like you, Tanner," she speaks softly. Something inside my chest feels like it's melting, or maybe coming to life again.

"I like you too, Bryn."

As we walk away, I bring it up. "What will happen to the bunnies?"

"We'll eat them." He doesn't even look at me as he says it.

My heart sinks. Somehow it feels just as wrong as eating Voley, or other humans.

I feel Dusty's hand on my arm, a concerned expression on his face. "It won't happen with these ones. Rose wants to breed them a few times and build a population first. So you don't have to worry yet."

When we get back to Dusty's house, Daniel is sitting cold-faced in a chair, with a rifle across the table. There's no trace of his earlier warmth. My first feeling is terror—something's happened to Russell.

"What is it, Dad?" Dusty asks.

"Word of a raid at the Twin Peaks settlement."

"Shit, that's pretty close." Dusty hangs his head. I keep quiet, wondering if they're referring to face eaters, and try to contain my fear.

A pretty older woman with long brown hair steps into the room from the hallway. She sets a tool belt loaded with hammers and screwdrivers on the table with a grunt, then plops into a chair and sighs. When she looks up, her deep brown eyes fix on me.

"Twin Peaks is a small settlement. No reason to think they'd attack here. Just stay alert." She speaks to Dusty, but her eyes are glued to me. Her strong jaw works back and forth on a piece of gum as she reaches out a muscular arm. "You must be Tanner?"

I lean forward and shake her hand. She nearly crushes my fingers.

Daniel finally looks up from his rifle. "This is Linda, head of construction here at Blue City. And my better half."

"Nice to meet you." Linda nods, then quickly turns to Daniel. "You need anything before I shower?"

"No, I'm good."

"Thank god. Pour me something strong if we've got it." She stands, then looks at me again before she leaves, flashing a brief smile. "Ten broken pipes, six clogged chutes, a failing rain ditch, and two collapsed tents. All in a day's work."

Dusty directs me into a room divided by a flap. "We'll sleep in here."

I hesitate. "I need to see Russell first."

"I'd let him sleep. Don't worry, he's completely safe in the infirmary."

Everything I've learned has taught me not to trust such proclamations, but something about his voice, about my entire day here, eases me.

The bedroom has blue walls and ceilings like the rest, lit by three candles on a warped pine bureau. It's a bit colder in here, and there's a metal bunk bed. "You get top, so Voley doesn't bother you."

"Were your dad and Linda talking about face eaters?" I ask, hoping he'll dispel the dread building in my imagination.

"There've been a couple raids nearby, only on really small settlements. Don't worry, we're well armed here." He doesn't sound concerned at all.

Somewhat relieved, the call of sleep sends me up the thin, creaking ladder to the top bunk. I flop over and sink into the mattress.

So soft. How people slept every night, before the rain.

Dusty blows out the candles.

"Do you know the names of all those plants?" My voice cuts through the darkness.

"Maybe." He sounds like he's teasing me. I hear Voley jump up onto his bunk.

The day goes through my head. It no longer feels like a dream that will end, but instead, like I'm waking up from a nightmare. I think about Voley and the bunnies and then I realize—I can't believe I forgot to tell Dusty about the whale.

"Dusty I saw a whale, in the rain sea."

"Impossible." His voice is soft and muffled.

"I really did. It shot up water, just like whales do."

This time Dusty doesn't answer. He's already snoring. I tuck my hands under the pillow, the smell of grass still on my fingers. I breathe it in over and over, trying to capture it, until I fall asleep.

14

ROOK

8 YEARS, 4 MONTHS

Rook blinked in disbelief at the date of his father's letter. It was only a few weeks old. Adrenaline cleared the fog of alcohol from his brain.

They're still alive!

His long-dead hope reignited, and in the next instant, he was racing up and down the empty hall, hoping to catch whoever had left the envelope, but no one was there. The urgency was too great anyway. All that mattered was getting to Canvas City. His mother was alive, but she was sick, and he needed to bring her medicine.

Marrow had joked when he'd left the party that he was going to spend the night working at the lab. *Maybe he's still there.*

"ROOK, ARE YOU OKAY?" Jonathan, the third meteorologist under Franklin, looked up as Rook burst into the lab, gasping for breath.

"Is Marrow here?"

A puzzled look formed on Jonathan's face, but he gestured affirmatively toward the hallway.

Marrow's face warped with surprise, and then concern, as Rook barged in without knocking. "Rook, did something happen at the party?"

"They're alive." Rook breathed heavily, his hands shaking.

Marrow's eyes narrowed in confusion, wrinkling his pale, freckled forehead. "What?"

"My parents are alive. My mother's sick. I need to bring her medicine." Rook's fingers sweated against the letter in his pocket, his heart thumping out of his chest.

"Alive? How? Where?" The shock wore off Marrow's expression, and he cocked his head quizzically.

"Will you help me?" Rook's voice rose in pitch. He began pacing. "Please!"

"Of course I'll help you." Marrow's tone grew sympathetic as he rose from his chair and put his hand on Rook's arm. "Do you know where they are?"

Rook nodded quickly. "A settlement called Canvas City. I need to bring her antibiotics."

Marrow looked at the ceiling and breathed out a long, frustrated sigh. "Canvas City? That place is a hundred miles from the nearest shelter. There's a reason we don't go directly to smaller settlements—they're very dangerous. You're our best meteorologist. I can't afford to lose you."

Rook felt a rush of whiskey-fueled defiance. "If you have to replace me, I understand. I need to do this."

"I don't think I *could* replace you." Marrow shook his head.

"Please, sir, I've given everything for this company. I won't be able to function, knowing they're still out there, that she's sick."

Marrow's voice softened. "If you do this, I can't guarantee your safety."

"I know the risks, and I promise I'll come back," Rook lied. If he found his parents, he wasn't sure if he could ever leave them again.

Marrow tensed his jaw. "Okay. I'll arrange it. Antibiotics and a boat. You deliver them to her, say hello, and then come right back."

Rook couldn't help himself. He hugged Marrow, thanking him and crying into his shoulder.

Finally, Marrow stepped back. "Do you have the letter with you?"

Rook handed it to him, and Marrow read it slowly. "I'm sorry about your mother," he said calmly, giving it back. "But maybe this is a miracle.

I think you'll reach her in time to help." He smiled. "I'll have your passage ready for tomorrow morning."

"You don't know what this means to me!" Rook extended his hand. Marrow shook it firmly, and Rook turned to leave. Halfway out the door, Marrow said, "Rook, one more thing. Who delivered the letter?"

When Rook turned back, he saw a look of consternation tightening Marrow's face. It lasted just a split second, and as soon as they made eye contact, his smile returned. He added warmly, "I want to know who to thank."

"I'm not sure, sir. It was under my apartment door when I returned home. But I know my dad's all-caps handwriting. It's definitely him."

"No worries. Good luck, Rook, and I'll see you in a few days."

Rook nodded and left. After getting home to his apartment, he frantically threw a pile of clothes together and packed. The alcohol and adrenaline were fading, bringing into sharp relief a mix of anxiety and hope. It was a miracle they were alive, like Marrow said, but what if he got there too late to save his mom? The last thing he felt was tired, but he'd need to try to get some sleep. Forcing himself to lie down, he reread his father's letter. Taking in the words slowly this time, he stopped at the first line, blinking to be sure he was reading it right:

I AM WRITING ONCE AGAIN, AS I HAVE EVERY YEAR . . .

Every year?

A sick feeling began splashing up his gut, pooling into his throat.

It had to be that Canvas City was too far off the grid for those other letters to make it. Or maybe they'd been at a farther settlement before Canvas City. That would explain it. The letters were lost en route to bigger settlements before Yasper could pick them up. When was the last time any of his friends had received a letter? He couldn't remember. But then, like him, they'd lost their loved ones.

He was overthinking it, that was all. As he finally began to drift off, the image of Marrow's face, when he'd asked who delivered the letter, appeared in his mind. It was just a fleeting second, but Marrow had almost looked upset.

By dusk the next day, the Yasper ship was navigating through the debris around Canvas City. A row of shingles, the frame of a playset, deformed children's dolls, all manner of detritus glued together, bobbing in a plastic soup.

Utility poles poked through the water first, and then roofs appeared. Rook watched anxiously as the ship pulled close to the banks of what had once been a suburb. A network of fires winked in the gloom, illuminating endless tents surrounding crumbled houses.

Rook threw his duffel bag, which contained some clothes, a small bit of food and water, and the precious antibiotics, over his shoulder and climbed into the waiting rowboat that would take a small crew ashore.

"Marrow must really like you to risk our necks coming to this hole," an auburn-haired, beak-nosed young man said as he joined Rook in the boat. Rook had hoped Captain Lawrence would take him, not only because this other captain had been rude the whole trip, but also because he wanted to ask Lawrence the question that had been bugging him since he'd left Marrow's office last night: Was Lawrence the one who had found and delivered his father's letter? If so, Rook wanted to thank him.

Rook ignored the captain's jab. "How long will you stay and trade?"

"We're a hundred miles from the nearest shelter," the captain said sharply. "This is no-man's-land. One hour, tops. Don't keep us waiting."

They rowed in and disembarked. Rook tailed the captain and a crew of three up the fractured asphalt of an old highway that rose from the water. Two dirt-faced old men approached from the nearest tent, long frayed beards drooping down tattered ponchos.

Rook spoke first. "Excuse me, do any of you know a Thomas Wallace?"

Their faces twitched as they studied him. "Not every day Yasper comes directly to us," one of the men said, sounding giddy.

"Thomas Wallace, a former sheriff?" Rook pressed.

The other man's eyes opened wide. "That cocksucker?"

Rook's stomach flipped. "What did you say?"

"He's here, still meddling in other people's affairs. Stays in Shit Shed, past that row of cars, up Tire Hill." The man pointed to a bend in the highway where a barren hill rose, dotted with naked trees. "Tell him he ought to get the fuck out of town before his luck runs out."

Seeing the seriousness in the haggard man's eyes, Rook's excitement turned into fear. Why would anyone hurt his father?

Heart pounding in his chest, he jogged quickly toward the line of rusty cars. Shoddy tents and canopies covered the open spaces between dilapidated houses, the air thick with the stench of rotting garbage and feces. Bedraggled faces stared warily as he pinched his nose and weaved between piles of sodden furniture, steel sheeting and dirty foam, buckets and bottles, metal canoes holed with rot.

"Yasper!" someone shouted.

Glancing right, he spotted a young woman springing to her feet, eyeing him from underneath a canvas canopy. A ring of people dressed in black plastic, seated around an oil-drum fire, watched her approach him.

"Hey!" She darted closer. Pink sores pocked her face between ratty strands of brown hair. "You got any?"

"What?" Rook froze in a panic as her sunken eyes drifted to the duffel bag slung over his shoulder.

"Red." She spoke as if scolding him.

He stepped back. "No."

"Your suit's got a *Y*, don't it?"

"He's lying!" An older man walked up, his dirt-crusted jowls hanging loosely around a large abscess.

"I'm with the weather team." Rook held up empty palms. "I'm here to help my parents."

Disappointment creased her welted face.

"Weather team?" The man blinked filmy eyes. "I'm good at that—you ready? It's going to rain tomorrow." He broke into laughter. "Can you hire me?"

"If you want to trade, the shipping crew is there." Rook pointed, holding his breath. To his relief, they spotted the ship in the water and started toward the shore.

He hurried on through the ragged maze of tents that dotted the mudflat at the base of the hill. The shed stood at the top, as big as a house but without a single window, smoke rising from a metal chute on its roof. Discerning a makeshift staircase of tractor tires embedded in the hillside, he started toward it.

"Hey, you!"

Fuck, not again . . .

A tall man stood in the doorway of a tent only a few feet away, wrapped in black trash bags stitched together like a rain suit. Light glinted off something in his hand.

"You trading Red?" His dark eyes looked like slits cut out of his sunken cheeks.

Rook kept walking. "No, I'm here to see my father."

"Stay where you are!" The man raised a long knife. It was huge, more like a machete.

Rook turned to run, but the man was upon him, his giant hands clasping Rook's arm.

"That's a big bag you've got." The man pointed his machete. "I just want to peek inside."

Rook didn't care about the food and water, but the duffel held the antibiotics. If this crazy man saw pills, he might think they were Red.

"I'm not a trader, the traders are at the shore." Rook stepped blindly backward, terrified of losing the medicine.

"Not interested in trading." The man raised the knife to Rook's neck.

Up close, despite the dirt and sores, the sallow face looked familiar, but adrenaline blanked Rook's memory. "I don't have Red! These are supplies for my parents."

"You won't mind if we look, then?" He beckoned to two stocky men who were emerging from the tent.

Even if the crew's in earshot, they won't see me through the fog. Dropping the duffel was the only way to escape.

"Back the hell up, Gerry!" came a shout from atop the hill.

Gerry? The name echoed in Rook's head.

A hunched figure wearing a dirty orange rain cloak was pointing a rifle at them from the top of the hill.

"Go inside, Sheriff, before you catch a cold," Gerry mocked.

Dad! Rook wanted to scream, but he was frozen with fear.

Rook's father raised the rifle. "You act like you've never seen me shoot. Forget I can't drill a hole through a rabbit's temple at fifty yards?"

Gerry lowered his knife, cursing under his breath. "You're dead before the week is out, hear me, Tom? I warned you not to interfere with us again." He stormed off in the direction of the tents.

Rook put his head down and bolted up the tires toward his father. The man he found at the top of the hill was almost unrecognizable: eyes recessed, glassy and bent, his skin sagging in deep-cut lines around his brow and mouth.

"Rook . . ."

Trembling with shock, Rook went to hug him. "Dad!"

"Not while they're watching." His father kept the rifle between them, eyeing the bottom of the hill.

From the eaves of his tent, Gerry and the other two stood stock-still, glaring.

"Come on." Rook's father led him to the shed door.

Rook watched sadly as his father walked with a heavy limp. "Dad, your leg?"

"Been this way for years. Doesn't slow me down."

The building was smaller than it looked from the outside, and so crowded with people that Rook could barely move. Muted conversations mixed with an acrid smell of fuel, smoke, and body odor. Two small stoves glowed in the middle of the room, hooked to fuel tanks, with a couple of children huddled around them. Others sat wrapped in dirty blankets, despite the mugginess of the room. A long row of silver propane tanks lined one wall, and everywhere were candles glowing from shoddy fixtures. Steady drips of water fell from the roof into a few buckets. Near the back, figures crowded a row of rotted mattresses.

"Is Mom here?" Rook's gaze jumped from face to face.

The room quieted as pale and greasy refugees turned to look. Three middle-aged men and the rest women of different ages, maybe a dozen people in total.

"You shouldn't have come." His father's eyes watered.

"I had to. I got your letter."

His father's lips quivered as he wiped his cheeks, then leaned in and wrapped Rook in his arms with surprising strength. "My boy."

Everything felt surreal, a dream within a nightmare.

"Come see your mother." His father gestured to a corner mattress where a blanket hid everything but a shock of frizzy hair.

"Mom!"

Rook's joy evaporated as he knelt by her weathered face. She looked like she hadn't been out of bed in weeks. Her cheeks were red and puffy, and her lips were dry and cracked. Dark grime and sweat soaked her patchy skin and matted her hair.

She opened bleary eyes. "Rook?" She struggled to her elbows. "Oh my God! My baby, my baby!" She sobbed as Rook scooped her in his arms.

She felt too hot, too frail. "I'm here now." Rook kissed her oily cheek. "I'm here." Immediately he unzipped the duffel and retrieved the large cylinder of pills.

"What's that?" She squinted, wheezing to catch full breaths of air between words.

"It's amoxicillin."

Rook's father teared up. "This is a miracle." He brought a pail that had been collecting rainwater by the mattress. She leaned back and swallowed two pills.

"There's enough for a couple full courses." Rook smoothed his mother's gray hair out of her eyes. "In case you or Dad get sick again."

"My sweet boy. You're so handsome. How I've missed you." She paused to draw a sharp breath as tears slid down her face. "It's dangerous here. I always told you never to come. It's safe at your job."

A loud *pop* sounded outside.

"You hear that?" Rook's father's forehead wrinkled with anger. "Yasper has to waste bullets on those animals just to attempt business here. I don't know how the hell you got them to come, but they'll never return. You should go back—"

"Why did you stop writing us?" His mother wiped her face with the blanket. "We sent so many letters, we thought you were . . ."

"I stopped getting them seven years ago. I thought you were gone, too."

"We never stopped writing. Every chance we got, we sent a letter to the nearest Yasper trade station," his father said.

Rook tried to piece it together. Dina had lost contact with her family shortly before Rook had, then Gene. Had their families' mail been lost, too?

The door opened, and a middle-aged man with curly black hair and thick stubble approached Rook's father, urgency in his voice. "We need to trade that Red back to Yasper. I just talked with one of the crew. They'll give us three canned peas for it."

"Trade it back?" Rook looked in surprise at his father. "Why don't you take it?"

"Christ no. They steal our food, so we steal their drug when we can," his father spoke matter-of-factly.

They? What the hell was going on?

His father flashed the dark-haired man a look of concern. "Gerry and his boys are riled up right now. I better go with you, Christopher. Charlie, Frank, and Mike, too."

"No, Tom, you're too slow. I'd rather go alone, it'll draw less attention," Christopher said confidently.

Rook's father lifted a small metal safe from behind the mattress. It broke Rook's heart to watch his dad's hands tremor as he entered a combination and withdrew a familiar bottle marked with a black *Y.* He dropped the bottle of Red, with its distinctive Yasper packaging, into Christopher's hand. "Take my rifle, at least."

"No, that's our only gun. Keep it here, in case they try to come mess with you." Christopher's dark brown eyes dipped to his waistband, where he flashed a small knife, and he rushed out of the shed.

"Is Gerry stealing your food?" Rook felt dumbstruck that his dad's best friend could be the same man who'd nearly cut his throat. Gerry had been his father's most trusted deputy, the kind man who'd come to his brother's Little League games, who'd dressed as Santa for Christmas once. How could he have transformed into that maniac?

"That drug is evil." His father frowned. "It's destroyed him. Destroyed so many of us."

"It's the worst thing that's happened to us." His mother cupped her hands together. "God help us."

Rook felt his stomach falling out from under him. He thought of the woman who'd approached him, how obsessed she'd been about getting it, and then Gerry, too. It was the same behavior he'd seen in his brother at the depths of his addiction. "It's helping, though. They've always told us it's helping. Why wouldn't it be helping here?"

"They take too much and don't realize how hungry they are until it starts to wear off. By then, they're out of food because they've traded everything for more of the drug." His father sat on the mattress, arm around his wife. "Frank and his family saw it happening at another camp before they came here. From what we've heard and seen, it's happening everywhere Yasper ships the drug. It turns people into monsters, even good men like Gerry. It's going to destroy our chance to survive this."

Rook struggled to process what he was hearing.

"They lied to you, son." His father shook his head. "It's been getting worse and worse for years now. I put it in my letters. No wonder you never got them."

"They cut the letters off . . ." Rook felt himself reeling, trying to recall conversations he'd had with Ed, with his friends, things Marrow had said at the meetings. Something that would negate this, something that would make it not true. Nothing came, and his mind blanked. "They didn't want us to know." He looked at his mother, his eyes watering.

"It doesn't matter now. What matters is that you go back where it's safe," she said. "Even if they lied, they'll keep you healthy there. That's all that we care about. Anyone in this camp would trade an arm for a job at your company."

A wave of darkness and despair crashed down on Rook, squeezing the breath out of him. He'd trusted Ed and Marrow so completely, and because of that, he had helped to spread the drug as much as anyone else at Yasper. Looking at his parents' beaten faces, it started to sink in that he'd done this to them.

"I'm so sorry." He hung his head in shame. All those years imagining how proud they would have been of him. And to see them now, like this, was too much to bear.

His father gently touched his arm. "You can't blame yourself for what you couldn't have known. You said it yourself, they cut everyone off—"

A high-pitched shriek interrupted his father, who cocked his head to listen, putting his palm up. "Quiet!"

A staccato of distant shouting sounded outside. It went on for a few seconds, loud then soft, until a long, guttural moan punctured the air.

His father grabbed his rifle and began limping toward the door.

"Dad, where are you going?"

Rook's mother wrapped her arms weakly around Rook, crying. "Please God, we don't deserve any more of this!"

His father beckoned toward the three stout middle-aged men with dirt-smeared faces. "Frank, Charlie, with me." They hopped up, knives in hand. "Mike, stay and guard the door." And then the three left the shed.

Rook watched the door shut, struck with confusion and fear. He'd never been in a real fight, let alone against men who had knives and were eager to use them. But the look on his mother's face, her stabbing sobs, shattered his paralyzing fear and self-pity. He had to do something.

"Rook." She clung to his leg. "Stay here."

"Dad can barely walk, I can't let him go down there!" He pulled away from her weak grip. *If something happens to Dad while I sit here . . .*

Ignoring her pleas and Mike's cautioning, he went outside.

Mist clumped low to the ground, the visibility so poor that Rook could hear them before seeing them, down at the bottom of the hill.

"No!" his father bellowed.

Rook raced down. On the ground, a body lay submerged in the mud.

Lying face up with his hood off, messy hair across eyes locked open in horror, Christopher's hands were wrapped around the handle of a knife stuck into his ribs.

Rook's father dropped down and slid his arms under Christopher's motionless body. Rook glanced side to side nervously, expecting Gerry to leap out at any second.

"Help me, damn it!" His father's arms shook, trying desperately to summon enough strength to lift Christopher.

But Rook couldn't take his eyes off the shadows moving inside Gerry's tent, just a few feet away.

"Dad, he's dead." Rook kneeled in the mud, peeling his father's hands off. "We have to go back, or he'll kill us, too!"

His father pounded his fist into a tire, then picked his rifle out of the mud and swept it over the silhouettes inside the tent.

Words choked in Rook's throat. "Dad, *please*. We can't leave Mom."

Frank and Charlie helped Rook pull his father to his feet and toward the tires.

"You boys leaving so soon?" Gerry's voice sliced through the darkness.

Rook's stomach dropped when he turned back to look. Five men in black rain suits, the tallest one in the middle, stood outside the tent.

His father tried to raise his rifle, but Rook bear-hugged him. "No, we're outnumbered. Mom needs us."

"Now's not the right time, Sheriff." Frank hooked his father's arm. With Charlie's help, they dragged him uphill.

As soon as he stopped struggling long enough for them to let go, Rook's father turned one more time to look down the hill at the men standing there. "You're going to pay for this in blood, all of you!"

"You got a lot of propane in that shed, Sheriff," Gerry hollered back. "Ain't you worried about a fire starting in there?"

Before anyone had time to react, Rook's father raised the rifle and fired. Somewhere in the darkness, the men laughed.

15
TANNER

"Good morning," Gloria greets me in the infirmary.

"How is he?"

"Getting good rest."

I go over to Russell, buried in his pillow. "Hey."

He slowly lifts his head. "Tanner?"

"How do you feel?" I grab his hand.

"Like I really slept." He rubs his eyes, his foggy expression becoming serious as Gloria walks away. "We can't stay here. I have a bad feeling."

I'm shocked—*a bad feeling?* "Russell, the veneer is everywhere here."

"This isn't Leadville." He breathes deeply. "We need to get back to the boat."

I want to tell him everything I've experienced, show him that we don't need to rush to leave this place, but I'm too angry.

"Have you forgotten that you were dying, and I was in the boat, rowing and bailing alone? Can't you see what's happened? It's a miracle you're alive. We've got food and guns, and people here who want to help us."

He rubs his temples like he's getting a headache.

"I can't do it alone again. You almost killed both of us." I keep my voice cold. "You have to stop worrying and rest. When you're better, you can walk around with me and see this place for yourself."

He sighs. "That's fair."

"You have to believe me, the veneer's alive here. In Dusty and his dad, and Voley, and Rose—"

"You *think* it is," he cuts me off. "But you can't be sure, can you? We've been to places like this before. Remember the settlement in Indianapolis, how perfect you thought it was? They turned out to be cannibals. Maybe you're seeing all the bright colors here, but not the thing that's producing them."

"I was ten years old in Indianapolis! I'm old enough to know the difference now." I narrow my eyes. "What if this is as good as it gets?"

He groans. His eyes look glassy.

I realize that now's not the time to argue with him and that I'm jumping to possibilities I don't even know we'll have, or that I really want. Even if Blue City allowed us to stay permanently, to make this place our new home, are there enough pieces of the veneer to sacrifice Leadville? Wait until he's better. "I'm sorry. You need to rest. I'm going to help Dusty in the greenhouse."

He nods, pulling himself into a fetal position, and then he's still.

On my way out, Gloria stops me. "Is everything okay?" She sounds alarmed.

"He has a headache. Please take good care of him."

Her soft gaze holds mine, and her words seem sincere. "He's in good hands."

"Thank you." I walk out, afraid that if she looks into my eyes too long, she'll sense the problem is bigger than a headache.

By the end of the week, forty filtered pots line the wall of the greenhouse, all created by me. Each one is filled with cuttings, little green sprouts spreading into the water, sucking in the bright light, growing.

"It's quitting time," Dusty says, mimicking Rose. I hit him with an overly enthusiastic high five like the ones he gives me.

It's strange how normal the daily routine feels after only a week.

Each morning, after checking on Russell, I wake Dusty, and for two hours we pull asparagus and potatoes and chard and beets, carefully transplanting cuttings into empty soil before heading to the grub tent. It's our only big meal each day and I've started taking advantage of second helpings. Dusty keeps telling me I'm gaining weight and that I look good, making me blush. And of course, Voley follows us everywhere.

Each day, after we finish eating, Dusty checks in with his dad. Daniel's usually busy managing Blue City, keeping track of food, making sure everyone has clean clothes, seeing that wood and fire get divided evenly. He even left for two days on a scavenging run into the ruins of Salt Lake City and brought back a lot of scrap piping that Linda is going to use to shore up some of the tarps.

Dusty says I'll be able to help her with the construction. I've watched her at work a few times, and she's incredible with her hands, replacing rotting pipes and patching every tarp hole with ease. Once, I got to help, spending a few hours building rain ditches and replacing smoke chutes. I'm sure I could learn as much about construction from Linda as I have about plants from Dusty and Rose. She's so tough, and it makes me want to get stronger.

After talking with Daniel, Dusty and I make the rounds, walking the shoreline to check for signs of boats, then back to the greenhouse in the afternoon to make new cuttings. Rose is usually there, and sometimes Philip, a friendly guy with the longest hair I've ever seen on a man. Bryn spends most of her time waiting for new whiskers to poke out of the baby bunnies' cheeks. I can't leave without her demanding that I look at how much they're growing. Sometimes she asks me to cut up vegetables for the mama bunny.

By the time we're home, I'm dead tired, but Dusty and I talk until we fall asleep, one-upping each other with every interesting thing we've done in our lives. I always win.

It surprises me how much I love talking. Russell and I used to talk a lot, or I used to ask a lot of questions and listen. But our conversations died off over the last few years, frozen on the thread of getting to

Leadville. Now, I find myself impatient for the next time I get to hear Dusty's laugh.

I'm ready to crash hard after the greenhouse tonight when Dusty turns the wrong way on the road home.

"Where are you going?" The sky's dark and most of the bustle inside the tarps has died down. A few fires flicker, but the road's empty.

"Can I show you something?" Before I can think, he grabs my hand.

He's touched me before, but never like this. His fingers wrap mine tightly, pulling me close. The strangest, happiest feeling washes over me, just being connected to him. I squeeze his hand as he pulls me between two tarp houses, through an alley that exits into the dark wasteland.

"You're going to be so surprised." He lets go of my hand and starts to jog. Voley bounds ahead, like he knows just where we're going.

"Is this safe without your rifle?" He's let me shoot it a few times for target practice when we've finished work early, but suddenly I wish I had my own.

"We'll be back in ten minutes." Dusty dashes up a hill. I run to catch him, spraying my rain suit with mud.

Panic churns in my stomach as the blue tarps grow distant behind us. But my anxiety vanishes when I reach the summit, where Dusty's looking back and forth eagerly, grinning.

The flat brown sea stretches to infinity. Mountain ridges rise up beyond the island, and there, directly down the hill, is an open bay. A tan dock extends from the bank with an enormous barge and several smaller boats tied alongside it. The barge looks like it's been put together from random pieces of metal and wood, with two high masts in the center. Limp coils of canvas hang down, which must be makeshift sails. It looks far from seaworthy, but Dusty is squirming with excitement.

"That's our fleet! The smaller boats have propane outboard motors. Linda converted the engines so they can run on alcohol, too." He's shouting like I should have reacted by now. "Look how big the barge is." He spreads his arms. "We built it. Isn't it amazing?"

"It *is* big." I can't help feeling like that thing would go under at the smallest crashing swells.

"There's something else I wanted to tell you." Dusty grows even more excited. "I talked to my dad. He said if you two want, you could have a home here after Russell's better."

My heart leaps, but my guard automatically goes up. "Your dad really said that?"

"You've proved yourself. You work hard. You shoot better than me." He's smiling like a child, expectant eyes studying me under the lip of his hood. "Do you really believe it's going to be that much better in Leadville?"

I have to admit that deep down, part of me hoped this would happen. Each day it's been a little easier for me to feel it, that this place could be similar enough to Leadville to give up the dream. But Russell . . .

"I don't know if Russell would want to."

"Well, you could stay. You're old enough to decide for yourself, right?" Dusty's words sting, so much that it makes me feel guilty for dismissing Russell's gut feeling about this place. He's never been wrong before, and maybe I'm stupid to second-guess him.

"I would never leave him." My words hang like daggers.

Dusty's smile vanishes. "I didn't mean anything by it."

"I can't decide anything until he's better."

"I'll help convince him." He steps closer. "Once he's better, it'll be easy. He'll see what it's like here."

I watch Voley splash through a mud puddle so I don't have to look into Dusty's beautiful eyes.

"Do you know how rare it is to be us?" He rests his hand on my arm.

I give in and look at him. "Us?"

"How often do you see people our age?"

He's right. I've seen more of the world and know it better than he does. Just meeting Dusty and the few other children living here has made me dream about when kids went to school, when you could have lots of friends your own age. Impossible to fathom.

"And even rarer, someone who laughs at my jokes," his voice cracks. Suddenly, for the first time since we met, he looks nervous.

"I don't laugh at your jokes." I keep my voice like steel.

"Okay." He narrows his eyes suspiciously and pushes his ears out with his hands. "But what about this?"

"What's that face supposed to be?"

"It's how Voley looked when I told him I liked you."

No. I won't smile.

"He was very skeptical." He bends down and rubs Voley's ears.

"No he wasn't, Voley loves me!"

"He was. He's skeptical of people without pets."

"No one has pets. I hadn't seen a dog in—"

"It's just . . ." he interrupts, voice wobbly.

I feel ready to burst, to open up about my fear that this place might be too good to be true. I want to tell him that, except for Leadville, places like this aren't supposed to exist anymore, that it's all a con, and somewhere along the way, we're going to be used up for something evil, some broken imitation of the veneer.

But I can't get my thoughts out because he pulls me into his arms.

It's almost too much, the same warmth from when he held my hand, only a thousand times stronger, but I can't find the will to push him away. Rain bounces off his hood into my face. Am I betraying Russell, just by feeling this?

Dusty lifts my chin so we're eye to eye, so close I can feel the heat of his breath against my lips.

"You don't think it's all pointless?" I say it, my gnawing fear that whatever this feeling between us is, it's useless because it doesn't help keep us alive, keep us moving, keep us heading to a place where it isn't raining.

Confusion blanks his face.

"I mean love." It falls out of my mouth like a forbidden artifact from Philadelphia, something long ago laid to rest, a taboo. I want to take it back, but it's too late.

"I'm not sure what love feels like." He becomes serious. "But I've seen it in other people. I know it's not pointless."

Things start to blur together, like we're mirrors, reflecting the same energy. "I don't know what it feels like either."

He watches me for a long time, dark eyebrows raised hopefully as the rain pelts us. A tiny star of light hangs in his hazel eyes. I don't know when it happened, but our bodies are so close that my stomach is against his. Like an electric shock, his hands glide up my back. I can't help it—I embrace him, holding the solid curves of his shoulders, and we kiss.

When we pull apart, it feels like time's stopped. There's an uncertain look on his face.

"Come on." He turns around, jogging back toward camp. I follow him, in shock. My body hums, vibrating and mute.

Could I stay here, if Russell decided to leave? *No.* Never. But I run as fast as I can, so afraid I'll lose Dusty, lose this feeling. Before I can recapture it, we're back inside his house.

Daniel's still up, cleaning his rifle. Linda sits across from him at the table with a book spread under a candle.

"Festival's tomorrow." Daniel puts the gun down. "You were supposed to help Linda this evening."

"Shoot, I forgot." Dusty squares to attention.

"Be sure you're awake early to set up the extra tents," Linda speaks calmly without looking up. "Don't worry about going to the greenhouse. Rose knows I need you for this."

"I will." Dusty waves me into the bedroom, curling his lips down like he screwed up. I wonder if it's that he forgot to help Linda, or that he regrets kissing me. Voley follows at our heels and tries to hop on the bottom bunk.

"No, boy." Dusty stops Voley and grabs a towel to wipe him down.

I hang my rain suit and climb right up the ladder, desperate to be close to Dusty but suddenly anxious with Daniel and Linda so near, and even more nervous that he's changed his mind about me because our kiss didn't feel like he thought it would. Why else would he run away afterward? I hide under the covers, trying to forget it happened. Dusty quietly gets into bed.

Five agonizing minutes pass without a word. It's driving me crazy. I need to hear his voice. I'll know just by the sound of it.

"Dusty?"

"Yeah?"

"What's the festival?"

"A few times a year we have a celebration, kind of like how there used to be holidays."

My stomach flips. I don't really want to hear about the festival, just what he feels about us. But his voice sounds relaxed, relieving some of my dread.

"You can dance, right?" he asks cheerfully, like nothing went terribly wrong between us on the mountain.

"I don't dance."

"Well, Terry is going to play his ass off, and Philip's a virtuoso on the drums. Dad tries to play harmonica, too . . ." He trails off, then speaks softly. "So you better dance with me."

I feel a jolt of elation. Everything is okay.

"I'll try."

"Good. Oh, and Voley says good night."

"Good night, Voley."

Exhilaration tortures me for an hour before I get sleepy. Each time I recount all the things that make Leadville better than this place—the electricity, the real buildings, the blue skies, the grass and stars at night, the silence of no rain—it feels impossible to give it up, not after we've come so close. But then, the kiss plays again in my head, uninvited, and I'm fearful that this really is as good as it gets. I'm sure, just when I can hardly keep my brain awake any longer, that I hear Dusty tossing and turning, too.

16

ROOK

8 YEARS, 4 MONTHS

"Son, are you up? I want to talk to you privately." Rook's father gently roused him, then beckoned to the shed door when he opened his eyes.

Exhausted from a nearly sleepless night, Rook nodded and rose. Stepping groggily around the sleeping refugees, he followed his father outside.

The early-morning clouds were bright, and most of the fog had burned off, providing a clear view of Canvas City. A scattering of gray tents crowded the base of the hill, dotting the landscape down through crumbling suburban streets. Surrounded by trash, tents, tarps, and more canvas shelters, the cracked lanes of asphalt ran between sagging residential facades right into the waterline. The settlement looked empty and was eerily quiet.

With a shudder, Rook glanced at the site where the murder had happened. There was no sign of last night's struggle, just a hair-raising feeling that somewhere very close, Gerry was high on Red, watching them. The boiling guilt that had prevented Rook from sleeping much of the night seemed to amplify in daylight. *His* company, *his* work, had caused this.

"Up here." His father climbed tires to where the hill flattened out at the top.

A collage of green dumpster lids formed a road into open wasteland, surrounded here and there by stands of naked trees.

Once a forest, the gnarled trunks were the only sign of that former abundance. No bird songs, no squirrels climbing trees. At Yasper, there'd been constant noise—thrumming machines and generators, clinking lab instruments, speakers playing music. Even outside, the white noise of the power plant and refinery always rumbled. It had been enough to trick Rook, to make him forget that the world hadn't continued on just fine. Here there was nothing but the rain, no suggestion of Earth's former beauty and color.

On the horizon, a city skyline veiled in fog appeared to stand on the water.

His father pointed. "That's where we go."

"That city way out there?" Rook shivered, certain he wouldn't have the guts to travel that far in some flimsy boat.

"There's years' worth of food in those ruins, if we get it before the water does. We have a few skiffs with outboard motors. You saw how much propane we have in the shed, where Gerry and his boys can't get to it. With no storms, the trip takes two days. Every few weeks we hit a lode, somebody who stocked up like I did and never lived to use it."

"I can't believe you go out there." Rook pulled his hood down tighter.

"It's the only way we'll make it. By being more stubborn than the rain itself." His father stepped through a stream, splashing up mud. "But Rook . . . this damned drug."

The drug had plagued Rook's mind, too, as he tossed and turned all night, reeling from the shock of Christopher's death. He'd been duped so badly, all those years with no idea what was really happening. He thought again of that moment before he left, that frown on Marrow's face.

"Before I came here, my boss asked me who delivered your letter. Thinking back on it now, I could swear he looked upset. Just for a second, on his face, I saw it. But I didn't connect the dots until I got here, heard it from you and Mom, saw it for myself." He choked back the horror on Christopher's face, now etched into his mind, and tried to compose himself. "I feel horrible. Dad, I'm so sorry. I failed you. I failed everyone."

"That's bullshit." His father eyed him crossly. "You didn't fail us, you did the right thing. Probably saved your mother's life. She felt less feverish already this morning." He raised his eyebrows sympathetically. "Don't beat yourself up. You couldn't have known because they didn't want you to. They stopped delivering letters years ago to make sure you wouldn't know."

Rook racked his brain for something else he might have missed: a conversation with Ed, a data sheet, a report at one of the Family Meetings, anything that might have tipped him off to Yasper's cover-up. If there had been any clues, he'd missed them all.

Losing his family had deepened his trust in Ed and Marrow. They'd taken such good care of him. "Every year they gave us reports about the drug, how important it had become to the company, and how much it was helping refugees. It was all bullshit."

"Helping?" His father laughed hard. "The hell kind of help is that? What about when all the company's customers are dead?" His forehead creased as he raised his voice. "What about human decency?"

"I don't know what to say." Rook felt the urge to apologize again, something inside him desperate to receive his father's forgiveness. "I don't know what to do."

"Christ." His father lifted his hood and let the rain fall into his mouth. "We can't stop the storms. But if we work together, we can prevent starving to death, freezing to death, our common enemy. But this drug shit's split us apart."

"I thought Ed and Marrow cared. I misread them from the start, or maybe they changed. It just doesn't make sense. I don't understand why."

"It makes sense to me. Way I see it, you're either good at heart or you're not. That's what I've learned through all this. The rain just exposes who you really are." His father chuckled at the sky. "Kind of ironic, right? Your boss is doing what I did before the rain. God, I regret it. All those years I *prepped*." He mocked the word. "Saving up supplies, thinking only of your mother and me. That's your *why*. Your boss decided it was each man for himself, and to hell with whatever it costs the rest of us, as long as him and his people are taken care of."

"But you shared when it mattered!"

"I shouldn't have needed the rain to make me start." His father lowered his voice and looked at the ground. "And I shouldn't have gone so hard on your brother. Maybe he'd be here now if I hadn't said the things I said . . . if I'd been a better father."

The show of emotion took Rook off guard. The frailty in his father's eyes, the genuine sadness, was all so unlike his dad. The rain had beaten his old man down, weakened him, but in the end, it was the others' drug use that was breaking him. He was powerless against their addiction, as he'd been against his son's, and it must have felt like he was reliving the same failure.

Rook placed his hand on his dad's shoulder. "We tried everything we could, for years, and he kept hurting us, stealing from us. We had to go hard on him. If you're calling me on my bullshit, I'm calling you on yours. You were, you *are*, a great father. I don't care if you believe it or not."

His father chuckled. "If I was, it would've been hard for anyone else to tell. Couldn't keep you and your brother at peace for an hour."

"Stop it." Rook couldn't help raising his voice. The self-pity was so unlike his dad that it angered him. "I don't want to hear any more of that crap. It wasn't his fault or yours. When we were kids, I was the one who whined every time he tried to get me off my computer. I was the baby, and I didn't understand that he was just trying to build me up, get me to face my fears and make me tougher. That's how he showed his love."

"He did love you. I'm glad you know that. He loved all of us in his way, even after the drugs made him a stranger." His father sighed, patting Rook's back. "The first few years of the rain, people asked me to sort things out, called me Sheriff. That's all changed with the drug. Everyone's tribalized, thinking they'll last longer that way. Last night you saw it—*God* . . ." He stifled a sob. "Son, I brought you up here because I need your help. I need to ask something of you."

"What?" Rook's heart raced. His father never asked anyone for help. What could he help with here, except maybe comforting his mother?

"Your mother and I talked, and we both agree," his father said calmly, pausing to make eye contact. "You should go back to Yasper."

"Go back? I can't leave you again!" It felt like a punch in the gut. Even if he was useless here, his father didn't look invincible anymore, and this place was so dangerous. He would find some way to help them stay safe.

"Calm down and listen, okay?" His father raised a palm. "There is nothing your mother wants more than for you to be safe, more even than seeing you and having you close. As selfish and fucked up as your company is, you look healthy, and they're the reason for that."

"Well, you and Mom aren't healthy. You're older, and barely surviving here. I can't turn my back and—"

"Don't you dare say it," his father snapped back. "I'm a goddamn sheriff of the law. Did you forget what I told you when this all started? *I can protect your mother.*" His fingers clenched the rifle so hard they turned white. "You're not built for this place, Rook. You're not built for life here. You're built to use your mind, to work on a computer, to use science. But most importantly, you have what no one else in this godforsaken settlement has, or any other settlement, for that matter. You have a lottery ticket, a way out. You have your job."

Rook didn't need his father to tell him he wasn't built for this place, wasn't tough like him or his brother, nor even as tough as his mom. It hurt enough to see his parents finally, alive but in danger, and to be told he was useless. "I can learn, whatever it is, *I'll learn*. If I have to go scavenge in that city, if I have to fight, I will. I can make a difference here. Those people at Yasper lied to me, had me doing things that harmed you and Mom. I can't go back and face them again."

"You're taking it the wrong way, son. I know you could learn, and you could make a difference here. Look, I agree with your mother, your job is your ticket to safety, but I've got my own, selfish reason for asking you to go back, and I don't plan on discussing it with her."

Rook drew a blank, his injured feelings momentarily replaced with confusion.

His father took him by the shoulders. "You're the only one who can fix this problem from the inside. Go back, like nothing's changed, like you agree with what they're doing, if it comes up. But you fucking destroy this drug. I don't know how, but if there's anyone with a chance, anyone smart enough to find a way to stop it, it's you."

Rook struggled to find words for the clashing emotions inside of him. His father was the most independent person he'd ever known, and he had never asked anything of Rook before because there was nothing he couldn't do for himself. But now, the watery-eyed desperation on his father's face, the vulnerable wilt in his voice, inflected with hope . . .

His father pushed Rook's hood back. "I know you must be feeling a million different things, but try to put your emotions aside. Trust me to protect your mother, and go back. If you really want to help us, this is the only thing to do. And I believe in you. I believe you'll find a way."

Destroy the drug? Rook couldn't even begin to think of how. If Ed and Marrow had been lying all this time, there'd be no way to reason with them. His father seemed to see something in him that Rook couldn't see in himself.

He fought back tears and spoke through the knot in his throat. "I can't stand the thought of not seeing you again, after thinking for so long you were both gone."

"If it's what God wants, you'll find a way back to us," his father said with conviction. "You figure out a way to get rid of that shit, and it will make it safer out here for us. If you can't do it, at least you'll have tried, and your mother will have her wish, knowing you're healthy and taken care of. Son, I hate myself for asking this of you. It's selfish of me because I wish I could do it myself, but I can't. I need *you*."

Rook looked down at the mud, flooded with conflicting thoughts: fear of staying in Canvas City, fear of leaving his parents and going back to Yasper, fear that if he did go back, he'd fail. Finally, he looked up. "I hardly got any sleep last night. I need to get some rest. I promise I'll think about it and let you know tomorrow, okay?"

His father grinned, ruffled his son's wet mop of hair, then pulled his hood back down. "Let's get out of the rain." He gestured for Rook to follow him back to the shed.

As the bottom of the hill came into view once again, a shiver ran down Rook's spine. He'd been groggy when he first saw the spot Christopher had died, and he hadn't stopped to think where the body had gone. "Did somebody retrieve Christopher's body this morning?"

His father remained quiet until they reached the shed door. "No. It's not the first body to disappear either. It's high time I dealt with Gerry."

Rook watched his father's face tighten with anger. "What are you going to do?"

"Get rid of him," he said matter-of-factly. "Tomorrow morning. Me, Frank, Mike, and Charlie."

Rook's heart jumped. "You don't mean kill him?"

"I'll give him one last chance to change, but he won't. Before old Rupert passed, he said, 'Tom, watch after my son, Christopher.'" His father's voice quivered. "I didn't. It won't happen again."

"But the violence will escalate."

"It's been escalating. This is the only way to slow it down a bit. Christopher's not the first life they've taken over this drug. I should have done this a year ago." His father's face hardened.

A noise, maybe footsteps, sounded from near one of the tents at the base of the hill. They swung their heads around, but no one was there. Rook felt panic tightening his chest as he followed his father back inside the shed.

ROOK SPENT THE DAY resting by his mother's side, recalling happy memories with her when she had the strength to speak. His father came and went, patrolling outside the shed and preparing for the confrontation with Gerry. Soon darkness fell and everyone took to bed, but Rook had no luck making up the previous night's lost sleep. Despite his mother's excessive warmth, he couldn't shake the chill crawling over his skin. He slipped out from under her arm and sat by the stove. Probably past three in the morning by now, he guessed, angry at his brain for staying awake when his body felt so tired. The shed was dark and quiet except for the snoring and the patter of rain on the roof.

Everything he knew about the drug played through his mind again. The chemistry wing pressed the powder into tablets in the same building where he worked. Ed had told him that the raw material for Red was stored in the basement, below the chemistry wing. If it was all in one place, surely that made the drug vulnerable. But how?

Frightening questions popped into his head. What had happened to Christopher's body? Was leaving his parents and returning to Yasper the right thing to do? Could he conceal his anger at the company, his old friends, long enough to find a way to destroy the drug? His swirling thoughts finally centered on the most imminent nightmare. His father was going to confront Gerry. The thought of violence shook him to his core, but how could he live with himself if he didn't go along? It was the only thing that seemed clear. He had to go with his father in the morning.

When another hour had passed and exhaustion finally dampened his adrenaline, Rook crawled under the blanket beside his mother, tossing and turning until she groaned from all the movement. Then he lay still in the darkness, envying the snorers around him, until he finally drifted off.

THE SOUND OF TEARING metal woke him. Opening his eyes, he saw his father handling a dented can of peaches. Beside him, his mother was already awake.

She strained for breath. "Rook, my baby, I'm so glad you're healthy." Pale and sweaty, she leaned in to kiss his cheek.

Two young children, a boy with dark freckles and a girl with wavy strawberry-blond hair, wandered close enough to bump the edge of the mattress. They fidgeted, staring at the can.

"Lisa, Randy, get back here!" Frank swooped out his arms to gather his children.

"I'm sorry," said a lean woman with crop-cut hair as she helped wrangle them.

"They're fine, Jean." Rook's father rotated the can, showing the label to the kids. "You can have the syrup, okay?"

"Peach syrup!" Lisa squealed, hugging her brother so hard he whined.

"No, Sheriff." Jean waved him off. "We take extra when we need it, and we have enough right now."

His father ignored her, scooping out three slices and handing them to Rook's mother, then he gave three to Rook. Nectar oozed down Rook's fingers as he shoved them in his mouth and felt the sweet liquid soothe his dry throat.

"If something's canned well, it never goes bad." His father chewed the last of them, then gestured for Lisa.

Lisa grinned, revealing a wide gap between her front teeth. Randy looked away, covering his face with one arm but peeking through.

"What do I want you to do?" Rook's father held out the can.

"Share with my brother!" Lisa snatched it. Rook's father winked as she tilted it to catch the stove light, examining how much syrup there was. Randy jumped forward, no longer shy, squirming as she put it to her lips.

"Thank you, Sheriff." Jean smiled softly. Frank nodded, his arm tightly around his wife.

Maybe it was just the sugar, but Rook felt a wave of hope that maybe he could make things right. This place was dirtier and more dangerous than he could have imagined, but families were holding on to their love. If he went back to Yasper and destroyed the drug, he'd be giving his parents, every refugee, a better chance. It was the only way to make up for all those years he'd helped it to spread, and the only thing his father had ever asked him to do.

"You don't need to come," his father whispered. "But I'm letting you know we're going to see about Gerry, and I love you." He kissed the top of Rook's head.

"Dad, I'm coming."

Before Rook could pull on his rain suit, Frank was handing him a kitchen knife. Rook took it in his hand, wincing at the idea of pressing it into somebody's flesh.

Frank, Mike, and Charlie stood ready to go, but first his father brought them together to kneel by his mother's bed, where she was flipping through a dirty Bible. Others in the shed sleepily rose as she read aloud by the light from the stove and candles. Rook took his father's calloused hand on one side and his mother's, cold and clammy, on the other. The prayer was soothing to Rook, a deceptive feeling given the dread pulsing through his body.

Her haggard voice stopped and started, wheezing at times, but she finished the passage. It was about compassion. "God be with you, and everyone in this camp. Be careful."

Rook turned to his mother. “Don’t forget to take the medicine!”

“I already did.” She wearily blew him a kiss and lay down. “You stay back, behind your father, okay?”

Rook admired her ability to maintain her faith at a time like this, and he urged himself to be like her. If she could be strong now, so could he.

The hill was deserted, and dawn’s early mist overhung everything. Only a few fires smoldered near the shanty tents at the bottom of the hill. His father led them down the tire path, and Rook fell to the back, nausea fizzing in his gut as they drew closer.

The sun brightened a band of clouds on the horizon as they waded through the muck toward Gerry’s tent. Shadows were moving inside it.

They’re awake.

Rook had prayed that they would at least startle Gerry, but that was impossible now. His stomach flipped, hoping his father would turn back, reformulate the plan, but he just kept walking.

The shadows froze.

Rook’s heart pounded as he sped up to his father. “They see us—” His throat clenched shut.

“We’re okay, they don’t have guns.” His father held a finger to his lips, then took a step onto the wooden pallet leading to the tent-flap door.

A figure, eyes shadowed under a hood, pulled back the flap and looked out, then quickly disappeared inside. The shadows shifted fast, and Rook heard them whispering.

Gerry emerged, his yellow-ringed eyes cold and vacant. “You’re up early.” Two others crowded the entryway beside him.

“Just here to talk.” Rook’s father lowered the rifle.

Gerry’s hand dropped to the handle of the machete sheathed against his waist. “With guns and knives?”

Something didn’t feel right. Why wasn’t his father pointing the gun?

“We come to give you another chance.” His father sounded calm and empathetic, raising the barrel slightly so it was aimed at Gerry’s knees.

"A chance?" Gerry sneered, flicking his head side to side at his gang. "What a joke you've become, Sheriff."

"You killed Christopher." His father's peaceful tone had vanished.

"No, I didn't." Gerry's eyebrows bent with anger.

"Who did?"

A smirk spread across Gerry's face. His fingers danced over the knife. "Anyone know?" He side-eyed his companions.

They shook their heads, eyes wide in fake dumbfounded expressions.

"Sorry, Sheriff. Looks like we can't help." Gerry shifted from one foot to the other, his smirk tightening into a tense glare.

"Where's his body?" Rook's father's voice cut like a razor.

"You losing your memory, old man?" Gerry raised his brow. "I just said we had nothing to do with it."

"You won't mind if I search your tent then." His father took a step forward.

Dad, don't! Rook wanted to scream, but panic siphoned the words out of his throat, seized up his muscles.

Gerry pushed his chest into Rook's father. "You still think you're the law?"

"Damn it, Gerry, how many people did we scoop out of the floods? How many lives did you save—"

"Shut up, Tom." Gerry scowled. "That's over. Not everyone can survive anymore."

"You've changed into something awful," Mike muttered from behind them. Rook squeezed the handle of his knife as sweat loosened his grip.

"I did change," Gerry said. "You know what else changed? Everything. And none of you accepted it. You think the morals we used to have matter now? Sheriff's holy-law-and-order, pretend-the-rain-never-started bullshit? When you all die, it'll be because you *didn't* change."

"Enough!" Rook's father pushed Gerry aside and stepped toward the tent.

Rook stepped forward to stop his father, close enough to catch a glimpse inside the tent. Rusty brown streaks covered the floor.

"There's blood inside the tent," Rook whispered.

Gerry shoved Rook hard, knocking him down into the mud. "Go home, all of you."

Rook rubbed dirt from his eyes to see his father raising the rifle.

"I'm coming in," he said, "one way or the other."

Gerry gestured up the hill with a tilt of his chin. "Your wife's up there, isn't she? I hear she's real sick. You should be caring for her."

"Don't talk about her again."

Rook struggled to push himself up from the mud. He could see the rifle shaking in his father's hands.

"It was self-defense." Gerry's voice softened. "Christopher tried to kill me, over something I said."

"He would never!" Mike pushed forward.

"Swear on my mother's soul." Gerry raised his palms, machete pointed at the sky. "If you leave us alone, we'll leave you alone. There's a different way you want to live. I'll respect that. But I'm not going to let you pretend to enforce law here anymore."

"Last chance." His father's finger curled around the trigger.

"You gonna shoot an innocent man?"

Disoriented but finally standing again, Rook raised his knife. If he was going to die, he might as well use it.

Suddenly Gerry cocked his head up the hill, put two fingers in his mouth, and whistled loudly. Rook twisted to see two dark figures running atop the tire trail, barely in view. Silver light glinted off something in their hands, then they disappeared inside the shed.

Rook's father spun around, horror on his face. "They're going inside! Get up there! Protect your mother!"

Blinded with panic, Rook dashed wildly toward the shed. The rifle cracked loudly behind him, but he couldn't look. Screams erupted from the shed. He kept his eyes on his feet so he wouldn't slip, desperate to reach his mother.

A muffled explosion reverberated from atop the hill. Rook heard footsteps rushing alongside him, and then Frank was yelling the names of his children.

Bang.

Bang.

Bang.

Two men in black rain suits stood in front of the shed, each of them swinging something at the door.

Hammers . . . they're boarding them up inside!

By the time Rook reached the shed, Gerry's men were dashing away to higher ground. When he saw the door, his stomach turned to liquid. Two planks were nailed across it.

"The propane tanks!" Frank joined Rook, pulling at the planks as loud popping noises sounded within.

The smell of something burning drew Rook's eyes up. The chimney was billowing black smoke. Mike and Charlie arrived and grabbed at the boards, but they were nailed on too tightly.

"Mom!" Rook backed up and rammed his shoulder into the door. A shock of pain lit through him, and he crumpled to the ground.

High-pitched shrieks began to mix with the shouting and heavy pounding from inside. Dark smoke rolled off the roof in waves, and flames began licking out through the siding. The whole shed was catching ablaze.

"Dad!" Rook spotted his father hobbling frantically up the tires. As he neared the top, his foot slipped on the muddy rubber and his rifle went flying downhill.

A loud crack drew Rook's attention back to the shed. Someone's leg had broken through part of the fire-weakened wall. A wave of heat poured out, a body fell through the smoke. Then two more, soot-covered figures clambering over each other as blood-curdling cries grew louder inside.

"Get out! Everyone out!" Rook remembered with horror learning in his meteorology studies that not even heavy rain could put out a house fire. Shouting for his mother, he pulled his shirt over his mouth and staggered into the burning shed.

Blazing streaks blinked against thick smoke. Blue flames rose from the wall where the propane tanks had been stacked. He strained to see the back of the room, the mattresses, but dizziness blanched his vision. Coughs sounded, but he couldn't see where. In his last moment of consciousness, he stumbled outside.

The pain of searing plastic woke him, his rain suit melting into his shoulder. He ripped it off, pain pulsing along his arm as skin peeled off with plastic and fell sizzling to the earth. After dropping and coating himself in mud, he raised his head to scan the faces groaning around him.

His mother was nowhere in sight.

"Why?" Rook heard his father sobbing.

Gerry was standing over his father with the rifle. "I warned you to leave us alone countless times! But you just couldn't quit!" Gerry pushed the barrel down into his chest.

Rook swiveled his head around, frantic for help, but Mike, Charlie, and Frank were pulling the wounded away from the fire. Ignoring the pain of his burns, Rook stood and charged at Gerry.

Gerry swung the rifle up. "Easy, boy." Rook froze as it pointed toward his belly.

"Where's your mother?" his father cried out, looking up from the mud.

Rook shook his head, hot tears clouding his vision.

"You son of a bitch!" His father lunged for Gerry's legs.

"No, Dad!"

Gerry whipped the barrel back down and fired.

With a long moan, Rook's father slumped between two tires. Someone's arms wrapped Rook up from behind before he could move any closer.

"Enough, Gerry, please!" Mike pleaded.

Gerry glanced at Mike for just a second, then back at Rook's father. "You're no sheriff."

"Fuck you," his father groaned, holding his hip.

"There is no law here . . . you understand now?" Gerry's voice wobbled. "Do you hear me? Next time you come near our tents, *everyone* dies!" He turned abruptly and disappeared down the hill.

A loud crash loosened Mike's hold on Rook. A plume of ash shot into the sky as the shed roof collapsed. Fire was licking up the outside walls now.

Rook ripped off his shirt to try to stanch his father's bleeding. His hands shook as he pressed the cloth against his father's blood-soaked waist. "Someone, help me carry him!"

Mike hooked his arms under Rook's father, and together they lifted him. Staggering up the hill, they laid him under a ratty strand of roof, hardly enough to keep the rain off.

"Go get your mother." His father's eyes rolled back in his head.

Rook felt himself collapsing inside. *It's too late.* But his father said it again, angrily, and Rook joined the others in pulling the living farther from the fire.

17
TANNER

Linda barks orders all afternoon until the new section of tarp is finished, extending the grub hall by thirty feet. I take in the empty floor, imagining it filled with partyers.

Dusty walks toward me, wiping sweat from his forehead and leaving a new smear of mud. "Did you check on Russell this morning?"

"Yes, he's going to come to the party!" It's a miracle, he's well enough just in time for the celebration. I planned to show him what this place really is, but now he'll see it for himself. All of Blue City will be here.

The smell of garlic and onion wafts from the corner where Terry and Caroline, another cook, have three large silver kettles going. Plates and utensils are already laid out, alongside cups and liquor bottles.

"When's he coming?" Dusty unfolds the last chair and sits down.

"Gloria said she'd wake him," I say just as Gloria walks in, followed by Bryn.

"He's up!" She glows. "A little slow from the downtime, but he'll be a hundred percent in a few days."

"Is he here?" I squirm, eyeing the entrance.

"He wanted to go for a walk to get his muscles warm before he has to deal with the dancing," she chuckles.

Immediately I want to cut out and find him. If he walks too far from the tarps, or gets up to something, taking things in without me, he might not see this place right . . .

Dusty places his hand on mine under the table. "Hey, he's fine. But if you really want to find him, I'll come."

It's the first time he's touched me, other than a high five, since we kissed. It scares me how much he's learning to notice what I'm feeling. I hold his hand for just a second and then pull away.

"No, it's okay." I stand up. "Russell can take care of himself." The words only feel half-true. Since Sioux Falls, it's been me taking care of him. But this place and its people have earned my trust. Let it go, I tell myself. He'll get here.

I wander over to where Philip is setting up. His long hair hangs over his drums as he positions a cracked gold cymbal. The rims of the drums are rust orange, the surfaces scratched to white. He adjusts a stool and pulls them closer.

"Hi, Tanner." He twirls his sticks. "Ready to kick this thing off?"

"I'm so excited!" And it's true, as long as I ignore my worries about Russell. A loud thump reverberates as Philip slams a stick down. Heads turn, smiles all around as Terry carries his guitar over.

A rush of commotion sounds from the doorway, yellow rain suits filing in fast. I watch, listening to the drums pound, hoping that Russell's dirty gray rain suit appears soon. The chairs fill up, some faces I know and some I don't. He'll be with the next group, I tell myself.

"Food's ready!" Caroline shouts from behind a kettle.

Dusty taps my arm. "Want to help dish it out?"

"Of course."

By the time almost everyone's served, I'm dying to sit down and eat. The atmosphere is contagious—everyone smiling and laughing, people I don't know introducing themselves as I hand them their stew. Bryn jams the line, updating me about three new whiskers on Little Buddy, the runt of the litter. The band steps up the tempo and Dusty hums along.

Then he slaps me on the back. "Look who's here!"

I see Daniel first, rifle strapped around his chest like usual, holding Linda's hand. Then my heart leaps. Russell's behind them in a shiny new rain suit. My hand shoots up, waving like a crazy person, flinging stew from the ladle. His face lights up and he waves back. I can't believe how good he looks. They fall into line and I start preparing Russell's bowl.

"Am I late?" Russell raises his eyebrows, trying to look serious.

"You're out of bed!" I hand him the bowl.

"Sure are fitting in fast." He cracks a wide grin. My heart wells up so much I can hardly take it—there's color in his face again, and he looks happy like he used to be.

"What do you think?" Daniel asks as Russell eyes the room.

"I really don't have words." Russell shakes his head. "It's been years since I've seen anything like this." He lifts a spoonful into his mouth. "This tastes great! Tanner, did you help make this?"

"I wish." I point to Terry, who's bobbing back and forth, eyes closed as he strums. "How are you feeling?"

It takes him a moment to snap out of the trance the music has him under. "No better than if I'd gone to Jefferson Hospital." He beams, looking back to the band. "I wonder if I can still play."

"You two look hungry." Daniel nods to me and Dusty. "How about we sit down and eat?"

A new melody starts up and Russell pauses on the way to our table, mesmerized.

"You coming?" I call.

"They're really good." His eyes still look far away as he joins us at the table.

Chatter grows as people finish eating, a steady buzzing underneath the music. I can't even hear the rain unless I listen really hard. After I shovel down the stew and stand up to stretch, Daniel puts something on the table. A piece of blue-and-silver metal.

"I'll be damned." Russell picks it up. "You play harmonica?"

"Try to," Daniel laughs with a shrug.

"Do you mind?"

"Not at all."

Russell puts the harmonica to his mouth and blows a harsh note.

"I need to get them to change key." He gets up and walks toward the band with barely a trace of his limp.

"He sure sprang back to life, didn't he?" Linda grins. I nod and chase after him, catching up in the wide space between the tables and the band reserved for dancing, still empty.

"What do you think?" I hope he'll read my mind, but he just smiles mischievously. "Well?"

"You were right, Tan. It really is here." My heart could burst. He sees the veneer, too.

"Dusty said he talked to his dad, and we could stay if we want to."

"Hey." He takes my shoulders, studying me with concern. "We're not abandoning Leadville. We'll still get there. But for now . . ." He sighs. "After walking around here, talking with people, I can't stop thinking about what you said—maybe we should stay a while, in case it *is* as good as it gets."

Then a bittersweet expression forms on his face. I feel the same thing. Leadville is so close, and for a moment I forget what we've found here and return to the familiar fantasy of blue skies, our rainless city in the mountains. I still believe I'll find a place where the sun is shining.

Russell raises the harmonica. "Want to hear me mess a song up?"

"Of course!"

He hurries over and leans close to Terry's ear. The music slows down, then dies. There's a loud count of *one, two, three, four . . .*

When the music starts again, the notes of the harmonica slice a melody through the rhythm. Russell bends his knee and taps his foot, his cheeks sucking in as he bobs side to side. He looks like a little kid, but it sounds good. I feel so relieved, so happy just watching him, that my own feet start moving a little bit.

Someone touches my back.

"You don't dance, huh?" Dusty mocks. "You're the first one out here!"

He starts matching my sway. Bryn's bundle of black hair comes loose as she bounces over to us, twisting in her cute red-and-white polka-dot dress. She clacks her black shoes on the floor. They look brand new.

"You're a great dancer!" I shout at her. "I love your dress."

"She only wears dresses for the festivals." Dusty sneakily locks his fingers with mine. I feel a hundred eyes on us, and my first instinct is to go sit down, but then I see they're actually looking at Bryn, cheering her on.

The music booms fast and heavy as Dusty lifts my hand and twirls me around. "You're a natural."

Voley crawls out from under a table, watching curiously as Bryn crisscrosses the dance floor, spinning until she's so dizzy she falls down. Even people in their seats are moving side to side now.

Caroline joins us next, and then Linda explodes onto the floor, the first person with real dance moves. The faces start to blend together as we're pushed to the edge of the room. The song finishes and the crowd bursts into applause. I clap so hard it stings. Russell's talking in Terry's ear like they're best friends already, and then Terry hands him the guitar. Bass notes alternate and Russell starts singing, Terry adding a harmony.

"*A long time ago these dreams first fell behind us . . .*"

Russell's eyes fall on me as he belts the song, and then I remember—it's the one he sang to me when I was little, back when he had a guitar in Pennsylvania. My feet start again and I watch Linda carefully, trying to learn how she moves like that.

With a grin as wide as his face, Dusty grabs my hand and swings to his left, bouncing us in a circle. My hand goes up and he pushes my shoulder, spinning me so fast this time that my knees buckle, but he catches me.

For a moment, as he pulls me up, we're practically hugging. "Let me try it again." I back away from him, suddenly wishing we were alone and I could stay that close.

By the time five songs go by, I need to sit down before I pass out. Everyone else must be fueled by alcohol because they show no signs of slowing down. Neither does Russell, despite the sweat glistening on his forehead.

"Want to get some air?" Dusty follows me out of the crowd.

"I'd love to."

We grab our rain suits and find a spot out back to huddle underneath the eaves of the tent.

He turns to me. "You're pretty good, you know?"

"Yeah right." Then, before I can tell him how wonderful this night's been, that it's the happiest I think I've ever felt, his hands curl softly around the back of my head, and he kisses me. I kiss back, hard and deep and sweet. My hands run through his wet hair, and he pulls me in, a perfect fit against his chest. Part of me wishes I didn't have the damned rain suit on, that I could feel his skin against mine. A new song starts up inside the tent and feet stomp in unison as the heat from Dusty's mouth melts away every thought in my head.

"I like you a lot." He abruptly pulls back. "I've never felt like this before. It makes me nervous."

"It makes me nervous, too."

The thought pops into my head—we could sneak away while everyone's partying. I argue with myself at first, that it's too soon, but all I end up thinking is that there's no guarantee of another chance.

Fuck it. "We should go to your house."

He looks startled. I kiss him again, and this time, I pull him around the side of the grub hall. Firelight and silhouettes blink beside us and it feels like my feet aren't touching the ground.

"What about Voley?" He sounds alarmed.

"Your dad's there."

And then, I'm racing. His hand slips out of mine and we splash through the mud. I giggle. Before I know it, we're inside.

We both glance around nervously, but no one's home. He pulls off his rain suit, and I do the same, throwing it to the floor. The next thing I know, he has my hand, pulling me into our bedroom. His fingers grasp at my sweater, begin sliding it up.

My eyes close, feeling each hot breath against my neck and then his gentle touch wandering over my body, sending electricity through me, and I can't help it—I pull his shirt off and feel the curves of his chest and stomach. The air's cold until we're pressing into each other, his skin warming mine.

Together we fall onto the blanket. I feel like I might lose consciousness as his hands run over me. The rain hits the roof above our heads, and again and again we find each other, in our eyes, mouths, and bodies, and I want nothing ever to happen again but this.

A faint popping sound freezes us. Then another.

"Do they fire guns at the festival?" I whisper.

"No." He darts off and brings back my sweater. "Come on!"

Everything crashes through the earth as I dress and then pound outside after him. Cold droplets soak me and I realize neither of us remembered our rain suits.

No, no, no . . .

Down the road, people are dumping into the street from the direction of the festival. A scream splits the air, then another gun blast.

"Fuck!" Dusty spins around. "My rifle."

He grabs my hand for a second and then lets go, barreling back to the house. I spin around too fast and slip. As I scramble to my feet, two gangly figures in tattered rain suits burst out from a nearby tent into the street, right behind Dusty.

Face eaters.

"Dusty, behind you!" I run toward them.

The taller one chases Dusty, but the other stops in the middle of the street and spreads his arms to block me.

I veer left at the last second, close enough to catch a glimpse of the crazy eyes, the sunken cheeks. His fingers reach out, snagging at the back of my sweater and then sliding off as I bolt past. Dusty disappears inside the house, the face eater right behind him. My lungs are on fire as I sprint to catch up.

There's a loud crack and light flashes from the doorway.

I almost stumble over the face eater's body as he falls backward, and my eyes lock with Dusty's, his face white with terror.

"Duck!"

I throw myself down and the rifle blasts again. Loud groans erupt from the second face eater.

"Grab a gun!" Dusty waves to Daniel's gun rack. I find a black pistol and spin around. Footsteps trample loudly through the connected tarps, then shouting.

"This way." Dusty leads me down a corridor. I stay close, listening for any sound that more are coming.

Something crashes to the floor in a nearby room, followed by a scream. It takes all my willpower not to shout for Russell at the top of my lungs.

Dusty glances at me when we reach the doorway to the next room. "Ready?"

I nod, both fists tightening around my pistol as he enters in front of me. I aim just below eye level, wondering how many bullets I have but afraid to ask.

Boxes and crates are scattered on the floor, and there's an oil-drum fire sending smoke up the chimney, but the room is empty.

Dusty pivots. "Damn it, where are they?"

A quick succession of gunfire rocks through the settlement. Voices call out, but I can't understand the words. My hands shake, sweat sliding the gun out of my grip. I've never had to fight them without Russell.

"They're in there." Dusty moves into the next room.

When I catch up to him, I hear terrible moaning sounds. Before I can search the room, something's on my leg, clutching at my ankle. I kick and kick again until I'm free. It's a downed face eater, blood pooling from its chest. Downed but not dead, slugging along on the floor, still enough life to come for me.

"Fucker!" I take aim and fire two bullets into his back. He groans loudly but keeps moving. I point at his head, ready to shoot another two bullets, when Dusty pushes my arm down.

"No! Save ammo." He steps forward and swings his boot hard, splitting the face eater's head with a sickening crunch.

He looks at me anxiously. "They must have stolen a big supply of the drug. It keeps them going after they should be down."

"Shit." My gut sinks—it's the same thing we've been seeing since South Dakota, like the face eater who came at me even with Russell's knife deep in his belly. At the thought of Russell, terror flips my stomach. What if he's stuck somewhere alone?

Dusty twists around as footsteps clap behind us.

Turning, I see two mud-brown faces charging, one of them with hair to the waist, a woman. My finger eases off the trigger because it catches me off guard. I've never seen a female face eater.

Suddenly, she stops running and raises a pistol.

I drop to the floor right before the bang. From the ground I stretch my arms and fire for center mass. She bends over, clutching her stomach. The other one charges forward, hands balled into fists. Dusty's rifle cracks above me and the second face eater staggers to the ground, but both of them keep crawling. I look away as Dusty runs up and starts to stomp on their heads until they're limp.

"Help!" comes a loud cry as I stand up.

"That sounded like the infirmary—guard this hallway so they don't sneak up behind me." He runs off.

I stand at the edge of the doorway, just my head and gun poking out, keeping an eye on the twitching face eaters. An eternal minute passes, but no one else comes.

A distant shout sounds from somewhere behind me. Panic kicks my gut. *Dusty* . . . I can only watch the corridor a few more seconds before I'm convinced he needs my help. I run after him.

The infirmary walls are sprayed with blood, and Dusty's nowhere in sight. I spot movement in the corner, the torn rain suit of a face eater bent over someone in a bed. Gurgling noises sound, broken by a loud bang that glazes my vision to white. My hearing disappears, replaced by a high-pitched ringing. I'm sure I've been killed, but there's no pain. When my sight comes back, the face eater is slumped lifelessly over the bed. I turn, still half-blinded, and see my savior—it's Linda.

"Go that way!" She points to a door on the far side of the room, but I hesitate, listening to a shouting voice. It sounds like Dusty, and it's coming from another direction.

"Now!" She furiously throws her arms.

"Where's Russell?" I ask, but she's done talking to me and kneels by an open flap, facing out into the wasteland. Her rifle blasts once, twice.

Christ, how many are there?

As she reloads, I dash through the doorway she pointed at and enter a large supply room. Three aisles of metal shelving take up the whole left side of the room, stacked with boxes to the ceiling. Some of them are scattered on the floor like there's been a scuffle. Opposite me, at the other end of the room, another door leads deeper into the tarps.

I swing my pistol around at the sound of a frightened voice.

"Tanner!"

It's Russell. A miracle.

I can hardly see him, hidden in the farthest aisle. Sprinting forward, I squeeze between the crates to reach him where the last aisle dead-ends against the wall. Immediately he starts pulling boxes off the shelf and stacking them in front of us.

"What are we gonna do?" But I realize he's walling us in, so I help make it higher. After a minute we're out of sight except for tiny slits to see through.

"Get behind me." He rips the gun out of my hands. "No noise." Switching between two slivers in the crate wall, he eyes both entrances to the room. The distant scuffling noises move closer, feet stamping, shouting, gunfire, but I can only see Russell's back, hear his heavy breathing.

"Be ready." He nudges me, but I don't know how because he took my gun.

I eye the crates, hoping I can pry one open to find something sharp. Then I see it—half-hidden under a pile of boxes in the next aisle over, there's a metal sheen on the floor. The tarp flooring is cut away around it.

"That might be a cellar." Russell sees it too and moves two boxes apart on the lowest shelf. "Can you fit through?"

"I'll try." I bend down.

"I got your back," he says as my head pops through and I twist awkwardly onto the ground. Russell nods for me to inspect the floor.

I slide the boxes carefully but they get stuck on the edge of the metal. Bracing myself, I push harder until they slide too fast and I slip. My palm smacks the corner of the metal, and I pull back in shock.

Cold, I mouth to him. The metal is freezing, so cold that frost has melted on my hand.

He frowns in confusion. "Stay there." He squeezes past the box wall and runs around to my aisle.

We lift the boxes off the shiny flooring, revealing a steel ring attached to the metal.

"It's a door." Russell runs his finger across the frost, leaving a wet line. He grips the ring and pulls up. At first, nothing happens, like it's locked, but then, after another tug, it groans open. A cloud of frost curls out from a cellar.

I can't see anything inside, just darkness. Then as my eyes adjust, I discern strange shapes, reddish in color, underneath a layer of frost. Russell drops the door before I can duck my head in to look more closely.

His eyes are wide with shock. "Meat."

"It can't be," I finally speak. He doesn't reply. "Let me look."

He shakes his head like he's figured it out in that three-second glance. "Quiet." He turns toward the sound of incoming footsteps, holding his finger up angrily, and I shut up, thinking the worst. Dusty and his family wouldn't eat people, but what was down there, cold and hidden?

"You hardly looked."

"I saw. They're chopped, wrapped in frozen blocks, and . . ." His hoarse whisper fades as the footsteps enter our room.

It's Daniel, thank god. He walks past the first aisle, swinging his head around frantically. I throw my hands up, but he looks the wrong way.

A face eater flies into the room after him, hands circling his neck.

"Daniel, get down!" Russell slaps away a crate for a clear shot.

Daniel wrenches at the face eater's fingers, choking.

"Get down!"

He finally hears and sinks to the floor, the face eater falling right on top of him. This one has no hair on his head, his scalp red and scraped. The thought of an old face eater crosses my mind just for a second, the horrible possibility that someone could live that way for a long time, as Russell aims and pulls the trigger.

18

ROOK

18 YEARS, 9 MONTHS, 3 DAYS

Dear Mom, Dad, Big Brother . . .

I don't know why I'm writing this. I guess I'm hoping you'll all hear me better if I write things out. Maybe it's just for me, so I know clearly what it is I have to do now before I kill myself.

I know it's hard to hear me talk about suicide. Mom, if you've been watching as everyone we knew from the shed died or became like Gerry, while I took care of Dad these last ten years, hiding us away in the city ruins so the drug-addled maniacs (whom I loathe myself for helping create) didn't eat us, then you must understand. Now that Dad's with you again, this existence will be too lonely, hollow, wet, and cold. But I'm not coming home yet.

Dad, would you believe that after all that time, arguing every time we saw a Yasper ship that I should leave you, let you die so I could go back to Yasper, that they returned to this shithole four days after you'd gone? Maybe you had a hand in that? It's taken way longer than you wanted, but I'm finally going back to destroy the drug. I was able to get them to radio in, and Marrow remembered me. I'm going to do what you asked of me so long ago, and what I promised as you lay dying. I hope you forgive me for not going sooner, but I couldn't leave you to die alone in this awful, rotting place.

Maybe I'm delusional, but I don't care. I feel determined, more than any time before in my life. This is my last chance to make things right before I return to you all. And it goes back way before the fire, before the rain ever started. My whole life, I wanted to make an impact the way you all did. I never could, though. And to think how proud I was of myself at Yasper, how proud I was that you were proud of me . . .

I can't wait to see you all, to laugh about this somehow, but not until I destroy the thing that took you both from me. Maybe I should have listened, Dad, let you die years ago and done this sooner. The truth is, I was scared. As horrifying as it was seeing the drug destroy everyone around us, seeing those empty souls mutilate and eat each other, I was more scared to be alone again.

I remember where the Red is stored, and even if I have to burn the whole compound to the ground, I'll do it. Then I'll come home, because outside of keeping my promise, there's nothing else to live for. And at least I'll know I did something that gives humanity a better chance of surviving to see the sun shine again.

Living like we did, cockroaches in the city ruins, was only possible because you taught me how to, Dad. Even paralyzed from that bullet, you guided me. If you can just send a little more guidance now, and courage, I promise it will be enough.

Big bro, I'm sorry I pushed you away, didn't try to rebuild the relationship after so much time passed. I hope you beat your demons in the end, and I'm sure you're at peace now. I can't help thinking back to before the drugs, when we were kids. You tried to build me up. I fought you tooth and nail when you pulled me outside to experience the world outside my books and computer. Truth is, I wanted to be able to do all the things you did, I was just scared. I didn't have what you and Mom and Dad had. And I held on to that resentment. God, I should have let it go when you were knocked off your feet, but I didn't. It took me living through hell to see how petty all that was. I'm sorry I was envious that I never got the girls like you did, jealous that you traveled the world while I stayed in Colorado. I just want to know what happened, how it went for you in the end. I promise, when we meet, I won't chicken out if you want to wrestle like old times.

It's strange, I just didn't think it mattered that we grew so far apart after you left Colorado. Somehow I always thought we'd reconnect, become best friends later in life. Funny how things go. So if you can lend me some of your toughness, too, I could use it.

I hear the horn down on the water. It's time to go. I love you all, and if my old pup Bartleby is up there, tell him I love him, too. You won't be waiting for me too much longer.

Love,
Rook

19
TANNER

Russell fires again, and the face eater rolls off Daniel.

I rush out and help Daniel to his feet. "Where's Dusty?"

"I don't know." He rubs his neck. "I saw him—"

He can't finish because Russell points the gun at both of us.

"Move, Tanner." Russell's voice is calm.

I recognize his stone-faced expression. He's going to shoot. "Russell, please don't!"

He flicks his head at the sound of incoming footsteps. "Watch the door, god damn it!"

I have no choice—I move away from Daniel and into the doorway, my heart thumping as they talk behind me.

"Why?" Daniel's voice shakes.

"Don't fuck with me." Russell's tone is ice cold. "I saw what's down there."

There's a silence before Daniel answers. "Our population is getting too big. We can't sustain ourselves on the greenhouse and scavenging alone. But we just started trading for it. We didn't kill for it, and we don't take the drug here."

Trading for it? I don't understand, but I feel my heart collapsing. Russell was right the whole time—the veneer here was all an illusion.

"Enough," Russell says flatly. "Give me the boat keys."

I have to turn around. Daniel is staring blankly at Russell, blood dripping from his lip.

"Russell, don't hurt him!" I yell, but approaching footsteps distract me. Darting back to the doorway, I see Linda coming. Her face washes with relief as she spots me.

"Keys!" Russell shouts. I hear the clinking of metal, the keys trading hands.

"Tanner." Linda inspects me head to toe as I block her from the room. "More are coming, we have to get to North Tent now!"

"Is Dusty okay?" I peer over her shoulder.

Before she responds, Daniel hollers, "Linda!"

"Daniel!" She pushes past me to find Russell aiming at Daniel. "What are you doing?" Linda takes a moment to react, then raises her own pistol at Russell.

"Listen," he says, pointing back at her. "We just want to leave. We need a boat. I'm not going to hurt anyone."

"Shoot him!" Daniel yells at her.

Linda's gun flashes and bangs and I jump away, out of the line of fire. Another blast sounds behind me, followed by a thump on the floor. My heart stops.

I turn back, certain Russell's dead, and almost trip. The rubber sole of my boot slides over a pool of blood. It's Linda, not Russell, groaning from the floor, reaching for her pistol a few inches from her hand.

"Grab it," Russell orders, pressing his gun to Daniel's temple, holding him as a human shield. I can't do anything but stare down in shock at Linda, desperate to help her somehow.

As Russell takes a step back from Linda's spreading blood, Daniel spins free and charges into him, knocking them both into one of the shelves.

Instinct takes over and I kick Daniel's ribs with everything I have, but he's still able to squeeze his hands around Russell's neck.

Dropping to my knees, I scramble for Linda's gun, turn, and squeeze the trigger. The bullet rockets into Daniel's side. His hands loosen first, and then he slumps off Russell.

"Get up, get up!" I grab Russell's hand.

It takes him a moment to regain his breath, but then he snaps up and starts toward the far exit. "Come on!"

"We're taking a boat?"

"Yes, run!"

We pause as we enter another storage room. Russell scans the room to be sure it's clear, but I'm in shock at the horrible thing we've just done. I want to run back and help Daniel and Linda, but it's too late now. It all happened so fast.

"Keep an eye behind us." He grabs a canvas sack from one of the shelves and starts throwing in everything he can get his hands on. Water, cans, bottles, small boxes. He's trying to give us a chance on the endless sea.

"People coming." I tap him as footfalls and voices get closer. Then I spot them entering the room behind us—tarpers this time, not face eaters. Most of them have rifles, and Dusty is leading the pack.

I move to the edge of the door, hoping he won't see me.

"Tanner!" Dusty spots us.

An outcry starts behind him as they discover Linda's and Daniel's bodies, but Dusty's oblivious, his eyes locked on mine, calling out to me at the top of his lungs.

"They'll think it was face eaters." Russell shoves a bag into my hand. "Don't lose it on me, okay? We have to get to their boats—do you know the way?" He slings a second sack over his shoulder.

I pause for a moment, just long enough to hear Voley bark. Dusty calls, "Tanner, I'm here!"

Russell jerks me so hard I almost trip. "Now!"

I swing the bag over my shoulder and run, unable to look back. I can't. It hurts too much to know what I've done, what I'm leaving behind.

We break through the cocoon of tarps into the dark wasteland. I hear barking, Voley chasing after us like it's a game. I lead Russell toward one of the mud hills.

"Where are you going?" Dusty hollers, not far behind.

He still hasn't figured it out. Maybe none of them ever will. I turn my head to yell at Voley.

"Go home, boy!" But he keeps chasing, like he has to protect me. "The docks are this way." I point, recognizing the summit I visited with Dusty.

We crest the hill, the rain sea stretching before us, a black and silent forever, then descend toward the spit of rocky shoreline with the huge, ramshackle barge and the motorboats.

Russell reaches the water's edge first. "Here!"

I follow him onto a floating wooden dock, then glance back to take in the spread of land behind us, breathing hard. My heart breaks. Voley and Dusty are speeding down the hill after us.

Russell hops aboard one of the motorboats and I follow him.

Dusty has to realize now that we're stealing a boat. I can't take my eyes off them as Russell tries each key in the outboard motor. "Come on, come on, damn it," he grunts.

Dusty shouts but I can't make out the words. It's just him and Voley dashing down the hill together. Then, at the top of the hill, three more people appear and start down.

"Shit, they're onto us." I shake Russell. "Make it work."

"I'm trying!" The keys jangle, but the boat won't start.

The three new figures aren't wearing yellow rain suits, and they don't seem to be running with Dusty and Voley. No—*they're running at them.*

"Face eaters!" I smack Russell's arm.

He's in his own world, trying the last keys on the loop. I can't wait for him. I lift my pistol and point into the rain, but the boat's rocking too much for a clean shot. Leaping onto the dock, I run toward the bottom of the hill to warn Dusty and Voley. "Behind you!"

I hear Russell shout, "Get back!"

The motor roars to life, but I can't turn around now.

"Behind you!" I yell again. It takes a moment for my words to register, but finally Dusty sees the maniacs closing in, almost sliding down the mud after him, their arms flailing. Dusty must have lost his rifle because his hands are empty, and he can't turn and fight. He sprints after Voley, who reaches the dock first, barking, his hackles raised.

"Run faster!" I point and shoot, but the face eaters only speed up, like they're enraged by the gunfire.

"Get in the fucking boat!" Russell slaps the hull.

Dusty makes the dock and I stand aside. "Go, go, go!"

Taking a last shot, I aim and fire, hitting one of them. He spills into the mud.

I jump in the boat after Dusty and Voley. Russell turns the wheel, the engine rumbling, and fixes his pistol on us. For a moment, I think he's going to shoot Dusty, but the gun bangs and Dusty's still alive, clutching my arm. He's shooting past us at the face eaters. Another one goes down.

Russell spins, hits the gas, and a rush of white foam blasts from the stern.

More dark figures crest the hill, and a chorus of gunfire erupts in the distance as we launch into the bay. The remaining face eaters crumple into the mud. It really is tarpers coming this time, but they're too late for us. We're already past the barge monstrosity, leaving the ugly fake hope of this island behind. I feel sick to my stomach watching Blue City disappear, the most beautiful illusion of the veneer I've ever known.

"What the hell's going on?" Dusty demands.

I look shamefully at the confusion wrinkling his face. He still hasn't figured it out yet, even as Russell steers us into open water. Then it comes. The painful recognition slides over him as the coast grows smaller, the tarpers' calls inaudible.

Russell slows the boat after a couple of minutes when he's sure no one's pursuing us.

He turns to face Dusty. "What do you know?"

"What the hell are you doing?" Dusty squints, throwing his arms wide.

"What do you know about the bodies in the floor?" Russell sounds callous, no sympathy for what we've just done to him.

"The what?" Dusty's eyes widen.

The lump in my throat finally disappears. "He didn't know!" I can't help the pleading note in my voice.

"Why are you stealing a boat and leaving?" Dusty turns from Russell to me. "Why are you doing this?"

Russell returns to the wheel. "Because we're going to Leadville. That's where we've always been going. And you don't have to become a face eater to survive, do you understand?"

But Dusty doesn't. "Colorado? This is crazy. It's suicide! The currents are too strong, it's too cold—there's nothing out there!" He looks at me desperately, like I have the power to stop this.

"It happened so fast, the face eaters came, we had to run." I search for words. "We didn't want you to follow us!" The color drains from Dusty's face like I've stuck him with a dagger.

Then Russell gives him his options.

"You can still make it back to shore," he says calmly. "Get off and swim back if you want. Otherwise, you're stuck with us until we hit land."

Voley whines, circling the boat nervously, uselessly shaking off the rain. Could they swim back that far? I glance at the mountain rising from the sea behind us and think about how cold it is in that water. The rain is freezing, but the sea is so much worse.

It kills me that I've given pieces of my heart to these two. Russell warned me never to lend out my heart, not while the veneer's stripped. If you do that, you'll slip and fall, he said, and you may never get up. But I screwed it all up, and now I'm torn in half. I care so much about what happens to this boy and his dog. I watch Dusty think through his decision.

He finally looks right at me. "I can't leave my dad behind."

"Off," Russell orders.

Dusty looks terrified, and I think he's crying, or maybe it's the rain, as he takes off his shirt and jumps into the sea. Water splashes back at me and the truth hangs on my lips, but I'm paralyzed and can't say it—that he's risking his life for nothing, that his dad's dead. Then Voley, as scared as he is, jumps right in after Dusty. I watch them start to swim. Voley paddles right beside him, working through the freezing brown, back toward the distant barge.

Russell doesn't watch. He turns and steps on the gas. The propeller blasts them with foam.

I can't look away. It seems like they're going to make it back just fine. Their movement is steady, but my heart starts skipping, a deep sadness I've never felt before eating me alive. Maybe Russell's wrong. Maybe it's not black and white, and if people don't murder for their meat, it can be okay sometimes. And then Voley's head goes under the water.

He can't keep up. It's too cold.

Dusty swims toward his dog instead of the shoreline. They get smaller, wrapped up together now, one tangled mess of struggling and splashing, not even halfway back to land. Then they both go under. They come back up. They're drowning together.

20
ROOK

18 YEARS, 9 MONTHS, 6 DAYS

The bright fluorescent lights startled Rook as he entered the Yasper lab. His eyes slowly adjusted to the sterile white interior, the tidy shelves, steel equipment shining on worktables, the tan-suited employees typing on computers. There was no rotting trash, none of the rancid flood odor that caked everything in Canvas City and the city ruins. It was surreal to be standing here after a decade. The place felt both alien and exactly as he remembered it.

Having showered in his new apartment and donned fresh rain gear, Rook was blending in already, and almost no one took notice as he walked through the drug production wing toward Marrow's office. A few familiar faces gawked, but their names eluded him. They didn't matter now, anyway. He'd come back for one reason only.

Heart thumping, he knocked on the door.

"Come in."

Marrow sat behind his desk, messy with books and papers, his skin still the same pale red hue as his hair, which had thinned considerably. His dark eyes looked tired yet alert, and the weight of age had pulled his face down in heavy lines.

"Rook, I can't believe it!" Marrow stood up and vigorously shook his hand.

"Mr. Marrow, I can't begin to express how grateful I am." Rook cringed, unused to social interaction, fearful Marrow would see through him.

"Have a seat. Did the guards set you up in a new apartment?"

"Yes, as soon as I arrived. I had the best shower of my life."

"There's no one left—*no one*—with credentials like yours." Marrow's face glowed with relief. "You were second to Dr. Franklin when you left, correct?"

"That's right." Rook dug his fingers into his palm until it hurt, anger rushing up at the man in front of him. He couldn't confront Marrow about the deception, how the drug had led to his parents' deaths, and the deaths of so many others.

No, not now. Hopefully, the Red was still stored just a few hundred feet away in the lab's basement, and until every ounce of it was destroyed, Rook had to fly under the radar.

"As the shipping crew told you, Dr. Franklin's no longer with us," Marrow said with genuine compassion.

It sounded strange to Rook, who over the years had come to think of Marrow as almost a figment of his imagination, a one-dimensional villain. "He was a great man." Rook's initial adrenaline began subsiding. Marrow had no reason to be suspicious. No one would, until they found him hanging in his closet.

"Finding your way back here, right after Dr. Franklin has passed, is a sign." Marrow slapped the desk. "A sign that we'll continue to prosper. There were times I doubted if I could keep the company going. Franklin's death seemed insurmountable, but here you are!"

"It's a great responsibility, sir."

"And with that responsibility comes benefits you didn't have before. First, you'll have all-hours clearance to the lab." Marrow handed Rook a black key fob and a piece of paper. "Jonathan and Cleo are still here. They'll work under you in the weather lab. We still have a small network of radio repeaters and weather stations operating via longwave radio. Our computer intranet is still running smoothly. Anything you need is yours. Here's Franklin's log-in." He gestured to the paper.

"Log-in?"

"To Franklin's computer. It's yours now." Marrow beamed. "Of course, now that you have access to classified files, anything we discuss stays between us." His expression flattened. "Understood?"

"Of course."

"Good. Hopefully, everything comes back to you. Aside from the daily route forecasts, your main priority is to continue Franklin's investigation of the dropping temperatures. He was working to determine if the ice will continue to get worse around the compound. If so, I want to be ready to move our base of operations off this island."

"Yes, sir." Rook had long pondered the same question. When the rain began, the climate had grown hot, constantly muggy and uncomfortable. Not one winter had been cold enough to produce snow. But during the years in Canvas City, and then in the city ruins, temperatures had gradually dropped. At first, he'd hoped things were reverting to normal, but they kept dropping until it felt like summer, spring, and fall had converged in one long, mild winter. Last year there'd even been sleet during the summer. Traveling east, from the city ruins to Yasper, it had only grown colder. From the deck of the ship, he'd seen the sheen of growing pack ice.

"Good . . ." Marrow studied him quizzically. "You are happy to be back?"

"Happier than words can express." Rook swallowed. "My parents both passed. I was stranded in a decaying city. I never thought I'd see a Yasper ship again."

"I'm so sorry for your loss. You know I have no blood family either. My employees are my family." Marrow's voice softened, and he narrowed his eyes. "You must have seen firsthand how some weak-willed people out there are misusing our miracle drug."

Words caught in Rook's throat. "I saw some of that."

"It's become all too common in the smaller, cruder camps. It's important that you know it's not like that at the big shelters, and it's not like that here. The places that remain civilized use it responsibly, and it helps them a great deal."

"Of course," Rook swallowed, harder this time. "I wanted to get to a big shelter, but I couldn't move my father. I'm so grateful to be back—somewhere civilized again."

Marrow seemed happy. "I've asked Cleo to refamiliarize you with the compound. I'll check in with you again soon."

"Thank you." Rook nodded and left the office, nervous at the thought of seeing his old poker buddy.

Walking through the laboratory, he noticed something else, besides age, that had changed in the workers' faces. Their eyes all looked alike: large dilated pupils, no trace of their irises, the telltale sign of Red use.

He felt a pang of fear. Had the drug turned them into maniacs like Gerry? Clearly, the place was still running smoothly after all these years, so the drug must not be affecting employees the way it had the refugees out in the floods. Still, a sadness hung in Rook's heart, the feeling that they were all lost.

Before he could reach Dr. Franklin's desk, someone tapped his shoulder. He turned to see an attractive woman with a close-cut crop of curly black hair.

"Cleo . . ."

"You're not a ghost?" She put her arms around him.

His instinct to tell her everything was strong, but he stopped himself. It would jeopardize his mission. No one could know.

"God, I can't believe it." She gestured to the main exit. "Join me for a walk around the compound?"

He was curious to see what Franklin had left behind, and even more eager to get down into the basement to explore where the drug was stored. "*All-hours clearance*," Marrow had said. But it would be better to snoop around at night anyway. Maybe a walk around the compound, seeing how much things had changed, would be helpful.

"I'll be damned!"

Rook turned to see another familiar face gawking at him.

"Gene?" His old friend had grown thin and bald, his big pupils contrasting with puffy pink bags under his eyes. "How are you?"

"I get booze and tobacco once a year now, how do you think I am?

But thanks to Marrow, Red's always on tap. We'd have all killed ourselves by now without it."

Rook stomached his revulsion, scrambling for something safe to say. "Do you still play poker?" As he remembered the old gang, nostalgia flooded in, shaking his solitary mindset. But things wouldn't pick up where they had left off. As soon as possible, he would destroy the drug and rejoin his family.

Gene soured, pursing his lips. "I wish . . ." He looked ready to say more but instead patted Rook's shoulder. "I have to get back to a batch of Red I'm pressing. Let's catch up soon."

As Cleo led him outside, Rook glanced down the hallway, past Marrow's office, to the basement door. "Speaking of Red, I remember we had enough raw material in the basement to make it for almost two decades. It's still there, in the basement, right?"

"Sure is. At this year's Family Meeting, Gene announced he's found a way to concentrate the formula. With how few milligrams each dose requires now, there should be enough powder downstairs to last at least another ten years. Incredible, isn't it?"

"Jesus Christ." Rook felt a wave of nausea.

"Hey, it's a good thing," Cleo said as they stepped into the rain. "Thank god Marrow had the foresight that first year to ship all his chemicals here. It could have all been lost in the floods."

"How is Ed?" Rook's stomach twisted at the thought of the two-faced man who had once been the shepherd of their little gang. Ed had protected Rook, cared for him when he'd been depressed, but he'd lied to him, too, countless times. Whenever the drug had come up, Ed had assured Rook that there were no negative side effects.

"I hardly see him," Cleo said. "He stays holed up in his office, with his equipment and his scribbles, trying to one-up Gene and concentrate the drug even more. I think he wants the spotlight back after all the praise Marrow heaped on Gene at the meeting."

People are eating each other over this drug, and Ed's making it stronger? Rook pinched himself to keep it together.

"And Dina's still managing the power plant, wearing her poker face even though we haven't played in years," Cleo said flatly. There had once been so much expression in her voice, so much life in her face. It was what had attracted him to her: her ever-present smirk; her quick, mischievous wit; her glowing eyes. Now, her face was rigid and fixed, pale, just like her voice.

This must be what the drug had done to them here. It hadn't made them violent because they didn't have to trade their food for it, but it made them lifeless just the same.

"What about Captain Lawrence?" Rook wanted, after all these years, to thank Lawrence for having been the only one at Yasper who did right by him.

"The shipping crews are never here. With all the ice slowing them down, they leave an hour after they return to unload. They've got the toughest job."

Continuing down the main road, they passed the faded siding of the cafeteria building and the plexiglass-paneled grow house, finally reaching the power plant. White smoke still billowed from its gargantuan cooling towers, making Rook shudder. *All this energy at Marrow's disposal, all the good this electricity could do, and he uses it to rob the refugees of their last shreds of humanity.*

Rook's eyes fell to the concrete foundation, where dark cracks spider-webbed up from the base. Despite Marrow's genius, he couldn't stop the rain from taking its toll on buildings, even here.

"I never thought I'd see you again," Cleo said, interrupting his musings. "I can't fathom living out there that long. What was it like? How did you survive?"

"The violence was . . ." Rook stopped himself. What could he tell her? This wasn't Cleo anymore. Her eyes were black. She was loyal to the company. "Horrible. I got numb to it, did what I had to do to take care of my father in the city ruins after my mother died. I scavenged for scraps, rationed them, and we hid. After he died, I didn't know how long I would make it, but a Yasper ship—"

"Did you at least have Red?"

"No." Rook gritted his teeth. *And that's the reason we didn't become cannibals*, he wanted to yell, but he just glared silently at the cracks in the foundation.

"I can't imagine living without it." Cleo shook her head sympathetically. "Being here, with a little Red to ease the mind, it feels like nothing ever went wrong."

"And no one takes too much?" Rook pictured the psychotic, twitching faces of Gerry and his gang with a chill. He remembered how, after the fire, Mike and Charlie had started using Red, and how quickly it was before they needed more and more.

We had to leave them, Dad. It wasn't safe anymore until we were alone in the ruins.

"Dosing's strictly regulated. Everyone's aware of the side effects now."

Now. Rook tried to choke back his emotions, but he could feel himself slipping, losing control.

"That's the problem in those tarp towns," Cleo continued. "They take way more than the suggested dose and—"

"That's because it's hell out there! No one's enforcing dosing guidelines. No one cares." All the attraction that Rook had once felt for Cleo was gone. She wasn't the same; nobody here was. Maybe it wasn't their fault, but it would make it easier to keep his distance.

Cleo's forehead wrinkled in confusion. "I didn't mean anything by it."

"Sorry, forget it." Rook took a deep breath and turned toward the last buildings on the compound, the fuel storage casks. An orange rain suit was walking between the casks. The site stored fifty-year-old uranium in casks, from before the power plant was converted to steam, but no one had ever needed to work in that area before. "We're manning the old fuel site?"

"Dina's had one of her workers keeping an eye on it for a few years, ever since the last earthquake."

Rook's gut dropped. Were the same cracks he'd seen crawling up the power plant also spreading up the spent nuclear fuel containers? "I want to take a look."

Cleo shrugged and followed him past the white-suited, machine-gun-wielding guards posted at the entrance to the power plant.

Rook eyed them anxiously. "Security's up a lot."

"Better too much than too little, right?"

A fractured concrete path branched off toward the pearl-colored casks, mud seeping through its cracks. At the end of the road, Rook peered through a chain-link fence at the giant barrels, eight in total.

The orange rain suit, walking toward a utility shed between the casks, spotted them and paused.

Rook strained to see a face under the hood. "Would he mind if I asked a question?"

But the orange suit was approaching already. Under the dripping hood, Rook saw it was a woman, roughly his age.

"Can I help you?" She squinted from the other side of the fence. Droplets of rain dripped from her hood, one of them catching the tip of her nose and hanging there. From what Rook could see of her face—a sharp jawline, full lips, and rosy, unblemished skin—she was pretty. But it was her eyes, full of color, that nearly stopped his breath.

"My name's Rook Wallace. I'm the new head of the meteorology team."

The shipping crew who'd brought him back, the guards, the lab workers, Cleo and Gene, even Marrow, all had the same dark, glazed eyes, but this woman's eyes were clear and green.

You don't take the drug! he wanted to exclaim. But not with Cleo here.

"I'm Luce." Her chin dipped, and her hood cast a shadow over her face. "Is something the matter?"

"I wanted to ask about the condition of the fuel site. I just saw the cracks in the power plant, and we never used to have anyone working here—"

"Used to?" Her eyebrows knitted with confusion. "I've been working the fuel site for years."

"Right, I'm sorry. I worked under Dr. Franklin during the first eight years of the rain, but I left to take care of my parents. I just got back."

Luce did a double take, her eyes narrowing in shock. "You were out there for—"

"Ten years."

"Wow, that's admirable." She sounded impressed. "I don't remember you. I worked in the power plant until I got posted here. Anyway, there're no problems. I have an easy job."

Rook surveyed the casks. In the gray murk, they appeared alien, the wombs of some sleeping radioactive fossil. "I guess they're built to last forever."

"Not one breach since the plant switched to HTGR," she said optimistically, turning to look at the casks.

"What's HTGR?"

"High-temperature gas-cooled reactor," Luce explained.

"Ah, I always thought it was a steam plant."

"And there's a reason they don't pay me to predict the weather." Dimples formed on Luce's cheeks as she smiled.

Rook felt suddenly unmoored. How long had it been since he'd been attracted to a woman? He fell dumb.

"Rook." Cleo tapped her leg anxiously. "We better get back to the lab."

"You said you're in charge of meteorology?" Luce asked, oblivious to Cleo's impatience. "I'd certainly be interested to learn more. Maybe you can tell me why the hell it keeps getting colder."

"That's actually the project I'll be working on. And I'd be interested to know what kind of radiation I'm getting exposed to." Rook thought he saw a smirk on her face, but it disappeared as Cleo interrupted.

"Thanks, Luce." Cleo began walking away.

"Let's talk another time," Luce said.

Her green eyes pulled him in. Was there someone here he could trust? He hadn't talked—*really talked*—to anyone but his father in so many years. "I'd like that."

"I eat in the caf at noon and eight most days."

"I'll make sure to find you." Rook found himself unable to wipe the grin from his face as he waved goodbye.

Luce took a yellow instrument from her pocket and walked back into the fuel site.

"I think you should be careful," Cleo said when Rook caught up to her.

"What do you mean?"

"Marrow wants the weather projects to stay classified, doesn't he?" She sounded spooked.

Marrow *had* said that, but what had Rook given away? No details, just the existence of Franklin's project. "You're right. I'll be more careful."

But he'd already decided he would meet with Luce again. She'd made him feel more alive in one minute than he had in ten years. And she seemed interested in him. Maybe she'd noticed his eyes, too, and realized that he wasn't on the drug either.

Back at the lab, Rook thanked Cleo and went to Franklin's desk in the alcove of the weather room. Powering on the computer, he punched in the log-in Marrow had given him.

Username: RFranklin
Password: nimbus414

As the computer logged on, he took stock of the information he had. Cleo had confirmed that the raw powder was still stored in the lab basement. His new clearance should get him through the basement doors. He could go at night when the place was empty.

But how to destroy it?

He'd fantasized for years about setting fire to the lab, finding explosives to blow the whole building up. *If it comes to that, that's what I'll do.* The security guards had to have an armory somewhere.

A directory window popped up on the computer screen. Big block folders cluttered the desktop, more hard-drive directories than he'd ever had access to when he'd merely been one of Franklin's technicians. The climate project was clearly marked, but Rook couldn't help hovering the cursor over the other folders.

Do I have access to every file on the network?

He struggled for a moment with what had once been second nature, then remembered the hot-key command to "select all." Rook glanced over his shoulder and, seeing that no one was paying attention, typed in a search:

Red drug Yasper

His jaw dropped at all the results. He scanned them, his pulse quickening, until one caught his eye: "Complete Red Abstract." He quickly opened it.

A headline ran across the top of the page:

ABSTRACT ON RED SYNTHESIS BY EDWARD BOWLING, COMPLETED 2 YEARS AFTER THE RAIN BEGAN

Rook's heart leaped into his throat as he scrolled, scrutinizing the bold section headings until one of them froze him.

LONG-TERM EFFECTS OF RED DISTRIBUTION

This abstract concludes that the distribution of Red, if successful, may destroy the communities that become dependent upon it, given the limited resources available to refugee settlements, the lack of regulated dosing, and its potential for physical addiction.

Marrow's signature was scrawled underneath, next to Ed's.

Motherfuckers. Rook's stomach soured. Ed really had lied from the beginning; he'd known how much the drug would hurt everyone, hurt his parents. It was no different from what the Sacklers had done to his brother all those years ago, lying about OxyContin's addictive potential for abuse. No wonder Marrow had stopped all incoming mail.

The mail . . .

Rook had often thought about who might have delivered his father's last letter, but there was never really a question in his mind.

Of course it was Lawrence. He'd broken protocol to search for Rook's parents, and then, in delivering that letter, because Rook's mother was dying, he'd broken it a second time. Most likely caught hell for it, too. It was clear in hindsight that Lawrence was the only person Rook could ever trust here, and he'd never even thanked him.

Then, Rook saw the answer—how to destroy the drug—staring him in the face. It was so obvious, so simple and ironic, that he could smack himself.

He read the same passage three times to be sure:

BREAKDOWN OF RAW POWDER MIXTURE FOR RED

Keep raw powder in a dark, cool, and dry place at all times. Avoid exposure to sunlight and, most importantly, water. Component powders are water soluble and will clump upon contact, leading to molding that will render the product unusable.

Rook struggled to contain his excitement. If there was a way to flood the basement, the drug would be gone forever.

Dad, all I need is the rain . . .

21

TANNER

Russell looks over when I start to cry. "It was his decision."

I cry harder. "They're going to die!"

He doesn't reply.

I start taking my waterlogged sweater off, stripping down to my tattered undershirt. "I'm going in."

And at that moment, I know how much Russell loves me because I feel the boat start to turn, and then we're gunning a straight line for the two struggling forms.

We stop fast. Russell bends over the rail next to me and helps haul them out of the water, soaked but alive.

"You're not going back, kid." Russell glares at Dusty and turns the boat around.

Dusty can't reply because he's heaving for air. Voley recovers long before Dusty stops shivering. I watch Dusty's hazel eyes and bluish skin, moving close to warm him, not caring if Russell sees.

"It's okay. You're safe now." I hold him, pulling up my shirt to warm him against my skin. The rain feels colder than it has all week. We left too quickly, without our plastic suits. And we don't know if we're going the right way.

But Russell's alive, and we're still together. I try to maintain hope as I scan the boat to take stock of our supplies. A rolled-up nylon tarp, a single mast with a sail curled around it for when the gas runs dry, two pistols, and the bags we stole. And a boy and his dog.

WHEN DUSTY STOPS shaking so much, I pull the tarp out and tie it to the mast to create a canopy. His breathing stabilizes, and I can't help but feel okay for a moment, like somehow everything will work out in the end. Leadville does exist, and this was all meant to be. But Russell's on edge, and he'd kill me if I jinxed us, so I keep quiet. Maybe I'm delirious from everything that happened in Blue City, but I don't care. Voley gives me a bunch of kisses, like he was never scared to die. As soon as I feel a bit of warmth returning, Russell calls out.

"Get up here." I can tell something's wrong by the tone of his voice.

He doesn't have to explain. As soon as I look at the horizon, I can tell the sky's too dark, even for dusk—perfect black instead of the usual gray. *Please, not now, Poseidon.* A fork of lightning startles me, illuminating a giant thundercloud. The blue-and-white flash reveals distant waterspouts spiraling down to the sea.

"Looks big," Russell says. "We'll steer away from it, but be ready."

I feel the boat rocking as he talks. The swells are already starting. Just the thought of big waves makes me queasy, sending me to the rail in case I throw up.

"We're gonna be okay." He rubs my back.

The boat rolls a little as Russell steers a new line through the water. The storm shifts to our right at last and I get back under the tarp with Dusty. He's soaked, still in just his underwear, his clothes crumpled on the bench.

He looks up at me, eyes wide like I owe him an explanation, but no words come to me. A clap of thunder hits and Voley scurries in, licking Dusty's nose as if urging him to stop the noise.

"He better get his clothes on," Russell hollers. "And start pumping."

I'm almost glad to get up and pump because I don't want to feel the guilt burning a hole in my chest every time I look at Dusty. The rain pools slowly in the boat but the scuppers take care of most of it. When I turn around, Dusty's up, wringing his clothes out.

"What's going on?" He sounds angry, speaking loudly so Russell hears.

Russell doesn't reply, but I know exactly how he wants me to handle it. I can't tell Dusty the truth about his parents because we don't know how he'd react, if he'd try to hurt us. But part of me thinks there's no other way but to tell him, or else the twisting feeling of guilt will grow and eat me up forever.

"Hey!" Dusty waves his hands. "Someone tell me what the hell's going on? This is insane!"

I look past him, unable to make eye contact. "We're going to Leadville."

"You brought me out into this shit!" He eyes the storm. "And Voley, too!"

I glance at Russell's cocked head, making sure he's paying attention in case Dusty loses control.

"You're going to act like you can't hear me?" Dusty steps out of the canopy, right behind Russell. "We helped you, and you run at the first sign of trouble?" His voice shakes like he's as shocked as angry.

I step closer to Dusty in case he lunges at Russell.

Russell swings around but speaks calmly. "Relax, okay? There's a storm coming, and I'm trying to keep us from capsizing."

The boat rocks hard from a swell and I grab the rail to keep from stumbling. My imagination starts spiraling out of control. I picture the white water rushing toward us, taking aim. But the rain sea is still dark on the surface, and nothing's breaking yet, no foam.

"Take me back," Dusty says with a firmer voice.

"What are you going to do about it?" Russell puts his hand on his hip, touching his pistol.

Dusty bites his lip and stares him down, but gives up and sulks away. The boat crests a swell and drops quickly as thunder cracks in triples.

There's so much anguish on his face and it's killing me. Compassion swells inside, my too-deep feelings for this boy and his dog. I go back under the canopy and sit with him. "We didn't mean for you to come."

He looks disgusted, and it tears me apart. What we had between us is gone already, a short-lived fantasy. It was beyond my control, a spell pulling me into Dusty's orbit, trapping me the moment I touched him. No, it started even before that, when he showed me how to grow flowers. And just then I realize that what we did to Daniel and Linda is somehow just as wrong as eating human meat. It makes me feel desperate for apology and forgiveness, as if those things alone could fix what's broken between us.

Dusty lies flat on the opposite bench and covers his head with his hands, like he can leave this all by going to sleep. Every few minutes the boat rocks and Voley whines, but Dusty stays quiet and motionless.

I try to summon my courage, but I just can't bring myself to say anything yet, so I return to Russell. "You're just getting better, you need to sit down out of the rain."

"Thank you." Russell moves the second I offer, his eyes half-closed. I feel guilty I didn't relieve him sooner.

I have to ask. "Should we tell him?"

He sighs like he's conflicted about the same thing. "Keep the storm on our right" is all he says, and then he leaves.

WE CRUISE UP AND DOWN the endless swells until I notice my hands getting numb. The storm's as big as ever, covering the whole sky, but it's way out there, miles from our small tub. And we're passing it. The thunder grows softer, relieving me enough to notice how hungry I am.

Russell and Dusty both look asleep as I grab one of the sacks. Voley's at the rail, his tongue hanging out and staring at the rollers, no longer nervous but terribly curious about the sea.

I find a box of hard crackers, open a tube, and devour them all. Something sounds behind me and I hold my breath, paranoid that Dusty's awake and he's going to try something. He appears out of nowhere right next to me and sits down in the passenger seat.

"Did you plan it all along?" His voice wilts.

The swells have died down, along with my fear of dying in a rogue wave, enough so that I can glance away from the horizon to look at him. His big hazel eyes bore into me. Maybe somehow I can save what we have between us still. I struggle for the courage to tell him, but my voice comes out cold and emotionless. "The only thing we planned was getting to Leadville. Nothing else. It was planned a long time before Blue City."

Dusty's face sours. "So you steal whatever you need to get there?"

"We do whatever we have to."

How can I tell him his parents were cannibals? That he was probably eating it too . . .

"We wanted you to stay with us." His voice cracks like he's going to cry. "Didn't you want that?"

"I've never wanted anything more in my life." My voice feels brittle, unable to handle all the feelings flowing to the surface. It catches me off guard, and instead of using my better judgment, doing what Russell would want me to do, the words come out of me. "Dusty, your parents are dead."

"What?" His expression blanks, then he narrows his eyes at me.

"They were killed in the attack. We panicked. There were too many face eaters. We ran because we thought we were going to die, too. I didn't want any of this to happen."

"Why did you say my parents are dead?" He stands up, condemnation in his voice.

"Because we saw it." And then, before I can admit the horrible thing Russell and I did, I lie. "The face eaters killed them right in front of us."

"No, no, no . . ." Dusty leaves his seat and walks a quick circle, hands grabbing his hair. "You're lying, why would you say that!"

"I'm not lying! Russell was there too. There were too many. We ran."

He starts shaking his head, pacing back and forth, when Russell emerges from the canopy.

"Is it true?" Dusty's voice weakens as he turns to Russell.

Russell looks half-asleep, but he must have overheard at least some of our conversation. I bite my lip and look at him, mouthing *I'm sorry* with my head turned so Dusty can't see.

"They're gone, kid."

“I want to go back!” Dusty stomps his foot, desperately swinging his head to me, then back to Russell.

Russell’s hand goes to his pistol but he speaks calmly. “You’re not going back. If you want to go back after we get to Leadville, you can take the boat.”

Dusty breaks into loud sobs. Voley begins whining at his heels. He bends down and wraps his arms around his dog. Every ounce of me wants to comfort him, and I get up to go to him, but Russell shakes his head at me.

The sobs grow louder before they soften, and after what feels like an eternity, Dusty retreats to the canopy.

Russell comes over, rubbing his temples like his headache is back. “Did you tell him it was us?” He speaks softly.

I want to be strong for him, but I can’t stop from tearing up. “I said it was the face eaters.”

He nods and takes over for me at the wheel. I watch him steer, hoping he has the words to make sense of this, to comfort me, but he doesn’t say anything, and instead he starts coughing.

“Please eat something.” I bring him the food sack and then work the pump to try to distract myself. Nothing helps though, no matter how I try to turn my head off, and I force myself to get under the canopy and lie down.

Dusty is completely still on the other bench. Voley’s somehow curled up small enough that they both fit. My fingers work restlessly over the grooves of my pistol, wrapped in both hands on my stomach. Words keep passing through my head, things I could say, but nothing makes sense. Everything feels broken, and for the first time, thinking of how close we are to Leadville doesn’t make me feel any better. Eventually, my exhaustion slows the thoughts until they’re just a steady feeling of sadness and pain, and I drift off.

It’s still dark when I wake up. The bench across from me is empty. Dusty’s gone, and so is Voley. Slowly I come to, rubbing my eyes, wondering how long Russell's let me sleep. Then I throw my head back and forth, checking the deck and the bench for my pistol.

It's gone.

Panicking, I look toward the front of the boat, but the sail's been raised, blocking my view from this angle. Without the engine or the thunder, it's perfectly quiet except for the rain.

I hurry out toward the bow and—there's Dusty, standing behind Russell with his arm outstretched, pointing my gun at the back of his head.

22
ROOK

18 YEARS, 10 MONTHS, 2 DAYS
SUNDAY

Rook stared at the noose hanging in his closet.

He'd been back at Yasper for three weeks, and he'd thought everything was in place for him to go forward with the plan. It had come together almost too easily, but now something was wrong.

First, he had put Jonathan and Cleo to work managing the daily shipping forecasts. During the days, he worked on Franklin's climate project and occasionally updated Marrow to keep suspicions at bay. Running almost purely on adrenaline, he'd forsaken sleep, sneaking out across the dark mud hills to surveil the nightly routines of the security guards. After spying for three weeks, Rook was confident in one scheduling weakness: from midnight to 4:00 a.m. on the weekends, there was only a single guard at the lab, a burly man who often fell asleep inside the front foyer. The rear entrance was unguarded.

It was the perfect window of opportunity to get into the basement unnoticed for four precious early morning hours on Saturday or Sunday. Even if he were caught, as long as it wasn't in the act of sabotage itself, he was sure he could lie his way out of it: forgotten documents, computer files left unsaved, a book from the meteorology library.

And finally, at three o'clock that morning, he'd worked up the nerve for a trial run. After disabling the alarm using Franklin's security pin, he'd snuck in the back, armed with just a pen flashlight and his lab ID card. He clicked open the cellar door with his fob, and there, down the stairs, was the sea of red powder, visible underneath the plexiglass lid of a large metal vat.

Right above it, almost as if by design, a PVC pipe carried rain from outside to the filtration tanks. All he had to do was steal the fire axe from his apartment hallway next weekend. Open the vat lid, climb up on its rim, and crack the pipe. Water would pour down all night, and by morning the drug could never be made again. After that, the noose he'd tied on his first night back at Yasper was waiting for him, right there in the closet.

But Luce . . .

They'd met for dinner almost every evening, and Rook found himself thinking of her whenever he drifted off to sleep. She was the increasingly painful reason he was hesitant to push the plan forward. The last step didn't make sense anymore. Luce made him not want to die.

He touched the yellow nylon cord, curled his fingers around the knot. *This was so simple before I knew her . . .*

More than her beauty, her hopefulness drew him to her. She still believed people were good at heart, that they'd live to see the day the rain stopped, and that things would one day go back to the way they were. All the things Rook once believed, too.

But what attracted him most was her strength in not taking the drug. She'd told him she was afraid it would dull her, numb her to the joy that would come on the day the rain stopped. It didn't matter if it was naive. When she'd said it, that was the moment he'd started falling for her.

There was only one thing about Luce that bothered him, and it grew worse each time they met. She believed Yasper was still helping people, and it killed him inside. He desperately wanted to tell her she was wrong; he had come so close several times.

Touching the rough grooves of the noose, Rook wondered if there could be a different ending. Maybe Luce would believe him, and . . .

We could escape together.

He punched the wall of the closet in frustration. If he cared about her at all, he wouldn't subject her to the life he'd endured for so many years out in the floodwaters.

And there was something worse, something he could hardly believe, except that he had seen it for himself, right inside Marrow's desk.

He could have just left the lab after reconnoitering the basement, right back out the way he'd come in. But something had stopped him, pulled him toward Marrow's closed office door. Trying the knob, he'd found it locked. Heart beating out of his chest, his hand had brushed the sturdy plastic of his ID card hanging from his neck. He was only seven when his brother taught him how to pick locks. Of course, he'd never done it maliciously, just when he'd locked himself out of his own home. But at that moment, something compelled Rook to push the thin edge of the card into the crack between the door and the latch. The card bent and wiggled, and the latch compressed. He turned the knob and shone the pen light across the dark room. It seemed like the obvious place to look, inside those desk drawers.

That fucking monster, he'd thought after reading and understanding what Marrow's documents meant. Even in their deaths, the victims of his company had no peace.

Glancing away from the noose and at the clock on his wall, Rook saw he was late to meet Luce for tonight's dinner. His mind flipped back and forth as he pulled on his rain suit. *I can't do that to her, can I?* This had to be goodbye. The last time he ever saw her. Then, he'd get the job done at last.

"Sorry I'm so late." Rook brought a bowl of vegetable mash to their usual table in the corner. Besides a few scattered workers, the cafeteria was empty.

"I'm impressed!" Luce opened her eyes in surprise, her bowl already empty. "I thought you were too uptight to ever be late."

"You're finally catching on to me," Rook laughed, his anxiousness flickering away as she brushed her curly brown hair out of her eyes and chuckled. There was an aura about her, a gentle optimism in her smile, that put him at ease. "How was your day in nuke town?"

"Same as every other day, unfortunately." She grabbed his hand, looking concerned. "Your knuckle's bleeding!"

He hadn't even noticed that his skin had broken when he'd punched the closet wall. "I don't know how I did that," he lied.

She rubbed his hand, a sarcastic frown forming. "Well, it looks pretty bad. You might not make it."

She had touched him softly and quickly before, on his forearm or his shoulder, but tonight he felt completely unprepared. Getting to know Luce had brought so many unexpected feelings, desires he'd longed for in his old life but that had died in the rain. To be touched, to be flirted with. To have what his mother and father had.

The mission was so simple: destroy the drug and disappear from the world. Rejoin his family in peaceful rest. At least it had been. Now, whenever he was around Luce, Rook found himself desperate to keep their friendship growing. After so many years alone, this kind of bond had been unfathomable, and he felt keenly aware of how fragile it was.

Such a strange feeling to care about someone so much, an old-world emotion he'd been sure would never return. Twenty-two years old—that was the last time he'd had a girlfriend, felt a real kiss, made love to a woman. Now at forty-three, it felt like a lifetime ago. When he'd first arrived back at Yasper, it had seemed a terrible idea to be honest with anyone, but from everything he sensed about Luce, she could be his ally in this, if he could just get the truth out.

"Hey, what's wrong?" Her eyebrows bent with concern.

I want to tell you so bad. Rook looked into her eyes, on the verge of speaking.

"Nothing." He looked away. She had to know he was lying, but something was still preventing him from being vulnerable with her. Something besides the fact that it would hurt her to know the truth. Besides the rain, the only constant in his life had been that everyone he ever loved went away in the end, and it scared him to death that it could happen again.

"Okay, you don't have to tell me," Luce said. "But I would hope you trust me by now. We're the only ones here who don't take the drug. At least to me, that means a lot."

"It does mean a lot." Rook poked his spoon into the bowl, meeting her eyes. She'd never acknowledged what was growing between them, and neither had he, but now she'd said it. His heart sped up. Words started to form in his head, sentences crawling from his brain toward his throat.

"If you could have any superpower," she asked, changing the subject, "what would it be?"

"What?" She'd caught him off guard. All the things Rook was preparing to say scrambled at the absurd question, the goofy grin on her face.

She rolled her eyes. "What do you mean, *what*? It's a simple question. You really don't know a person at all until you know what their superpower would be. It reveals a lot."

"You're not kidding?"

"Stop stalling!" She dropped her hand on the center of the table, inches from his. "You have to pick the first thing that comes to mind, or it won't be honest."

It happened without thinking: he slid his hand closer so that it was touching hers. "Okay, easy. I'd be able to take care of all the dogs."

"The dogs?" Her brow wrinkled.

"I know, it's weird. I had a mutt growing up, Bartleby. I had trouble making friends in school, was never quite sure how to act in social situations. But Bartleby, he always understood me. We were best friends. Back then we lived on a highway, and one day he ran out onto the road . . ."

"Oh, I'm sorry."

Rook felt the warmth of her fingers locking around his. The hardened interior he'd built up while living in the rain was dissolving. He tried to suppress a wave of giddiness as he curled his fingers around her palm. Looking up, he half-expected her to pull her hand back. But her green eyes didn't flinch, and she waited, a soft look of understanding on her face.

Sighing, he took himself into the memory. "When the rain first started, my mom was bringing strays back to the house, until my dad made her stop. They didn't have room, with all the refugees. I remember—"

Rook felt a sadness so old and powerful it made him shiver. Luce gently squeezed his hand.

"When I was little, and I first learned that dogs who aren't adopted had to be put down, I got depressed for about a year. I'd see adoption ads and just cry. I couldn't understand why grown-ups let it happen. They had the money and the power to help. I swore that when I was grown, I'd do something about it. I had this crazy plan to take in a hundred dogs. When I got older, I forgot about it, got caught up in school, then my job. When Mom told me she was saving them, I remembered my promise, but it was too late. I had nightmares about where they were all sleeping at night, how they were going to make it if the rain didn't stop . . ."

He turned away, trying to hide his watery eyes.

"I like your mutant power very much." Luce pulled her hand back to wipe the tears in her own eyes.

"I didn't mean to upset you." Rook dried his cheeks. Her question had taken him by surprise, cut to something deep inside his spirit, and exposed it, like a crack in a dam, ready to burst any second. Seeing her cry, feeling her care for him, destroyed the last of his uncertainty. The truth was crystal clear, and undeniable. *I can't kill myself. You make me not want to die, Luce . . .*

Suddenly she stood up, her eyes on the wall clock. "Shit, is it really that late? I have to be back at the fuel site in six hours. Be here on time tomorrow, okay? I hate having our dinner together cut short."

He stood to hug her. "It won't happen again. See you tomorrow." The words came out without thinking, leaving the truth burning on the tip of his tongue as she walked away.

Sitting alone at the table, he felt the things he wanted to say sliding back down his throat, choking him. It was the same sick feeling, the isolated darkness, that had been growing ever since he met her. Keeping everything inside was eating him alive.

Fuck it, he thought. *Things are complicated, anyway.*

Leaving his dirty bowl and spoon on the table, he chased after her into the rain.

LUCE WAS ALMOST to her apartment, the building across from his, when Rook caught up to her.

She spun around at the sound of his footsteps, her hands up and eyes wide. "Jesus, you scared me!"

"I'm sorry," he breathed heavily, jittery with nerves. "Listen, I have to tell you something."

"Tell me what?" Her face creased with confusion.

Rook spotted a white rain suit about twenty feet away, one of the security guards, walking in their direction. "I didn't come here to head up the weather project." He leaned in and spoke softly. "I came back to destroy the drug."

"I don't understand."

"It's turning people into monsters. They trade everything for Red until there's nothing left to trade, nothing left to eat."

Luce shook her head, squinting. "That can't be—"

"Yasper stopped delivering letters from the outside so we wouldn't know." Rook eyed the guard, almost within earshot now. "I can't talk here. Can you come to my apartment?"

She hesitated, biting her lip and looking over his shoulder.

"Please, trust me." He took her hand. To his relief, she made no attempt to pull away, and they went up to his room.

Luce paused at the door. "You're not going to murder me?" It sounded like a joke, but her eyes flickered with nervous energy.

"How did you know?" He waited, hoping for a smile. She stared into his eyes, seemed to sense something in them, and went inside.

The apartment was bare: white walls, a small table with two chairs next to a twin bed, a lamp, and a small bookshelf. Rook rifled through the shelf, grabbing paper printouts and spreading them on the table.

"What's this?" Luce bent over them.

"I've wanted to show you for weeks." He ran his finger down to a sentence on the first printout. "This one's a report from Ed Bowling, about Red."

> This abstract concludes that the distribution of Red, if successful, may destroy the communities that become dependent upon it, given the limited resources available to refugee

> settlements, the lack of regulated dosing, and its potential for physical addiction.

“See, it’s dated from two years after the rain began. They knew all along that it would harm people.”

“It can’t really . . .” Luce took the paper and reread it. “But at the Family Meeting—”

“Fuck the Family Meeting. It’s a lie. Marrow doesn’t care about anyone out there anymore. He hasn’t since the government collapsed. I wouldn’t lie to you, Luce.”

She kept shaking her head, a faraway look in her eyes. Rubbing her knuckles over her face, she sat down and cupped her head in her hands.

“I know, it’s a lot to take in.”

Her words came out wobbly and fragile. “I’ve spent my whole life, since the rain, believing I was helping.”

“So did I.” Rook felt his face heating up and tears welling in his eyes as he took the chair next to her. It was horrible to see her like this, and selfish to have told her.

But she deserves to know.

She sniffled sharply, wiping her nose. “You wouldn’t trick me about this?”

“I would never. Besides stopping the drug, you’re the only thing left in this world that I care about.” Whatever shell had hardened around him in the city ruins had completely broken. “You mean so much to me, Luce.”

The pain on her face eased as she took in his admission, but then her eyes began darting over the paper again. “Maybe this is wrong. How can we be sure?”

“I saw it with my own eyes when I was out there. My dad’s best friend, Gerry, turned into a monster. Him and so many others. The first night I was there, Gerry killed someone over the drug. My dad tried to stop him, but . . .”

Luce placed her hand on his arm as he forced out the painful memory.

“Gerry burned my mom alive.” Rook’s voice went flat. “He shot my father and left us for dead. Dad couldn’t walk after that. One by one, everyone else I knew started using the drug. We escaped to nearby city ruins, living like cockroaches, surviving on scraps for years until he passed."

Luce put her hand over her mouth. "I'm so sorry, I had no idea."

"When the Yasper ship finally came back after all those years, it was a sign, a chance for me to do something. I just never thought the son of a bitch knew from the start what the drug would do. And there's something worse, something more recent." Rook pointed out another page. "I pulled this from a folder in Marrow's desk."

TRADE DIRECTIVE 118.1,
17 YEARS AFTER THE RAIN

Yasper will henceforth accept trades in fresh cadavers, which have become a necessary commodity given the scarcity of food. The following provisions will be strictly adhered to for both the sanitary inspection of meat and its preservation using salt and, when possible, ice.

Willem H. Marrow

Luce shot up from her chair, her hands over her mouth, and rushed to the bathroom. Rook listened to her repeated hacking as he waited outside the door.

The toilet flushed.

Looking at the ceiling, Rook replayed the memory of the first time he'd seen it happen. That awful morning when they'd confronted Gerry. He shivered at the image of the blood smeared along the tent floor, the remains of whatever they hadn't eaten of Christopher's body.

"I know it's disgusting, but it's been happening out there for years. The drug pushes them to it. Marrow must have seen the dead as another market, another resource for the company to exploit."

The door opened. Luce's face was flushed red, her eyes wet and puffy. "Does this mean we've been eating—" She closed the door again quickly, then vomited.

"I don't think so. Marrow can sustain employees on the grow house alone, so why waste meat on us? Plus, going into the ruins is dangerous, and he'd want to avoid his own employees having to do it. He knows the addicts have become cannibals, so maybe he trades the meat for engine parts, oil, propane, whatever valuable salvage they gather for him."

Luce came out of the bathroom, wiping her nose. "What are you going to do?" her voice cracked.

"I have it figured out now." Rook pointed to the page about water destroying the drug. "All I have to do is flood the basement where it's stored." The full truth, that he'd been planning to kill himself afterward, wasn't important anymore. "And then, I'm going to leave. I'd love for you to come with me."

Luce started to pace back and forth, rubbing her temples, sobbing softly.

"If you don't want any part of this, I understand."

"No," her voice wilted, tears dropping to the rug. "I want to help, I just don't know what I'd do without this place. There's nothing for me out there. I don't have anyone left. I don't want to go to a shelter."

It tore him to pieces to see her falling apart. "You don't have to help me, and you don't have to leave here. We can pretend I never told you."

"Are you serious, Rook?" She gave him a cross look. Her eyes were hazy and red, but her glare was clear enough. "I'm sorry. I just need time to process this." She sighed deeply.

"I survived out there." He stood close to her. "It's possible. And once I've destroyed the drug, and people stop taking it, it should become a little easier."

He waited a long time, but she just stared out the window. He tried gently touching her back. She turned to him with a look of deep despair. "There's something I'm not supposed to tell you either."

Rook's gut dropped. "You can tell me anything." He tried to speak casually.

"I'm under strict orders not to . . ." she stammered. "My contract stipulates I'll be kicked out of the company. But now—"

"If we're in this together, we can't keep secrets anymore."

"There's a leak, in one of the nuclear storage casks." She shut her eyes. "I've hated keeping it from you. No one knows but me, Marrow, and the head of the power plant, Dina."

I knew it . . . Guilt swirling in Rook's gut transformed into something worse, a head-to-toe wave of terror. They'd thrown her to the wolves as expendable personnel to monitor the radiation. No one cared about her exposure, so long as she warned everyone else before it got too bad.

"Why you? How much radiation have you been exposed to?"

"It's not that bad yet. But if there's a big storm, or another earthquake . . ." She tugged at her hair. "I always suspected they put me there as a punishment. What other choice did I have, though?"

"Punishment?"

"For not taking the drug. Maybe it's in my head but . . . I've always felt frowned upon for refusing, like an outcast, until I met you."

Luce pulled out a small yellow rectangle from her pocket. It looked like an old handheld video game, but when she turned it over, Rook could see the lettering: GEIGER/DOSI.

"It's a Geiger counter and dosimeter in one unit, powered by lithium-ion batteries. It reads local radiation levels, and also how much total I've absorbed." Rook looked at the number displayed on a small LCD screen: *.92 sieverts*. "It's not that high, I promise." She sounded insincere.

"What's too high?" He frantically tried to remember anything from the nuclear meteorology course he'd taken in college.

"It doesn't get really dangerous until it's between 4.2 and 5.6 sieverts. I'm nowhere near—"

"That fuck, Jesus Christ!" Rook balled his fists. "You have to stop going there!" It was the first time he'd ever lashed out at her, and he tried to backpedal. "I'm sorry."

She shook her head. "I'm okay. I would tell you if I was in real danger."

He pulled her into his chest. "All the more reason for us to get out of this place!"

"I have to be back at work in less than six hours, and I'm going to feel awful if I don't get a little sleep."

"Get some sleep then. You don't have to decide anything right now. Can you come back tomorrow night? The only part I have to figure out is how we escape after I destroy the drug."

Because that wasn't in the plan at all.

Luce nodded but made no move to leave. For what felt like an hour, he held her, wanting to say so many things, his fears and his small bit of hope, hanging by a thread, that they could have some kind of future together. But none of the words that passed through his head seemed right.

Luce sniffed and wiped her eyes. "Okay, I'll eat early and meet you here at eight o'clock."

"It's going to be okay." The words came out reflexively, halfhearted and weak, and after she left, Rook knew he shouldn't have said anything at all. He should have kissed her.

23
TANNER

"No!" I jump forward at the sight of the gun in Dusty's hand.

Russell jerks up, like he'd fallen asleep at the wheel, then turns to see the pistol in his face. He puts his hands up. "Dusty, don't."

"Take me home," Dusty says limply, shaking badly enough that I'm afraid he'll accidentally shoot. But he doesn't get the chance because Russell's fist slams into his stomach, then slaps the gun out of his grip. Russell kicks it my way, then shoves Dusty back.

Dusty's so off-balance from the gut punch that he knocks into the rail and crumples to the deck. Voley leaps on top of the passenger seat, barking frantically.

Dusty lies completely helpless, curled up on the ground, crying. My heart breaks because I understand—I would have done the same thing if I was in his shoes.

"Son of a bitch!" Russell shakes his fist. He continues to curse, but it breaks into a coughing fit and he holds his chest. Each hack sounds worse than the last, like his insides are being cut apart. I shove him into the seat and hunt around for water, crackers, anything to make it stop. Finally, after a minute where all I can do is hold him, it does.

"Are you okay?"

"I'm fine," Russell wheezes.

I see just how much of the veneer Russell is clinging to, much more than he lets on, because he extends his hand and helps Dusty to his feet.

"Look at me." Russell stares close into Dusty's bright red face. "You can't take this out on us. We didn't mean for any of this to happen."

He's right, and I wish I could tell Dusty the full truth—that Russell didn't plan to kill anyone, and neither did I. Things just got out of control. It happened too fast. But Dusty will never understand without having seen it himself.

"I'm sorry." Dusty lowers his eyes in shame. Voley jumps down and whines at his feet. "I'm really sorry . . ."

I want to hold him, to hug him and tell him there's nothing to be sorry for, but he quietly sulks back under the canopy.

"Are you okay?" I ask Russell.

He grimaces. "Can't stop shivering."

"I'll take over, go rest."

He goes under the tarp and right up to Dusty. "You know how to work a primer stove?"

I can't believe Russell's talking to him like nothing happened. Dusty looks as startled as I am. We've all forgotten how cold we are, completely numb and near frostbite. Russell pulls the stove from underneath a small hatch. "There's hardly any fuel for this, let alone the engine, so we have to use it sparingly." He closes the hatch.

Dusty finally sits up. "Yeah," he mutters, then gets to work.

"Which way are we headed?" I holler back.

"Into the sunrise. Just a little to the left, but mostly straight at it. A straight line, all the way to Colorado. The Rockies, you hear me, Tan?" Russell cheers me on, like some new spirit of life has come into him, excited about Leadville for the first time in forever. The old familiar hope. "There'll be fire for you when your shift's up."

I steer a line toward where the light's hitting a few bands of gray and wonder how far we've gone, what our speed is. Watching the rain makes me think of the number that only ever gets bigger, total rainfall, every inch piling up until the entire world is drowned. And we just have to get to Leadville before that happens.

I glance back at the glow of the primer stove in the center of the boat, a beacon of life and warmth. A nylon blanket is hanging from one rail of the boat to the other. The sides drape down, and I realize they've built a fort while I'm out here freezing. I want to end my shift right this moment. But Russell needs the sleep, and even though Dusty seems to have given up on going home for now, I'm hesitant to let him have a turn at the wheel. I keep the blooming sunlight in front of me, happy that there's no more sign of the storm.

"Hey," a voice comes, again and again, raising me from sleep. I hear the rumble of the engine as I open my eyes, remembering that Russell relieved me. He must have turned the engine back on to cover more ground during daylight. When I sit up, there's Dusty, seated right next to me.

"How long have I been sleeping?" I shake the life back into my arms.

"A couple hours. I steered after Russell, he just took over again. He'll get you when it's your turn. You can go back to sleep."

I wonder why he woke me up just to say I can go back to sleep. "Why'd you wake me up?" I poke my head out to be sure that he's not lying, that Russell really is out there.

Dusty takes a long time to speak. "It's just hitting me, that they're gone, you know?"

In truth, I don't know. Russell's the only family I've ever had, and as many times as I've imagined him dying on me, he's never failed to regain his strength.

"But Dusty, we're still alive." My guilt floods back in, making it impossible to watch the sadness on his face. I look at Voley instead. "Who knows what happened back there. There were so many, they might have killed everyone in Blue City."

He moves closer to the primer stove, closer to me. I still feel wary after what he did, despite my gut telling me he's no longer a threat, and I scoot back. But then he just pushes right into me, his legs against mine. A flash of electricity zaps through my body, and I'm wide awake, nervous Russell can make out our silhouettes touching.

I almost draw back from his touch, but I can't. I can't bring myself to.

"Do you believe in heaven?" He sounds exhausted and weak. "My dad did. I guess I kind of do. I've been trying to tell myself I'll see him again."

I struggle to answer because I've seen nothing in my life that makes me think a fantasy like that could be true. "I believe in Leadville. I guess that's kind of like believing in heaven."

"How so?" He doesn't sound comforted.

"I mean, we have hardly any proof that Leadville exists." I think of the rumors, the radio broadcast Timothy heard. "But we believe in it anyway, just from our gut mostly. If it helps you to believe in heaven, then I think that's a good thing." I almost tell him I talk to Poseidon, and how even though he's not real, it helps calm me down when the waves get bad.

Dusty sighs. "I think heaven is more likely than Leadville."

I finally look him in the eyes. "You don't buy any of it?"

"It's raining everywhere," he says. "Maybe in Europe, or China, or Australia, it's not raining anymore. But in America, it's raining everywhere. We got hit the hardest."

"Hit?" I wonder where he's heard this one.

"By a comet. A lot of it's still up there, circling the Earth, dumping ice that turns into the rain."

"I've heard that one before," I snicker.

The sad look on his face warps into confusion. "So what do you believe happened?"

"The people who ran the world stopped caring. They did this to us, not a comet. Do you know about the pollution they used to make?"

"Why would people stop caring about their own homes? That makes no sense. Every bit of nature that's not mud, every bit of *life*, is the most precious thing there is." He speaks confidently, full of conviction. I don't even care that he's wrong—it's how much he believes it that makes me remember what I love about him. A picture forms in my head, his hands digging through the soil, the way he cared about those plants. I stop myself from sliding further, from thinking of the sweetness he showed to Bryn, to his parents, to me.

"Because it meant more money." I steel my emotions, trying to recall what Russell taught me. "Every country was in a never-ending race to have the most money, more and more like they could get richer forever. Protecting the environment got in the way."

"But there's always been money, for thousands of years. The rain and the earthquakes happened all at once."

"That's because technology came all at once." I think of the dead computers I've seen, the abandoned cars, the ghost factories we passed in the East. How they were all once alive. "Everything was done at human speed for thousands of years until technology. In just the last hundred years, we became capable of destroying the world a million times faster. Things kept speeding up until something broke."

"Broke?" He sounds intrigued.

"Something in the atmosphere rotted away, and the sun started burning the Pacific, evaporating the ocean and sending it up into the sky like a big vacuum. And it gets slung through the clouds and dumped down here."

"Maybe you're right. I guess it doesn't matter now, anyway," he sighs. "Nothing matters."

"Well, the how doesn't matter until we get to Leadville. All that matters is staying warm and dry. There can't be veneer without those things first."

"Tanner!"

Russell's yell jolts me and I scramble outside, Dusty right behind me. We freeze when we see the horizon.

Boats.

"Are they face eaters?" I strain to see, but they're too far away, a tiny fleet moving slowly over the brown sea toward us.

"No telling yet," Russell speaks softly.

No one says anything, and we just wait. Voley lets out a bark.

Russell gestures to Dusty. "Shut him up."

Dusty tries to lead Voley under the canopy, but he's not having it.

"Gun?" Russell looks at my empty hands.

I quickly pull it out.

"If all those boats have face eaters, there'll be too many." Dusty anxiously looks at Russell's pistol. "I don't even have a weapon."

"They're not motorboats. They look like whaleboats, rigged with canopies. Listen . . ." Russell cuts the engine and cocks his ear. "No noise."

"This far out, with no engines or sails?" I ask.

"You're right." Dusty bends over the rail like he'll be able to see better.

"This feels off." Russell shakes his head. "We're close enough, we should be able to see them. Standing, moving around, something."

But there's nobody. No one moving. No one steering. No oars hitting the water. Something strange is going on out there and we all seem to feel it together. It's like all—I count quickly—seven of them are ghost boats. I crowd in under the tarp, shivering after being spoiled for hours by the warmth of the stove.

Russell wraps his arm around me and rubs my back.

Dusty fidgets as we drift closer. "We better steer clear of them."

Russell ignores him, and I recognize the determined look on his face—he's made up his mind to figure out what happened on those boats. There's a cold silence, nothing but the rain pattering the swells, so constant that it's like there's no sound at all.

"Turn the motor on!" Dusty stamps his foot. "We're heading right for them."

We glide slowly up a swell, then back down. I startle as Russell turns the engine on and brings us right up to the two closest boats. I raise my gun, but Russell only half-raises his, like he's already certain there's no one aboard.

The boats look old, the wood worn and chipped. I lean over the rail and look in. Three benches and two oars under a dirt gray canopy, not a soul on board.

"Empty." Russell jumps right into one of them. He paces and then leans out toward the next one. "Empty here, too." He starts scouring under the seats.

"God, be careful Russell!" My nerves rattle with each step he takes as the boat wobbles back and forth under his weight.

"These are good. Catch." He throws an oar at me. "It'll burn after it dries." Dusty leans over the rail next to me, and Voley pushes between us to get a glimpse too. Russell rows himself toward a third boat, hell-bent on checking each one.

"Bring her around," he calls. I take the wheel and give it gas.

"What happened to them?" Dusty no longer sounds frightened but mystified. I've seen mile-long body-jams, dead cities flooded five stories high, and schools of empty boats, and I know better than to care what happened to them.

"Something killed them," I say matter-of-factly. "You really haven't traveled, have you?"

"I've been to Salt Lake City, Grandview Peak, and King Mountain," Dusty counters defensively.

We motor alongside Russell, and he jumps back in, proudly holding up a small plastic duffel bag and an automatic rifle. "Don't know if it'll still work. I'm gonna salvage them all. Tanner, pull up to that next group."

I steer toward another cluster of boats as Dusty asks Russell the same question. "What do you think happened to them?"

"It doesn't matter. They're not here." Then, he leaps over the rail again.

As Russell drifts farther away, the last two ghost boats float past us. Dusty stands up on the rail.

"What the hell are you doing?" I watch him steady himself.

"I'm not scared." His voice cracks like he's nervous as hell, and I know he's choking it down, trying to prove that he's brave. He jumps right in and ducks to search the floor.

"Tanner." Russell holds up another oar. "More firewood." He tosses it at me, but the boat he's in has drifted too far and it lands in the water. As I hang over the rail to pull it out, a dark shape rises behind Dusty.

"Dusty!"

The figure behind him latches onto his shoulders and pulls him backward. Dusty twists, but they both fall, splashing into the water between our boat and the ghost boat. The hulls bang into each other, and they disappear below.

Voley barks furiously as I push the throttle to ram the ghost boat so Dusty doesn't get trapped underneath the hulls. *No*—the propeller could slice him apart. Cutting the engine, I run to the rail and look down. The water is too brown to see anything, and then I hear a knocking sound, right underneath my feet, something banging against the bottom.

"Where's Dusty?" Russell squints, frantically looking around, but there isn't any time to explain.

I stomp down on one side, trying to wobble the boat so Dusty can escape to the surface. A hand pops up, and tightly clasping the fingers, I pull. But right away I know—the skin's too frozen and rubbery. A pockmarked face bursts from the water, gasping for air, the welted complexion and bloodshot eyes of a face eater. Dusty kicks to the surface beside him, spitting and heaving.

I try to wrench away but the face eater's hold on me is too tight. The only thing I can do is slam my hand into the side of the boat, again and again, until he finally slips off and his body goes under. Dusty's arms stretch toward me. I lean out as far as I can, latching onto him and pulling until he can climb up. He rolls into our boat and breathes heavily from the floor.

"Get back here!" Russell shouts from his boat, drifted almost thirty feet away now.

"Dusty, go to the stove!" I sprint to the wheel and push the throttle until we're close enough for Russell to jump in.

"What happened?" He breathes fast, taking the wheel and driving us into open water.

"A face eater was in one of the boats." I rush to Dusty, terrified that after two times in the water he'll have hypothermia.

He hyperventilates until he's got his breath. "I'm . . . okay."

When I look up, one of the distant ghost boats is rocking wildly.

"Stop the engine!" My words are lost in the roar as I watch Dusty's attacker climb up and flop back into the ghost boat. He stands up, soaking, his shirt ripped and hanging down around his legs. "Russell!"

Russell finally turns around and sees what I see.

"Don't leave!" the man yells.

Russell cuts the engine and turns so that we're drifting again, parallel to the face eater. The current pulls us apart, and he grows smaller but doesn't stop calling out, waving his arms wildly. The words become too garbled to understand.

Dusty staggers to his feet. "He tried to kill me."

Russell raises his pistol and takes aim, but something about it feels wrong. I push the barrel down.

"What the hell are you doing?" Russell narrows his eyes.

"Let him live."

Dusty watches, speechless.

"He's already gone." Russell aims again.

I watch the face eater sit and cup his head in his hands, and even from this far away, I hear him sobbing. I put my hand on Russell's bent elbow. "He's not worth the bullet."

Russell sighs and puts the pistol down, then returns to the wheel. The engine sparks, and we kick off until the sobbing blends into the rain. By the time my heart stops pounding in my chest, every last ghost boat has disappeared behind us.

24

ROOK

18 YEARS, 10 MONTHS, 3 DAYS
MONDAY

Rook lay awake for most of the night in his apartment, turning over the plan in his head. Only the last step had changed: running away with Luce instead of ending his own life. By dawn, his chest was buzzing with hope. As long as she decided to come with him, everything would work out. Restless, he rose from his bed and went to the closet.

I don't need this anymore . . .

Taking down the noose, he ran through the escape in his head. Ten years ago, he'd helped Dr. Franklin build an animated map showing future flooding and erosion of the Yasper compound. At that time, the company had used two harbors, East and South, but the map had forecasted that East Harbor would become unused after erosion brought South Harbor much closer to the compound. It would be a long hike to reach East Harbor, and he'd have to steal a raft and drag it along, but they'd be able to leave the island unseen.

Smash the water pipe, rendezvous with Luce, and hike to East Harbor.

The soonest window to strike, when security at the lab was down to a single guard again, would be midnight on Saturday, five days away. It felt like forever, but he needed the time anyway, to hash out the last details. Make sure East Harbor wasn't being used, find a boat, collect food for the trip, and figure out which direction to steer on the open water.

Glancing across the lab, Rook saw Cleo's eyes glued to radar images on her screen, managing a shipping reroute to somewhere in Wyoming. Jonathan was mapping out a report about shoals to avoid in a rescue mission. In stretching their routes farther to find new settlements to trade with, Yasper had wrecked a ship somewhere near the Wasatch Range, way out in Utah.

With both of his subordinates busy, Rook loaded the map he'd created ten years ago. He hovered the cursor over the Print icon, then pressed it. No one noticed as he entered the hall between the chemistry and meteorology wings, then keyed his fob to the printer room.

Empty, thank God.

He approached the first in a row of printers and picked up the blank sheet. Turning it around, he saw the map. There, clearly marked with a small blurry square against the waterline, about a three-mile walk from the compound, was East Harbor. In his hand, the map looked exactly like he remembered and confirmed what he'd hoped: East Harbor was now unused, in favor of the much closer South Harbor, where the southern edge of the island had eroded.

We have our escape route, Luce!

He'd thrown so much at her last night, and he still couldn't promise her they'd get anywhere safe after they left the compound. But at least he'd thought everything through, and she could make an informed decision. If she didn't want any part of it, had changed her mind and wanted to forget she'd ever met him, then he'd deal with that, too. Glancing at the clock, he saw he had just ten minutes before she was due to meet him at his apartment.

Heart racing, Rook folded the map into a square, put it in his pocket, and looked down from the clock to the door. It was cracked open, and someone was staring in at him.

"Ed." Rook could barely get the word out through the zap of adrenaline rushing through his body. Inside his pocket, his hand clutched at the map. *Did he see what it was? Would it mean anything to him, anyway?*

The man who'd once been Rook's closest friend now looked like a different person, rail thin and haggard with age. His previously neat salt-and-pepper goatee had grown unkempt and frizzy. The few times they'd crossed paths, Ed had acted like he hardly remembered Rook.

"How's the project going?" Ed sounded tired, but his black eyes were alert, flicking side to side. His former teasing, brotherly personality had vanished, as it had with Cleo and Gene; whatever had once made them convivial was now sterilized by the Red.

"Going okay." Rook clenched the paper and swallowed, pulling his lab coat closed.

"Good." Ed looked him up and down but didn't speak further.

Rook worried that his perspiration would give him away. *Why is he blocking the doorway?*

"Marrow's looking for you," Ed finally said, blinking too many times, though the rest of his face remained expressionless. "It's urgent."

Shit. Luce was probably already heading over to his apartment. If Marrow kept him too long, he might miss her.

Ed moved aside, holding the door open without another word.

Steeling himself, Rook thanked him and headed toward Marrow's office. He knew what Marrow wanted, and he was prepared. Marrow had been asking for updates about Franklin's weather project, and Rook had procrastinated. If he went into Marrow's office with nothing to say, suspicion might follow, but finally, today, he'd spent hours reviewing it, enough to be knowledgeable. *Just in time . . .*

THE FRUSTRATED LOOK on Marrow's face confirmed Rook's suspicion.

"Do you know why I called you in?" Marrow asked, getting straight to the point.

"Dr. Franklin's project." Rook felt his heart thumping. "I know, I told you I'd have an update last week."

Marrow nodded slowly. "It's been nearly a month, and you haven't given me anything substantive." He worked his jaw back and forth, eyeing Rook skeptically. "The shipping crews are reporting so much ice around the compound that it's making it hard for our ships to get in and out." He raised his eyebrows. "Please tell me you've at least read through all of Dr. Franklin's notes by now?"

"Of course, sir." Rook swallowed. His throat was too dry. *Just summarize it. All you need to do is buy time. One week.* "Franklin theorized that a shift in the Earth's rotational axis, by way of the convection of molten rock in the planet's core, could cause the climate to cool, but he couldn't confirm it because of an inability to compare star positions, due to the constant cloud cover. I can continue to crunch numbers, but in the end, without a clear sky, I won't have an answer."

"Precisely what I hoped you'd say!" Strangely, Marrow's frustration seemed to vanish. He smiled widely.

"I'll spend this week doing calculations. By next Monday, I should have a probability and—"

"Your calculations can wait!" Marrow clapped his hands together proudly. "A more expedient solution has presented itself. You're going on an expedition to test Dr. Franklin's hypothesis right away."

"An expedition, sir?" Rook's gut dropped. *No, not now . . .*

"As luck would have it, one of our shipping crews reported clear skies in Nebraska this morning. Cleo checked the closest weather buoy we have to that location, and it looks like there might be a small window of time to get you out there and chart the stars. This is ideal, given Franklin's hypothesis, correct?"

Marrow was right. If the constellations were visible, and not where they should be—where they were before the rain—it would reveal the new location of the geographic pole, and the direction of its shifting position. The thought was terrifying, that the earthquakes had thrown the Earth off-kilter that much, enough to place Colorado in the path of a newly forming arctic biome.

"Yes, it is." Rook felt his chest caving in as he searched the office walls for a clock. *I'm sorry, Luce . . .* "When would the expedition start? How long would it last?"

Marrow was already picking up the radio receiver on his desk, ignoring Rook's questions. "Good, then you're leaving right away." He pressed a few buttons and pushed the receiver against his ear, then held up a finger. "If I have to move the whole fucking company to a new island, then I want to do it as soon as possible. I'm radioing down now to let them know everything is good to go."

Rook felt a spike of urgency. He didn't want to delay the plan, but there didn't seem to be any way out of this expedition.

Marrow tapped his fingers impatiently on the desk, waiting for someone to answer. Then he spoke. "It's Marrow. What ships are docking tonight? I need the best available captain . . ." A moment of silence passed. Marrow's eyes were pinned on Rook. "Lawrence is? Well, then put him on! . . . Alright, let him know Rook Wallace will be down there first thing in the morning with one of his technicians. Get the boat prepared to launch."

Lawrence?

The name brought a quick wave of shock—Rook thought he'd never see or hear from Lawrence again.

Marrow set down the radio and approached Rook. "Don't look so worried." He cupped both hands around Rook's. "It's only a couple days. Pack whatever equipment you need and be down at South Harbor by six. Captain Lawrence will meet you there. Thank you, Rook."

Rook left the office feeling badly shaken. An expedition out of nowhere, and now he was going to miss Luce. Maybe if he hurried, he'd still catch her.

Walking back through the weather wing, he tried to stay calm about the upheaval of his plans. The next opportunity to sneak into the lab wouldn't be until the coming weekend anyway.

I'll be back in time. Maybe I can somehow make this work in my favor.

An idea struck him: he could overpack food supplies, and then stash them back at his apartment after the expedition. Captain Lawrence had been the one person who'd risked his neck to help Rook, more than once. He would finally be able to thank the captain for delivering his father's letter, and surely Lawrence would have an idea where there were settlements that had no Red users. *A place for us to live, Luce.* Maybe Lawrence could even help them get a boat.

Stopping at Jonathan's desk, Rook jotted down every piece of equipment he would need for the trip. "Make sure all this is packed up for me before you go home tonight, okay? You're coming with me tomorrow on a trip. Marrow's order. And bring double the food supplies I've written here."

"A trip?" Jonathan looked confused.

"Bring everything to South Harbor by six a.m. Remember, double the food supplies. No telling how many days we'll be gone if the weather kicks up." Rook slapped the note on the desk and left before Jonathan could ask any more questions.

Jogging up the road, Rook caught sight of a silhouette in the fog, someone walking from his apartment building toward the one across the street.

"Luce!" He sprinted toward the orange rain suit.

Her face was flushed with exhaustion, and her hair hung messily across her face. "I waited at your door and you weren't there. I got scared."

"I'm sorry."

"What's wrong?" Her eyes locked to his.

"I'll tell you inside."

Once they were in his apartment and had stripped off their rain suits, he told her about the next day's expedition.

"Oh god." She sat down on the bed. "I don't want you to go." Her voice edged on tears.

"I should only be gone a few days." He sat beside her. "Then, when I get back, I'm going through with the plan. And I still want you to come with me." He tried to shake the feeling of anxiety, to sound strong for her. "But Luce, you don't have to be part of this. We can pretend we never met."

"No." She stared defiantly, sounding angry. "I thought about it all day, and I'm going to help. What this company is doing to people, what this radiation is going to do to me if I don't get out of here . . ." Her voice shook, as if her strength would give out at any moment. "I'll do it."

"You're sure?" Rook half-expected the determination in her eyes to fade, but she nodded immediately and confidently.

Here she is, so close to you. And this time tomorrow, she'll be a hundred miles away. His heart fluttered, a confused swirl of emotions. Without thinking, he caressed her arm.

Her breathing quickened, and she looked down at his hand.

"I'm sorry." Rook drew back.

Then she leaned forward and kissed him. He pulled her close, and they kissed again, longer, holding each other gently.

When they finally let go, Rook felt like he was about to wake up from a dream. But Luce was right there, smiling, the tip of her nose touching his. "I've wanted that since I first saw you."

She let out a tired laugh, but there was sadness in her eyes, the understanding, Rook was sure, that everything would be so hard now.

Drawing a deep breath, she slid closer. "I never told you what my mutant power would be." Her voice wavered between tears and laughter.

"You want to tell me now?" The timing seemed absurd, but he found himself laughing, some kind of hysteria seeming to take over, shielding him from what loomed ahead.

Luce ran her fingers over his palm, her eyes growing distant. "Remember I told you I had an older sister, Maddy, who got sick?"

Rook followed her eyes to the ceiling.

"I still miss her, all the time."

"I wish I could've met her," he said.

"It's one of the reasons I never took the drug. I'm afraid I would stop missing her, you know?"

He did know. He'd seen Gerry first, and then others, lose their love and compassion for those they once held dear as the drug numbed every emotion away. It was one of the reasons he'd never taken the drug either.

"After she died, and we had this beautiful service for her, with all her pictures hung up, I started having these nightmares. At first, it was just her, but then it was all the people close to me. They would get hurt somehow, and I'd watch them deteriorate, like I was strapped down, watching a horror movie. The nightmares eventually stopped, but they always stuck with me. And that's it—I wish I had the power to heal people, to stop them from leaving me like my sister did."

"It's a beautiful idea." Rook felt chills run through his body. He tilted Luce's chin up. "If we destroy the drug and get out of this place together, maybe we still can."

She wept softly into his shoulder, and he held her. Then she started looking back and forth at the walls.

"What is it?"

"It's so bare in here. We should do a drawing together and put it up, so it doesn't feel like an asylum."

"You draw?"

"I love to draw. Before the rain, I dreamed of doing a gallery exhibition someday. Instead, my apartment here became my gallery. The walls are covered with landscapes of the world before the rain, or at least what I remember the world looking like."

"I'd love to draw something with you."

"I bet you stink." She nudged him, her eyes red and puffy.

"Better than you," Rook lied. He was a terrible artist, but already he was scheming. If Marrow was right about the weather buoy, there would be enough clear sky to see the stars. It had been almost twenty years since he'd seen a clear sky. He could draw Luce a picture of the constellations.

"We'll see about that." She pushed him down, the full weight of her body pressing him into the bed.

"When I first came back here . . ." He shuddered at her warmth, and then words he had never meant to say rushed out. "I had a death wish. I wanted to kill myself after I destroyed the drug. But you changed my mind."

Luce stared down at him, her face wet with tears, a look in her eyes like she was waiting for him to say something more.

To hell with it, he decided. He rolled her over, kissing her neck, pulling her shirt up. She let out an uneven breath. Rain struck the window, and thunder rattled somewhere in the distance as they made love. A storm was brewing.

25
TANNER

Dusty takes over for me at the wheel, and I head under the canopy. Russell's got a can of beans heating over the primer stove. He nods, and I shovel them into my mouth, watching him root through the bag he found on the whaleboats.

"Anything good?" I ask.

"I got the rifle unjammed, and there was ammo. Can opener, scraps of paper, some pills, I don't know what they are. Another knife. A small radio. A broken GPS, I think."

"GPS?"

He raises a yellow brick of plastic. "Before the world went to shit, you could look at this screen, and it had a map on it—that would tell you where you were."

"Anywhere in the world?" I snatch it.

"Pretty much. This one looks old, before cell phones. God knows why they brought it. Satellites have been dead almost twenty years. Maybe for luck?"

I tap the small silver screen, then toss it down and pick up the black rectangle near his legs. "I wonder if the radio works." I spin the device around. There's a long cutout on the back where batteries are supposed to go.

"There's a radio?" Dusty hollers. Without the motor running, he can hear everything we say.

"It needs batteries." I wave it at him.

"I'm good at fixing electronics." He sounds excited. "We had unopened lithium batteries in Blue City."

"There's something else." Russell's face is smoky and shadowed, but the edges of his lips curl up. He's happy. And he hasn't coughed in hours. Whatever they gave him in Blue City, maybe it was enough to kill the parasite inside him.

"Well?" I tap his arm as he stalls, grinning.

He slowly uncrumples a piece of paper. It's a map.

I move closer. "What are all those numbers? And the squiggly circles?"

"Elevations." He points at a circle. "Each ring delineates a different height."

I try to look for names of states, but it's nothing like our old map. "It's confusing. What's it a map of?"

"This is better than that wet old thing we left in our tent." Russell drags his finger over something. "Look." He taps a spot in the bottom corner, and I see: COLORADO.

I grab his arm. "Is Leadville on here?"

"It's more than on here. It's *marked.*" He brings it up closer to my face. "Do you know what this means, Tan?"

I can just make out the tiniest lettering. "Someone did mark it!"

There's a small circle around the town. *Leadville.* My heart starts to race. Handwritten numbers show the elevation: 10,152 feet. But the map doesn't say anything about how high the water is there.

"That's the place." He nudges me. "The destination, kid."

The boats had been trying to get to Leadville. They'd marked it on a map. I stand up, trying to hide the tears welling in my eyes.

Dusty comes over, Voley at his heels. "What's wrong? What is it, Tanner?"

"This is it." I hold up the map for him. But he doesn't smile. At first, I think it's because he's sad about Blue City, but then—

"Could it mean they left Leadville because there was nothing there?" His tone drops. "Why else would they be drifting so far west of the spot they marked?"

Russell shakes his head. "Don't you see? These boats made it to Leadville, when there were people on them. Hell, they might have been in Leadville for a long time. But they broke loose—in a storm, or maybe the lines were cut—and they drifted out. That's why there was no crew. These boats drifted to us all the way from Leadville!"

Dusty blinks. "But there was a person!"

Dusty's suspicion begins to contaminate me. "Russell, he's right."

"One person," Russell says firmly. "A face eater. Maybe he was exiled, or maybe he cut the boats loose to steal them and was swept out by the current." He pulls me into his chest and kisses my forehead as I repeat his explanation to myself, trying to believe.

I pull back just enough to look into Russell's eyes. They're big and bright and filled with hope again. "How far away do you think we are?"

He shrugs. "Can't be more than a few hundred miles."

"It makes no sense for those boats to drift all the way from Leadville in a tight pack on the open sea," Dusty says, "unless they had people in them to manage their direction. Unless something happened just before we found them."

All the horrible scenarios roll through my head. Maybe they got to Leadville, and there was nothing there—everything was under the rain. And they just moved on, or were forced off. Exiled. Maybe they got there and it's nothing like we think it is. A settlement of face eaters, maybe even a clean-cut one like Blue City.

There'd be nowhere left in the world to try for. And we'd have to starve and die, or live like everyone else, giving up the last bits of the veneer we have. As I watch Russell stare at the map, tracing its lines, figuring something out in his head, I can't help but voice my fears.

"Russell, what if—"

But Voley cuts me off. He barks, and I turn to see him standing on the pilot's chair, hackles raised. At first, I think there's nothing out there, but then I realize—he's barking down, at the water.

All three of us crowd around the wheel, and no one says a thing as we watch bodies bob lifelessly over the swells. Russell turns the wheel to pull alongside two of them. One has his eyes open, looking straight up into the rain. They're swollen, absorbing too much salt maybe. But it's not the eyes I get stuck on. It's the open chest. And legs. And arms. Empty cavities, scooped of all their muscle. Bloated sacks of flesh emptied to the core.

I look away, nauseous.

For all I've seen of rotting corpses, I can never get over this kind. The ones with teeth marks.

We glide past the rest of the bodies, twelve in total. Some look normal, but they're the ones floating facedown. And I know their carved-out rib cages are exposed to the depths of the sea, that somewhere deep under the murky brown, the whale sees the mutilation on its way up for air.

Dusty sounds shaken. "Well, now we know where the people from the boats went."

Russell looks undisturbed, and I know he's debating whether to search their clothes, their pockets, for anything that might be useful.

"Alright," Russell sighs. "We'll go back." Dusty's face lights up, probably thinking that Russell means Blue City, but then Russell adds, "I'll try to talk to him."

He means the face eater. I can't help but smack him. "Good thing you didn't shoot him!"

Russell smirks, and we speed away from the corpses. Soon they're indiscernible from the swells. We follow the sun, heading back the way we came.

"Keep your eyes peeled," Russell says.

I scan the fog on the horizon. "What are you going to ask him?"

"If they were going to Leadville, or leaving."

Dusty stands behind me, shivering. "I've never known a face eater to have a conversation."

"This one's still human enough to beg for his life. And we have food. Let's hope he's hungry."

It's only a few minutes before the boats appear in the distance. Then, as we get closer, it's strange because there's only one now. The rest have gone. But it keeps getting bigger and bigger. I shake my head. It's much too big to be one of the whaleboats.

A sick feeling crawls up in me. "Russell . . ."

Dusty reaches the same conclusion. "That's not the right boat!"

There's a swath of cloth, black as night. Then, the sound of a distant motor. Two more triangles emerge from the fog. Trimmed sails. A line of dark smoke rises from the ship. And I see figures, even from this far away, moving on deck. The ship must be six times as long as ours, its deck at least that many feet off the water.

Russell swings the wheel. "Hold on."

We swerve, kicking up foam, and then we're speeding in the opposite direction. Russell pushes the throttle until we're flying over the swells. The propeller spits foam behind us, but the boat doesn't get any smaller.

"They're following us." I tug at him.

But he's transfixed, gripping the wheel, the motor whining in protest.

"They're the ones who killed those people, aren't they?" I cringe. Russell ignores me.

Dusty disappears, and then he's back. "A little to the right. Keep our back to them." He's got the rifle in his hands.

26

ROOK

18 YEARS, 10 MONTHS, 6 DAYS

THURSDAY

After three days on the icy water, each more gray and stormy than the last, a miracle occurred. The rain softened to a drizzle, and the sky opened up, a wide rip in the clouds. Cheers rose among everyone on deck, but Rook stood mute, awed by the sunlight—real, actual sunlight—bolting through in long beams, all the way to the surface of the water. A wave of happiness, tainted only by the sadness that Luce wasn't with him to see it. After dusk, the firmament filled with stars, brighter than he'd ever seen them. Mesmerized by the beauty, Rook stood with the others, the moon bathing the deck in ghostly light, unable to fathom how he'd once taken the night sky for granted.

As he wiped away tears, his throat grew tight, his chest so full it might burst at any moment. But laughter came instead, total relief.

They aren't gone.

Somewhere in the back of his head, Rook heard voices. He turned to see hugs going around, more emotion than he'd seen from any of the drug-addled employees since he had returned. The radiance above seemed to be eroding their numbness, sparking new life.

"They're still there!" Lawrence clapped Rook on his back.

If only Luce could see, they could draw the stars together and, when morning came, lie on the deck and feel the sun on their skin. It was too painful to think about. They'd made love. And within hours, he'd left her behind, back with all the radiation.

But this trip is a good thing, Rook reassured himself. Seeing the stars made him feel sure of it.

The voyage was taking longer than expected, but they could still carry out the plan the following weekend. One extra week shouldn't hurt. And Luce had taken the map, even volunteered to hike down to the old East Harbor to scout the area. She'd said she liked to jog anyway, so it wouldn't be suspicious, and he was happy she'd get away from the radiation for a while.

Jonathan had packed double rations, which were already transferred to Rook's bags. And in his idle time on the ship, Rook had managed to say hello to Lawrence. The captain had been too busy navigating the ice to have a genuine conversation, but he acted friendly enough. As soon as Lawrence had some downtime, Rook could thank him for delivering the letter from his father.

There was some color in Captain Lawrence's eyes, nothing like the full irises he and Luce had, but a sliver of blue was still there. Maybe he wasn't taking much of the drug. It gave Rook hope that Lawrence might help him again, give him guidance about where to find a safe settlement.

Once the ship anchored alongside Yasper's Nebraska weather buoy, Rook set to work. The buoy itself was anchored by chain and concrete, giving Rook the point of reference he needed. First, he identified three familiar constellations: Ursa Major, Ursa Minor, and Orion. Using a sextant, he carefully measured each star and its distance from the horizon. For the next four hours, at intervals, he repeated the measurements, double-checking every number. Finally finished, he stored the notes in his bunk and breathed out a long sigh. All that was left was to get back to the servers at the Yasper compound and compare the star positions to where they had been historically. If they'd moved, the Earth's axis was shifting.

Adrenaline made it impossible to sleep, so Rook sat on the deck and traced the starlight for Luce. The drawing looked nothing like the real thing, nowhere as exact as the numbers he'd measured. With a sigh, he folded it into his pocket, then stayed up as long he could, watching the small winking lights until exhaustion finally pulled him to his bunk.

WEATHER KICKED UP the next morning, rocking Rook awake. Quickly reaching the deck, he saw what he feared. Clouds blanketed the sky. He'd overslept, and they'd turned around to go home. It was over already.

The sky darkened, and the waters turned white with chop. Rook balled up on a bench, seasick, unable to enjoy the afterglow of the stars and the moon. It took another two days for the water and his stomach to calm, and when it did, he was left anxious and restless. They'd be home soon, and he still needed to talk with Lawrence.

The very next time Lawrence was alone at the wheel, Rook seized his opportunity.

"How we doing, Captain?"

"Except for all this damned ice?" Lawrence waved a hand across the horizon. Bluish chunks gleamed on the water, their fractured veins stretching as far as the eye could see. "I'm doing fine. I might ask your stomach the same thing."

Rook tensed. "I've never been more excited to see mud in all my life."

"Well, we're past the storm now." Lawrence sounded upbeat, re-invigorated. "Be anchored before you know it."

Rook stepped close, waiting for eye contact. *Now or never.* "Hey, I wanted to thank you for delivering that letter from my father. It meant the world to me that I got to see them again. I can't tell you how much I appreciate everything you did for me back then."

Lawrence drew back, surprised. Then his gaze grew distant, like he was digging through memories. "Oh, yeah, I caught hell for that." He frowned. "How'd you know it was me?"

"You risked your neck searching the settlements for me. I couldn't think of anyone else who would care enough to break company policy after letters were stopped. Thank you."

Lawrence's face scrunched as if in pain. "Marrow chewed me out a good one."

Rook saw vulnerability, a chance to connect. "But cutting us off from our families was wrong, and you knew it. You did something about it."

"Honestly, I can't say I don't regret it. It was the last time I did anything like that." Lawrence looked off, sighing. "You're right. I didn't agree with it then. I hadn't caught up to Marrow in how we needed to view things. But now I know . . . he did it to protect us. After it became clear the rain wouldn't stop, he knew a lot of people would try to help their folks, be heroes, and get themselves killed."

"Maybe so, but it should have been their choice to make. You gave me my choice."

"I give you credit." A look of admiration spread over Lawrence's face. "If I had folks out there, I don't know if I could have done what you did."

"You risk coming out here all the time." Rook looked across the deck. Two crewmembers were at the stern, chatting. Jonathan fumbled with weather instruments on the deck. It was time to go for it. "Thanks to you, we'll last a lot longer. Most of the settlements you visit out there are pretty dangerous now."

"I'm sure you appreciate it more than most, having seen them yourself. We're damn lucky to work for Mr. Marrow." Lawrence made a face of disgust. "Thankfully Marrow chose to refocus everything on protecting us. The rest of the world's turned to savagery."

"You don't have to tell me." Rook gritted his teeth, summoning courage. If Lawrence had come to view things the way Marrow did, asking for help would be risky. Still, he could tread lightly and try for information, at least a general direction for him and Luce to sail. "But there have to be at least a few settlements that aren't so violent, that don't use the drug? Maybe farther away from Yasper, places the company doesn't reach too often?"

For a moment, Lawrence studied him, as if concerned. Then he seemed to relax. "I know a few, a couple hundred miles to the west, in Utah." His voice shifted lower. "Like you said, far enough we don't make it out there to trade very often. They're a ripe market for Red if we were just a little closer. If Marrow decides to relocate because of the ice, let's hope we move in that direction."

"Where exactly in Utah?" Rook spoke a little too urgently.

"Out by the—hey, you're not planning to take off again?" Lawrence chuckled, but he narrowed his eyes suspiciously. "I hope you didn't spread that around, about the letters. Last thing we need is bad morale at a time like this. Our family needs to stick together."

Rook felt his face heating up as he forced a laugh. "Of course not."

"Good. We have to preserve ourselves, no matter the cost. So don't get any ideas. We need you with us," Lawrence winked, then turned to the sea without another word.

No matter the cost . . .

The words stung, made Rook sad that Captain Lawrence had become part of the problem. At least he'd learned they should travel west, toward Utah. That was a start. Turning around to head back to his bunk, something caught his eye.

On a shelf running along the cabin wall was a row of notebooks. The lettering on the spine of one in the middle stood out: *Albert Lawrence, Settlement Trade Records*. With a quick glance, Rook noted that Lawrence was gazing silently out at the water.

The exact locations of all known settlements had to be in the log. Heart thumping in his chest, Rook inched closer. In one swift movement, he snatched the book and tucked it into his waistband. Then, spinning around, he breathed a sigh of relief. Lawrence's back was still to him, and Jonathan remained outside. No one had seen a thing.

"Well," Lawrence said, breaking the quiet. "Did you get what you were after?"

"What?" Rook clenched his fists.

"Did the stars say the compound is going to freeze up? Are we going to have to move the company?" There was no trace of anger in Lawrence's voice.

He doesn't know I took it. Rook tried to speak calmly. "I won't know until we get back. I have to compare my findings to data at the lab."

One of the crew entered the wheelhouse. "We've got an oil leak, Captain."

"Alright. I'll take a look after we anchor." Lawrence turned back to the horizon.

The logbook dug into Rook's skin as he walked out of the wheelhouse, his whole body vibrating, ready to give him away. But no one bothered him as he returned to his bunk and lay down. When he was alone, he secured the logbook inside one of his bags and tried to sleep.

THE LAST DAY on the ship was a blur. Rook made small talk, enough to get by, but every noise made him jump. He was terrified Lawrence would ask where his book was, but the last night on the water came and went, and he never said a thing.

Yasper's island came into view under thick cloud cover. They anchored and disembarked just after dawn, and while everyone else gathered up their things, Rook said quick goodbyes and hustled off the dock with his bags.

His nerves had just started to settle when he heard someone's angry shouting behind him, back at the dock. Was it the oil leak, or had Lawrence discovered his logbook was stolen? Rook sprinted toward the apartment buildings. Farther down the road, the power plant loomed, the fuel site out of view behind it.

Luce . . .

Desperate as he was to see her, his body protested. Seasickness had kept him from getting any good sleep for a week, and he was filthy. And if Lawrence had noticed the logbook was gone, then Rook needed to read it and get rid of it as soon as possible.

27

TANNER

Foam spits into my face as I lean over the stern beside Dusty. Out from the protection of the canopy, the rain slaps us as we watch the phantom ship slice through the swells like a razor. It's gaining on us, despite Russell giving our engine everything it has.

"They're on deck again!" Dusty hollers as two figures appear. I think I see something in one of their hands—a gun or something else, I can't be sure.

"And?" Russell shouts from the wheel.

"They're too fast, we can't outrun them," I yell. Voley won't stop barking, fixed on the horizon as if he knows just what's at stake.

"They're the ones who did those bodies like that, aren't they?" Dusty keeps his eye against the rifle sight.

I think of the bodies, hearing Russell's voice. *There are no coincidences.* "Has to be."

Dusty stays still as ice, staring down the biggest man on the enemy deck, his finger gliding down the barrel and touching the trigger.

I think about what'll happen if he misses. "Do you want me to take the shot?"

"I got it." But he doesn't sound sure.

Spray blasts us after every swell we crest, stinging my eyes and making me shiver. We glide up a high one and drop hard. Salt coats my tongue and wind beats my face. This is it. It boils down to this.

And then, when they're so close I know I could hit them, Dusty lowers the rifle.

"What the hell are you doing?" I grab for the gun.

He pulls back.

"Russell!" I yell.

"No—look." Dusty points. "The flag."

I look at the black sails. Then, lower, on the deck, I see it, a white flag in one of their hands. "It's a trick!"

"How do you know?"

"You saw the bodies!"

"What's going on?" Russell cuts in. He can't leave the wheel. We're going too fast.

I run to him. "They raised a white flag and Dusty won't shoot."

Russell's coughing when I reach him, purposely trying to muffle it. "How close?"

"In range."

"Take over." Russell waits until my hands clench the wheel and carefully slides out. "Keep her straight into the swells." He rushes off.

"Shit." I tighten my fingers and sit down, realizing how big the sea's become. Or maybe it's just how fast we're moving. Either way, the wheel's trying to turn on its own, and I can't take not seeing what's happening behind me.

I hear Russell and Dusty talking, but I can't make out any words with the wind screaming. I turn my head for a second, unable to look long enough to see anything more than a blur. My heart pumps faster, waiting to hear the gunshot.

"Shoot them, Russell!" I scream, picturing the bodies, the floating shells. And I know that'll be us next unless I hear the gun go off soon. But nothing happens. I can't help it—I twist my head around for too long. The boat veers left, almost smacking the next swell sideways. I swing the wheel to straighten us out again as Voley starts howling.

"For Christ's sake, what the hell's going on!"

Russell yells back, loud and clear even above the numbing wind, "Shut it off, Tan!"

"What?" I can't believe what he's saying. How can he give up, too? I think for a second that Dusty's turned on him again, has him at gunpoint. His ticket back to Blue City.

"Tanner, kill the engine!" Russell yells louder.

I push the throttle down and we go into a long glide. I hold the wheel firmly as we cruise up another long roller, and then, after we slow enough that I'm confident we won't flip, I rush back to find out what's happened.

When I reach the stern, Russell has the rifle now, but he's not pointing it at anyone. It's aimed down at the water. The black-sailed ship is practically in front of us, six feet high off the water, with three men on deck, no weapons, one of them waving the white flag. Russell's just holding the rifle limply at his side, completely useless, giving up over a white flag. I can't believe it.

"Give me the gun." I lunge for it.

He whips it out of my reach and stares me down, a look that means I'm supposed to trust him. It's another one of his gut feelings. I know he's usually right, but this one's too hard to buy. We've never been this close to Leadville, and he's putting it all on the line, everything we've been clinging to, for a damn piece of white cloth.

The ship pulls up right alongside us. Then Russell raises the rifle, and relief comes back that he hasn't given in yet. He points it at the men watching us from their bow. They stare down without a trace of fear. The one man keeps waving the white flag. Then all of them raise empty hands.

Russell hands me his pistol and I aim at them, too.

"If they make one move . . ." I curl my finger around the trigger.

"Easy now," Russell whispers.

We rise and fall on the waves, studying each other's faces. I try to work out whether they're face eaters or not from their appearance. *Those bodies had teeth marks.*

One of the men on the deck shouts to us, but I can't understand the words.

Russell replies, "We don't need any help, thanks. You can head on wherever you're going."

The biggest man, to the right of the flag holder, looks like a giant compared to his crewmates. "I'm afraid we don't mean to help you," he says in a deep, scratchy voice. By his tone, I know he's in charge. Rain splashes off his long black beard and onto his plastic suit. "We wanted to know if you might help us."

"Just enough supply for ourselves." Russell shakes his head. "Sorry." We keep the guns trained on them.

"Not interested in supply. Just talk. Can you tell us anything about the South?"

Despite the tension choking my throat, and the fact that our lives are hanging in the balance of a sudden movement, Russell laughs. I don't get the joke, and I think he's lost his mind.

Russell reins in his laughter long enough to say, "There's likely no country to the south. It's all rain."

"There most certainly is," says the big man. "Rainless country at that." His black beard is wild and untrimmed, but his skin is rose-colored and clear. All of them are vibrant with life. The same way Dusty looked when I first saw him, when he was the one pointing a gun at us.

"Bullshit," replies Russell. "We saw those carved-up bodies. Can you explain that?" I watch his finger dance on the trigger. I know the sound of Russell's voice, and they seem to get it now, too. He's ready to shoot, even though it's clear now that if they are cannibals, they're not the crazy kind.

There's a long way to fall before you become a face eater, with slippery steps along that slope. The ones we first saw in South Dakota were on one step. Blue City tarpers on another. These three might be halfway down. Maybe not mad on drugs yet, but stripped of the same rules, the ones Russell and I know still matter.

The big man motions to the skinny one without the flag. He must have ordered him to do something because he runs off.

"Keep him in sight," Russell says, but it's impossible to see where he went.

The big man just looks at us and says, "Bait."

Russell's face lights up like he understands something from that single word. Dusty flinches as the skinny man returns, and my finger starts to squeeze the trigger, but then I see he's got something big and shiny. It's a net, and the skinny man raises it high into the air so we can all see. Only it's not empty. It's stuffed and moving.

Dusty shouts, "Drop it!"

"Jesus." Russell staggers into me. I put my arm on his shoulder, half to support him and half because of the shock at what I'm seeing. "Fish. Jesus, fish." It really is. A net full.

We've known since Indiana that fishing was useless. There's something about the way the floodwaters carry chemical pollution. We used to see large surfaces of water crusted with dead fish on top. Eventually, there were none at all. They died off, just like wild animals and outdoor plants.

"For how wretched those cannibals looked, the fish think they taste great," says the bearded man.

Russell stands straight. "Lower your guns."

I'm angry that he's being so stupid. "No, Russell."

"How did you know?" Russell asks the big man. "How did you know we weren't—"

"Because face eaters aren't men," he says. "And you are a man." He winks and motions toward the side of our boat where Voley hangs over the edge, calmly watching and wagging his tail, wind blowing his ears back.

"Man's best friend," Russell mutters. "Of course."

"Can we talk below deck," the big man says, "or do we have to do this over open water? We're pushing on south, but we'd like to talk. Like to know what you've seen. Trade you food for information, if you've a mind to eat."

Russell doesn't tell the man we've never been south of here, only to the west in Utah and the north in Wyoming. Instead, he motions for Dusty and me to huddle close, as if we're part of the decision-making process now.

"What do you think?" he asks us. I feel him getting greedy. He wants information on Leadville. But it still feels hard to trust anything the men have said. When I look up, the smallest man, the one with the flag, is staring hard at me.

"I don't know," Dusty hesitates.

"Your dog does." Russell nods at Voley.

That's why it's so quiet. Voley's stopped barking.

I let the thought of the fish creep in, that they'd really let us eat some, but I can't shake my wariness. It's usually Russell who's most cautious of strangers. I remember what he used to tell me—that more than exposure, the rain kills with the desperation it causes. He's becoming vulnerable to it now, I know it, getting reckless because we're so close.

"We need to keep going," I protest. "Let them talk to us over the water, not on their ship."

"Rain's getting colder," calls the big man.

Finally, Russell decides. "You two stay here. Keep the guns. I'll go talk to them. There's an extra canister of propane we can trade for food."

"We need that gas." I glare at him.

"They're catching fish. Do you know what that means?" Russell blinks.

I can't answer because I don't remember the last time we caught fish that weren't diseased or dead.

"It means the waters are healing here," Russell says. "Maybe I can get us a rod and tackle. Still a lot of miles to Leadville."

I think of the whale, and I know he's right, but I can't let him go alone. "To hell with it," I say. "If you're going, I'm going."

Dusty looks terrified. "You want me to stay here alone?"

"Do whatever you want." Russell looks at Voley, our boat, then back to the three waiting men.

"Just because we're getting close doesn't mean we can start trusting people again," I mutter. "You've got to remember that." I half-mean Dusty because we'll be trusting him as much as the strangers if we leave him alone with our boat.

"I know." Russell leans in close and kisses me on the forehead, making sure the men see it for some reason. Then he turns to the big man. "Throw us a line."

The man sends one of his crew to grab a rope ladder, and in a couple of minutes, we're tied together with the strangers, for better or worse.

28

ROOK

18 YEARS, 10 MONTHS, 12 DAYS

WEDNESDAY

A noise jolted Rook awake from a nightmare. Panicked, he looked around the room. The apartment windows were dark, the room itself barely visible except for the flickering light of a candle on the table. Captain Lawrence's logbook still lay on his stomach where he'd fallen asleep reading it.

He eyed the clock.

Shit! He'd slept all day and missed Luce.

Then the noise came again, a knocking—not from the dream at all, but his door. Springing up, he tucked the logbook into his bookshelf and darted into his kitchen nook to grab a knife. Slowly he approached the door.

"Rook, are you in there?" Luce spoke softly.

Thank God! He quickly opened the door, his nightmare coming back to him as he frantically looked her up and down. In the dream, she'd been wasting away from radiation, ugly boils eating her alive, but there she was, in front of him, her skin clear and her green eyes vibrant.

"You're okay!" She pushed her way inside, and before he could say hello, she wrapped him in her arms and kissed him.

"I missed you." His fingers ran through her hair.

"I missed you, too." She shut the door and began taking off her rain suit.

He couldn't shake the horror of the dream. "How's the fuel site?"

"That can wait." She lifted up his shirt and pushed him down on the bed.

Everything uncertain in the world, and in his spirit, was suspended by the touch of her hair across his face, the smell of her skin, the taste of her mouth.

WHEN IT WAS OVER, Luce leaned off the bed, pulling her rain suit from the floor.

"I brought you this." She took something out of the pocket, a small yellow plastic brick.

Rook took the device and examined it. He'd seen one in her hand when they first met.

"It's the same as mine," she said. "It'll tell you how much radioactivity is in the area and keeps track of your total absorbed radiation."

ROOK WALLACE. "You etched my name in the bottom?"

"So we don't mix them up. It's for the walk to the harbor."

Rook remembered the plan. "Did you go?"

"You were right, it's abandoned. And . . ." Luce smiled mischievously. "Some old wooden boats were left behind, with oars. Old, but they don't have holes. We can take one to get off the island." Something darkened her expression. "And I discovered another reason why Marrow abandoned that harbor. The rain channels drain along the old road that leads there, and the nuclear leakage is flowing in that direction to the shoreline. It's pretty bad in some spots."

Rook felt the horror of his dream again, the terror of seeing Luce disintegrate like that. It had been so real. "How high is yours now?" He remembered the number, .92, etched into his brain from the last time she showed him.

She pulled her device out and showed him the screen.

"1.02, that's too high!" Rook shuddered. "I don't want you going back to the fuel site, okay?"

"You said we could do it any Saturday, at midnight, right? That's only three days away, and then we'll be gone." She kissed him. "Tell me about your trip."

"The whole time I wished you were with me. We saw the sky. I felt the sun on my arms, saw the moon and the stars."

Her eyes opened wide. "God, I wish I'd been there, too."

Rook remembered the logbook. "I know where to go when we leave here." He brought it over from the shelf and opened it in his lap.

"Wait—this says Captain Lawrence?"

"I guess I'm a thief now. Look." He opened to the page he'd been reading before falling asleep. "This is from a few months ago."

2/13, 18 Y.A.R.
Blue City, Wasatch Range—East of Park City
40.6461° N, 111.4980° W

List:
Unrefined oil—3
Misc. building materials—9
Canned goods—12
Propane—3
Misc. medicine—2
Ammunition—3

Notes:
Organized, peaceful settlement. Their leader, Daniel Garrison, did not have interest in trading for Red. Request permission to provide free samples on a future visit. Smaller settlements are fleeing here from Salt Lake City area, and Daniel said they may have a need for food eventually, due to population aggregation. Says they have ammunition/weapon reserves to trade. Advise a future trip with salted meats.

"Lawrence said it himself. Blue City is a safe settlement, but he wouldn't tell me the exact location. Now we have it." Rook watched her hesitate like something was wrong. "Luce, they don't take Red there. We just have to head west until we see the mountains."

"But did you read that? They don't give up until they hook everyone on that shit, even the people who don't want it." She pounded her fist.

"*Shhh!*" Rook put his finger to his mouth, taking her hand. "It's okay. We're putting an end to all that soon."

"I'm sorry," she said. "It's still sinking in that they lied to me for so long."

"They won't be able to hook them. Only three more days, remember?" Inside, though, Rook felt paralyzed. He wanted only to stay next to her, in the warmth of the heated room, on a soft bed, pushing away everything that now hung over them. So many things could still go wrong.

Pulling Luce down on the bed, he cradled her. They breathed together softly for a long time until it sounded like she was falling asleep. Drifting into his own dream about the stars, he remembered.

"I have something for you." He retrieved the drawing and held it up for her.

"Hmm?" She groaned, opening one eye.

"You were right, I do stink at drawing."

"Oh! It's the stars." She sat up and took it. "You made this for me? It's beautiful."

"I couldn't stop thinking about you. Luce . . ." He leaned close, heart fluttering. "I think I'm in love with you."

"You *think*?" She blinked.

"I am."

"I love you, too."

They made love again, and it felt different from before, slower, every touch deliberate, as if it would be the last. Afterward, they lay intertwined in warm silence until it grew late, and Luce said she had to go.

"This Friday night?" She sounded confident as she pulled on her rain suit, but Rook saw the uncertainty in her eyes, a reflection of the same fear he'd been feeling all night: *they might never have a moment like this again.*

"It's a date." He tried to match her optimistic tone as he stood to hug her. "Meet me here at eight, so I can give you the supplies." With a last kiss, she was gone.

Mom, Dad, give me strength, Rook prayed as he tucked the yellow device into the pocket of his rain suit. *I know this won't be justice for what happened to you, but it's the closest I can get.*

As he lay in bed, his thoughts became muddled. Hovering at the edge of consciousness, he saw Luce reappear. Some faintly aware part of his brain seemed to know what was happening, tried to warn him. *It's just another dream, it's just another dream.* But the warning grew softer, dissolved, replaced by a steady gurgling. It sounded like water. She reached out to him, opening her mouth to say something. No sound came out, not even breath.

Luce!

He desperately needed to help her, but his body was stuck, wouldn't listen to any command he gave. The gurgling intensified. Then he saw the source: it was her skin, boiling and popping, oozing from open sores. Where her eyes had been, there was only white.

29

TANNER

Russell hands Dusty the rifle and goes to the ladder first. The big man helps him up. I worry they'll try something as soon as he's aboard, but nothing happens.

I go next, fighting back the feeling that I should stop trusting Russell. After all these years, everything that's happened from Philadelphia to Blue City, I'm skeptical that there are any good people left in the world.

Dusty changes his mind as soon as I'm up. "Can I bring my dog?" He gestures to Voley.

"All are welcome." The big man hangs over the rail and holds out his arms. Dusty hoists Voley high enough for the man to grab him with ease, then climbs up.

They lead us casually across the wooden deck, like they don't even mind that we've brought our guns. I tell myself it's a sign that they're real people, that they understand our need for caution.

We're led down a staircase to a large room below the deck. There's a rush of warmth, like a cocoon, softening my apprehension. The skinny man leaves at his boss's instruction, and the rest of us find a seat around a worn table. Wooden bunks line either side of the room, with loads of shelving between. Near the table a fire stove is going, much bigger than ours, a steel pipe running its smoke out through the hull. I tell myself to stay alert because the warmth's like a drug, slowing me down too much.

I watch enviously as the bearded man and his short partner sit down in their gray plastic suits. They've got it good here. Then I smell it, even before I see it—the salty aroma of fish. The skinny man returns with a loaded tray of them, flashing blue-and-gray scales, and immediately lays a metal grate over the stove flame.

"More proper to talk over food." The big man smiles, getting up to cook. I watch him season the fish with salt and pepper, and in a few minutes, there are more of them than I thought were alive in the great brown sea, piled on plates in front of us.

I speak first. "How'd you catch so many?"

"New water, I think," the big man says in a deep and hoarse voice, handing out forks and knives. "Maybe a path from the Pacific Ocean. That's my guess. It's good and bad. Means more fish, but a lot less land left in this country than I'd like."

"So you used face eaters as bait?" Russell starts his fact checking.

"We've had more than a couple run-ins with cannibals since coming from Montana."

All the way from Montana! I want to say, but I keep my mouth shut and glance at Dusty and Voley. Voley's quiet, sitting at Dusty's feet by the rifle. Still close enough to be used. Voley's calm is a good sign. Dogs sense evil, or I've always heard it said. And he isn't making a sound.

"When we spotted them, they were already eating each other," the big man explains. "So that's an opportunity for bait. Every time we hit a group of them, we skin and gut them. Just like you would a fish. Because that's what they are, somewhere down there on the food chain. Not humans anymore. They gave that up with their choices."

I try to make sense of using people for bait and glance at Russell to get his read on it, but he's already digging into his food. When I look back, the big man's eyes are on me.

"Don't you feel sorry for them either, young lady. They're too low on the ladder to deserve any of your sympathy. See, we don't eat people," he speaks with conviction.

Somehow he knew what Russell needed to hear because Russell clinks his fork down and gives his full attention.

"Don't get me wrong," the man continues, stroking his massive beard and eyeing Russell. "I understand that the rain's made people sink to it, the necessity to waste nothing. Hell, if it got to be the only thing between me and death, I might do the same. But it hasn't. Not yet. And I intend to make sure it never does."

"Where are you heading?" Russell asks.

"The Rainless Land."

Russell smiles at this. I feel it too, another confirmation of what Timothy told us. My chest swells with hope, the certainty that we were right to believe all along.

Giddy, I speak at the same time as Russell. "You mean Leadville?"

"Heard it would be in Colorado somewhere. Maybe farther south. We don't know. That's why we're talking with you."

"Why'd you leave Montana?" Even in my excitement, I can't help but pry.

Dusty slides closer to me, accidentally knocking the rifle to the floor. The bearded man and his crewmates flinch like Dusty's going to try something, but then they just lean back again.

"Before that long tale, I'd like to know your names." The big man leans forward, his rosy cheeks rising with his lips, beard still dripping. "At least, I'll give you mine." He removes the hood of his plastic suit. The darkness of his beard is mirrored in long curls that fall to his shoulders. His eyes are brown, surrounded by wrinkles, but alive. "Ernest." He looks pleased with himself. And that's all he gives us.

The room becomes awkwardly quiet. Ernest looks much older than Russell, but stronger for the aging rather than weaker. He waits patiently, chewing fish, but Russell doesn't give our names.

"We've been a crew of three for a while now." Ernest turns to one of his mates, putting him on the spot.

My eyes fall on him, the short one who stared at me from the deck. He's looking at me again. I can tell he's a bit older than Dusty, but a lot younger than Russell.

His soft blue eyes and open posture give an appearance of innocence. "Clint," he says in a thin and raspy voice.

The third man, lean and wiry with smooth copper skin and sleepy eyes, speaks next. "Call me Lemmy."

One by one, starting with Russell, we mutter our names.

"And him?" Ernest looks under the table.

"That's Voley." Dusty pets his nose.

"It's good to meet folk without the dark eyes," says Lemmy.

"Dark eyes?" Russell asks.

Ernest chimes in. "Those are the ones I've most heard called face eaters, who've started using too much of the drug."

"So that's all true then, about the drug?" Russell confirms what I already knew from Dusty.

Ernest points to the corner of the softly glowing room. Against the planking of the hull rest several crates, one of them marked with a giant *Y*. "That's the stuff right there."

"Why do you keep it?" Suspicion sharpens Russell's voice.

"It might come in handy. I don't know how. Once they slip into that stuff, it takes away their hunger, distorts it to something else . . . They're numb. Then pain doesn't deter them much, and that's the tricky part. At least, it's been that way through Montana and Wyoming. I can't speak on parts elsewhere."

"Have you taken it?" Russell's voice cuts like a razor.

"Of course." Ernest sounds calm.

Russell's scowl forms fast as he studies the faces of the captain and his mates. I look too, but none of them have dark eyes.

Ernest laughs like he knows the look of judgment well. "And I'll never touch it again. Unless there comes a time when I have to eat a body to survive. Or go some long distance over the ground without the strength to do it. But there's no sense figuring on that until it happens, right?"

Russell doesn't reply. He's unsure, and so am I. Part of me is curious about what the drug does, what it feels like. Can it really take away hunger and pain? I've never taken anything besides antibiotics and Tylenol that we've been able to scavenge. But it is, after all, the face eaters' drug, the ones who are completely stripped, no veneer left. Taking it can only mean moving one step closer to them.

"If you haven't figured it out yet, I'm not one of them. You can relax a bit, if you'd like to. Although I know you won't. And I don't blame you. If you hadn't had that dog on board, we would have opened fire on you." Ernest looks to Voley. "God's honest truth," he says with love in his voice. "And God's been with this ship since it sailed. It's no coincidence your dog was in plain sight."

Dusty nudges my leg. I trace his line of sight to Clint and look away immediately because his bright blue eyes are still on me. The fact he knows I see him doing it doesn't even break his stare. Guys have stared at me before, but never this persistently. It's so creepy that I can't help fidgeting in my seat.

Ernest snaps my attention back. "To your first question, Tanner, we left Cooke City when supplies ran out. Used to be relatively dry there, and warm. Rain was lighter. I swear to hell it was. And a hell of a lot warmer. Then things really took a turn. More and more of the people we knew, some of them we loved, turned to cannibalism. What else could we do? Maybe the waters would have gotten better if we'd waited, but there were no fish then. The talk of leaving started, all of it based on some old broadcast."

"Broadcast?" Russell gasps.

"Something that come over the radio. Probably ten years ago."

My eyes glue to Ernest, thinking of the radio we found in the face eater boats. I wonder if it works, if anyone still sends broadcasts.

"Someone was talking about the Rainless Land—"

Russell's loud coughing cuts Ernest off.

He pauses and looks Russell over. He's making an assessment of his health, like I've been doing for weeks. Maybe Ernest needs to know how easily he could take us out if he has to. Or he sees how weak we've really become, that our guns are just props holding us up so the wind and rain don't blow us away. But he said that face eaters would have eaten a dog before taking it on a sea voyage. Long before that. So he's made up his mind that we're not the enemy, and that maybe we're the same as him.

"What else did the broadcast say?" Dusty asks, shifting his attention from Clint.

"The voice was breaking in and out of static," Ernest explains, "claiming there were places to the south that were safe havens. And on top of a few mountains, not even raining."

Russell can't contain himself any longer, and he blurts out everything we know about Leadville.

Ernest doesn't seem to recognize the name.

"That's your Rainless Land," Russell finishes.

"I don't know." Ernest shakes his head. "That broadcast was years ago. But a lot of us in Cooke City got to talking about our long-term options. There's nothing left of the law in all of America, you know?" He chuckles. "So the idea for a grand expedition started to eat at us. It took years to get the boats and all the supplies together. We had—how many did we have when we set out, Clint?"

All eyes turn to Clint, his silent gaze finally upset as he looks up in thought, his face twisting with sadness.

"Let me think." Ernest slaps a palm on the table, drawing the attention off Clint. "Fourteen ships total, that was it."

Clint recovers his composure and nods. Ernest describes their staggered departure, how his ship *Resilience* left with five other ships in her group.

"We lost many a good man and woman." He rocks back, searching for something inside his jacket. "You all left in a hurry, without rain suits?" He raises his eyebrows. "I don't care how good your canopy is. You won't last long without plastic."

We're not ready to answer, though, because we don't know what he's looking for under his shirt. But it's just a tiny wooden tube, a pipe. Russell sighs.

Ernest waits for us to talk, as if he wants our story before he's finished with his. He takes out a small bag and a box of matches and puts them on the table. He stuffs the pipe with tobacco, lights it, and looks again at Russell, waiting.

"Where are the other ships? The rest of your crew?" Russell presses.

Ernest draws from his pipe and exhales a pungent cloud of smoke. "We lost them in a monster sea. Biggest waterspouts I've ever seen." He whistles. "It was black as night. Our crew, God rest their souls, were lost, swept overboard. No sight of the other boats when light finally come." He seems lost in thought as he puffs, sadness on his face. "They might have reached the Rainless Land, for all we know. More likely they're on the bottom."

Russell understands and waits. I look back at Clint, expecting his blue eyes on me again, but they're not. They're closed now. Something painful on his mind, too. Memories. The bane of people with hope.

Finally, Ernest speaks, the pipe dangling from his lips. "So we couldn't do anything else but sail on, right? We're making a go of it, anyway. The three of us. Keep her flying. See what we find."

Ernest is done, even I can tell. He won't tell us any more. He grunts as if to say that's the reason we're all sitting here—to exchange information. What we know. So that some kind of hope can be kept alive, despite how painful it is.

Russell tells our entire lives in a few minutes. He only spends a moment on each city. How the water rose, the flash floods started coming all the time. Food dwindled. The chaos of panicking millions. He tells about how much worse it got: Philadelphia, Pittsburgh, Indianapolis, the Great Lakes, Sioux Falls, Rapid City, Wyoming, but he stops before Blue City. He knows Dusty's hanging on every word. Then he returns to Leadville.

"It's the same as your Rainless Land," Russell says. "I grew up in Colorado. But I haven't been in twenty-five years."

"So you've come all this way for the same thing as us?" Ernest looks impressed. "And what a greater distance, too."

"We didn't mean to at first," Russell admits. "A lot of years were spent just heading to higher ground. Then we heard the same thing you did. Someone told us about a broadcast."

"Land where it's not raining?"

"The same."

"I'll take that as a good omen."

When Russell doesn't continue, Ernest asks how long the law lasted out in the East.

"There was anarchy a few months after everything went dark. Some people tried to keep it going, self-policing, but the groups split into factions. Infighting for resources, gangs claiming safer territories for their own. There was plenty of food, though, so no one went around killing each other to eat."

A great silence descends on the room because all the information that we were hoping for, and that they were hoping for, seems like dead weight. It amounts to nothing. Nothing more concrete than what we'd each already known. And all of a sudden, the thought seems as obvious to everyone else as it is to me—we're completely useless to each other.

Ernest just leans back in his seat, like he's been doing every few minutes, takes another smoke, and looks us over. "So then it's settled, isn't it? You won't get far in that little boat. The water keeps rising. It's getting colder."

His meaning is clear, and I see Clint react in surprise, as if the suggestion is as unexpected to him as it is to us. Dusty's eyes go wide, like Ernest means to gut us too, clean out our insides and throw them in a barrel for fish bait. His hand stretches toward the rifle.

"No, boy," Ernest clarifies. "We need extra hands. I mean for you all to join us."

Dusty freezes, and I look at Russell. He locks eyes with me and nods. Without a word, he's telling me he trusts them and asking me if I trust them, too.

It still sounds like a trap, in part of my mind, but I haven't heard a man talk the way Ernest does in a long time, confident and optimistic despite the rain, the exposure, and the cold. I trust Russell though, so I nod back.

He slides out of his seat. "We'll get our stuff from the motorboat."

Ernest tells Clint to help us bring everything aboard. "What's it run on?"

"Propane outboard."

"We should keep it then, take shifts steering it behind the *Resilience*," Ernest says. "We don't know what we're up against, do we? A man from the North and a man from the East."

Russell nods in agreement. He waves for me to come, then follows Clint up into the rain.

"Hold on a moment." Ernest walks toward the shelves lined with gear and barrels. He fetches a fresh gray rain suit and tosses it to Russell. Standing at the stairs, Russell takes it and just nods.

He can't say thanks. We haven't shown them our worth yet. And that's the way of things. Nothing comes for free. But Russell puts on the plastic anyway and heads up.

"Let's go," Russell calls, and I know he's speaking to me.

"Got more, hold on." Ernest tosses rain suits to Dusty and me. Mine's dirty and too big, but there are no holes, and it'll keep the welts off my skin. Ernest and Lemmy head up, leaving Dusty and me alone.

We look at each other as Voley stands at attention, ready to chase after everyone.

"I can get that radio to work." Dusty's eyes are already scanning the shelves. "If he has batteries, I can get it to work."

I believe him for some reason. Ernest's optimism is contagious. He acted sure that we were going to be okay without ever saying it. It was just the tone of his voice. And I saw it filling Russell up. We're so close to Leadville, and it's starting to infect me, too.

After everything's in, I lie down in one of the bunks. Voley jumps up and nuzzles me with his cold nose. The warmth and the soft glow of the stove make me drowsy until I hear footsteps coming down.

It's Dusty. He doesn't say a word, just sits on the floor, the radio in his hands. He opens the back and puts a battery in. Voley and I watch him hold one up to his mouth and lick it.

"What the heck are you doing?" I sit up.

"Trying to get the radio working. Sometimes it helps get the last bit of juice out." He twists toward me, smirking. "Want to try it?"

"No." I recoil. But it's the first time I've seen him joke since we left Blue City, and I don't want him to stop smiling.

"Tastes good, too." He walks over and holds the battery in front of my mouth. "Stick your tongue out."

I shove his arm away. He opens his eyes wide and sticks his own tongue out like an idiot.

"You better quit." I can't help but laugh. It's been so tense between us. I want to melt back into what we felt in Blue City before everything went wrong. Then it slips out of me. "Dusty, Russell found meat in a freezer before we left Blue City."

"Meat?" Dusty's smirk vanishes.

"That's what he saw."

"That's impossible! I told you we don't eat people." His eyebrows cinch together with anger.

"I know what we saw. Maybe you just didn't know."

"I don't believe that." He huffs and retreats to the opposite side of the room, fiddling loudly with the radio. "Shit, they're no good!" He drops the dead batteries and starts rummaging through the shelves.

"Have you ever heard anything come over the radio?" I want to test how mad he is.

"I spent weeks listening in Utah." He sounds more sad than angry, like he's secretly considering the possibility that Russell was right. "Nothing ever came on." I lie down and drift off while he searches.

Someone taps me awake. Dusty. His eyes are wet like he's been crying.

"Are you okay?" I sit up and instinctively take his hand.

He leans down and hugs me. He's squeezing too tightly, like I'm going to disappear. There's no trace of anger from what I told him earlier.

I finally break the silence. "No luck with the batteries?"

"I'm going to ask Ernest if he has unopened ones." He loosens his arms, quickly kisses the top of my head, then leads Voley up into the rain without another word.

I pause and look around the empty room. The warmth is with us again. Despite everything, we're still going. I feel relieved that I told Dusty, told him as much as I'll ever be able to. But it hurts knowing we lied to him, and it feels so selfish. *What good would him knowing that do though?* If he knew, he would hate me. And he kissed me—he doesn't want to lose what's between us. As I pull my plastic suit on, I'm struck by what feels like a memory.

My mom. I feel like I can see her for a second. It's strange because I know I don't have any recollection of her. I was too little when she died. But the thought has produced a face I can't recognize. It's still there, deep in my mind. The feeling of her love. That I had a mom once.

I see her plainly now. She's warm and right next to me and gently touching my hair. *I love you*, she says. And then I shut my brain off, or it shuts down on its own, because it's all made up. Delirium from hunger and fatigue.

You have to stop cracking, I scold myself as I climb the stairs into the cold. I know I've been slipping ever since I met Dusty. I haven't told Russell, but he's guessed it. I know he has. And the problem is that Russell's cracking too. We're both getting soft, and there's nothing yet that proves we're any closer to hope than we've been in years. It's all an illusion until we're standing under blue sky.

30

ROOK

18 YEARS, 10 MONTHS, 14 DAYS

FRIDAY

It took three days to finish his comparisons, and the results had shaken Rook to his core.

Dr. Franklin was right: the geographic poles were shifting, and Colorado was going to keep getting colder until the rain turned to snow and the floodwaters froze. By the new positions of the stars, Rook had determined that the compound's latitude, thirty-nine degrees at the start of the rain, was greater than forty-four degrees now. Because no one else had taken measurements, there was no way to tell if the rate of polar drift was steady or accelerating. Either way, the island would become ice-locked.

After the shock faded, an old anger resurfaced. Rook could still hear the propaganda: climate change is not our problem. It's not a problem at all. *How much pride we humans took in our power to manipulate the environment, the power that supposedly exalted us above all other species.* If only the people who wielded that power had known how much they'd actually underestimated it, how ignorant they really were.

Rook had been subconsciously clinging to the smallest hope that the Earth might heal in his lifetime, but now that was extinguished. Maybe future generations would see that, but not his. *It doesn't matter now anyway.* He pushed the anger away as he headed for Marrow's office.

He'd considered lying to Marrow, letting the company ships get stuck in the ice, frozen into one big irradiated glacier. One last fuck-you. *No, there are still many innocent people here.* Besides, tonight was the night. The Red would be destroyed, the company's ability to spread the addiction crippled, and that was revenge enough. It was the justice his father had expected of him, and that he owed his mother. But probably it would mean the most to his brother, who'd fought so long to free himself from drugs.

Help me get through one more conversation with this shitbag, Rook thought as he knocked on Marrow's office door.

"Come in." Marrow's eyes lit up at the papers in Rook's hands. "You've finished?"

Rook sighed, choking down the sick feeling buzzing through his body. He held up his packet of calculations. "Dr. Franklin was right. The data fits."

Marrow's face flushed. "Fuck." His head sank into his hands. "You're sure?"

"I'm sorry." This was the last time he would ever see Marrow, and it took every ounce of willpower to keep from accusing him of selling out his humanity, of killing Rook's parents.

Marrow rubbed his temples. "How long do we have until we're locked in?"

"Maybe a few months, maybe a year? There's already a lot of ice on the water. We saw plenty on the expedition."

"Alright." Marrow drummed his fingers on the desk. "That's it then. I'll speed everything up."

"Sir?"

"I have to move the damn company, don't I? If our ships can't get in and out, how can we keep trading Red?" Marrow slammed his fist down on his desk, startling Rook, but the look of exasperation slid quickly off his face. "I'm sorry. I was hoping Franklin was wrong."

Keep trading Red? You selfish . . . Rook edged toward the door, anxious to leave before his disgust and anger exploded. "Anything new I should work on?"

"Just stay on top of the forecasts. We'll lose contact with our closest settlements when we move, and I plan to trade as much as possible before that happens. Squeeze every last bit out of these savages."

Did he really just say that?

The worn and aged faces of his parents flooded Rook's mind, then the memory of their love, their struggle, their doomed attempt to hold on to the morality that guided them in the old world. He heard his mother wheezing her way through a prayer of compassion, saw his father offer up what scarce food he had to a little girl and her brother. Despite their awareness of the futility, of the rain and the drug working together as an implacable force that shredded the humanity of everyone around them, they had desperately held on to their small community in Canvas City. Made it their life's purpose to stave off the savagery that they watched envelop Gerry, then Charlie, Mike, Frank and Jean and their children. And this fuck, Marrow, in his fortune and years of insulation, had pronounced it a mere choice—a refugee's decision—to embrace a barbaric existence, as if even Gerry hadn't fought with every fiber of his being to delay the inevitable debasing that forces outside his control, the momentum of natural disaster and Marrow's evil, were racking upon the better angels of human compassion and empathy.

Marrow's words ricocheted violently in Rook's head, disintegrating the last of his self-restraint until a burning impulse possessed him. Marrow needed to feel the pain he'd caused, take responsibility for the hypocrisy he'd conned them with, even if only for an instant. "My parents were those savages," Rook said, "and the drug killed them, because you stopped caring."

"What?" Marrow's mouth opened in surprise. "Red doesn't kill anyone. Everyone here takes it, and is it hurting us? If your parents took too much, then—"

"People here don't have to trade their food for it! That's bullshit and you know it."

Marrow drew back with a panicked expression, picking up his radio handset. Then, radio halfway to his ear, he froze. "You've been through a lot, haven't you? Grieving for your parents twice, I can't imagine. But how can you accuse me of not caring?"

Rook snapped out of his rage at the sight of the radio, the thought of being taken by security. He cursed himself. How had he lost control now, this close to leaving?

"I'm so sorry, sir," he backpedaled, evening his tone and putting his hand to his forehead, pretending to be shocked at himself. "I didn't mean that. Hearing you call them savages just made me . . . My parents weren't savages, they were good people. It's the anniversary of their deaths, and it's been really hard today," he lied.

"What I need you to understand," Marrow said firmly, lowering the handset, the panic in his face easing, "is that you're one of a rare few. Anyone not lucky enough to work here *is* going to die, one way or another—disease, rising water, famine, exposure. You can't blame me for the fact that the world has reverted to survival of the fittest. It's no one's fault. And I apologize, I shouldn't have called them savages. I'm frustrated. I didn't want to move the company so soon."

Rook forced a sob and slouched his shoulders, slumping against the wall, tucking his hands into his pockets to appear unthreatening. "I just wish things could be the way they were in the beginning, when I first started here."

"We all do. But that's not realistic. *We* will be the last ones, when the floods cover the world. *Our family* will have enough to live on, for our *children* to live on. If resources were spread evenly, what do you think would happen? Everyone would have enough for a short time, and then it would be gone. They'll die either way."

"Children? Our contract stipulates no relationships."

"I haven't told anyone yet," Marrow said softly. "But that's going to change. We *have* to have children. I've seen you with that power-plant worker in the cafeteria. You seem to like her. Doesn't that change everything for you, make it worth it?"

The possibility of staying at Yasper, of having a family with Luce, sprung into Rook's head for the first time. Could he stomach being a party to the drug if it meant a secure future with her?

"Listen, really listen, Rook." Marrow leaned forward. "When the government funded us, it made sense to help. But they're long gone, and so is their aid. Our humanitarian efforts died with them. I'm the only one who saw it early enough to adapt."

"You did, sir."

"The good news is that I have a solution for you, for all the horrible things you're feeling. You don't take Red, am I right?"

Rook stammered, then nodded.

"If I didn't take Red, my emotions, my memories, would haunt me, too." Marrow breathed deeply. "The drug gives us the power to survive. Yes, it comes at the cost of some people using it improperly, many of whom are less fortunate than us. But we can't save them anymore. You need to make a choice, Rook. I've always liked you. That's why I brought you back the moment I learned you were still alive. But you need to decide whether you want to be among those whose children live to see the day the rain stops. Or whether you wish to go back out there."

Rook swallowed, a chill making his hair stand on end. If he and Luce could have children who lived to see the rain stop, to see the Earth heal, maybe Marrow was right. *But is it worth being part of a future created that way?*

Marrow surprised Rook by getting up to hug him. "I want you here with us," he said sincerely. "But I can't decide where your loyalty lies. You're free to leave. The next shipping crew can drop you at whichever settlement you like."

Rook took a long breath, trying to dampen the jitters pulsing through him. Through the tangle of confused emotions, he knew what he had to say. "I want to stay. I want to have a future. This is my family."

Marrow clasped his hand over Rook's. "I know it's hard for you, not only losing your parents, but having seen firsthand what the country's turned into."

Rook nodded, wiping his cheeks.

"I was once very angry at how ugly the world has become. This is a better way to deal with it." Marrow took a Red tablet out of his pocket. "It will fix everything you're feeling."

Marrow's dilated black eyes followed Rook's hand as he took the tablet.

"I'll try it." Rook went to put it in his pocket.

Marrow grabbed his arm. "There's no need to wait for relief. Take it now." He handed Rook a mug of water from the desk.

Knowing better than to hesitate, Rook quickly stuck the pill into his mouth, drank, and swallowed.

Marrow beamed. "You'll feel better soon, I promise. Your work is invaluable. *You* are invaluable. Your home here is well deserved, and permanent."

"Thank you. I'm going to get right to work on the forecasts." Rook gave him a firm handshake, making sure to maintain eye contact, and then, with a huge inner sigh of relief, left the office.

As soon as he made it down the hallway, he turned calmly into the bathroom and spit the tablet into the toilet. Then, bending down on his knees, he threw up.

"ROOK!" Luce was glowing when Rook opened the door for her that evening.

"It's eight already?" He let her in, confused.

He'd fallen asleep after work, thinking of the strange conversation with Marrow, unable to shake the appeal of Marrow's offer. Something was preventing Rook from letting it go. He'd planned to bring it up with Luce, even if just to hear her laugh it off. But here she was, smiling, on the night they would carry out their escape, and it stopped his thoughts dead in their tracks.

"Look." Luce entered and dipped her head down, revealing soft white powder speckling her hair. Rook put his hand on it, melting the snowflakes.

"It was raining when I—"

She dragged him to the window. Snow was falling in wavy arcs, a thin layer of pure white already concealing much of the dirty brown. It looked so peaceful. She pressed into him from behind, her heat flowing through him. If only they could stay connected like this forever . . .

"Do you feel ready for tonight?" she asked.

He dropped his head, sighed, and closed his eyes.

"What is it?" she asked.

"Something's bothering me." He struggled for the courage to tell her. "When I gave Marrow the report about the stars today, he told me he was changing a policy. He said if we have children—if any employee does—it won't be a breach of contract anymore."

"Children?" Luce recoiled.

"The idea has been in my head, and I can't get it out. What if we could have a life here together and . . ." Rook trailed off as Luce's face soured.

"This is an awful world. What makes you think I want children?"

It stung, but more than that, Rook felt like an idiot. *She's right.* They'd never talked about children, and *I love you* didn't imply anything. Though it felt like years, he'd only known her a little over a month.

"I'm sorry." He looked away, tearing up.

She turned his face back to hers. "It's not that I don't think you'd be a great father. I'm sure you would be." She stopped to collect herself, easing her tone. "But Marrow is evil. That's the man you'd want protecting your child?"

The words tore through him. Even considering Marrow's vision of the future—for a chance at security, a family with Luce—went against everything they believed in, everything Rook had promised himself and his parents. *How could I be so selfish?*

"You're right." He leaned into her, unable to keep from crying. It had been an excuse, a way out of the plan, a means to avoid his fears. As wrong as it was, it hurt to let the fantasy die.

Luce kissed his cheek.

His eyes fell on the axe lying by the bed. "I'm ready to do this. We should go over the plan one more time."

They went carefully through each step. First, Luce would go back to her apartment, bringing everything they needed in two bags: the coordinates to the settlement Blue City, copied from Lawrence's logbook; the map to East Harbor; and the extra food Rook had acquired from the expedition. She'd wait until twelve fifteen, then bring the supplies to the old road that branched away from the power plant toward East Harbor. There, she'd wait for Rook.

Rook would stay at his apartment until midnight and then, with the axe concealed under his rain suit, cross the mud hills and sneak to the back entrance of the lab. There would only be one guard at the front of the building, and he'd have no trouble getting in with his key fob, same as he'd done before. He'd head down to the basement, open the vat of chemical powder, then climb onto the rim of the vat to reach the water pipe. From there, he'd axe the PVC pipe, causing water to flood down directly onto the drug. Sneaking out the way he'd come in, he would head toward the power plant and meet Luce on the old road at twelve thirty. They'd hike to the boats and leave. By the morning, when the broken pipe was discovered, the entire supply of the drug would be ruined forever, and they would be free.

He embraced her. "I wish I could be there tomorrow to see the look on their faces." They turned together to look out the window at the carpet of white accumulating on the mud. Rook traced a drift of snow as it swirled down. "I thought it would be months until the first snow."

"I wish we were down there." She sounded playful, as if what lay ahead didn't matter.

"We have time." He nudged her, happy to procrastinate a little longer. "Unless you stink at snow angels?"

"Better than you." With a smug look, she handed Rook his jacket.

"Let's go." He gathered up the two bags of supplies that Luce would take, then took her hand and led her down to the first floor. In a moment they were outside, through a back door to a secluded alcove behind the building.

Rook hid the bags behind a dumpster as Luce ran ahead, planting fresh tracks in the muddy snow. He stuck his tongue up into the frost. *If I could make time freeze, this would be enough . . . If I could just have this.*

A blast of cold mush stung his cheek, and he heard Luce's laughter.

"Hey!" He scooped up a snowball and chased after her, laughing. "You're done for." He cocked his arm and threw, but she ducked just in time, and the snowball sailed past her.

"That the best you can do?" She grinned.

He ran after her, caught her, and wrapped her in his arms. They fell to the ground, lying there entangled, staring up at the snow. The cold faded, and everything felt warm again.

He poked her nose. "You look like Rudolph."

"Get out of my space!" She spread her arms, up and down, and kicked her legs. "Well?"

Rook stood up to look. "You might be good at drawing, but that's a *horrendous* snow angel." He dropped back to the ground to start his own.

Luce stood over him, watching. "Okay, there's *one* thing you're better at." Then her hand whipped around, and another snowball exploded against his forehead.

"Not fair!" He grabbed her legs, and she spilled on top of him.

"I don't want to go anywhere," she said, steam rising with her breath.

"Me either."

They lay entwined until the snow coated them and Rook felt her shiver. It was time to go.

He brought her the bags. "I'll be waiting for you. See you on the road to East Harbor at twelve thirty?" For the first time that night, he saw nervousness in her eyes.

"Twelve thirty."

Rook waved goodbye and watched her walk out of sight. When her footprints had filled with fresh snow, he went inside to watch the clock.

31
TANNER

Days slip by until it's nearly been a week. As much as I try to keep my guard up after Blue City, it isn't working. Ernest's infectious confidence and Lemmy's calm determination give me hope, and I see the same feelings happening to Russell. Ernest feels like an old friend to both of us. Besides some weirdness from Clint, who keeps staring at me when he thinks no one is looking, I feel happy on the *Resilience*. Maybe it's just knowing we're united by the same goal—getting to Leadville.

Russell's up in the wheelhouse as usual with Ernest and his crew. Dusty and I hang below deck tinkering with the radio again. It's the same thing—no life—when all of a sudden, static erupts out of the speaker.

"I got it!" Dusty claps. Voley congratulates him by chasing his tail and kicking bad batteries across the planking.

We move in closer and bump into each other. It's the first time we've touched since he woke me up with a hug almost a week ago. I don't move away and neither does he. We just huddle close, listening.

The radio crackles in and out, my gut fluttering, ready for someone to start talking. It's pure static, but at least it's on. We wait forever and nothing comes.

"Let's conserve the batteries. These were the last ones I could find." He shuts it off.

Ernest lumbers loudly down the stairs. "Don't tell me you got it working?" He walks over to us, puts one hand on my shoulder, the other on Dusty's, then bends to inspect the radio.

"Yeah, but there's nothing but static." Dusty flicks the radio back on for just a second, so Ernest can hear the white noise.

"Good man. Well, keep checking it, and let me know if anything comes on." Ernest's smile is so wide and goofy, his teeth so big and crooked, almost glowing against the black of his beard, that I can't help but laugh.

"Don't you laugh at me, young lady, or there'll be not a grain of salt for your dinner tonight. Hear me?" He pats our shoulders as Russell appears at the top of the stairs.

"I can help again with dinner if you want." Dusty sounds eager. Throughout the week he's grown less troubled about leaving Blue City, more present in the moment. Falling in with Ernest seems to be giving him a new purpose, or at least a distraction.

"You're good at more than just cooking, I hear. Growing plants, too? What about you . . ." He turns to me. "I hear you're a dead shot with a pistol? Tell you what, you both teach me something when we get to Leadville, and you can have all the spices you want. Deal?"

"Deal," I answer for us.

Russell comes into the room, smirking like he's been bragging about me. Not just me—Dusty, too. I turn away because my face must be getting red, but it makes my heart jump. Watching Russell's growing friendship with Ernest, the way they talk like pals from before the rain, makes me happy. They're both after the same thing in Leadville—a life that, since they are older than us, only they knew. It's opening Russell up again, and I suspect that maybe he's starting to really care for Dusty, too.

"You want to take another look?" Russell holds the map up for Ernest.

They sit at the table near the stove light, poring over the map, discussing the best path to Leadville. I lie on the bunk next to Dusty. He closes his eyes. I do too, but I listen.

Russell's talking about Timothy again. Then something about his brother and his parents. I can't make out the words, but just his tone makes me sad. He's talking about them like they're still alive. It's impossible, and I wonder if my deepest hopes would sound impossible to other people, too. I've always kept them to myself, all the things I yearn for after we reach Leadville, after we find the veneer. Maybe we need our impossibilities to keep going, though. If Russell's willing to start saying his out loud, I wonder if I should, too.

I turn to Dusty, admiring his thick eyelashes, the peaceful look on his face, when another set of footsteps comes down the stairs.

"Hey, Tanner, it's your shift." Lemmy waves to me. I wave back and head up into the freezing rain to steer the motorboat behind us so it doesn't run into the ice, or the *Resilience*.

Lemmy's quiet, and he acts like Ernest but with fewer words. When he does talk, he smiles, but whenever I see him alone, he always looks melancholy. They all must have lost so much in the storm Ernest talked about. Maybe their entire families, but I would never dare ask. Just the laughter and friendly conversation this past week make me feel like we're all filling a void through each other. The same thing that started to happen in Blue City. And I'm more okay with that now because Leadville has never been closer.

I expect Clint's awkward stare as I climb down to relieve him from the motorboat, like every other time we've been together, but he doesn't even glance at me.

"Thanks," he mutters and climbs up.

Dusty is suspicious of Clint, and I wonder if he said something to him, or told Russell or Ernest about the staring. I feel guilty at the possibility because I know it's just that Clint's attracted to me. I've felt it before from men, but it's hard to tell that to Dusty because he's probably just jealous. One thing Dusty said really did give me chills though—the way Voley acts around Clint. Voley goes up to everyone on the ship, looking for attention, but for some reason, with Clint, he keeps his distance. There's something else, too—it's usually Clint who Voley watches when we're eating dinner.

I get distracted almost immediately as a huge slab of ice skims past.

The bergs, as Ernest calls them, have been appearing more, and getting bigger. I grip the wheel tight and keep my eyes peeled for another long shift.

Dusty and I are making up the bunks the next morning when Russell comes ripping down the stairs. He hasn't coughed in days, rejuvenated by the fish. Or that's what he thinks it is, anyway. He's even been talking about running again after we reach Leadville. And by his beaming face, I know that's what he's come to talk to us about.

"According to Lemmy, we're going to be there tomorrow. At the least, close enough to figure out a way in. You hear me, Tan?" He ruffles my hair.

His grin widens as I let it sink in, part of me still hesitant until I actually see it. But he's brimming with excitement, and I feel it flow into me. All our long shots, the terrible and endless moving, finally coming to an end. Russell extends his hand toward the boy who tried to kill him. Dusty still doesn't know how things ended in Blue City. And we haven't talked more about it either, an unspoken decision between Russell and me. Our own ugly truth. Russell keeps his hand hanging until Dusty finally takes it, smiling like our belief in Leadville has finally got to him, too. They shake hands furiously, both of them nodding, and Dusty starts to laugh. It's the first belly laugh I've heard from him since the night we kissed, and I drink in the beautiful sound of it—it's peace.

I want to squeeze him too, jump on him in the bunk. But I can't. It's all too overwhelming. As I think about our wonderful turn of fortune, something startling becomes clear. The man above, Ernest, must be Poseidon himself. He has to be.

I half-believe in the old gods because I don't see any reason they're less real than the other ones, and they must finally be repaying us for all the time we've gone without sinking to the lowest level. We've never eaten people. We've kept some sense of right and wrong, and that's the foundation, everything the veneer's built around. I can't help thinking that this ship, this crew, it's all here to reward us for what we've endured—the rain, the wet, the cold, the empty driving force that compels us to live on even though we don't really know what for.

As I watch Russell give Dusty a hug, it smacks me in the face—our whole struggle has been for this. A sense of family. Community. Love. Being here for each other. And all the armor that's helped us survive, as we reach the doorstep of Leadville, is thrown out the window. We're heading toward something more than Leadville—we're heading toward being real living people again. And my guilt about what happened to Dusty's parents feels like it's turning into something else, a duty I owe him, to protect him through this.

"I'm proud of you for sticking this out," Russell tells Dusty as I grab Voley's paws to celebrate. He doesn't get any more detailed than that, and he falls quiet, watching both of us. Then he reveals it, what he's been holding back. "You ready to see it?"

And I'm completely ruined because I get it, they've already spotted land. While we were down here toying with the radio, the reality of the dream was in their sights above. I can't get mad though, I just sprint past them. Russell laughs as Dusty chases at my heels. And Voley somehow gets there first.

It's unreal. The vast range of the Rockies spans the entire horizon. I don't have to ask. Everywhere in front of us are the spiking peaks and tabletops of the mountain range. Most of them rise high above the water, as if the rain sea is much lower than it was in Wyoming. I can't be sure until we're closer, but it looks like the most land I've seen since Indiana.

Water slaps my face but I don't pay it any attention. I can't. It's so much colder than it's ever been, but the view's paralyzed me more than any cold water could, and I throw my arms around Dusty in a fit of joy. Ernest grins through his pipe, a man of endless fish and tobacco. Poseidon himself.

Ernest says what we already know. "Over that pass somewhere"—and he points to nothing I can see—"is Leadville. It's in there. Maybe a bit of trial and error, but we'll find it."

Russell has had plenty of time to work on Ernest, and he's sold that Leadville is his Rainless Land now, too. They don't seem to care that the sea is thick with ice and that rain is pouring from the sky as hard as ever, everything freezing cold. The sight of the mountains is enough to squash any doubts. The matter of the face eaters—whether they had been coming or going from Leadville—isn't brought up. It's a downer, a remnant of the hopeless past. The lawless, reckless life of gloom. Ernest and Russell are on the same page, and they'll have none of it anymore. They believe together.

And then Ernest proclaims that he sees part of the Rainless Land. "Look." He hands me a pair of worn binoculars.

"Where?" I lift them to my face.

"No rain, Tanner," Russell says, but all I see are the towering slabs of mud and rock.

Ernest turns my shoulders. "Look for the white."

And then, I spot it. Between two crossing lines of mountain, there's a patch of white. So unlike everything around it that I can't believe I didn't notice.

"Not quite what I thought 'rainless' would mean," Ernest sighs contentedly. "But if the weather can change once, it can change again, farther in."

I look in awe at the slope of white. The sky above it is still gray, but I know he's right. It can't be raining there. The snow looks like a pile of salt spilled over the slopes.

"Is that snow? That can't be what they meant, though. Snow instead of rain?" I turn anxiously to Russell.

"No," Russell says. "The sky's blue in Leadville. We just can't see that far from here."

"He's right." Ernest bends over the rail. "We're too far to know."

Dusty takes a turn with the binoculars. And then, he hands them back to Ernest and hugs me again. He pulls away suddenly when Russell comes up behind us.

"You're fine." Russell puts his hand on Dusty's shoulder. His other goes to mine. He understands, and he's okay with it.

Clint and Lemmy come up. I catch Clint's glance but look away. I can't think of him now. I can think of nothing but these gorgeous mountains. All of them ours.

"Here's how it'll go." Ernest waves a hand over the mountains. "If there's no Leadville, if it's all bullshit, then we'll make our own town. Find a good bay and make shelter. There're enough fish to be had in this sea. We'll build up a nice place to live in the mountains."

Looking at the jagged slopes, his idea sounds crazy to me. Still, the way he says it gives me comfort, makes me believe that this man will stop at nothing.

"Alright, that's enough. Your turn on the boat," Russell tells me. "We've got to speed up a bit while there's daylight. Be careful of the ice."

I slip out of Dusty's arms and head to the stern. Once I climb down into the motorboat, the *Resilience*'s motor starts up. I steer from behind and keep the motorboat straight, following the ship, imagining the distant Rockies growing bigger. The mountains spread out like arms to welcome us. Then I see the first crusts of ice on the water, long and thin and clear, cracking apart as the *Resilience* hits them. In the distance, I spot bigger bergs. One of them looks blue.

"Pull up!" Dusty appears, hanging over the stern railing. "I have something to tell you."

I have to turn on the engine and push the throttle to get closer.

"Dare me?" He hops the rail and hangs from the rope ladder.

"Dusty, stop it!"

But he leaps right down. The motorboat rocks and we almost catch a wall of water.

"What the hell are you doing? You could have sunk us!"

But it's obvious why he did it because he pushes me against the wheel and wraps me in his arms, leaning forward, his eyes bright, the color of wet stone. His fingers curl behind my neck and pull my lips into his. We kiss and I can barely see where I'm steering. All I can think is that I do love him, and I'm sorry for everything, though I can't say it out loud. I didn't light the spark again, but the fire was still there. It's okay now. Everything's okay.

Even though the rain is colder than I've ever felt, I feel nothing but Dusty's warmth, the heat drawing me into his chest. And in a moment of joy like nothing I've ever known, as I look over his shoulder to steer, I see from the corner of the deck. Clint is watching.

32

ROOK

18 YEARS, 10 MONTHS, 14 DAYS

FRIDAY

Buzzing with built-up adrenaline, Rook glanced at the clock on his apartment wall one last time.

11:59. *Time to go.*

He made his way out into the frigid wind, cutting across the mud hills as snow swirled off the ground in small plumes. The axe felt cold against his skin, tucked into his waistband underneath a jacket. A hundred meters away, he could see that the main road was empty. Only the red dots glowing atop the distant cooling towers broke the darkness.

Every few steps he glanced around nervously, but the compound seemed deserted, almost peaceful. He worked through his nerves, rehearsing how it would go. *Same as last time, in and out.* By morning, the drug would be gone forever, and he and Luce would be on the water.

The dark outline of the lab came into view, its roof frosted with white. The windows were dark except for a few dim lights. Visible in the front foyer was a silhouette, that of the lone, heavyset security guard, seated in a chair.

Everything had built to this moment. He would prove that his mother's and father's lives had meant something. He would end the spiral of addiction he'd seen in his brother, and then in Canvas City. He would see Luce soon and know they'd done the right thing when no one else was left to do it.

Please stay with me, give me the strength, he prayed to God, to his family, to anything that might be able to hear him as he silently crept around to the back entrance.

The key fob clicked, and he was inside.

His pen light offered just enough illumination for him to walk without bumping into anything. Moving fast, he followed the path he'd taken the last time he broke in: through the chemistry wing, down the hallway past Marrow's office, all the way to the basement door on the left.

Holding his breath, he raised the key fob again. The basement door clicked open. He slipped in and shut the door behind him. The basement had no windows, so he could use the room lights without anyone noticing. Groping along the wall, he found the switch, flipped it on, and descended the old metal stairs.

The large windowless room opened up on his left, a concrete-walled labyrinth of ducts and pipes. Then, rotating, he saw it: the enormous, rectangular green metal vat stretching the length of the room, as high as his shoulders, sealed with a thick plastic cover. He walked up and peered inside. There was the drug, a sea of red powder underneath the clear plastic lid.

Setting down the axe and gripping the edge of the lid, he pushed up. It didn't budge. Wedging his palms under the lip, he squatted and put his legs into it.

Open, damn it!

He felt his body heating up, his heart racing, sweat running down his forehead. Time was wasting, and he had to get it open. Then he spotted the latches. On each corner of the vat were clamps holding the lid down.

Duh . . .

They unhooked easily, and the lid popped up. With a grunt, he slid it off, smacking the floor with a loud echo. Chemical stink instantly filled the air.

Rook eyed the ceiling. Three pipes went directly over the vat, two black and one white. The white PVC pipe in the center would be filled with water.

Heart pounding, he hoisted himself up onto the utility table that ran alongside the vat. From the edge of the table, he could step onto the rim of the open vat, where he'd be high enough off the ground to reach the pipe.

Then, with his foot halfway over the edge of the four-inch rim, the dune of powder directly below his toes, Rook froze.

Fear pulsed through his body, tensing every muscle. He'd been dreading the thought of falling in, inhaling a concentrated dose of Red, probably enough to kill him. Battling his nerves, he tested one foot on the lip. It felt firm. Four inches would have to be enough.

He put his other foot on the rim. Swaying side to side, he reached out and grabbed the closest black pipe with his left hand, then grabbed the axe with his right and swung.

He struck hard, and then again, until finally a fracture formed in the white pipe, one tiny drop of water falling, directly into the powder below. Feeling his excitement grow, he cocked back to blow the whole thing open.

And as he started to swing, the room went pitch black.

Rook froze in the darkness, fumbling for his pen light, his fingers clenching the pipe so he wouldn't fall into the vat. A noise sounded in the darkness. He strained to hear it.

Creaking metal.

The stairs.

A wide beam of light cut through the darkness. Turning around to jump down and hide, he was blinded by the piercing glare of a flashlight.

"Get down!"

"I can't see." Rook blinked.

"Down now, or I'll shoot!"

He leaped. Something clipped his elbow, the pain coursing up his arm before his head smacked a hard surface, and everything went black.

33

TANNER

We have the slowest, happiest dinner. I could eat fish for the rest of my life. Voley lies at our feet, patiently waiting for scraps. Everything is warm under the deck.

"The Earth must be healing." Ernest raises his fork and winks. "Because I keep catching fish."

"Thank god," Russell says. It's the first time he's said that in so long.

"Lemmy's the best fisher in Montana." Ernest pats Lemmy's back as we slowly suck the flavor out of every morsel.

Lemmy shakes his head. "I can't take all the credit. The filth of the floods must be wearing out."

"We should have the general area of Leadville in our sights tomorrow," Ernest says, eating with his mouth open. "There's enough stove fuel for two more weeks, more than we'll need."

Russell turns excitedly to me and Dusty. "We spotted some landmarks today, and I think we have our position figured out exactly in relation to the city."

"The inlets between mountains are too shallow to take the *Resilience* in." Ernest puts his fork down, a far-off look in his eyes. "Good thing we brought your motorboat, eh? We'll have to take it in, find a spit to land on, and hike in on foot."

“I’m going to check the horizon before last light.” Russell stands. “Dusty, take dishes for me tonight.”

Ernest heads above deck with Russell, and Lemmy shrugs and follows. Clint remains at the table with us, long after we’ve finished eating. It’s like he senses that Dusty and I want to be alone and he doesn’t like it. We wait, in case he wants to talk, to say anything at all.

“Seems almost too good to be true, doesn’t it?” he finally says.

I want to kick him. He’s a downer, more and more irritating to be around. I’ve even heard Ernest arguing with him. I thought I overheard yelling about the drug crates, but I can’t be sure. I could see him doing it though, sneaking into that stash when no one’s around and taking a pinch. Eating just enough so no one notices.

Clint waits for us to react.

“I’m going to mess with the radio.” Dusty stands and heads to the bunks.

“It’s your shift, isn’t it?” I ask Clint. I know it is and he does, too. In another ten minutes, Ernest will come down and holler if he’s not on the motorboat.

Clint fidgets at my hint for him to leave. He stares at me with his pale blue eyes, searching for something that I don’t have. But it’s not time to start making accusations, the night before we get to Leadville. I can’t mess things up. He’ll be easier to deal with on land. That’s what I tell myself.

He puts his palms flat on the table, refusing to go. There’s always got to be something, some idiot who doesn’t get it. And now it’s this asshole.

He glances at Dusty, hunched over the radio on the bed. I hear it click on, and the static starts up. Voley stays by me under the table, whining for scraps. The last thing I want to do is turn my back to Clint, but with Voley here, I know I’m okay. He’d protect me if anything happened. He’d strike Clint dead in a heartbeat.

Voley licks my hand, like he’s letting me know that my thinking is accurate. Then Clint pushes his hair back and sighs.

“You look just like her,” he says under his breath.

“What?”

"I'm sorry." He stands up and leaves.

"Did you hear that?" I turn to Dusty. He barely looks up, busily turning knobs on the radio.

I go over and lay my head in his lap, and then start to drift off, forgetting Clint and thinking about how even my dreams have started to change. They're no longer the shapeless, dark nightmares of South Dakota and Wyoming. Now, I see us all growing old together somehow. It's too much to dwell on while I'm awake. I get too fearful. But in the dream, it's all so natural and expected. Like that's the usual way things go. People living full lives . . .

The drone of radio static carries me away.

34
ROOK

18 YEARS, 10 MONTHS, 15 DAYS

SATURDAY

A stabbing pain throbbed in the back of Rook's head. He tried to touch the spot that hurt, but his hands wouldn't move.

"Luce." He opened his eyes. *We were on the boat, almost to Utah.*

But when he looked around, he saw his apartment. Everything was the way he'd left it: bed unmade, closet open, a half-empty glass of water on the coffee table. How had he gotten back to Yasper?

His stomach flipped as his memory returned.

The lab basement lights turned off . . .

Dizziness turned his vision white as he tried to stand, and halfway to his feet, something snagged. *Ouch!* His hands were bound behind him, fingers touching warm metal. Tied to the radiator.

This can't be happening, he thought, struggling against the bindings. But the more he twisted, the more his wrists burned.

Did they have Luce tied up somewhere, too?

Voices talked nearby.

"He's conscious," someone spoke. A guard in a white rain suit appeared from the kitchen nook, holding a machine gun.

Then another person stepped out. A horseshoe shock of red hair and wide black eyes.

Marrow.

Rook watched silently as Marrow rolled his fingers into his palms, curling and stretching them, unable to stop fidgeting.

"Tell me this is all a mistake." Marrow took a seat by the radiator. "Tell me you didn't betray your own family, Rook. Tell me you were fixing that pipe, not smashing it."

Rook fumbled for words. Marrow asked again, angrily, but Rook's mind went blank. His head rocked with pain. Everything was foggy. He needed a lie, an angle—anything—but it wouldn't come.

What could he say? He'd been caught with the axe, hadn't he?

Rook hung his head. The pain was unbearable. His hands were losing feeling, and he desperately wanted to ask about Luce.

"It's a shame." Marrow's demeanor relaxed, like he was already over it. "I liked you so much, that's why I rehired you. I *still* like you, and I sympathize with what happened to your parents. It upsets me terribly because I thought we had an understanding. I thought you were honest . . . I believed you." He slowly shook his head, keeping eye contact. "Why the pipe?"

There didn't seem to be any reason to keep it from him. "Flood the basement."

"Flood the base—*ahhh*." Marrow let out a long breath and then chuckled. "To ruin the drug . . . That's very clever, and a terrible oversight of mine, structuring things that way. I'll be sure to reroute the water pipes at the new compound."

"New compound?"

"I guess I can tell you, though I wish it were on better terms." Marrow stood, gesturing with his hands. "I've found a place to move the company. I'm taking my most loyal employees, and my boats, and starting over. It'll be a smaller operation, but more importantly, sustainable."

"Are you going to kill me?" Rook sank to the floor, eyes flicking side to side for anything that could help.

"Kill you?" Marrow drew the words out as if they hurt. "You think I'm a monster?"

Rook looked away at the wall.

"Of course I'm not going to kill you. Whether or not you survive after I'm gone, that's another question." Marrow folded and unfolded his arms, pacing the room. "You were supposed to come! I had already selected you. Even after you shouted at me about the Red, I still trusted you. It wasn't until Captain Lawrence called me after you'd left, and informed me that you might have stolen one of his logbooks, that I realized something was wrong. He told me just in time, too. Otherwise, I wouldn't have put a tail on you before you broke into the basement, and your plan would have succeeded."

"Where are you going?"

Marrow pointed at him with a small laugh. "You're already scheming again, aren't you? I guess it won't hurt to tell you a little. I'm taking a select contingent of employees, an even ratio of men and women whom I trust most. We're going somewhere it's not freezing, where we have enough supplies to last generations. Maybe not as much electricity without the power plant, but that's being taken care of. I cornered the graphene panel market on speculation, just a year after the rain started. Do you know what they are?"

Rook shook his head weakly, the weight of his failure setting in. He'd been so close. The pipe had started *dripping.*

"Solar panels that harvest energy through rainfall. Brilliant, right?" Marrow cupped his hands together proudly. "I didn't expect to leave this soon, but some things are even more urgent than the growing ice. In your absence, Cleo detected a hurricane with the weather buoys. It's heading toward us, due northwest, and it's big enough to do some real damage. You see, the nuclear fuel site's compromised, and I don't want to be here when the storm arrives. The radiation will be everywhere." A look of sympathy crossed his face, quickly replaced with a scowl. "My true family, and my boats, will be long gone when it hits."

"Are you leaving the drug behind?"

Marrow gestured for Rook to stand. "Look out the window."

Rook rose until his bindings snagged. He could just make out a line of white rain suits pushing wheelbarrows down the road. The wheelbarrows were covered, but he knew what was inside. His heart sank.

"It's backbreaking work. But they know that coming with me is worth it. *They* are loyal."

"What about everyone else? You're leaving them here to starve?" Rook banged his hands violently against the radiator, trying to rip his bindings.

A look of amusement grew on Marrow's face. "No. To survive. See, Rook, that's what this is about. You want to save everyone, but the greater good is doubling down on a few, not gambling on the many. We will outlast this extinction event." Marrow paused, scrutinizing Rook closely. "You do realize that's what this is, don't you? An extinction-level event."

Rook glared back. "Because of your company, it might be."

"It's a shame. You could have brought Luce, who seems to fascinate you so much. You would have been happy." A quizzical expression formed on Marrow's face. "What if I trusted you one more time, and offered you a bunker at the new compound?"

The words stunted Rook's anger for a moment, his dead fantasy reanimating, almost taunting him, before Luce's words echoed through his head: *That's the man you'd want protecting your child?* She'd been right, and it had taken her saying it for him to realize it. There was no way he would accept a future under Marrow's twisted vision of the world.

Summoning every ounce of his disgust, he spat at Marrow. "That's what I think of your offer. I know you're trading human bodies. You're the worst kind of monster!"

"You really hate me, don't you?" Marrow stepped back, his voice softening. He whistled for the guard. Rook's heart fluttered as the man aimed his rifle. "I am not a monster." Marrow tapped his chest. "The rain requires that we buy and sell what is valuable to our market. Just because something was sacred before the rain doesn't make it sacred now."

"You're a fucking coward." Rook struggled halfway to his feet, grinding his teeth.

"I'm sorry our relationship, both business and personal, has come to an end. Where did you hide Captain Lawrence's logbook?"

"It's gone. I burned it."

"Search the room," Marrow said coldly.

The guard flipped the bed and tore the pillowcases off the pillows, throwing them across the floor. He knocked the table over and smacked the chairs to the ground before pulling everything off the bookshelf. A large encyclopedia bounced open on the floor, and the logbook tumbled out.

"Got it." The guard picked it up from the floor.

Marrow took it. "Stay in the hallway and guard the door until I send word that we're ready to depart. If he calls for help, kill him. No one gets in to see him. Understood?"

"Understood, Mr. Marrow." The guard nodded and left.

"Wait! Just untie me, please," Rook pleaded.

"I am sorry, but you chose this. I sincerely hope you survive. Goodbye, Rook." With a flick of his hand, Marrow closed the door behind him.

Rook slumped against the radiator. There was no chance of destroying the drug now. The only thing left was a small hope that Luce was okay, that somehow he would see her again.

The windows grew black as the day wore into night, but Marrow had left the apartment light on. Rook had to close his eyes to find some darkness. He twisted into the least uncomfortable position he could, tormented by thoughts of Luce, his failure, and the feeling of his pulse beating through his stinging wrists. Throughout the night, his throat swelled with dryness, and the only thing he could think to do was pray—*God, please keep Luce safe*—over and over, until he fell asleep.

HE AWOKE TO an acrid odor the next morning. Squirming into a seated position, he felt the cold where he'd wet his pants. Above the noise of wind and rain, he heard shouting from outside. Rising by degrees as the numbness in his legs wore off, he peeked out the window. Thick cumulus clouds flashed against the horizon, lightning illuminating monstrous thunderheads. The snow was gone, melted into pools of slush over the main road.

Then he spotted the source of the noise.

A sliver of the main road was visible between the apartment buildings, and a procession of rain suits walked past. He counted thirty people, maybe more, some wearing tan rain suits, some white. Rook strained to catch sight of Luce's orange plastic, but it wasn't there.

Maybe she isn't going. No, of course she isn't going. Unless he made her . . .

The last rain suits marched out of sight in the direction of South Harbor. Marrow had been true to his word. They were leaving just in time for the storm.

A clap of thunder rattled the walls.

"Hey! Anyone there?" Rook checked to see if the guard was gone.

No sound came from the hallway.

"Help! Somebody please get me out of here!"

He hollered until his voice grew hoarse, and then, steeling himself to the pain, he writhed against the radiator. Warm blood ran down his fingers. There was no escaping, and no one was coming. Old prayers cycled incessantly through his brain, a mechanical repetition, until his mind slowed down and he lay his head against the metal, drifting in and out of fitful sleep.

A LOUD SHATTERING startled him awake. When he opened his eyes, shards of glass covered the floor and coated his pants. The storm had smashed the window. Urine blended with the rain, soaking him through. He stretched slowly until feeling came back to his legs, then stood enough to shake off the glass. Peering outside, he saw it was night again.

Wind whipped the rain into his face. He opened his mouth and swallowed, then swallowed again, the rawness in his throat easing for a moment. A few glints of light were visible outside, reflections off the floodwater covering the main road. Loose wires swung wildly, slapping loudly into utility poles. A few of them lay toppled. The hurricane had arrived.

He searched for a sign of life in the abyss, shaking his head each time the wind blew his hair into his eyes, imagining he would spot Luce. Shivering and drinking until he could swallow without too much pain, he waited.

"Hello!" He screamed until it felt like his throat was on fire.

As if in response, the light overhead flickered. He turned to see the ceiling lightbulb fade to the shape of a glowing coil, then disappear, leaving him in total darkness.

"Fuck!" He slammed his back into the radiator. The metal felt cool. Was it dead too, just like the lights?

You'll freeze to death before you starve . . .

A wave of panic surged him into action, one more struggle to rip free. He tugged and twisted viciously until fresh scabs tore loose and spilled blood down his fingers. Finally, he slid to the floor, unable to bear any more pain.

At some point during the night, half-asleep, he felt something icy brush his neck. He opened his eyes to see snowflakes drifting down. It was such a sad way to die, chained to a hunk of metal in an empty room, not knowing where Luce was.

You're not going to die here.

Was that her voice?

He squeezed every muscle in his body, hell-bent on fighting the growing numbness and lasting just a little longer for her.

35

TANNER

Dusty's asleep next to me when I wake up. It's dark in the cabin because the stove is on low, but still warm. No one else is down here with us. Voley's sleeping at our feet, curled tightly into a ball. And I think I'm dreaming when I hear a voice I don't recognize. It's coming through white noise.

The radio! Someone talking on the radio! I listen, my brain on fire for every syllable.

". . . everything out. Again, do not approach the area surrounding central Colorado. I'm reporting one last time. The old Fort Saint Vrain nuclear fuel has leaked. Don't approach. The radiation is everywhere. Repeat, radiation levels are high. We've evacuated. If you've come this way, we've moved everything out. Again, do not approach . . ."

And then, as magically as it appeared, the voice cuts out, returning to a wash of static.

I start shaking Dusty. "The radio said not to go!"

He rubs his eyes, glancing around confused. "What are you talking about?"

"The radio came on—it was a warning, it said don't go into central Colorado, that there's radiation."

I'm in disbelief at my own words. We're at the doorstep. How could someone tell us not to come in?

"We have to tell Russell." I slide off the bed.

Dusty cocks his head to listen to the white noise. "You probably dreamed it. Let's go back to sleep." He's already giving up, too groggy to be concerned. Voley's ears perk up, upset we've disrupted his peaceful rest. I give Dusty a death stare and repeat what I heard.

"Jesus, Tanner. Are you sure?" He finally sounds awake. "If you tell them that, you know what it will do to them."

"I want to go more than anyone!" I slap the bunk, hurt that he'd say that. Even Dusty's lived some small version of the veneer, his whole life in Blue City. Everyone but me has had a real life.

"I'm sorry," he groans. "I know."

Of course Russell will be upset, but the message was clear—*do not go to central Colorado*. Exactly where Leadville is. I feel the whole dream, too good to be true, shattering inside me.

"What's radiation?" I ask.

"I'm not sure, maybe it's dangerous?" Dusty scratches his head. "I heard there was a great dam called Hoover, a wonder of the world, Linda said, somewhere in Nevada. They got their electricity in the old days right from the running water, like magic. But I never heard much about radiation."

He doesn't know a damned thing. "Keep the radio on," I tell him. "You hear me? Keep listening. Wait for it to come back."

"What are you going to say?" Dusty calls as I dart up the stairs.

There's no time to answer. I have to ask Russell about radiation, what it means. I don't have to tell him why I'm asking. I can wait to see if it's really something to be afraid of.

The rain cuts like frozen daggers as I cross the deck. I half-want to stop and peer out at the horizon to see how big the ice on the water is, but it's too dark anyway. And the swells that I could barely feel below deck drop my gut out from under me as I enter the wheelhouse.

Despite the cold and the rising wind, Ernest and Russell look delighted to see me.

"By morning we could be on the outskirts of the city," Ernest says to Russell, who nods, holding Ernest's pipe. They've been celebrating. I think I see a bottle of liquor, but Ernest moves to block my view.

Russell knows me too well and immediately loses his smile. “What is it, Tanner?”

“What do you know about radiation?”

He looks dumbfounded. “Radiation?”

“I heard Dusty tell a story about it,” I lie. “Something about how they used to get power in the old days. They either used big dams, or they used radiation. But he doesn’t know anything more about what it is. I thought maybe you remembered.”

“Hey, calm down. Why are you breathing so hard?” Russell knows I’m lying. Ernest doesn’t, and he starts to tell a story about a place somewhere in Russia, across the world. He says a funny word—Pripyat. A story about an old ghost town. It was the radiation that did it. Killed everyone who lived close by. There are all these details that don’t make sense. The only word I understand is *exposure*. I know it all too well.

“You can’t see it.” Ernest folds his arms, his face somber. “It’s an invisible killer, but more deadly than anything else if you take too much of it.”

Russell must see the color draining from my face, but Ernest hasn’t noticed yet. He’s still buying my story—the random curiosity. Russell hands him the pipe and ushers me out into the icy rain. It stings, his words slicing right through me with it.

“What the hell’s going on?”

“Dusty left the radio on. We fell asleep but I woke up and the radio was talking. It was a man saying not to go to central Colorado, that there’s radiation.” I choke the words out. “It means we can’t go to Leadville, doesn’t it?”

I wait for him to say no, that it doesn’t mean that, but he runs right past me, like I’m a ghost all of a sudden. All my hope collapses as I chase him below deck.

When we enter the dry warmth, Voley and Dusty are at the table. Dusty grimaces. “The batteries are starting to go.”

Russell picks up the radio. “What else did it say?”

Dusty looks up, startled. “I haven’t heard anything.”

“You didn’t hear it?” Russell’s eyes go wide.

Dusty looks at me for guidance, but that’s enough for Russell. He knows it was only me who heard. We listen to painful static for another five minutes. Finally, footsteps come down the stairs. It's Ernest. He surveys us all crowded around the white noise.

"Well?" His face wrinkles. "Someone going to give me a clue?"

I tell him everything.

"Maybe you were dreaming," Russell says. He's reaching now. Part of him already believes me.

"I wasn't." I let him study my face to see I'm not lying. I can't say anything else. I have no evidence.

Ernest squints, deep in thought, and then his face lights up. "Lemmy worked as a lineman before the rain, monitoring power grids up and down the mountain zone. I bet he knows something."

He disappears, and in another minute he's back with Lemmy. Lemmy's already filled in, and he has a straight-faced verdict for us.

"There are no nuclear power plants in Colorado."

That's all he says, writing me off that fast. Lemmy's been kind to us, but I want to smack him because now everyone's written me off.

"Wait, no, I'm wrong. There was one." He perks up. "Called . . ." He stretches out into a long, paused thought. Finally, he comes back with a name that sets off a bomb in my head. "Fort Saint—"

I finish the sentence with him—"*Vrain.*"

"How'd you know that?" Russell spins, seriously alarmed for the first time since I told him what I heard.

"It's what they said on the radio."

"Impossible," Lemmy says. "The nuclear reactor was decommissioned a long time ago. Taken apart, all the radioactive components cut up and buried. Trust me, I—"

I can't stand it, so I cut him off. "You missed a word, they said it was called Old—*Old* Fort Saint Vrain. Was that part of the name?"

"No." Lemmy frowns in confusion. "Just Fort Saint Vrain, far's I recall."

Everything stops dead.

"How much radioactive material did they bury?" Ernest asks.

Lemmy shrugs. "I have no idea."

"No way they've got another nuclear plant built?" Russell turns to Lemmy now too for answers.

"I don't see how, not with the rain." Lemmy sounds cautious with his words. "My job was—I only worked power grids for a distributor. I don't know much about how the plants work. What's going on? Someone going to tell me what the broadcast really said?"

Ernest repeats my story for him.

"Sounds unlikely," Lemmy says. "Could be a ploy."

"I heard it," I say, almost in tears. And then, the radio crackles loudly. My spirit jumps because the white noise has disappeared, clear of any static now, ready for a voice to come in. Only it doesn't. Nothing comes. And instead, the radio dies completely. No more juice.

"What if *old* isn't part of the name?" The full message I heard comes back to me and I blurt it out. "The voice said the old Fort Saint Vrain nuclear fuel has leaked! Maybe they meant old fuel." Only Russell seems to understand me at first—that if Lemmy's right and they buried something with this radiation, the broadcast could have been referring to that. Old radiation that's come back to the surface. Something that could kill us all.

"No," Russell says without taking any time to consider it. "Can't be."

"We have to turn back," I argue. "It said *do not approach*, that everyone evacuated."

Russell looks away from me. It's too much to ask. He loves me, and he knows I'm serious, but with every ounce of his being he's denying me. He's wanted this for too long to hear reason.

"Tanner, we have to go. We finally made it here." For the first time, though, I have no doubt that he's dead wrong.

"You don't always know what's best for us!" I walk away to take a deep breath. "I won't go."

When I turn around, I see the realization sinking in on his face. That I'm going to be independent and stand my ground.

"Tan." He reaches out.

"You go then." It's hard, but I do my best to sound like I don't care what he does.

Ernest interrupts. "Tanner, if that's what you heard, it had to come from someone, right? Someone's still there." He nods at Lemmy. "I agree with you. I think it's a deterrent. Hell, we'd set something up like that if we had a safe home and wanted to keep people away."

"It was a fucking recording," I say. "The voice repeated itself. I'm sure it did. I heard it start over. It was no one. A phantom. A recording, nothing more. Leftover."

For the first time, they all look like they're considering the warning was real.

"They evacuated," I go on. "That's what the recording said."

No one speaks, like they don't know how to handle it. It's the most absurd possibility because the only exposure we've had to deal with before now is the rain and the mindless face eaters. Anything more than that is too unfair. Especially now, when we're at the doorstep of salvation. Russell says all that with his stare, telling me he can't let it go.

"You don't have to go," he says. "I'll scout first, take the motorboat in. You, and anyone else who wants, can stay here until I see it's safe." He seems to grow calm as he comes up with this compromise.

Ernest doesn't reply. He's seriously considering it.

Lemmy volunteers. "I'll go, too."

I feel only partly relieved because I don't want it to be Russell. *Send Clint, send Lemmy, send Ernest. Anyone instead of you, Russell.* But I don't say it. I'm frozen inside. Tortured. It's like what Russell said used to happen with the gods. When you weren't in their favor, they toyed with you like a game of chess. Bring you so close, every time, just to screw you in the end.

A giant swell rocks the boat, like we've fallen into a trough at a bad angle. Something bangs loudly against the hull.

Russell eyes the wall. "The motorboat."

"Christ, Clint, what the hell are you doing?" Ernest stomps above deck. In a moment the ship is gliding up and down like normal again, but I hear a new sound. It's the whining wind, cutting through the ropes above.

"Something nasty's blowing in." Lemmy follows Ernest up, leaving me alone with Dusty and Russell.

"Let Lemmy go," I plead.

Russell doesn't say no, but he's already decided that's the answer. I know from his face.

"Listen, radiation doesn't kill you right away. You have to be around it for a long time. And that might've been an old recording, Tanner." He touches my arm. "Hell, maybe a hoax to keep people away, face eaters. Trust me. We'll scout it out, and then we'll come back. If it's okay, then we'll all go in together."

"Russell, they said do not approach! We can go south, anywhere else," I argue. But whatever triggered him to listen to me before, to turn the boat around and save Dusty's life, doesn't work now. It's me or Leadville in my mind, and to him, I'm just panicking. A scared little girl.

"Everything's going to be okay," he pats my shoulder.

"It's not." I pull away, glaring. "You always know what's best, but not this time. Go if you have to. I'm staying here."

His eyes fall like he's wounded, and I know he's fighting his desire to see the old world, the one he left behind so many years ago, the one I'll never know. It's too strong for him to accept that I'm right.

I want to tell him what I've realized—that Dusty and Voley need me now. That he's taught me everything he knows, but now it's my turn to protect the ones I love, because they've never survived alone before. They don't know how, but I do, because he's shown me. He's given me that. I hug him, and it feels like goodbye.

"I'm going to come back, Tan," he says, but his eyes are watering.

I almost lash out, tell him no, he won't, but instead I focus on holding back my own tears. No crying.

After a long time, I let go of him.

"Get that thing working again, you hear me? Whatever you have to do." Russell points at the radio as Clint comes down the stairs.

Dusty nods, even though he knows it's impossible without new batteries. He takes the radio to the bunk and starts fiddling with it anyway.

36

ROOK

18 YEARS, 10 MONTHS, 17 DAYS

MONDAY

Rook blinked, adjusting to the daylight spilling over the apartment walls. Unable to feel his legs, he looked down. Snow covered his lap, new flakes still drifting in from the broken window. Why did he have to wake up again? In his dream, he'd been warm. Luce had been calling to him.

Then it came again, startling him. Her voice.

"Are you in there?"

"I'm . . ." The words caught in his throat.

"Rook! Can you unlock the door?"

He swallowed painfully. "I'm tied to the radiator."

A loud cracking sounded, and then again, until a fracture split the center of the door. An axe blade struck through and rocked free, splinters spilling into the room. The hole grew larger until Rook could see Luce on the other side. Finally, her foot smashed it down.

"My hands." He inched his stiff muscles forward.

"Hold still." She maneuvered behind him. "Okay, pull."

There was a popping as several plastic zip ties fell onto the snow. He was free.

The first thing he wanted was to hold her, but he could barely stand. And he'd soiled himself again.

"I'm disgusting." He took in the rancid smell and looked away in shame.

"Come on." She pulled a chair close and helped him sit.

He brought his blood-encrusted hands into his lap, staring with horror at the awful red cuts circling his wrists, and began to cry.

"Can you stick your leg out?" One by one, she worked his limbs back and forth until the feeling began to return.

Scooping some snow into his mouth to loosen his throat, he tried to speak. "Lawrence told him I took the log. He had me followed. Marrow's gone."

"I know." Luce's wet eyes blinked, her disheveled hair hanging down past the dark rings around her eyes. "That asshole quarantined everyone in the power plant and then took off. I came as soon as I could get out."

Hearing her voice again strengthened him. They were alive and together, a miracle. He slowly stood. Everything felt intact. He did a slow jumping jack to warm up, then another.

"We need to get you back to the power plant. The generator kicked in after the power died, so there's still heat there, and our food."

As she took his hand, his excitement at being reunited began to diminish. The plan had failed, and it had been his fault. What was left now? *Survival*, he thought. *As long as Luce is still with me, we will survive this.*

The snow was falling heavily outside. Fresh powder blended the road into the surrounding terrain, the lab building impossible to discern in the whiteout, but they trudged on, pausing for breath every few minutes, a terrible burning lighting up Rook's thighs as he pulled each foot from the snow. Luce forged ahead, carrying the axe. Each time he bent over to catch his breath, she turned and waited.

They followed her tracks all the way back to the plant. A rush of warm air hit as they made it inside, their feet clanking over grated floors, down a hallway into a large open-ceilinged room filled with panicked voices and dirty faces. Some were huddled in small groups, and others squatted in corners. With relief, Rook saw there were no white suits and no guns. Marrow hadn't left a single security guard.

Nor did he see Cleo, Gene, Jonathan, or any of his former aides.

They must have been among the selected. And we are the ones left to die, he thought as he listened to their tense chatter. *No, to survive.* His father would have refused to lose hope, would have found a way to help everyone live through this. If he had something to eat, some warmth and rest, he could be of help too, but his body ached terribly.

"I need to lie down for a few minutes." He took off his jacket to use as a pillow and lay on the floor.

"I'm so glad you're okay." Luce knelt beside him and squeezed his hand.

"I'm hungry." Rook closed his eyes, the heat making him drowsy. It felt amazing to stretch his legs and arms, to know Luce was there. In a moment, he was asleep.

A SHARP PAIN in his throat woke him. He swallowed, feeling a sore lump.

Please, don't get sick now . . .

He opened his eyes to a can of fruit on the ground by his head, already cracked open. Sitting up, he devoured it, the syrup soothing his throat.

Luce walked over. "You're finally up. How do you feel?"

"A little better. Thank you."

She knelt and spoke softly. "We have to figure out what we're going to do next."

Rook sighed. "I think we should help here. At least try. If things turn ugly, we can still go to East Harbor—"

"Rook?" a familiar voice interrupted.

"Dina," Rook spoke hoarsely, immediately recognizing his old friend.

Her face was drawn with worry, but she bore the same intimidating expression he remembered. "Looks like you weren't important enough to be chosen either."

"Did you know anything?" he asked as Luce helped him to his feet.

She frowned. "Not a thing. I guess where Marrow's going, he doesn't need someone to run a power plant."

"Fuck him." Rook shook his head. "We don't need him."

"Luce, I came over to ask if you'd come with me." Dina gestured toward a large group gathering on the other side of the room. "The snowstorm's over, and I'm going outside with some of the others to check for damage."

"Of course." Luce nodded.

"I'll meet you by the door." Dina started toward the crowd.

Luce turned to Rook. "You should stay inside, stay warm."

"Not if you're going." He swallowed, pain slicing down his throat. It seemed he'd traded his head injury for an infection.

She eyed him warily as he rubbed his Adam's apple. "What's wrong?

"Just a cold, I think." He stretched his arms, testing the soreness in his wrists. "Did you see her eyes?" He leaned in. "She's using Red."

"Everyone here is, except us. We still have to work together."

She was right. Scanning the room, Rook spotted a pile of canned goods and boxes in one corner. "Is our food for the trip in that pile, too?"

Luce sighed. "When the guards started rounding everyone up, I was still waiting for you on the road. They brought us here, and after they left, Ed made everyone dump their food, so it's all mixed together now. I still have the map and the coordinates in one of our bags, though."

Rook saw his former friend, arms crossed, guarding the food. "He thinks he's in charge?"

"Yeah, he does. I get a bad feeling from him."

"Me, too." Rook winced at the sting in his throat. A heavy, ominous sensation fell over him as he spotted a row of Red bottles by Ed's feet. His heart sinking, Rook realized that even Marrow must have had a bad feeling about Ed, to leave him and take Gene instead. *Christ, what'll stop them from taking too much now?*

Then something even more terrifying popped into Rook's head, Marrow's words before he left: "*The radiation will be everywhere.*" "Luce, the radiation. How bad is it?"

She frowned. "A lot higher than it usually is. I'm worried the storm might have broken a cask loose."

"That evil son of a bitch knew the storm would do this." Rook unzipped the pocket of his rain suit and found his Geiger counter still there. Pulling it out, he read the number on the screen. "Point-two-seven. What's yours at?"

She looked at her feet. "I lost it."

Rook's stomach dropped. "You're kidding . . ."

"When Marrow gave the order, security escorted me here immediately, and I dropped it. They wouldn't let me go back."

"What was it the last time you looked?"

She hesitated.

"Luce, tell me!" Panic surged as he remembered what she'd told him: sickness started at just over four sieverts, with a 50 percent mortality rate within the month. If she absorbed that much . . .

"Almost two," she said softly.

"Two!"

"It was *under* two."

He grabbed her arm. "We should all go to the apartments."

"The heat's off, we'll freeze," she refused, stone-faced. "This is the only building with a generator."

"There's furniture there. We'll burn it for warmth. The radiation's too high here!"

"Okay, okay. Let's see what the compound looks like first, now that the snow's stopped. I need to see if the fuel site is damaged. We'll decide after that."

They walked to where the crowd was congregating.

"Listen up!" Ed yelled with a raspy voice. He waved his hands quickly. The room quieted. "We're going to walk the compound and check the damage. Who are the electricians?"

Four people raised their hands.

"I need you to restore the main power."

"We tried already," one of them answered.

"Well, try harder!" Ed barked. "The rest of you—check all the rooms again. Food, Red, blankets, clothing, medicine, anything, pile it over there. Understood?" Some replied affirmatively and some nodded, but most stared blankly, as if the drug had numbed them to the horror of their situation. "We'll be right back."

The group divided itself, about fifteen staying and ten following Ed outside. Dawn's cloudy light reflected upon pools of slush and snow stretching in each direction. Ed led them toward the lab, but Rook followed Luce and Dina as they diverted to the fuel site.

In less than five minutes, they could see them: two pearl-colored fuel casks, hundreds of feet from their moorings, squashed against the rear fence of the power plant. One of the casks had a long crack, its dark uranium guts split open and washing in meltwater. A stream ran under it, all the way to the road's gutters.

Dina raised her Geiger counter. "No closer."

Rook watched the numbers spin rapidly higher. "We *cannot* stay at the power plant."

"He's right, especially with our cumulative radiation higher than everyone else's." Luce turned to Dina. "Yours can't be that far behind mine."

Dina frowned at the face of her device.

"It's not. I'm at point-eighty-eight."

Behind them, Rook watched Ed's group maneuvering slowly up the main road.

"We should stay together. Let's catch them." Whatever was salvaged, Rook needed to make sure Ed rationed it fairly.

They caught up where the cafeteria should have been. Ed's group was standing by the walls of its foundation, crumbled into the snow. Steel beams poked up dangerously from mounds of debris. A layer of ice shone on what had once been part of the floor. Broken chairs and tables were scattered, half-buried under the collapsed roof.

"It's all gone." Rook looked in disbelief at the ruins, then walked farther to see if any trace of the greenhouse remained. There was nothing. With horror, the truth crystallized. Whatever remained in the apartments, the power plant, and the lab, that would be it. There would be nothing else left to eat.

The wind picked up, and something stung Rook's arm.

He squinted upward. "Hail." The warm air masses from the hurricane were gone, the cooler air sinking, bringing back the cold. It wouldn't be long before the snow started again.

Ed approached, grim-faced. "Nothing here. Let's go back."

Others began circling around, repeating what was obvious. There would be little left to eat.

"The radiation's too high in the power plant," Rook warned him. Though Ed was as evil as Marrow, he didn't deserve to die. None of them did. "We need to go to the apartments."

"There are no lights on out there," one of the plant workers said, pointing to the darkened buildings in the distance. "No power. We should stay where it's warm."

"We can build a fire." Rook struggled to raise his voice, looking to Dina and Luce for support. "If we stay in the power plant, the radiation will kill us."

"He's right." Dina pointed to the plant. "A fuel cask's split open against the back fence."

"How long would it take for radiation to hurt us?" Ed blinked rapidly.

"At current levels, and without previous heavy exposure like Luce and I have, maybe a few weeks to see the first effects," Dina said firmly. "But once it starts, you'll get sick very fast."

Ed worked his jaw back and forth. "I still think we need to stay where there's electricity and food."

Rook threw his arms up in frustration. "Fine! Stay—" He lost his voice for a moment. "Stay and die. We'll take our share of food and go ourselves." The impulse he had felt to help these people survive, like his father had tried to do in Canvas City, began to slip away. Ed's drug-riddled glare reminded him too much of Gerry.

"Let's discuss it with the others, okay? Back at the plant." Ed sounded agitated, waving for everyone to follow him. Rook hung his head, desperate to go to the apartments now, but they needed their food. There was no choice but to follow them back.

Inside, everyone was gathered around the pile of supplies, which had grown slightly larger. Next to the bottles of Red, Rook spotted a small clear orange pill bottle. Thinking of his throat, he ducked down, and scanned the label.

Antibiotics.

"Hold up! No one takes anything until I say." Ed stepped in front of him, then gestured for quiet. "Listen up, Yasper family."

Voices died to silence as Ed explained the condition of the compound, Dina adding details about the radiation.

A tall, thick-bodied blond man replied first. Rook had never seen him before. "What she's saying is we'll be safe here in the heat, at least for a few weeks."

"Unless the cask rolls closer, or more break free," Dina warned.

"In my opinion, we won't be here long enough for the radiation to hurt us. My gut tells me that Marrow will come back for us in a few days," Ed said calmly.

Rook watched incredulously as the others nodded in agreement. "Guys, he's not coming back. Marrow's gone."

Ed shook his head. "I gave him two decades of my life. He would never leave his family behind."

"I talked to him, Ed, right before he left. He doesn't care about us!" Rook's throat felt like it was on fire. "He took Gene and the drug with him. He doesn't need you anymore!"

"Bullshit." Ed recoiled sharply, as if stung. Then, surveying the plaintive faces, he spoke with calm conviction. "He took the fleet into deep water so the ships wouldn't break up in the harbor. He'll be back."

A few cheers went up.

"You're delusional," Rook muttered.

"You all know the situation." Ed's face reddened, his once pudgy cheeks now gaunt, pulled down in a scowl. "I'll let you decide for yourselves. Raise your hand if you want to stay here for the time being."

One by one, every hand rose.

It was as Rook had feared. How could he have hoped to do what his father had failed at? No matter how well-intentioned he was, it wouldn't be enough to break the spell that Marrow and the drug had over them.

"It's decided," Ed declared. "We stay."

Rook had had enough. He gestured to Luce to get their bags, then took a step toward the food pile.

The brawny blond man stepped forward, arms raised to block him.

"No! The last thing we need is fighting." Ed pushed the man's tattooed arms down. "We'll find out, one way or the other, here at the power plant. And you in the apartments." Ed's beady-eyed gaze fell upon Luce and Dina, who stood apart from the crowd beside Rook.

Rook took a step back. "I don't want trouble, I just want what's mine."

"None of this is yours. It belongs to the company." Ed crossed his arms, glancing quickly around at the faces watching them. "But you were a good employee, and a friend. You can fill one bag. If you change your minds, and wish to come back to us, the food will be here."

A few people softly cursed them for robbing supplies as Rook knelt to fill the bag.

Ed raised his hands for silence. "It's okay, it's only one bag."

Rook quickly threw in boxes of dry grains and crackers and cans until the bag was full. He spotted the orange bottle of antibiotics and quickly snatched it.

Ed touched his boot to Rook's forearm. "The medicine stays with the group."

"I'm getting sick." Rook looked up at his old friend for sympathy but was met with a stony glare.

"There's only one bottle of medicine, and it stays with the majority. You can take a bottle of Red."

Dina reached for one immediately.

"No," Rook whispered. "Food's what's going to keep us alive."

"I'll get sick." Dina's voice cracked with desperation.

Rook sighed. "Just don't take more than you need."

He shouldered the satchel, and they walked down the hallway to the exit.

Rook turned around at the door. "We'll be back when we need more."

"The only supplies leaving this building are what's in there," Ed spoke coldly, pointing to Rook's bag.

I had two, Rook wanted to argue, but Luce grabbed him.

"We can't help these people," she whispered in his ear. "We have to go to East Harbor."

But we have half the food we had before, Rook thought. And now Dina was with them. Before he could say anything, though, Ed and the blond man, now holding a length of steel pipe, escorted them out.

"Good luck," Ed said and quickly shut the door.

THEY TRUDGED THROUGH THE SNOW to Luce's apartment building, the closer of the two, and dug out the door. A layer of ice coated the first floor where floodwater had busted through, but other than broken windows, the second floor appeared undamaged.

Rook eyed the common room. A few small sofas and two long tables stood along the walls. "Let's set up here."

"We should keep the food in one of the rooms where we can lock it up." Luce looked around nervously. Rook agreed, and they carried the bags to an empty apartment, then split up to bring back mattresses, chairs, and a few steel trashcans to make a fire. When the work was done, Luce took Rook's hand. "Come with me a second."

Rook glanced at Dina, half-asleep on a mattress already, fiddling with her bottle of Red. He left her and followed Luce up the stairwell to the top floor. She led him to room A41.

"This is my room."

The walls were plastered with her drawings, over and over again the same beautiful landscape: a river switchbacking down a wide range of grassy mountains, the sky filled with puffy clouds. A tremendous sense of melancholy crushed down on Rook as he looked at each one, until he felt Luce tugging him toward the bed.

"It's my stars!" he exclaimed. They were hanging right above her pillow. Tears pooled in his eyes as she pulled him gently around his waist. He pushed his face into her shoulder, all he could do to keep from crying.

"I'm sorry." His voice muffled against her skin.

"None of this is your fault."

"I came so close . . ." He thought of Marrow's offer, and it seemed like such a mistake to have refused it now. "It's cold. We better build a fire."

"I know." She lifted his face to hers. "I just wanted a minute alone with you."

If only he could make love to her, but his body was too chilled and achy, his damned cold on top of everything else. He kissed her neck anyway.

"I don't want sex," she spoke softly. "This is just as intimate."

Rook closed his eyes and tried to blank his mind, to think only of her presence.

She's with you now. Let that be enough . . .

Luce kissed gently along his jaw. The guilt of his failure flickered away just for a moment as she locked eyes with him.

"I love you."

37

TANNER

Russell finds me in the wheelhouse after his shift and throws his arms around me.

"Lemmy and I aren't going far, just deep enough inland to check for buildings, see if people are living there. If it's not a ghost town, we'll know there's no radiation problem." He tries to put me at ease. "The water's shallow so we're taking the motorboat in."

I don't have the energy to argue with him. "You trust Ernest to protect us while you're gone?" I step back, folding my arms.

"I do." He holds my gaze, unblinking.

"I can help you pack, at least." It's the only truce I can offer right now.

We carry supplies, some guns and knives, food, a bag of clean clothes, and a fresh tarp to Lemmy in the motorboat.

The cold rain prevents any sweat, but I feel exhausted when Ernest approaches us. "The weather's easing up. You should be good to leave at first light. There's nothing to do now but bring us in a bit closer."

Russell nods as I take in how huge the mountains are now, a long lead of water digging between them, growing narrower and narrower, riddled with blocks of ice. Something about how big it all is fills me with dread.

I look away and tap Ernest. "If you don't start dinner, I will."

He chuckles and pats my back. "You sure know how to make a man cook."

AFTER DINNER, Ernest, Russell, Clint, and Lemmy leave to look over the supplies in the motorboat one more time. I sit alone with Dusty and Voley, fighting off an urge to bring up the awful feeling I've been carrying since I saw all the ice crowding that little river into the mountains.

"Good boy." I trace the white stripe running down Voley's snout. He looks up, his sweet eyes closing in anticipation of the next pet. Each time my hand slides over his fur, his ears go down, popping up again just before my hand returns.

"Our daddy Russell has lost his mind." I tickle his ear.

Dusty jumps up. "I just thought of something. Maybe that GPS has batteries in it?"

He rummages around until he finds the duffel bag from the ghost boats. The GPS is still inside. I walk over and watch him play with it.

"There's an input hole. It must be a rechargeable device. That means we're out of luck." His finger runs along the edges and I feel my hope sink with his. "I'll try the old batteries one more time." He starts to put the GPS back in the bag.

"Wait, what's that say?" I reach for it. "Beneath the screen?"

He pulls it out again, studying it, and suddenly his forehead wrinkles. I can't tell what it is—from this angle I can only see the blank gray screen.

"Did you read this?" he asks, his voice dropping.

Slowly my eyes scan the small print beneath the screen. "Gamma Dose Rate," I read aloud. "What's it mean?"

"I don't know." He bites his lip. "I know GPS means Global Positioning System, not GDR."

I stare at the words. There's nothing else to indicate what the device is. Right away I realize, before Dusty tells me what he's thinking. "Maybe it has to do with the radiation." I almost trip on my way to the stairs.

"Where are you going?" Dusty asks, but I'm fueled with adrenaline and rush above deck.

I try to calm myself as I cross the boat, remembering to speak slowly. I spot Lemmy near the stern, inspecting a supply bag.

He looks up. "Hey, girl. You alright?"

I hold the device in front of him.

"Where'd you get that?"

"In the face eater boats. It was with the map."

He takes it into his hands and holds it up for better light.

"Do you know what it is?"

"It's a Geiger counter, I think. It records radiation levels."

My body shudders as I take it back. "Tell Russell to come see me when he's done on the motorboat," I say and hurry below deck.

"I can't believe it." Dusty stares when I tell him. "Do you think it means that the warning was real?"

"It has to." I fidget, impatient for the sound of footsteps coming down.

It takes a long time for Russell to finish up, and Dusty and I lie together on the bunk, waiting. He massages my head to keep me calm, and Voley manages to wiggle between us. It's stupid, but as I drift off, it feels like I'm surrounded by my family.

When I wake up, Russell is standing by the bunk. No one else is there. I can tell by the look on his face—Lemmy already told him.

"You can't go." I jump out of bed to grab the radiation device from the duffel bag.

"I already knew what it was," he speaks softly.

"What?" I spin around, the answer written in his frown. "We're supposed to trust each other with everything!" I kick the bag across the floor. "How could you? How could you keep that from me?"

His head hangs. "I made a promise that I would keep you safe. And that's what I'm going to do, by going to check things first."

"Even when you know it has to be true?" I pull the device out of the bag. "This thing is for radiation, and it was in those boats!"

"If it was just you, maybe I wouldn't go. We could stay on the ship, keep sailing. Find somewhere new. But there's something else." His face sours as if something's wrong with his stomach.

My heart quickens as he scans the cabin like he doesn't want anyone to see. Then he takes the thing from me and turns it upside down.

"I don't see anything. What?"

"Feel here." He pushes my fingers along an abrasion in the smooth plastic. "Read that."

My eyes take in the small cuts etched into the bottom.

ROOK WALLACE

I shake my head at him. "I don't know what that means."

"Wallace," he says matter-of-factly, like I should understand.

I take in the letters again.

"Oh my god." I hadn't even thought of it. No one uses last names anymore. I don't even know what mine was, if I ever had one. "*Your* last name is Wallace!"

"Do you see why I have to check what's there?" His eyes are glassy and he looks at the ground like he's ashamed.

"Rook Wallace?" I feel shattered. My voice shakes. "Your brother? Why the hell didn't you tell me?"

It makes sense suddenly, why Russell was talking to Ernest about his family as if they were alive. I want to hit him, but the way his face is screwed up, it looks like I already have. He stares at me like he's expecting me to forgive him.

"I grew up in Colorado." His voice becomes hopeful. "It's a sign, Tanner. Maybe he's alive. I have to go."

I try to find words. All this time he's kept their names from me—his daughter, his fiancée, his parents, his brother. The worst comes into my mind right away.

"What if he was on those boats?"

"I thought of that." He leans in and holds me. "Those were face eaters, not my brother."

I want to tell him he's wrong because we can't know who was on those boats, but he's never looked so fragile before, like whatever I say next is going to rip him apart.

"Okay." My voice muffles against his chest. "I understand."

"Ernest has a flare gun. I'm going to use it to let you know as soon as I do. If Leadville's abandoned, or looks like it's had a radiation accident, we're turning back right away. We won't be near it long enough for it to hurt us. I'll send the flare up, so you know. You'll see it from the boat, you'll know I'm safe. You'll know Leadville is no good, and we're starting over. Right here, together. Okay?"

"What if it is there?" My hope balances on a thread, the thought that Leadville might still be real, Russell's brother still alive.

"I'll turn around either way, I promise." He stands back, holding my shoulder and brushing a tear from his cheek. "One flare, it's no good. Two, it is. When you see it, you'll know we're headed back, and you'll know if it's there."

A rush of calm sweeps through me. This is about him now, finding out whether he has to kill some part of himself that's been stuck for almost nineteen years, the belief that his brother is alive. All this time I believed in Leadville for the future, he's been believing for the past.

"You promise you'll send the flares and turn back either way?"

"When I lost my daughter—" He clears his throat. "When I lost Audrie, and Elizabeth, my fiancée, I meant to end my life. But I found you. If there was a chance I wouldn't get back to you, if I had one shred of doubt, I wouldn't go."

"I want it to be real so bad." I squeeze him.

"Whatever happens, it'll be okay." His voice is strong again. "I don't show it, but I'm happy you found something you need with Dusty. If Leadville turns out to be wrong, then I'll have found the last thing I need, too."

I believe him with all my heart again. "I love you."

He holds me tightly. "Love you, too, kiddo."

38
ROOK

18 YEARS, 10 MONTHS, 19 DAYS
WEDNESDAY

Opening his eyes, Rook looked around the common room. Luce lay asleep on the mattress beside him. The fires still smoldered in steel trash cans by the open windows. Dina was gone.

What had that noise been?

Careful not to wake Luce, he slid out of the blankets. The sting of throat pain was joined by flashing aches throughout his body now, his cold having worsened over the last few days, delaying their escape to East Harbor. He'd wanted to go anyway because food would run out quickly, even faster now that Dina had agreed to join them, but Luce refused, unwilling to risk traveling through the snow and into the cold waters while he was so sick.

The noise came again, shouting, somewhere downstairs. *Dina.* Adrenaline muted his achy muscles and cleared the fog from his head. Grabbing the axe, he crept downstairs.

A wash of light filtered in from the lobby. Dina's silhouette stood at the front door.

"Dina!" Rook ran up to her.

She had both hands pressed against it. "He's trying to get in!"

Through the crack in the door, Rook caught a glimpse of a husky man in a tan rain suit, breathing hard.

"Please help me," his raspy voice pleaded. "There's nowhere else to go."

Rook took in the wide face, ice-frosted eyebrows, and thick beard, but he didn't recognize the man. "What happened?"

"Ed tried to kill me. They're going crazy."

"Christ, let him in." Rook pushed Dina off the door.

"He didn't bring anything!" She scowled.

"I don't care, let him in!" Rook winced at having to raise his voice.

"We have little enough as it is."

She was right, but he couldn't turn a frightened man away to die. Pushing the door open, the man squeezed inside.

Dina stood back. "Why didn't you bring your share with you?"

"He tried to tie me up," the man panted, his dark glassy eyes screwed up with fear. "He was going to shoot me. I had to run."

Rook's stomach dropped. "Shoot you?"

"He found a rifle in the lockers. Him and a few others have completely lost it, taking way too much Red. He tied some people up on the third floor—"

"Tied them up for what?" Dina's voice quivered.

"They stopped believing Marrow was coming back . . . argued about how fast the Red supplies were being used."

"Jesus Christ." Rook waited for the rosy-faced man to catch his breath.

Dina turned to Rook. "We've got hardly anything ourselves. What if more people come? We'll run out in no time." She looked suspiciously at the man. "You didn't bring any Red either?"

He shook his head. "Ed has control of everything."

Dina groaned.

"It's okay." Rook stood up straight, raising his palms. "Come up to the fire."

At the top of the stairs, Luce was awake and wide-eyed, a chair in her hands, poised to attack.

"No." Rook grabbed the chair. "He's not a threat."

Luce stepped back in confusion as the frightened man followed Rook and Dina into the common room.

"I'm Wayne." The man stood cautiously behind Rook and repeated what had happened, the look on Luce's face growing more distraught with each sentence.

Dina sulked over to a mattress near the fire. "I'm not giving up any of my food or Red."

"I'll share," Luce finally spoke.

"Me, too," Rook agreed, looking at Dina. "We're stronger as four." His words did nothing to shake the anxiety from her face. Rook wasn't sure he believed them either.

"Thank you." Wayne bowed his head. "I'll go into withdrawal without Red."

Dina grunted loudly.

"He can have what would have been our share," Luce said sharply.

"And if more come?" Dina snapped. "We need to decide now!"

"We let them in," Luce said.

"It was their decision to stay, to be radiated!" Dina yelled. "We warned them."

"It's not the radiation, it's Ed. You want us to act just like Marrow?" Rook's heart rate rose, making him dizzy.

"That's different." Dina shook her head. "We didn't have a choice. They did. They chose to stay." Dina fell silent as Wayne approached the fire.

"Wayne, did Ed search the lab yet?" Rook asked.

"Yeah, he didn't find anything. We went to South Harbor, looking for boats. There were none left." Wayne frowned.

Rook signaled Luce into the hallway, out of earshot. "What if Ed checks East Harbor?"

"He won't," she whispered. "It's too far a hike, unless they decide to leave the island."

"I'll be better in a few days." He took a deep, painful breath. "Then we have to go."

"What about Wayne?" She flashed a look of compassion.

"I haven't had time to think about it. He was scared for his life, I had to let him in."

"It wouldn't be right to leave him. We should all go, together."

"Yeah. We'll tell him the plan, and then he can decide for himself." Rook knew in his heart that she was right, but having so little food scared him. It was half of what they originally had, divided by four now instead of two. And Dina had a point. What if more people came? He felt faint, slightly nauseous with anxiety and illness.

Luce seemed to sense how overwhelmed he was. "Your only job is to rest. Don't think about anything else until you're better. I'm going to take care of us."

The conversation behind them grew louder.

"You think he'll hurt them?" Dina was asking Wayne.

"He lost his mind. I confronted him, told him we were on our own now. That's when they tried to tie me up."

"We'll figure something out." Rook staggered back to the mattress, light-headed. But they already had a plan. And he was the one keeping them from leaving.

Rook took Luce's advice to stay in bed, and after three days passed, he no longer had a choice. Whatever was infecting his throat and chest had only grown stronger, and the nights became unbearable. He woke up constantly, a sweaty and smelly mess, too hot and then too cold, burning his feet trying to stay warm, too weak to walk around.

Time passed in a haze. Luce comforted him around the clock, but his misery only worsened with the guilt that he was delaying them from leaving, and he was too much of a coward to tell Luce to go without him. If he didn't get better soon, they wouldn't have enough food to ration for the trip over open water.

He woke to voices in the middle of the night. It sounded like an argument.

"It's not my fault," Wayne was saying.

"Well, it's not me!" Dina grew louder.

Rook jerked up from his sweat-soaked pillow. "What is it?" A wave of nausea buckled him back down.

"Someone's taking extra food." Luce put her hand on his head.

"Christ, which one of you is it?" Rook rasped. "Do you want to kill us all?"

Wayne and Dina cast suspicious glances at each other. Their faces, like Luce's and his own, were caked with soot.

"How do we know it's not you, sneaking him extra because he's sick?" Wayne accused Luce.

"He's hardly been able to eat!"

Despite his body's protests, Rook dragged himself out of bed and walked to the food room. There were only three cans of food and one bag of rice left.

He stormed back into the room, but his breath snagged, and he bent over, hacking.

Luce reached out to him gently. "It's too cold to be up. Lie down with me."

"Thieves," Rook seethed as he got back under the blankets. Luce warmed him, slowly rocking back and forth. "It's my fault," he whispered to her. "I should be paying better attention."

She kissed his cheek. "It's not your fault. You're sick."

Sweat rolled into Rook's eyes. "I feel like I'm suffocating." He nestled against her chest. "If I die, I want you to be prepared. You have to try to go without me. Okay?"

She quieted him with a kiss, and he fell asleep.

THE NEXT MORNING Rook forced himself to try walking, but as he reached the window, he coughed up green phlegm, neon against the snow coating the sill. In a haze, he struggled back to bed.

The next thing he remembered, Luce was whispering in his ear, "I'm going to look for medicine and food."

"No—please stay with me." He felt like a child, afraid to die alone.

She looked sad, but her voice was firm. "I have to."

"No." He stretched his arms out to hold her.

"Fine. I'll stay. Get some sleep."

WHEN HE WOKE, his arms were empty.

"Where'd she go?" He frantically scanned the room. He stood up too quickly, dizziness returning stronger than ever.

"She went to look for food," Dina said softly from across the room.

"How long ago?"

"She's been gone since yesterday." Dina sounded sad, as if Luce were never coming back.

"Yesterday?" His temper flared, at Luce for lying to him, at himself for being sick and sleeping an entire day and night, and at Dina and Wayne for not going instead of Luce. "Why her? Why not you, or you!"

"My radiation level is just as high." Dina sulked, glancing at Wayne, who looked away, fear scrunching his face at the suggestion of going back outside.

Christ. She would have gone toward the power plant. Rook forced himself up. They looked on dumbly as he took the axe and left.

Desperation burned through his dizziness as he made his way, marching through blinding snow. He slogged on until the lab appeared, and very faintly beyond that, the shadow of the power plant. Stopping for breath, his strength suddenly evaporated. The achiness bent him to his knees, and a dark premonition began to strangle him: he was going to collapse and be buried by the snow. No one would even find his body.

Turn back or you'll die, you'll never see her again.

"Please, look for her," he scolded the other two weakly when he'd finally made it back. They dropped their heads, neither saying a word, and he collapsed on the mattress.

LUCE WAS THERE the moment he opened his eyes, like a miracle, the last bits of daylight catching snowflakes in her dark hair as she bent down over a bag, pulling out boxes of grain.

"Luce . . ." He tried to sit up.

"Antibiotics." She held out an orange bottle of pills, smiling wearily, her face bright red. Her hands looked frostbitten.

It was painful to talk, but Rook made sure she knew he was angry. "You said you wouldn't leave."

"There was a first aid kit in my work shed. Food, too." She pulled a pot of water close. "Take the pills."

"The fuel site!" Rook coughed. "You were there overnight?"

"I was trapped." Luce glared at Wayne and Dina, who looked away. "That blond guy walked around the perimeter of the power plant all night long, with a sawblade in his hands. I could hear him whistling. I had to wait."

"But, Luce, your—"

"Shut up and take them!"

He put two pills in his mouth and swallowed, desperately trying to push away his worst fear, the image from the nightmare he'd had the night they'd made the snow angels.

"There's enough food for another couple days." Luce sounded on the verge of exhaustion as she slowly sorted through boxes and cans on the floor, Dina and Wayne crowding close to watch.

Then, right in the middle of standing, Luce froze. The fire crackled, and Rook waited patiently for her to move. Her face wrinkled with pain, and she bit her lip.

"What's wrong?" He scooted close.

She answered with a cough, her hand covering her mouth just in time. When she dropped her palm, blood dripped to the floor.

"Baby." He put his arms around her and helped her onto the mattress. "Lie down."

"I'm just catching what you had," she moaned.

"No one eats anything!" Rook glared at Dina and Wayne as he stumbled off to hide the new food.

He returned and lay down with Luce, studying the red rings under her puffy eyes, the bright pink-and-white hue of her skin, angry at himself. "How do you feel?"

His thoughts worked quickly, rationalizing. Sure, she had some radiation poisoning, but if she'd caught his cold on top of it, that would explain why she looked so bad. He thought of her Geiger counter, now lost. There was no way to know if she'd breached the lethal threshold. He told himself that as long as her dose wasn't too high, she would recover.

She nodded, narrowing her eyes. "I saw something on my way back. Something in the snow."

He fought back the urge to scream at her for being so stupid, for going anywhere near the fuel site, but she was shivering, and he bit his lip instead, trying to contain his fears.

His cold and his earlier nightmare together felt like a great weight pressing on his chest, suffocating him. "You're taking some of these antibiotics." He withdrew two pills for her, wiping sweat from her forehead before it dripped into her eyes. "Can you eat something for me?"

"No." She made a face.

"Take them." Thoughts swirled in Rook's head, all of them too dark to speak, as he forced her to swallow the pills.

39
TANNER

In my dream I see the snow. Falling like angel tears, carpeting everything in white. I've never seen something so pure. Everything's supposed to be gray and brown and sad, but this place is unstained and unworn. At peace.

I slowly wake up and take in the hills and the distant mountains, all white without a trace of the muddy brown. The urge to run through the snow is too much. I hold my head to the sky and open my mouth. Where are the others?

When I swing my head to find my friends, I see something else. A darkness in the distance, spreading like black fingers, eating up the sky. A bubbling cloud I've seen somewhere before, but it's moving faster this time. Moving across the sky and consuming everything.

Something about the texture of the sky changes. A shiver runs down my spine—what's being eaten by the storm is actually skin. The dark fingers merge into one long curtain. And then, the whole sky becomes flesh, pale and matching the snow all around me.

Part of me registers that I saw the snow through Ernest's binoculars but have never been there yet. It clicks that I must still be asleep on the bunk, rocking inside the hull of the *Resilience*. But even knowing it, I can't wake myself up.

The sky continues to transform, no longer white and no longer black. It's a red, bubbling body. The snow disappears and the sky rips open, bursts open, big infected sores rupturing. And the rain is falling again. Endless, heavy rain. But it's red rain, pouring from the wounded flesh.

There is no healing for this sky, something in my gut tells me. No antibiotics. No cure. Just endless invisible death. The radiation. It falls on me and I need to wake up because I can't take it anymore, it's too hot, hotter than anything I've ever felt. I try to suck in air but there's nothing left to breathe. The blood is suffocating me. Suddenly, when I'm about to die, the white comes back. The sky is blue. I've only seen a blue sky once. It's so beautiful.

WHEN I FINALLY PULL MYSELF OUT of the nightmare, there's a face above me. Blue. But it's not the sky in my dreams. It's the blue of someone's eyes.

Clint presses a finger over his mouth.

"What's going on?" I squirm, feeling something pinning down my hands and legs. The wind howls above deck. I look around, but no one else is down here.

"I'm going to help you," he whispers, his face too close. "Be quiet."

I try to slide out from under him, but his hands push my shoulders down. He won't let me up.

I kick my knee out, aiming for his groin, but he shifts and I miss, then he pushes down harder. His hand covers my mouth. I scream but no sound comes out. I feel something, his other hand, working its way down my sweater, pulling it up, touching my pants. I can think of nothing but the face eaters and their madness. I bite like I'm one of them. I taste his blood, but he doesn't even flinch. He's got my pants down and he's finding my underwear. I can't stop him.

Where is everyone? My eyes dart around the room. Not even Voley is here.

"Quiet," he mutters, groping his way inside my underwear—I bite again. It's just enough to get his hand off my mouth, and the scream of my life comes out. His hand slams down on my face, and I see nothing but white light, the snow.

I wait for someone to save me. But no—they won't—he's already killed everyone else. It's just me and him on the ship now.

I hear footsteps. Clint jumps off my bunk and pivots to the stairwell.

It's Ernest. "What the hell's going on?"

Then his face warps when he spots me. I'm afraid that he's in on it, and that he's going to come in now and finish me off, and together they're going to steal the last bits of my soul.

He bolts forward, grabs Clint, and slams him into the wall. Clint goes for something in his pocket but Ernest punches him squarely in his nose.

"Remember that you did this to yourself," Ernest growls, standing over Clint's dazed body.

Another set of footsteps breaks the quiet. Through the dim light, I recognize Russell's form.

Ernest just walks away as Russell goes straight for Clint, glancing at me only for a moment to confirm his suspicion. He punches Clint again and blood spills down his lips. Yanking him to his feet, Russell shoves him at the stairs.

"What did he do?" Russell roars, looking at me.

It's Ernest who answers, the words like poison. "He was on her."

"Up!" screams Russell, nailing his foot into Clint's back until he's scrambling up the stairs on all fours.

Clint yells something about taking the drug. That he didn't realize what he was doing.

Russell yells back, "Shut up!"

Ernest follows them up. The only other sound I hear is a splash. And that's it.

I lie in terror, pulling my clothes back on and waiting for someone to come back to me.

When Russell returns, he bends down beside me, a look of horror on his face. "Are you okay?"

I shake my head no, refusing to open my mouth, afraid that I'll start cracking. He just sits by the bed as I quietly cry, unable to let go of his hand.

"You're safe now. You don't have to talk. I'm just going to stay with you."

I nod, stuffing my face into the pillow. For a long time, after the tears stop, I replay what happened. There's no making sense of it.

When Russell looks like he's falling asleep, I speak up, just to keep him awake with me. "Where's Dusty?"

He jolts upright. "On the motorboat. He'll be in soon."

I hug him, my way of thanking him for staying so close. He catches a tear from my cheek, and it all just starts to come out again.

He squeezes my hand and whispers, "If you do need to talk, just know—"

"No." I cut him off, fiddling with my pants, pulling them up even though they don't go any higher. All my clothes are on, covering me up, but I feel naked, like my skin is bare and prickling. I nudge Russell so I can pull the blanket higher and wrap myself into as small a ball as I can, waiting for the adrenaline to die down. It takes a long time, but I finally stop adjusting the blanket and start breathing slower. Russell hangs his arm around me, and we cling to each other until I'm calm enough to sleep.

At some point I wake up again and Russell's gone. Dusty and Voley have replaced him at the side of my bunk, both asleep on the floor. They startle when I sit up.

"I'm sorry I wasn't here, Tanner," Dusty speaks groggily. "It was my turn on the motorboat when it happened."

"Did Russell leave yet?"

"No, they're leaving in the morning."

I feel safe enough to say it, and I tell him what happened, how Russell threw him right off the *Resilience*. How Ernest let him do it, didn't put up a single protest.

Dusty touches my leg where it dangles off the bed and I jerk back instantly. He looks away, ashamed. I try to decide whether I should explain, but I'm still so spaced out that it wouldn't make sense anyway. And I don't want to. I just reach down and take his hand, letting him know I'm not mad at him, and then give Voley the pet he's been waiting for.

40

ROOK

18 YEARS, 10 MONTHS, 26 DAYS
WEDNESDAY

Rook swung the last apartment door open, checked the last cabinets. His strength was back, the germs destroyed by the medicine in just a couple of days, but what they needed most desperately was gone. He'd scoured both apartment buildings and the lab, to no avail. After tonight, there'd be nothing left to eat.

His heart sank as he returned with the verdict. Morning light spilled over Luce, in the same position he'd left her, tucked under blankets a few feet away from the fire. Small plumes of frost rose slowly from her lips.

The sight of her like this felt like a refutation of every prayer he'd ever spoken. The antibiotics that had cured him had done nothing for her. She'd only grown sicker. They were supposed to have left the island more than a week ago. Now there was no food, and she was too weak even to sit up.

Keep it together, Rook. There had to be hope—he knew he had to force himself to believe that, at least. Otherwise, he'd crumble right through the ground. He could feel it already starting. And if he let that happen, how would he manage to find food, to carry Luce to the boats?

"I have to go to the power plant." Rook warmed his hands over the fire, steeling himself. However crazy he'd become, Ed had told Rook to come back if he wanted to live in the power plant. If he could just pretend, get inside long enough to take some food . . .

Luce's eyes remained closed as she softly murmured, the same as she'd done since first falling sick. It was too much, and he had to act now. They just needed enough food for the trip over open water, and then he'd carry her to East Harbor if he had to.

"I'm going to get supplies," he said softly into her ear. She mumbled something and opened her eyes. "You stay and rest so you're better for when we leave." He pressed his lips against her greasy hair.

"I don't want you to go." With a groan she rolled onto her side.

He kissed her again and stood up. "I'll be right back."

As much as it hurt to ignore her pleas, he threw on an extra set of clothes, grabbed the axe, and started downstairs.

Footsteps pounded behind him in the stairwell.

"Rook." Dina breathed heavily, her once copper-toned brown skin muted to an ashen white. "She's not going to get better."

Rook scowled at her. Dina and Wayne had proven they could be trusted again. Not once had they taken more than their share of the food Luce brought back, and they'd allowed him to ration their Red so they wouldn't be tempted to take larger doses. Though he could sense their growing impatience to leave, they hadn't argued when he told them they had to wait for Luce to heal. But from the look in Dina's eyes, it was obvious what she was about to say, and it was the last thing he wanted to hear.

Dina reached her hand out in sympathy. "We have to—"

"Stop!" Rook recoiled. He needed a clear head to make it in and out of the power plant. The guilt that Luce had gone to the fuel site for *him*, crossed the threshold because *he'd* been sick, was too much to bear. He obliterated his shame with rage. "Get the fuck upstairs and take care of her if you're not coming with me."

She backed away quickly, terrified, and skulked up the stairs.

THE SNOW WAS FALLING fast and heavy, and at some places, Rook sunk in up to his waist. With his strength back, fueled by his determination to save Luce, he battled on until he could see the lights of the power plant.

A good sign: the generator was still working. His heart quickened. Stepping along the front walkway, he thought he saw a person in the gloom.

Yes, someone was outside, kneeling in the snow by the front door. A man, rocking back and forth. Was the snow around him red?

Rook remembered Luce's words. "*I saw something on my way back. Something in the snow.*"

Moving closer, he saw the blood. And then six bumps, dark forms half-concealed under the fresh powder. *Bodies*, Rook realized, lined up neatly, none of the faces visible. His stomach turned as he caught the glint of silver, a saw blade, moving back and forth in the man's hands. A soft grinding noise drifted out, and everything inside him screamed to turn around.

No, she doesn't have time! You have to do this.

"Hello!" Rook called out, his body humming with nerves.

The butcher stood up, bloody saw in his hand.

"I'm here to see Ed."

"Don't move." It was the blond man. For a moment, he bent his knees, as if readying to charge. Rook raised his axe, and the man flinched. Then, like an automaton, he turned and walked to the front door of the plant, disappearing inside.

Rook inched toward the pale frosted bellies exposed to the air, and the truth sank in—there would be no reasoning with Ed. Yet he couldn't turn back. Maybe there was time to run around the side, try to find another door . . .

The door clicked open, and Ed appeared, rifle in hand. The blond man followed him out.

"You're alive?" A look of shock animated Ed's face. He glanced at the bodies, back to Rook, then toward the distant mountains. "This is what we've come to . . . this is what happens to everyone. You know that, Rook."

Rook stayed silent, watching both men shift their weight restlessly.

"We didn't kill them." Ed waved his arm over the corpses. The words sounded as hollow as he looked, cheeks drawn in around cratered eyes. "They got sick."

"I don't care what happened." Rook tempered his disgust and stuck with his plan. "I've run out of food. I want to come back."

A pounding noise sounded from above. Looking up, Rook caught a shadow streaking across a third-floor window, followed by a muffled scream. *The ones Wayne talked about, that Ed had trapped.* They'd chosen to stay, but Rook could have tried harder, could have warned them that there was more than radiation to worry about at the power plant. He knew firsthand what happened when people ran out of food, had too much of the drug.

Ed grimaced. "I'm sorry, but that offer has passed, old friend. We have to ration very carefully now. Marrow's taking longer than I expected."

"What about a trade, then?" Rook raised a Red tablet he'd taken from Dina's bottle. "I just need a couple boxes of crackers and a few canned goods."

Ed squinted crazily at the pill. "Sorry, we can't help you."

"Please, Ed." Rook stepped forward. He felt sure now that they didn't have any canned or boxed food left anyway. But he was here, so he had to keep trying. Even if it was human flesh, it could be the difference between starving or surviving on the water. "Remember all those times you kept me going, when I wanted to give up?"

For a moment, Ed looked like his old self. His arms relaxed. His visage softened. Then he buckled over with laughter. The blond man stood stiff and eerily quiet, a frightening contrast to Ed's animated outburst. "Marrow will be back any day now." He swung the rifle up and pointed at Rook. "Now get the hell out of here, before I forget that we used to be friends."

Ed's eyes narrowed, and he fired at the sky. Rook turned around to leave. It was over.

"Wait," Ed said. "Get those pills, please."

Rook spun around to see the butcher stomping through the snow toward him, saw in hand. Rook cocked the axe back to swing.

"Don't do anything stupid now." Ed took aim. "Not just as I'm about to let you live."

There was nothing else to do. He'd failed again.

Rook dropped the axe and shakily extended his hand. With a malicious grin, the blond man scooped up the Red.

"I gave you a fair share when you left," Ed said. "Good luck, Rook."

41
TANNER

We're spread around the table by the warm glow of the stove. Tension is thick in the air as we finish our last breakfast together. I eat slowly, knowing that when we're done, Russell will be leaving.

Ernest breaks the silence. "I'm sorry, but I have to say this, and it can't wait until you get back." He looks at Russell and then directly at me. "I should have gotten rid of him before, when he first got into the drug, but I felt sorry for him. That's my own weakness. Forgive me."

I feel too shocked to reply. It's the first time Clint's been brought up in front of everyone. I feel the weight of their eyes and look down at my cleaned plate, fumbling for words.

Russell saves me. "No need to apologize."

"Weather's good," Lemmy says, trying to break the awkwardness. "Good a time as any, yeah?"

"You sure you can handle these two brats?" Russell jokes, but there's nervousness in his voice.

Ernest laughs from his belly. "Better company than you two."

Russell's eyes settle on me long enough that I know he's asking me something, too—if I'm still strong enough after what happened. But my feelings are the same, even after Clint. I smile at him and he smiles back.

We follow Russell and Lemmy to the stern. Dawn's light catches the big blocks of ice on the water. The *Resilience* is as deep into the valley as she can go without risking a shoal.

"I guess you'd call this a fjord now?" Ernest scans the river snaking into the mountains. "It's quite pretty. I'm sorry I can't bring you any closer."

"You'll send up the flares, right?" I chirp nervously, making sure I say the plural, determined to keep Leadville alive.

"You bet I will. Keep your eyes peeled for them." Russell winks at me, carefree like he's going out for a jog.

"Good enough." Ernest claps them on their backs. "Better make a go of it then, while the sky's holding up."

"See you in a day or two at the most." Russell shakes Ernest's hand very firmly, and I can't help but feel my heart sinking fast. It feels like a goodbye. He turns to Dusty, holds his hand out for a second, but then leans in and hugs him. He tries to speak softly, but I hear him loud and clear. "You two look after each other."

Dusty bites his lower lip and sticks his chin out a bit. "We will."

Next, Russell bends and rubs Voley's ears. "You're a good boy. Don't let them feed you too much while I'm gone." Voley licks his hand, agreeing. Then Russell stands and faces me.

"I'm okay." I try to sound strong.

"You do how I taught you, alright?"

Before I can reply, he wraps me up and squeezes the breath out of me. It half-scares me and half-comforts me to know he's got his old strength back.

"It's only two days," I whisper.

"Only two days."

And then, after one last flash of his handsome smile, he follows Lemmy down the ladder. They fire up the engine and untie the tether. Foam spits out and the propeller cuts a line through the water. And that fast, they're gone.

We stand in a huddle, watching them grow smaller and smaller until it's impossible to see anything through the haze of the rain. I feel myself growing smaller, too, all of my strength evaporating.

"The binoculars," I practically yell at Ernest. He whips them out of his pocket like they're on fire.

I catch the motorboat through the lens, traveling down the tiny lead of water to where it's just a sliver between the mountains. And then, the boat rounds a bend and disappears.

A prayer starts up in my head, uninvited, like someone else is speaking it for me. *Please help Russell find his brother, but even more, please bring him back safely.* Somehow it eases my pain to keep thinking the words.

"I forgot my pipe, if you'll excuse me," Ernest grunts.

I feel Dusty's hand on my shoulder as Ernest walks away. He just keeps his arm around me, very gentle and quiet, letting me watch the empty mountains for I don't know how long.

"Maybe it's not the best time to tell you, but there's a game I want to show you," he says long after there's anything to watch. He sounds completely innocent, but the idea of playing a game right now seems crazy.

I turn to him, confused, and wipe my eyes.

"I think it might help pass some time." He steps back, worry crinkling his forehead, and stammers, "Not until you're ready—I mean, unless you want to."

"Okay." I feel my dread lighten at the goofy, nervous look on his face.

He sighs with relief and takes my hand. "Have you ever heard of Dots? I promise you'll like it." Confidence is back in his voice. He smirks. "You won't win, but you'll still like it."

I try to smile. "I want you to keep me warm for a little bit first."

I lock my fingers into his as we walk away from the stern. Voley follows at our heels and brushes up against me. Dusty reminds me that right now we have a stove burning in a dry room below us with a bed and food if we want it, but I'm stuck on Voley's eyes.

They're so green.

I hadn't realized how much color was in them, and how strange it is for anything to be so vulnerable and loving. The thing I notice, that scares me, is I can't feel any of it—the love in Voley's eyes, the warmth of Dusty's hand and his words.

Even though he's no longer a threat, and gone forever, I start to get scared that maybe Clint took something from me with him. What if he stole my ability to feel secure, to feel safe, to feel love?

You're stronger than he ever was, I tell myself. *No one has that power over you.*

The voice in my head sounds like Russell's. It's exactly what he would say. And he's right.

Why did I let you go alone? We finally made it to Leadville, and I abandoned you.

I'm sorry, Russell.

42
ROOK

18 YEARS, 10 MONTHS, 27 DAYS
THURSDAY

Wayne and Dina watched quietly, waiting for answers while Rook placed fresh blankets over Luce and stoked the fire.

He didn't say a word. He couldn't yet. They must have sensed how badly things had gone because they had left him alone with Luce. He curled up next to her and rubbed her back, but she moaned in protest.

Stomaching his dread, he asked, "How are you feeling?"

"I can't get comfortable," she said, squirming.

Blackness was enveloping his insides, an all-consuming frustration at his failure. How could he tell her that now they would have to leave without food?

She cleared her throat. "I'm sorry I didn't tell you where I was going. You were so sick, I was afraid you'd try to come."

"I'm better *because* you went." He refused the apology like it was poison.

"I feel so sick." She labored to raise her head.

"How can I help?" It was a useless question. She'd used up the antibiotics, but more wouldn't help anyway. Even caressing her caused pain, and it felt like he was losing his mind.

"Just stay close." She pressed her nose into his shoulder. "Hold me."

Rook felt tears coming and pushed them back. "I don't want to hurt you."

"Please."

He placed his arms around her as gently as possible.

"Tighter," she said. "I want to feel you."

Slowly, he squeezed until she grimaced.

"No, don't let go," she protested as he loosened the already soft embrace. "It's good like that."

"Rook," Dina whispered. Rook turned to see her standing with Wayne, huddled on the other side of the fire, soot darkening their faces.

He knew what she wanted, but all he could summon was a scowl. There had to be a way to delay them from leaving, so Luce had time to heal. She *would* heal. His parents had prayed their whole lives. To the end, they'd both believed in the power of miracles. What else was there left to do?

Please, God, heal Luce. Mom and Dad—in case God's busy, please help her get better.

He waited until Luce was asleep to slide out from the blankets and deal with Dina and Wayne.

He squatted in front of them. "Can we wait a little longer?"

"The longer we starve, the weaker we'll be," Wayne answered.

"They were eating people, weren't they?" Dina's eyes bored into him. "If we stay too long, they'll come for us, too."

Rook put his head in his hands. They were right.

"We have to go, and . . ." Wayne rubbed his hands together for warmth. "If you don't want to leave her, we decided we're going without you."

"One more night." Rook stifled a sob in his hands, hardening himself to meet their wary eyes. "She needs time to recover."

Dina looked away. He thought for a minute she would say out loud what they were all thinking: that another day was pointless, that nothing could save Luce. But then, when all hope seemed lost, she turned back. "Okay, one more night." Wayne cast her an ugly look, but her words flew at him like daggers. "They let you inside when I wouldn't!" She glared. "You'd be dead already, so shut up."

"Thank you." Rook cupped Dina's hands in his briefly, then returned to Luce's side.

LUCE HADN'T TOUCHED the fresh water he'd brought, so he tilted some past her lips. Waking up with a sour face, she turned her mouth away.

"What's wrong?" Rook lifted up the blanket.

"Stomach hurts. I can't drink. Everything hurts."

The sky grew dark, and he caressed her hair softly as she drifted in and out, sometimes kissing her head and whispering that he was there. Each time she woke up coughing, he cleaned the blood, trying not to let her see how terrified he was. By the middle of the night, she couldn't stop tossing.

"I can't get comfortable." She twisted side to side.

He tried to turn her over, but it seemed to make the pain worse. Looking around the bare room, frantic for anything that could help, he saw that Wayne and Dina were asleep. They needed their energy for the hike tomorrow. What could they do anyway?

When he looked back down at Luce, he saw that where she had shifted her weight on the blanket, some of her bruised skin had come off.

Please God, help her, his mind refrained endlessly, but as the night wore on, the moaning only grew louder, her breathing heavier and sharper.

He slipped away as gently as possible.

She startled awake, face gleaming with sweat. "Where are you going?"

"I'll be right back. I promise."

She had cradled herself into a ball, whimpering, when he returned with a pill of Red in his hand. He glanced at Wayne and Dina, daring them to reproach him for giving away some of their stash, but they were still asleep.

"Rook," Luce panted.

"I'm here." He crushed the tablet and mixed it into a cup of snowmelt. "I need you to drink this, please," he repeated until she understood and opened her lips. Her face squinched at the bitterness.

"You need to drink all of it," he held firm, waiting for her to swallow each sip. The sun was already lighting the window by the time she'd drunk it all.

Then, very suddenly, her breathing eased, and the groans ceased. She became quiet and lucid.

"I'm hungry," she surprised him.

"I know." It killed him that he had nothing to give her. "Do you want to talk?"

"Yes."

Rook struggled a moment to get it together, to pretend for her. Finally, he thought of something. "Do you think they'll laugh when they find my art?"

"They'll laugh." She grinned wide. "You're terrible at drawing. But I love you anyway."

"I guess they will laugh." It echoed in Rook's head: *they.* There was no they left anymore. Not in all the world. But she was smiling at him. "There's something really important I've been wanting to talk to you about," he said in a serious tone.

"What is it?" She craned her neck.

"It's hard for me to bring up."

"It's okay, tell me." She sounded nervous.

"Do you . . ." He paused, forcing a stern expression. "Do you want to get a whole lot of dogs, or just one?"

"Duh." She flopped her head onto the pillow in relief. "A whole lot."

"Phew. I wasn't sure. Me, too."

"I think we should buy a plot of land," she said. "Dry land."

"I'd love that. Can it be a place just like the valley you always draw?"

"That's your favorite?"

"Yep, it is."

"It will be just like that."

He went on, trying to keep the smile on her face, until she grew sleepy.

"Do you want me to let you sleep?" he asked.

"I want to hear your voice. Keep talking to me."

"Okay. I know a story you'll like. It was in an old magazine I used to get, about a sanctuary farm that rescued animals."

"Really?"

"Yeah. This cute, nugget-headed Chihuahua was born without front legs."

"Oh no." Her face wrinkled.

"But they built wheels for him. Even though he was crippled, he looked so excited in the pictures."

She let out a long, happy sigh.

"His name was Roo," Rook said.

"He kicked with just his hind legs?"

"Yeah. And he became best friends with a Silkie named Penny."

"What's a Silkie?"

"A ball of fluff with a chicken inside," Rook laughed. "It's a breed of chicken that looks like a teddy bear."

She laughed until she coughed, and blood splattered onto his hands. By the time he returned with a rag, she had already fallen asleep.

He hadn't even noticed Dina was awake when she spoke. "She won't last much longer."

His rage at her for bringing up the truth had passed. The truth had become simpler; there was no way he would carry Luce into the freezing snow, or let her spend her last hours alone.

"I can't go. I have to stay." He looked at Dina long enough that she'd know he was serious.

"We'll wait." Dina turned to Wayne. He rustled a bit but didn't say a word.

Rook carried on, talking to Luce while she slept, hoping she could hear his voice, even if it was only for a moment as she slipped in and out.

By the middle of the day, the moans started again. It was time to give her another dose of Red. Once again, her pain eased.

"I'm so glad . . ." she began, speaking lucidly.

Rook held her hand and waited.

"That the rain was made less miserable for a while," she continued. "And my heart filled with happiness because I met you."

It tore him to pieces, but he refused to cry.

"Me, too," he said. "It's funny. In the beginning, I didn't even know if you liked me, or if I should kiss you."

She squeezed his hand. "I'm so glad you did."

Her breathing became very slow. He ran his fingers over her hair.

"I wonder if you would have married me—I mean, if we met before the rain," Rook said, uncaring whether Dina and Wayne overheard.

"Even with the rain . . ." Luce pursed her lips. "I would."

This time Rook couldn't stop himself. He leaned close and kissed her, pressing his nose into her hair and letting out a sob. The warmth deceived him. She was so alive. He nestled his cheek against hers so that their skin touched. He breathed in unison with her.

"I'm with you and I love you always," he whispered.

I'm with you and I love you always.

He repeated the words softly, the rhythm of waves lapping against a shore, until sleep overtook him.

When he awoke, it was dark outside. Something cold pressed against his cheek. He opened his eyes and right away, he knew.

"She's at peace." Dina stood, fully dressed to go, a satchel slung over her shoulder with whatever supplies she'd managed to scrounge up.

Rook looked at Luce, but he didn't see peace. Peace required life. This was nothingness.

"Will you come with us?" Dina and Wayne both edged toward the hallway.

Mostly he just wanted to lie down and die with Luce. Then, a sudden paranoia crept into his mind. What if someone who was starving found her? "I just need a minute. I'll meet you downstairs." He bent his knees, finding Luce disturbingly easy to pick up. Cradling her in his arms, he took her up the stairs to the fourth floor and followed the hallway to the end, apartment A41.

Inside, he stood mesmerized, his breath taken away by the walls covered with her landscapes.

They're beautiful, Luce.

When she was completely covered with blankets in her bed, underneath the stars, he turned to leave.

No, something was wrong.

He stopped at the door.

She was all alone, and he was leaving her.

"Our night sky," he said, just as if she could hear him. He took down his drawing of the stars from above her bed and placed it under her hand. Somehow, it made him feel like part of him would stay with her. He kissed her one last time on the lips and pulled the covers up.

For a minute, the only thought racing through his head was to take the remaining Red, to numb the pain.

No. She'd hate me.

Rook had burned the directions into his brain. *Turn right off the main road, walk through the snow toward the mountain that looks like a tabletop. That's where the road had once been. Walk until you come to the edge of land, and if you come out in the wrong spot, travel the coast until you find the boats.*

As they passed the power plant, Rook froze. Something gnawed at him, the scream he'd heard from upstairs. Ed still had people trapped. It was crazy to go back there, but for some reason, he couldn't keep walking. He'd had an excuse before—Luce was sick, desperate for him to get back. Now, she was gone. *What excuse do I have now to abandon them to die?*

"What's wrong?" Wayne twisted around in the snow.

"I have to go in." The words came out flat.

"Are you fucking crazy?" Wayne pointed at the mountainous terrain that lay ahead of them. "We have miles to cover. We can't waste time."

"He's right, we have to keep moving," Dina said calmly, only her eyes betraying how absurd the idea was.

But it was the only thing in the world that made sense to him. "I'll be right back." Rook started toward the fence.

"Rook, no!" She charged forward and grabbed his shoulder.

He threw her off roughly and went on.

"What the hell are you doing?" she said. "We need you to help us find the boats. You're going to get yourself killed!"

"If you're not back in ten minutes, we're gone," Wayne called after him.

Rook understood, but he was unable to stop himself now. It felt like he hadn't done anything in his whole life except fail every person he loved. If death were waiting in either direction, he would die this way, trying to free the people Ed had trapped upstairs.

He passed the mounds of snow near the door. No blood was visible now, but it was still clear what they were. He counted nine bodies. The lights were on inside, but not a shadow was moving in the windows, no sign of life.

Heat washed over him as he entered the door, and then, a pungent smell. Something noxious, rotting. He paused to listen, but there wasn't a sound. The stairwell would be on his right, he remembered, just before the big room they'd been in. The scream had come from the third floor. He just had to go up, free them, and leave.

When he reached the end of the hallway, at the stairwell, he froze again. Something wasn't right. There still hadn't been a sound.

He poked his head forward just enough to peek into the big room, and his gut dropped.

Blood covered the walls. Unable to help himself, he took another step.

Ed's rifle lay several feet away from his body. He was stretched out prone, a line of blood running into a pool. Another body lay on top of him. The rancid smell of decomposition was overpowering. There were more when he crept in further, some slumped against the walls, others facedown with their arms crooked. He recognized the butcher by his blond hair, slumped over Ed.

Christ, they killed each other . . .

He took cautious steps around the bodies, irrationally afraid he might wake them from the dead. They were riddled with red holes: one with three in his chest, another with one in the neck, another with a single line running from stomach to crotch. A slaughter. In the corner, where the supplies had once been, was a pile of bones next to a smoldering fire pit.

Very carefully, he lifted the rifle, unable to avoid glimpsing Ed's open skull. He looked around at the holes in the walls, then back to Ed, and it clicked.

They hadn't killed each other—Ed had gone berserk, and then killed himself.

"Hello?" he called out, hoping there was ammunition left in the rifle, pointing it around the room and expecting someone to jump out. "Anyone here?" His voice echoed back, and all was silent.

Then, he heard a noise. Startled, he twisted in a circle until it came again. It was coming from upstairs.

"I'm coming!" He rushed to the stairs. The cries grew louder, and then understandable.

"Help!"

Down a dimly lit hallway on the third floor, he stopped at the steel door. A sign above the door read Communications Room. The handle turned with ease, and he stepped inside to find eight gaunt, terrified faces, each person tied to a metal radio console.

One of them tried to stand up. Then another.

"Please, help us," a skeleton-faced woman rasped.

They looked like living corpses. The painful irony struck him: none of them would make it all the way to the boats. But that didn't matter. He untied them one by one. They stood slowly, groaning and bracing themselves.

"Water," a hoarse voice groaned.

"There's water outside," Rook waited as they helped each other out of the room. "We're leaving the island."

Rook was the last to leave, surveying the room to make sure no one was left behind, when the lights on the radio console caught his attention. It was an Excelsior control module, the same kind they'd used in the lab.

He wondered how much longer the generator would hold out, how far the repeater towers could carry a signal across the floodwaters, if anyone was still out there to hear it . . .

The power switch worked, and the broadcasting display lit up green. Bending over the dash, he found the Loop Broadcast toggle and flicked it on.

Lifting the receiver to his mouth, he mashed the red Record button and spoke.

"I'm reporting one last time. The old Fort Saint Vrain nuclear fuel has leaked. Don't approach. The radiation is everywhere. Repeat, radiation levels are high. We've evacuated. If you've come this way, we've moved everything out. Again, do not approach the area surrounding central Colorado."

The message began playing back. It was the voice he'd heard more than any other during his life—his own—yet it sounded like the strangest thing in the world.

OUTSIDE, THE FREED CAPTIVES were cupping snow in their hands and putting it to their mouths. Ahead, by the road, Dina and Wayne signaled wildly.

"We're going to East Harbor," Rook announced. "There are boats. It's your choice, die here or try to come. There's no food, but there's enough Red for all of you." He took the bottle from his pocket.

Suddenly, a few perked up.

"You have some?" one asked. "I'll come." The others groaned in affirmation as Rook dropped a tablet into each outstretched hand.

Dina stepped back with fright as Rook approached. "They're not with Ed?"

"Ed's dead." Rook felt strangely calm. "They're survivors."

"What if there's not enough—"

"Luce counted seven boats," Rook replied brusquely, and before Dina could protest, he trekked off the road, toward the tabletop mountain.

They left the main road behind and reached a windswept groove of snow that wasn't as deep. The marching grew easier, and Rook's head began to clear, clearer than it had ever been in his life. The motion of each step forward was the only thing to think about now. When the buildings grew small behind them, he looked back to make sure everyone was still following. A small miracle. All were there.

Something else caught his eye before he brought his attention back to his feet, a softly flickering fire in the second-story window of one of the apartment buildings. Their fire.

He looked two stories higher, to the dark window of a room all the way on the right.

"I love you always," Rook told Luce one last time, and then he put his eyes back down on the place where he would next step.

43

TANNER

Even if I wanted to, I can't get Dusty and Voley to leave my side. Not that I do, because Dusty's silly games have helped to pass the time. It's the fourth day, the fourth time I've convinced myself that I'll see Russell again, but the sunlight starts to fade too soon. Through the binoculars, I watch the distant patch of white. I almost expect to see small shadows crossing the snow in the mountains, but there's nothing out there.

"You ready to eat?" Ernest startles me. His voice is cheerful, but when I look, I see the sadness bending his face. He thinks they're not coming back.

"I'm not hungry." The truth is I haven't had an appetite since Russell left. I'm too nervous, and if I eat now, I might miss the flares. Ernest leaves and I watch the horizon. We've taken turns looking over the wide mountain range, waiting for a spear of light to ride up the sky, but the only change I've seen is the ice spreading across the rain sea.

The sound of quick feet patter behind me. Voley brushes close, wagging his tail, whining a little bit. He sits, and I let him poke his cold nose into my hand. He looks up, so needy for love, and I scratch his head.

Dusty appears behind him. "Ernest said you're not eating again?" After hiding it so well for the first few days, Dusty's finally letting his anxiety slip out.

"We need eyes on the mountain. I'll eat later." I lift the binoculars up to ignore him. I feel a light peck on my cheek, and then he's gone. Voley stays just another minute, waiting for me, but the smell of burnt fish must be too much because he leaves next. I watch the icy water and the snow on the distant mountains alone.

It's the longest thing I've ever endured, but I refuse to go to the resigned, hopeless place where Ernest and Dusty have started to go. Russell and I have never been separated this long, and as much as Dusty, Voley, and even Ernest treat me like family, proving I don't have to be closed off anymore, I can't find solace in it. I have to know whether or not the dream of Leadville will come true, whether or not I'm losing my best friend. Somehow, I feel him, walking just out of sight, probably near the snow that's growing too dark. He's alive.

The wind dies down some, but the rain's so icy that it doesn't help much. I flex my toes to keep them from going numb. One more time I pass the binoculars over the landscape, straining to see something.

A sudden flash of white blinds my whole view.

I rip the binoculars away, and there it is—a thin streak of light spears up and then bursts quietly into a tiny star.

I scream and jump at the fragments of light twinkling down, disintegrating, impossible to miss against the dark clouds. They hang for a long time, slowly dimming, as I hear Ernest, Dusty, and Voley stomping close.

They don't have to take my word for it like with the radio—this time, the last few sparks are still visible, falling down behind the peaks.

"Good old boys!" Ernest hoots, wrapping us both in his arms and stamping his feet.

Dusty nudges right into me, showing off his front teeth, as Voley starts barking from all Ernest's hollering. Then, we all stand together, wind bombarding us, ignoring the frigid, pelting rain, watching without a word.

It's a long time waiting for the second flare to come up, I don't even know how long, but Ernest is the first to leave. He just pats our shoulders, sighing heavily, and heads back down to finish eating.

"At least we know, right?" Dusty tries to comfort me. "He's alive."

I mutely shake my head. I can't begin to think of moving one inch—I train my eyes on the line where land separates sky, willing the second flare to burst up.

As much as I believed the broadcast, and even having seen the Geiger thing, I never really, deep down, lost belief in Leadville. I know another star is going to appear.

Dusty starts to shiver, and finally, he taps me. "I'm going to finish eating. It's too cold out here. Will you come?"

He waits a moment but gets the message and leaves. Voley follows him down.

I shiver until it's pitch black, numb to the wind and the rain, not a care for the onset of hypothermia. There's a fire right below, but I'm convinced that the freezing darkness will only make it easier to see the second flare. I wait and watch, scanning the sky for any sign of light. But the color of night stays unbroken, and I watch the sky for so long that there's no confusing it. There was only one flare. No Leadville.

Eventually, Dusty reappears. When he speaks, he's flipped his tone, stern and angry. "You better come down now or you're going to get sick."

I'm too numb to argue anymore. "I'll be right there."

Russell had been so sure that we would see blue sky again one day. And stars at night. Slowly, as the idea of Leadville finally starts to dissolve, I feel pressure to resist. To refuse to accept it. It hurts too much to think that I'll never see the world Russell and Ernest knew, a place rich with the veneer. It feels like the loss of everything. We must have gotten the wrong location.

When I descend the stairs and the warmth rolls over me and I see the big grins on Ernest and Dusty, so happy I've come inside, something else enters my mind. Maybe losing Leadville is the end of what was keeping me from living in the here and now. The hard shell that's kept me alive, waiting to be opened once we made it there, has already cracked. And it never would have if we hadn't gotten this far.

I feel ashamed of how selfish I've been. The flare means Russell is already on his way back, the only thing that should really matter. And Ernest, with his honesty and genuineness, along with his strong ship, might well be enough to stand in for Leadville.

"Hungry?" Ernest puts down the book he's been reading.

"Starving." I wait at the table as he prepares leftovers. Dusty and Voley move to the bunk and curl up in bed. As soon as I finish eating and make my way over to them, Ernest turns the stove off and blows out the last candle.

"You still think we can make our own Leadville?" I ask in the darkness. The question doesn't hang for more than a second.

"There's no question." I hear Ernest's bunk creak as he shifts his weight. "Now get some sleep. There's a welcoming party you need to rest up for."

"Thanks." I close my eyes, intertwined with Dusty and Voley, no room to stretch my legs out but I don't care. Russell kept his promise. He didn't risk it. Something told him it was a no go, and he turned around.

I WAKE UP from a nightmare. Wiping sweat out of my eyes, I feel a pit growing in my stomach, a bad feeling that stays even after the dream starts to dissolve. But some images stick a little longer . . .

It was Clint—I saw him grab the rope ladder after Russell threw him overboard, cling to it in the cold water, climb aboard the *Resilience* when everyone was sleeping. Then he was on the deck, crawling like the face eaters we shot in Blue City, dead but not dead.

As my mind fully wakes, the details blur. I'm left with just the feeling. A horrible knot in my gut and I can't place my finger on what it is.

Sitting up, I remember last night—Russell only fired one flare. He still isn't here yet. Who knows how dangerous getting back to the *Resilience* will be? Our dinner celebration last night seems like nonsense now. I can't understand why I was so hopeful then, and now I—

Loud hollering above deck triggers my adrenaline. Something bad's happened, and the dream was a warning. I kick upstairs without even remembering to throw my rain suit on.

Everyone's huddled by the rail of the ship, facing the mountains and yelling. Voley barks frantically. I run forward, expecting the worst, but Dusty turns around with an open-mouthed grin. He pulls me into him. I look out over the ice-crusted water.

There's nothing but gray.

But then I spot a darker shape on the river. It's moving fast, breaking through thin ice. There's someone in a boat. No, two people. Their hands are high, waving.

The sight of Russell and Lemmy shakes off the nightmare, the bad feeling that came with it, in a single instant. We wave back, cheering as the motorboat gets closer. *It was just a dream, Tanner. This is real.*

Losing Leadville doesn't even matter. All this determination to find a life that isn't about just surviving, finding the veneer, doesn't matter now. There is no veneer. Not really. But there *are* pieces of it, and we carry them.

Or maybe they're not even something we carry, I realize, because the man waving to me in the distance is himself one big piece of it. So is Dusty, so are Voley and Ernest and Lemmy. So am I. We are the pieces.

My whole life will be a struggle to survive. With Leadville dead, I feel certain of that. It'll stay hard, and get worse, I seem to know in my heart. Instead of dragging me down, the truth makes me feel free, alive. Just surviving is okay, as long as I survive alongside my pieces of the veneer.

Russell comes into clear focus, still waving and smiling even after Lemmy has started gathering supplies on the boat. His wave reminds me of the last time someone waved at me like that.

It was Bryn. She was so sweet and innocent. I hear her telling me she likes me, and I liked her, too. I thought I'd get to know her as she grew up, protect her, teach her. And now she's another piece of the veneer that's gone forever. Like the bunnies she made me fall in love with, like every other piece we've lost along the way, and it hurts my heart. Timothy, Rose, Linda, Daniel—the names run through my head, their kind faces. Some are only names—Russell's brother, his fiancée, his little girl. The last ones I just feel. They don't have names or faces, and they never will. My mother and father, brothers and sisters, aunts and uncles, grandparents . . . I thank them all.

When Russell and Lemmy are so close I can see the white of their smiles, I snap back to the moment. I reach down for Voley. He's so warm. My other arm goes around Dusty. He makes a soft, happy moan.

It's the people who are left, who are still with me—and not the place at all.

Not the place at all.

ACKNOWLEDGMENTS

This book has been a long and extremely difficult journey for me. I would not have reached the finish line if not for the help, encouragement, support, and love of so many people along the way. I would like to thank my steadfast and clairvoyant agent, Jenny Bent, along with the talented team at The Bent Agency. Jenny took a chance on my story and saw the forest for the trees long before I did. She worked tirelessly to help me get the story right, and then made sure it would reach readers. She not only invested years of time into honing this project but also reassured me and advocated for me throughout a publishing process that remains daunting and arcane to me. She made me a much better writer and editor, and she believed in Tanner's story as much as I did; because of her, I can say I am finally a traditionally published author and that my lifelong dream has come true.

Thank you to everyone at Blackstone Publishing who helped me fine-tune this book and get it ready for publication. Thank you, Daniel Ehrenhaft, for believing in my story and making this all happen; thank you, Sarah Riedlinger, for designing the perfect cover; thank you, Jason Kirk, for obsessing over every detail and seeing what I could not; thank you, Caitlin Vander Meulen, for helping me stick the landing.

Thank you, Samantha Bailey, for helping me through the dark times that come with endless waves of revision, and for teaching me to always trust that there will be light at the end of the tunnel. Thank you, Roselle Lim, for being there when I was stuck in doubt and uncertainty.

Before starting my traditional publishing journey seven years ago with Jenny, I self-published my first eight books. There were so many readers who helped me along the way, even if they didn't know it. First, to all my readers—every single one of you who read my stories, left me a comment or review, or sent me an email—thank you. You are the reason I write. Whether positive or negative, your words gave me the motivation to keep going (and thankfully, most of what you wrote was positive!). I kept writing because of your feedback. I can't overstate how vital hearing from readers has been, and continues to be, for my journey as an author.

To all the beta readers who slogged through the early and way-too-long version of this manuscript, thank you. A special thanks goes to Jules Gross for sending me wonderful notes. To all the fans of the original Rain Trilogy, thank you. To Lauren—thank you for reading Tanner's story when I first wrote it, many years ago. You woke me one night, crying over the pages. The impact of that will always stay with me—it taught me the power my writing can have on another human being.

To my family and friends who always supported and believed in my writing—thank you. Thank you to Sue, Ann, Ron, Tom, C.H., Kathy, James, Mackenzie, and Collins for the support and encouragement you've shown me throughout this process. Thank you, Pat, for giving me the idea for Rook's name. Thank you, Noni, for your love that's always with me; thank you, Pop-pop, Marie, Mom, Tony, Tommy, Laura, Karl, Amanda, Mary (future bestselling author), Jess, Lukey, Ariana, Bubba, Autumn, Jakey, Dylan, Jojo, and especially Paul, who tried to edit some of my earliest writing—thank you for slogging through that. Your encouragement and love have meant the world to me. Thank you, Kurt, for rereading one specific book of mine every year and reminding me that I have the talent to do this. And thank you, Rob, my man, who told me he knew it would happen for me.

Finally, I'd like to thank Caroline. Thank you for literally taking my hand and guiding me through some of the darkest moments (and weeks) I've ever endured, those days when it felt like traditional publishing was going to be just too hard. You knew the future each step of the way, and you were right every time. The impact of your love and support is immeasurable. Oh, and thank you, Winnie and Moon Pie, for unconditionally loving me in that very special, canine way of yours. To all those I do not have the space to thank—you are eternally appreciated.